DOUBLEDAY
CELEBRATES
100 YEARS OF
EXCELLENCE

Also by Peter de Rosa

REBELS: THE IRISH RISING OF 1916

VICARS OF CHRIST

BLESS ME FATHER

Doubleday

New York

London

Toronto

Sydney

Auckland

Peter de Rosa

Pope
Patrick

PUBLISHED BY DOUBLEDAY
a division of Bantam Doubleday Dell Publishing Group, Inc.
1540 Broadway, New York, New York 10036

DOUBLEDAY and the portrayal of an anchor with a dolphin
are trademarks of Doubleday, a division of
Bantam Doubleday Dell Publishing Group, Inc.

This novel is a work of fiction. Names, characters, places, and incidents either are the product of the author's imagination or are used fictitiously. Any resemblance to actual persons, living or dead, events, or locales is entirely coincidental.
Pope Patrick was previously published in 1995 by Poolbeg Press Ltd., Knocksedan House, 123 Baldoyle Industrial Estate, Dublin 13, Ireland.

Book design by Jennifer Ann Daddio

Library of Congress Cataloging-in-Publication Data

De Rosa, Peter, 1932–
Pope Patrick / Peter de Rosa. — 1st ed.
p.   cm.
1. Catholic Church—Ireland—Clergy—Fiction.   2. Popes—Fiction.
3. Humorous stories. gsafd.   I. Title.
PR6054.E754P66   1997
823'.914—DC20   96-31635
CIP

ISBN 0-385-48548-4

Printed in the United States of America
March 1997
First Edition
1   3   5   7   9   10   8   6   4   2

To my wife,
Mary

Acknowledgments

I am indebted to Bruce Tracy, my editor at Doubleday,
for his enormous enthusiasm and for having a sense of humor
Pope Patrick himself would appreciate.

Author's Note

Pope Patrick is only Pope Patrick; his views are his alone.

Pope Patrick

Prologue

The End of an Era

In the autumn of 2009, though he had been Pope for a mere thirty-one years, one fewer than Pius IX, the days of John Paul II were clearly numbered.

In a tiny shop in a small dark piazza near the Pantheon, Alberto Gammarelli, head of a firm that displays in its window the sign "Pontifical Tailors," was busy. He was packing a complete set of papal apparel into three cartons marked small, medium and large.

Bellini, a prestigious undertakers' firm, was preparing for embalming.

In workshops behind St. Peter's, Vatican employees, the *sanpietrini*, were constructing a triple coffin of cypress, lead and elm. As they sawed and planed the wood and forged the twelve screws of 14-carat gold for the lid, they whistled cheerfully. Employees receive one month's salary when a Pontiff dies and another when his successor is elected. By threatening to become the Immortal Father, the dying Pope had deprived them of precious income.

The pontificate of eighty-nine-year-old Karol Wojtyla, the first non-Italian in 450 years, had begun in 1978. Soon, he had traveled farther than all his 262 predecessors combined. With titanic energy and scarcely pausing for breath, he had scolded five continents—though not everyone took heed.

By 2009, 60 percent of parishes worldwide had no priest. In Rome, not a single vocation for ten years. Italy's birthrate was the lowest in the history of the world.

John Paul, never fond of the USA, was not surprised that the average age of American clergy was sixty-nine, a third of them gay.

A far greater disappointment was Ireland. In one decade, Mass-going was halved, five of the eight seminaries closed and 12 percent of priests were black missionaries from Africa. The Bishop of Limerick's efforts to make adultery a crime, even if it meant jailing the entire Cabinet, had failed.

Few women were among the Pontiff's fans. Always opposed to women's liberation, he said in one address: "Jesus, God's Son, became a man not a woman. Women can no more be priests than can . . . monkeys." However theologically precise, this off-the-cuff remark was not good psychology on his part. From then on, wherever he went, angry feminists carried banners inscribed "Our Mother Who Art in Heaven" and "A Monkey for Pope."

I n his pontificate the world had changed. Communism was virtually dead. Without core values, the wonder was it had lasted so long.

Soon after the breakup of the Soviet Union, the Russian Federation itself began to fall apart, starting with the brutal destruction of the Chechen capital, Grozny. After Yeltsin, inflation was so high ruble notes were still damp from printing when they were in use on the streets. There was no bread or milk in Moscow itself. The Mafia ran a black market in everything from vodka to porno movies.

China fared little better. In spite of draconian measures, the population spiraled out of control. There was massive unemployment, internal migration and social unrest.

The question was, who would be the new superpower to counter American imperialism? To the horror of the West, the answer was already present.

I slam was born under the harsh skies and flavorless air of the desert. Thirteen and a half centuries after the Prophet's death a great and ever-swelling chorus of voices was heard: "There is no God but Allah, and Muhammad is his Messenger." The ground shook with the pounding of sandaled feet.

When the third millennium began, Muslims at well over a billion, mostly non-Arabs, outnumbered Catholics; soon they would outnumber the Chinese. This was a new and more militant Islam. For the first time, not just the many terrorist groups but the Sunnis and the Shias, as divided as Catholics and Protestants, were as one.

The leader of the Pan-Islamic Fundamentalists was fifty-one-year-old Ayatollah Abdallah Hourani. To some, he was the spiritual successor to Ruhollah Khomeini. To others, the new Mahdi, or Expected One, a great religious Warrior, Muhammad's Avenger. Some said bushes, the very rocks, bowed down before him. It was rumored that he did not even swallow his own spittle during the daylight hours of Ramadan.

Usually black-robed, the tall and lean Hourani wore a long curved dagger in his belt. His thick black beard was threaded with silver, his profile that of an eagle in flight. On his left lid he had a big black mole; even when he closed his cold brown eyes he seemed able to see like a wolf. When he spoke, always slowly, the majesty and harshness of Arabic was magnified a hundred-fold by the gutturals, as if his voice emerged, not just from his well-like throat, but from trackless deserts and from ages past.

For six years, Hourani had been President of the Federation of Islamic Republics (FIR). It stretched from Algeria in the West to Pakistan in the East and south into Africa. Moderates like Rafsanjani in Iran had been swept aside. Secular Turkey had "converted" back to Islam and left NATO. There were no more women Prime Ministers in Islamic states. A couple of assassinations had seen to that.

The FIR tore up all treaties between Islamic and heathen nations beginning with the one made by Sadat with Israel in 1979.

In the year 2004, the West's greatest nightmare became reality: Saudi Arabia fell to militants. The King and hundreds of princes of the Family of Saud were executed like the Baghdad royal line forty years before. President Hourani proclaimed the new *djinna* (the rebirth of Islam), led by fanatical mullahs, ayatollahs and imams.

"Now," said Hourani, "we will write with the sword using infidel blood for ink."

In fact, he wielded something far more lethal than the sword. The FIR had amassed a vast arsenal of conventional, biological and chemical weapons.

More dangerous still, in Pakistan, Algeria, Iraq and Iran, the Federation had an ever-growing stockpile of nuclear weapons. Some had been manufactured from illegally imported plutonium; others were stolen or bought with petrodollars from the old Soviets, who had retained 27,000 nuclear warheads at the end of the Cold War.

In addition, militant Muslims simply stole abandoned Russian nuclear subs in the Arctic. Advised by Russian and European experts, the FIR was all the time improving its delivery systems at sea and in the air.

In an increasingly unstable world, it was the USA that felt the brunt of Islamic hatred.

In February 1993, a 550-kilogram bomb blew up the underground garage of the World Trade Center in Manhattan, New York, killing six, injuring a thousand. In 1996, nineteen American servicemen were killed by an Islamic fundamentalist bomb in Saudi Arabia. A few years later, bombs went off across America, in three tunnels under the Hudson on a single night, in the New York subway, in banks and state buildings from Chicago to Seattle. A dozen Zionist rabbis were murdered in New York alone. The press engaged in strict self-censorship when five journalists, who had written critically of the FIR, were found with their severed heads sewn on again back to front.

SWAT teams of FBI agents were not dealing with small-time terrorists mixing fertilizer and diesel fuel in big barrels with wooden spoons. This was an international conspiracy organized by militant Islam and far more ruthless than the Soviets of old.

The USA put all Islamic states on the list of outlaw nations. It increased annual CIA spending from $26 billion when Communism faded to $50 billion; it strengthened NATO after a decade of decline. It renewed nuclear tests and went back on its pledge to dismantle two thousand warheads a year. Most important of all, after killing off Star Wars under Bill Clinton, America spent billions resurrecting it.

F rom mankind's point of view, this was a disaster. The Vatican was far more spiritual. Things had gone rather badly for it since the end of the Cold War. The new Ice War, as the press called it, gave the Church of Rome a worthy foe.

Two great patriarchal religions eyed each other with a suspicion and hostility not known since Urban II initiated the Crusades in the Middle Ages. The Vatican was back in business.

J ohn Paul's last trips abroad had been a security nightmare, dogged by fundamentalist *hashishi,* or assassins. Now the oldest Terrorist of all was busy stalking him.

Behind the shutters of his room high in the palace, the Pontiff spent long days and restless nights. Monsignor Stefan Grabowski, his Polish secretary, silenced the six great bells of St. Peter's, stopped the fountains in the Square from jetting and hissing at night. Still the Pope found no peace except by bronchially humming songs of the Polish Uprising and saying the rosary.

The walls of his bedroom were hung with pictures of Marian shrines. Strangely, Our Lady of Fátima had ousted the black Madonna of Czestochowa in his affection. Each month, he sent Grabowski underground to the Secret Archive. He returned bearing the small steel "Fátima Box" with its three terrible prophecies and closed the door behind him. An hour later, he invariably found the Pontiff, his face lime-white, his hands even more trembly than usual, weeping copiously and muttering, "Apocalypse. Apocalypse."

To cheer him up, the Rome municipality paraded the fire brigade when free under his window for the midday Angelus. Grabowski had trained them to sing "*Sto lat, sto lat, niech żyje żyje nam,*" which is "For He's a Jolly Good Fellow" in Polish. The Pope, thinking they were miners from his homeland, addressed them in his mother tongue, telling them not to commit the sin of abortion. He also had an open line to Warsaw, where he spoke for hours, sometimes twice a day, to a silver-haired, long-retired and stone-deaf Lech Walesa.

The end came suddenly one early morning at the end of November. Dr. Vittorio Gadda, a small sad-eyed man with waxed mustache who smelled of peppermint and Gauloises, called out: "*Silenzio, per favore.*" The black-suited archphysician put his stethoscope to the Pope's chest. A dramatic shake of the head signaled, No hope. The tall gaunt Secretary of State, senior of the six cardinal bishops of the Roman Church, was summoned. Cardinal Montefiori found the Penitentiaries, black-robed Franciscan friars, already kneeling beside the bed.

John Paul, his eyes gray buttons in frayed buttonholes, confessed his sins. The Cardinal Grand Penitentiary anointed him and gave him viaticum for his last and longest journey.

Combative to the last, the Pope's final words, spoken in thirty-two languages, as though he were addressing an Easter Day crowd in St. Peter's, were: "Contraception is still *forbidden.*" Officially, the Vatican was to say he used Jesus' own dying prayer, "Into thy hands, O Lord, I commend my spirit."

Gadda, after testing for vital signs, declared with an operatic throb: "*Morto.*"

Montefiori, now *Camerlengo*, or Chamberlain, removed the white linen from the corpse's face. Taking a tiny silver hammer out of a bag, he tapped John Paul's starchy forehead, using his real name for the first time in over thirty years.

"Karol Jozef Wojtyla, are you dead?"

The corpse's jaw turned to the far right as if to answer, characteristically, No!

A pause and the ritual was repeated. Then a third time. Montefiori split the Fisherman's Ring with silver shears and hammered the Pope's seals to pieces to stop anyone forging papal documents.

After the Penitentiaries had washed the remains, Grabowski gripped the sheet embroidered with the white eagle of Poland and drew it over the Pope's head.

An aide phoned the Vatican Press Office. Within minutes of the Rome Bureau of the Associated Press putting the news out on the wires, messages of condolence poured in from Berlin, Paris, London, Dublin, Moscow, Warsaw.

The most heartfelt of all came from the U.S. Republican President. Roone Delaney, nearly a year into his second term, was in a deep sleep, having left instructions he was only to be woken up in the event of a nuclear attack.

President Hourani and his FIR Council kept changing their HQ to guard against a missile attack from the American fleet. Presently, Hourani was in Tehran.

Clad in white robes, preceded only by an aide waving a scarlet palm branch, he had walked the milk-white dawn to the mosque long before the *muezzin* called quaveringly from the minaret: "Allah is most great / I bear witness that there is no God but Allah / I bear witness that Muhammad is his Messenger / Come to prayer, it is better than sleep."

Beggars, some of them blind, leaped up from the ground where they slept on cardboard and drew *barak*, spiritual power, by touching his garments or kissing his hand.

Inside the mosque, the President, with hands joined and only his outer black eye showing, began by intoning, "Allah is most great." Soon, he was prostrate on his mat southwest toward Mecca in Arabia where the Prophet was born. With his turbaned forehead touching the ground, he became one spoke of a giant prayer wheel circling the world, its hub the sacred shrine of the Kaaba. One day, and soon, that prayer wheel would fulfill Muhammad's dream and become the wheel of world domination.

After he emerged, still barefoot, an aide whispered the news from Rome.

"At last," Hourani murmured, shaking the dust off his sandals, "the Satan of the Seven Hills has gone to hell."

Next day, Dr. Gadda and two morticians drained the papal corpse with a syringe and injected it with chemicals. The organs firmed up, the skin took on a fresh pinkish color. Gadda felt proud that the Pope looked more alive than he had for years.

The Penitentiaries clothed the body in papal vestments: white cassock with mozzetta, the waist-length cape buttoned up in front like a corset, and a red velvet close-fitting cap with an edge of white fur. Secured on the bier by unseen hooks, the body was transferred to the Sistine Chapel, where it faced the scene of the Last Judgment.

In the morning, the clergy of St. Peter's took charge of the body and dressed it anew in full red pontificals. They carried it through the Sala Regia and turned left down the four flights of Bernini's Royal Staircase with its Ionic columns, through the great Bronze Door and into the portico. Inside St. Peter's, the coffin rested in honeyed light on a catafalque in front of the Altar of Confession. Swiss Guards stood to attention at each corner as crowds filed by to pay their last respects.

It was the end of an era. Behind the scenes, curial factions were planning the future. Lobbying for the Pope's successor is forbidden. Yet top churchmen, while fully trusting in the Holy Spirit, were leaving nothing to chance.

Cardinals resident in Rome met in the Sala Bologna on the third floor of the Apostolic Palace to settle the burial arrangements.

Two Pope-makers emerged: Montefiori, the Italian conservative, and

Gonzales of Rio de Janeiro, a monkey-sized liberal who chanced to be in Rome for his *ad limina* visit. Both men, renowned for their integrity, took soundings. Montefiori knew the Curia better, while Gonzales represented South America and, therefore, half the Catholics in the world.

By December 4, the day of the funeral, all members of the Sacred College were in Rome. Few heads of state attended, but King Charles III of England happened to be on an official visit to Italy. Divorced, and no longer Supreme Governor of the Church of England after its disestablishment, he paid his respects by going into a kind of mystical trance by the bier.

The body, placed in its triple coffin, was lowered into the vault under the main altar to the singing of *"In Paradisum."*

For the nine days of mourning, the Princes of the Church continued their wrangling in the Sala Bologna, on back stairs in the Vatican, in international colleges and first-class restaurants around the city.

On the evening of December 14, ninety-two cardinals, looking like giant bougainvilleas, processed in pairs into what was to become a historic conclave.

PART ONE

Choosing a Successor

Chapter  One

The conclave area was sealed off, windows onto the outside world were covered with lead strips, passages to outside corridors were closed. The conclavists processed to the Sistine Chapel, headed by a server bearing the papal cross.

In the four-hundred-strong procession were cardinals, some of them with assistants. There were confessors, doctors, pharmacists, carpenters, plumbers, electricians, sisters, and Sergio Fantucci, a Vatican gardener, whose job was to look after the plants. CIA-trained security officers with scanners even frisked cardinals and confiscated their wrist telephones and their miniature TVs with tiny built-in satellite receivers. One had a TV concealed in his big ruby ring.

In the Sistine Chapel, Montefiori read out the rules of conclave. Many cardinals prayed humbly that while their robes like their sins were as scarlet, they soon would be white as snow.

"Ring the bells," called out Montefiori, and everyone retired to his room. Cardinals, in particular, were keen to see their quarters for which they had balloted in advance. For the next hour the Master of Ceremonies, with the Architect of the Conclave who had designed the accommodation, went round making sure that no unauthorized person was inside. Then, when all but one of the exits had been walled up, the M.C. called out: *"Exeant omnes!* Everyone out!"

The great door was shut. The Marshal of the Conclave locked it from without and the Governor of the Conclave locked it from within.

Cardinal Thompson of Westminster, a small white-haired Benedictine, stayed in the Sistine Chapel, praying before the High Altar. Wrapped up in God, he took no notice of the ten thousand square feet of Michelangelo's masterpiece on wall and ceiling which shone as new after its restoration by art experts. Thompson's reputation was mixed. A holy man, he was known to drink heavily and swim in the nude. Add to that a poor grasp of Italian and he was judged not *papabile*. As two Italian cardinals passed, one inquired of the other, "*Gesummaria*, why is that strange Englishman praying at a time like this?"

The eight U.S. cardinals were less than pleased with what were called their cells. A small curtained-off partition of a salon contained a prie-dieu, lamp, washbowl and pitcher, cake of soap and roll of shiny nonabsorbent toilet paper, desk, a hard chair, a plastic bucket and, finally, under a brass bed, a chamberpot borrowed from a local seminary.

Most of them had just vacated penthouses in the finest hotels on the Via Veneto. Now they were dispersed in galleries on three floors in what Thomas Cardinal Burns of New York, puffing on a Macanudo cigar, described as "a goddamn wooden horse trailer with nothing in it but a bed of nails and a piss pot for company."

It was cold, too. "Boy oh boy." Sixty-six-year-old New York, fresh from the delights of the Presidential Suite at the Grand Hotel, wheezed through his gavel-shaped nose. "Talk about Alcatraz." He rolled up the cape of his soutane to make a muffler of it.

Bob Flick of Boston, a pip-eyed seventy-year-old called "Knife," had brought an ample supply of Chivas Regal, Hershey bars and fiber laxatives. Visiting Burns, he quipped, "Some conclaves in the Middle Ages took years, Tom. Emperors burned down their palaces around Rome to make them hurry up or took the roof off the conclave."

"You don't say."

"I do say. Sometimes they left the Uncle Joes full to overflowing, even let dead cardinals rot inside to help the rest make their minds up." Flick held up a bottle of the brown stuff and winked. "Didn't wanna be caught out, Tom."

Chuck Runnell of Chicago was poring over the latest IBM minicomputer which he had smuggled in inside a chocolate box.

Temple of St. Louis, having recited his breviary like he was double-parked, burst in on him to complain that he was billeted next to a black guy name of Kawa from Zimbabwe or Kinshasa or some godforsaken place like that.

Runnell adjusted his green-tinted spectacles and tapped a button. It was Kinshasa, as if St. Louis cared.

Temple was not looking forward to the conclave. He had never got beyond *mensa* in Latin. Runnell, with a doctorate in theology from the Gregorian, promised to give him constant updates on proceedings.

"Thanks, buddy." Temple, a 280-pound giant with an enormous flat forehead, held up a deck of cards. "Let me know when the Spirit moves you."

That evening, Brian Cardinal O'Flynn, who did not belong to any clique, was in his cubicle sucking a dead pipe as he read the book that was almost as dear to him as his breviary, *Collected Poems* by W. B. Yeats.

Short, chunky, with cropped gray hair and eyes like peeled grapes behind wire spectacles, he was aged sixty-eight. He had spent the last thirty years in Rome, without ambition, unobtrusively working his way up the curial ladder. He was, an Irish colleague used to say, spectacularly ordinary, without the least "notion of upperosity."

Father Kerrigan, a handsome, brown-haired newly ordained six-footer from New York, tapped on the wood panel next to the curtain and entered.

"Hello, Frank." Cardinal O'Flynn had a soft flat Mayo accent.

"Can I get you anything, Eminence?"

O'Flynn shook his head. The only thing he was missing was Charley, his golden Labrador, who always slept on the end of his bed. Charley had to stay behind in the Irish College.

Kerrigan, a doctoral student, was substituting. The cardinal's secretary was in the Irish College, which was isolated owing to a severe outbreak of flu.

"How're your quarters, Frank?"

Kerrigan made a face. "It'll do for a day or two, I guess." Secretly, he was elated at his fantastic luck in being there at all.

"Call me at six-thirty?"

When Kerrigan left, O'Flynn undressed and settled down for the night. On one side was Cardinal Angelo Pavese of Bologna, seventy-nine years old, with a face like a gargoyle and the skin of a jellyfish. A few months more, and he would have been disqualified by age from attending.

"I am telling you, *Dottore*," Pavese was saying, in operatic Italian, "I must be moved out of here, *pronto*."

Vittorio Gadda murmured something soothing.

"I swear on my mother's grave," Pavese shrieked, "I am slightly incontinent."

Slightly deaf, too, O'Flynn mused.

"I can't get to the bathroom in time and this room has no window."

Dr. Gadda explained that the big room next to the bathroom had been won fair and square by New York.

"Bloody Yanks," sang Pavese, castrato-like.

Gadda pointed under the bed. "You will have to do with the *vaso da notte* and the plastic sheet, Eminence, like many others."

Though chairman of the Commission of Justice and Peace, Pavese refused for ten more minutes to accept his fate, until sleep overcame him.

Gadda retired to his room stocked with medicines and sat in his armchair, smoking a Gauloise. Inside a copy of a medical bulletin on anatomy he had concealed the latest issue of *Playboy*. It contained a surprisingly sympathetic obituary of the late Pope in which he was likened to an old foreign paterfamilias who had emigrated to a more liberal land:

There he remains the boss. He never goes out on principle, never learns the language or the ways of a new country which he feels is not his own. His children and grandchildren, whom he claims to rule with a rod of iron, are compelled to learn two languages, one for their new compatriots in daily life and one for grandfather. At home, they continue to nod and bow dutifully. Then go outside and behave like everyone else. So the grand old man goes on blindly convinced that his ways, the old ways, are best; and that his family are fortunate to have him to guide them on the road to righteousness.

The cardinal electors might look to a future Pope's learning or holiness; Gadda concentrated entirely on his state of health. In John Paul's last years, as his arteries hardened, he suffered from terrible nightmares. He often recounted them in detail to Gadda, who became something of an unwilling father-confessor.

Once, against a fiery doom-laden sky, John Paul saw millions of sacks of grain being emptied out of boats into a raging sea; and he knew this was seed, not of the earth, but of men, which had been sinfully wasted since his reign began.

In one dream, he wrote an encyclical banning artificial sweeteners, spectacles and false teeth. In another, he anathematized anyone who unnaturally inseminated unmarried cows. He forbade women to sing in the choir, basing his insistence on St. Paul's words, "Let women be *silent* in church." He imposed Polish as the universal language of the Mass. He condemned the Olympic Games for being too ecumenical. Inspired by an idea of St. Augustine, he imposed celibacy on *all* Catholics. Better to go out with an ascetic whimper than a nuclear bang.

On one particularly awful night, he dreamed he had made renegade Swiss theologian Dr. Hans Küng a cardinal and put him in charge of the Holy Office, where he promptly wrote a universal catechism distorting every article of faith.

John Paul awoke moaning pitiably and asked Gadda, who was keeping vigil by his bed, to call Grabowski, who came running.

"I want to name my successor. Someone reliable. Glemp."

His secretary, knowing that Glemp of Warsaw had died some years before, coughed politely as he offered him a glass of water. "It is against the law."

"I am Pope." John Paul held up a bone-shiny hand, showing the Fisherman's Ring. "I will change it."

"Against *divine* law, Holiness."

The Pontiff, dazed-looking like an owl suffering from hypothermia, sank back on his pillow.

"A-a-a-ah." An elegiac utterance.

Grabowski said tactfully, "You have done enough for the Church already, Holiness, without choosing your successor."

No wonder Gadda was now praying earnestly that the next Pontiff would be younger and healthier than the last.

Meanwhile, Thomas Burns of New York was in his room which he had won not by luck or prayer, but by honest bribery. Whenever he visited Rome, his pockets were stuffed with checks made out to cash for heads of congregations and for anyone else whose help he might need in an emergency.

Burns was entertaining his fellow Americans to a drink and a few rubbers. It was, he confessed, not exactly the '21' Club in Manhattan. At eleven, in a thick atmosphere of booze and cigars, Burns brought them to order.

"I'm backing Montefiori's candidate."

"Ricci of the Holy Office?" St. Louis said. Ricci was called "the Pope's Assassin." "That guy never had an original idea in his head."

"There is certainly that in his favor, Jan." Burns had built up a sturdy reputation as a two-fisted conservative.

"But," Temple of St. Louis persisted, scratching his pickled nose, "Ricci is like an old lady behind the wheel. He's so careful he's dangerous."

"Rio's choice, Frangipani of Venice," Burns countered, "is likely to call another Council and prock up the Church all over again."

"Prock" was the latest all-purpose word. It came into vogue after a New England senator, Fred Prock, admitted to having had more one-night stands than his calculator could cope with.

"We need a change," said Runnell, the intellectual.

"Change, Chuck?" New York was disgusted. "In a world where every goddamn thing has to be relevant, isn't it refreshing to have one decent thing that is unashamedly *ir*relevant?"

18

"Secret of the Church's success," snapped Flick of Boston.

"Right," agreed tall, bowed, white-haired Kamierz Sapieha of Philadelphia. When, as now, he was a bit tipsy on Polish vodka, his nervous facial tic trebled in speed. "Look at us, now." He pointed a long finger at his scarlet soutane. "Who'd bother taking our picture in an executive suit?"

"Abso-procking-lutely," said New York, with a characteristic lizard-like lick of his tongue. "I'm irrelevant and proud of it." He was still smarting at the *New York Times* description of him at an Academy Award function as "looking like a tropical fish in a bowl, colorful but not doing a lot."

"Does Ricci sympathize with the Third World?" Runnell asked.

"Trendy stuff." Burns exhaled alarmingly. "Don't forget America was poor when the procking Brits owned it. We pulled ourselves up by our buckles, which is what the Third World's gotta do."

"Right," Philadelphia said, scratching a neck webbed like a duck's foot. "Give 'em buckles and tell 'em, 'Start lifting.' "

"As I see it," Flick of Boston said, piously signing himself, "the Pontiff recently deceased was a sparrow-fart in many respects but he did convince folk they were sinners. They *like* that. These days, there's not enough honest-to-God guilt around."

"Sure," Philadelphia said. "Give 'em plenty of guilt, pray over them and, hey presto, we save 'em from an eternity in the sin bin."

Flick went on: "If a Pope allowed, say, contraceptives, that'd be the end of Holy Mother Church. Where there's no sin, there's no forgiveness, and we'd all be out of business."

"Bingo," said Burns. "Leave all the crap about social progress and justice to politicians and concentrate on spiritual things like—"

"Whiskey, anyone?" asked St. Louis.

O'Flynn switched off his bedside lamp and pulled the threadbare blanket over his ears. Down the corridor elderly clerics, coughing, spluttering, throat-clearing, spitting, letting off the occasional cathedral fart, were settling down for the night. Below, in Montefiori's room, and, above, in Rio's, O'Flynn guessed the politicking would go on and on.

19

He slept so soundly, he did not hear the commotion at three in the morning when Cardinal Pavese had to be rescued by two firemen. The old gentleman had set his bedding alight. He had to be hosed down and rushed to hospital with severe burns.

When O'Flynn left his cell in the morning, he saw the parquet floor of Pavese's room awash, false teeth ebbed and flowed on the tide.

"Jesus, Mary and Joseph," he whistled, "the poor feller wasn't joking about his incontinence."

Chapter Two

On the first morning, the cardinals concelebrated Mass in the Pauline Chapel. Afterward, they processed in twos along the Royal Gallery to the Sistine Chapel, whose floor was protected by a wooden base overlaid by thick wall-to-wall felt.

Foreign prelates were overawed at the splendor of the setting. Six candles were alight on the High Altar; there were others on the dividing marble screen and over each of their "thrones."

After O'Flynn, who was junior cardinal deacon, had locked the chapel door, there was a long pause. Montefiori was allowing any elector so inspired to call out a name which, under the new rules, they would have to vote on. But no one spoke.

The chapel furniture was covered in purple. In the middle of the floor were tables for counting the ballots. In front of the altar, flanked by two flat-topped marble pillars on which Fantucci the gardener had placed silver bowls with gold and yellow hyacinths, was a table. On it were two silver basins containing ninety-one small billets. Pavese's had been removed. He was not *papabile*, anyway. Not because of his age, since several Popes had been elected in their nineties, but because of his faulty bladder. Papal ceremonies can be very long.

The cardinals' names were inscribed on a slip of parchment. Each was slotted into a cavity in a lead ball and dropped into a big velvet bag which was then shaken. The Master of Ceremonies drew out three balls with the names of the tabulators which he read out: Warsaw, Rio, Munich.

Next, each cardinal was given a slip on which he put his name and motto. In the middle, after the printed words "I elect to the Supreme Pontificate the Most Reverend Lord, Cardinal . . ." he wrote the name of his choice.

To become Pontiff, in the early ballots, a candidate needs two-thirds of the votes.

First, the tabulators were to place their vote in the gold chalice, then the rest in order of seniority. Having folded the slip, they singly approached the altar holding the ballot at arm's length between the index and middle fingers of the right hand.

At the table, they genuflected and rose to say, "I witness before Christ my Lord, who is to be my Judge, that I choose the one whom I think most fit for office according to the will of God." They dropped the ballot into the chalice.

When all the votes had been cast, Warsaw shook the chalice. As each vote was counted, it was placed in a ciborium and then withdrawn one by one. The names of the elect were checked by the first two tabulators and, finally, read aloud by the third.

Several Italians showed up well. And with Berlin, Rio and São Paulo received two or three votes as a token gesture. The outcome, as expected, was inconclusive. The ballots were threaded together, placed on damp straw in the stove and burned. In the Square, black smoke issued from the polished silver smokestack. The crowd knew that God had not yet made up his mind whom he wanted as successor to John Paul II.

D ays passed and the novelty wore off. John Paul had been elected after only two days. No such luck this time round. Electors had walked tall into conclave feeling they were making history by electing Peter's successor, the Vicar of Christ. Now many of them began to suffer from claustrophobia and their language matched the color of their robes. In March 1996, John Paul had ruled that a conclave, after a week, was free to elect a new Pontiff on the basis of a simple majority. The present conclave, however, voted to stick to the older discipline and demand a two-thirds majority. Soon, many began to regret it.

Five or six cardinals had, at various times, received nearly forty votes but no one had remotely approached the magic number: sixty-two. Since Ricci, the Pope's Assassin, and Frangipani were the only two candidates in with a chance, neither of their backers, Montefiori and Rio, would budge.

Discussions continued into the early hours. Options were examined, compromises suggested. John Paul II had lived so long, not one cardinal had experience in electing the Supreme Pontiff. After sixteen ballots, the conclave was deadlocked.

Flick of Boston had run out of Hershey bars and was having to ration the hard stuff. Worse, before he left for Rome, he had booked himself into hospital for pre-Christmas surgery on his hemorrhoids.

"You shouldn't sit on so many committees," New York said. Sympathy, like good whiskey, was in short supply.

The revolving drum in the Parrot Courtyard was only used for essentials; foolishly, cigars and whiskey were not so considered. Flick now hated Michelangelo's fresco of the Last Judgment with all the fiber of his laxatives. Jesus looked to him like a weight lifter on hormones. Flick would have whitewashed the whole procking wall if he could.

As to the painting of the Creation on the ceiling, even Temple of St. Louis noticed that Adam had a navel. This showed Michelangelo might have designed everything in the Vatican from the dome of St. Peter's to the lettuces in the Gardens but he was theologically illiterate.

"How," Temple asked scornfully, "could a guy without a mother have a belly button?"

Runnell answered, "Same as a snake could speak without a voice box."

Overcrowding, the smell of stale tobacco and cheese-and-onion underpants, yellow puddles in the corridors on the way to the toilets whose plumbing was more primitive than the Mayflower's, the geriatric atmosphere was getting to them all. Old men hate the exclusive company of old men.

Burns kept saying that some underarm odors would make a skunk turn and run. One or two cardinals he could mention needed fumigation. He was also missing his pool table and his favorite TV soap from Australia.

23

"Jesus Christ," he said to his confrères, as they bunched together for yet another meal in the Borgia Hall of the Popes. "If this goes on much longer, I'm gonna vote for Stallone."

Sylvester Stallone, an old, born-again Democrat, had run for President a few years back. He claimed to be a bigger movie star than Reagan, why not? Burns had rooted for Roone Delaney in spite of the fact that he had been a disastrous Vice President and had mysteriously been unavailable for the Gulf War in 1991. Delaney, a Catholic, had won convincingly and rewarded Burns by having him read a prayer at his inaugural.

"You can't vote for a layman, Tom," said the flat-headed St. Louis.

"Can't I just?" retorted New York, his serpentine tongue popping in and out.

Runnell agreed with Burns. Many early Popes were laymen when they were elected by the clergy and people of Rome. So was Gregory X, the Pope who was behind all this conclave stuff. Obviously, cardinals did not have to vote for a member of the Sacred College. Even after the tenth century, subdeacons had made it to the papacy. They could certainly vote for Rottweiler, the former Prefect of the Holy Office, though he was too old to take part in conclave. Even a married man was a possibility.

"Never!" exclaimed Temple.

Runnell nodded. "Peter was."

"That," retorted Temple, "is why he denied his Lord."

"And that," said Burns, "is why, if he came back to life, I'd never let him be a curate in the Bronx."

All agreed that the idea of a man procking his wife in the night and making an infallible declaration in the morning was obscene.

"Besides," Burns said gloomily, "I don't suppose Stallone would accept."

They took to ruminating on a late-fifteenth-century fresco by Pinturicchio, *The Trial of St. Catherine*.

"The kid in front," said Runnell, behind his hand, "is Jofré Borgia, fourth son of Alexander VI. The broad on the left, second row, is probably Giulia Farnese."

"Right," Sapieha of Philadelphia said, his left eye clicking a dozen times in quick succession, "the Pope's you-know-what."

"*One* of his you-know-whats," Runnell said.

"Some dame," said Philadelphia.

"Yeah, Kammy." Runnell gave a snort of approval. "That golden hair went over some mighty fine landscape before reaching her dainty ankles."

"The swine Alexander," hiccuped Sapieha. "Worse than Henry VIII and Norman Mailer. And they had wives for each day of the week."

"Just five hundred years ago, in this very place," Runnell whispered, "Pope Alexander's son, Cesare, organized the Joust of the Whores and invited his father to attend. Rome's best pros did striptease, tearing each other's hair out when the Pope threw 'em horse chestnuts."

"A real swine of a pig," sighed Philadelphia, envious.

"By the standards of the time, Alexander wasn't so bad."

This was news to some. They were surprised when Runnell ran off a very long list of promiscuous Popes.

Benedict V, Sergius III and John X. John XII, who gave away gold chalices for one night of love and was murdered in the act of adultery by a jealous husband. Benedict VII, who went to God in similarly embarrassing circumstances. Benedict IX, the promiscuous teenage Pope who resigned the papacy in a vain attempt to marry his beautiful cousin. Boniface VIII.

Some were adolescents and some were the sons and grandsons of Popes, which was quite a record, seeing they were heads of a celibate institution. In fact, Runnell said, the Church was often much better off without Popes.

"Moving to Renaissance times," Runnell declared to his now open-mouthed audience, "take Innocent VIII. A real freewheeler. Had seven kids by seven different women."

"Go on," urged Philadelphia. This was *Dallas* with tiaras.

Runnell complied. "Julius II, three daughters. Paul II, three sons and one daughter. Paul IV, three sons. Gregory XIII, one son."

Philadelphia whistled in belief.

"Callixtus III," Runnell said, "did little for his bastards, but Alexander VI, he was a swell daddy."

They all agreed at the end of a spicy history lesson that the Borgia Pope was irreligious, engaged in orgies, spent millions like water, went in for multiform adultery, incest, nepotism; and, as for simony, he bribed his way into the papacy with promises of whores, palaces and mule loads of silver.

"But he didn't practice procking contraception," Tom Burns affirmed with his unchallengeable pulpit look, as if there was more to Alexander VI than just infallibility.

On December 20, they took the usual four ballots, each with the same result: Frangipani and Ricci level at forty-five and always one spoiled vote (*Eligo neminem,* I choose no one). It was the worst stalemate imaginable. More black smoke. St. Peter's Square was deserted, save for frozen cameramen and a few patrolling *carabinieri.*

The American bishops retreated to Burns's cell.

"Maybe this'll go on for a year," Flick moaned, peering through the stained-glass window of an empty whiskey bottle. "By then, I'll be sitting on a homegrown pneumatic tire."

Runnell said it took three years to elect Gregory X in 1271. It was this Pope who ordered that cardinal electors were to be locked in *con chiave,* conclave, meaning, with a key. They had to live in one big open room. After three days, meals of one course only. After five more days, nothing but bread and water. It worked. Gregory's successor was chosen in a day. Even big-bellied Burns thought a day's fast in such a cause might be worth a try.

In the Sistine Chapel, Montefiori pleaded with his fellow electors to give the matter more thought and prayer. He took another vote. The two leading contenders again polled forty-five.

In spite of laxatives, Flick was more constipated than Martin Luther. Seated like the Buddha on his Uncle Joe, he was spending fruitless nights reciting the sorrowful mysteries of the rosary. He would have greeted a bowel movement like the end of the Vietnam War. In spite of his solemn promise to vote for the best candidate, he would have backed Judas Iscariot if it speeded his return home.

In desperation, he decided to vote for the man next to him, who happened to be O'Flynn. After all, Flick reasoned, the guy comes from County Mayo, which is almost as Irish as Boston.

The result of the next ballot was announced forty minutes later. Ricci's forty-five was greeted with a groan, even from his supporters. "For Frangipani, forty-four." Cheers even from Venice's supporters. The first hole in the dike. Who would plug it?

"And, finally, one for O'Flynn."

"O'Flynn. O'Flynn?" No one had ever heard of him. After the murmurs came thunderous applause as if he had been made Pope by acclamation. Someone pointed out that O'Flynn was the junior deacon who shut the door to keep out unauthorized persons.

The cardinal from County Mayo shrugged. *It's a mistake, Lord, it has to be. Or a joke. There've not been too many of them lately.*

They broke for lunch. The U.S. party no longer complained that the food did not match the decor. Sure, it was pasta again. Rope-thick macaroni that would anchor a battleship. Wine that tasted of urine from someone with kidney trouble. Hard-boiled eggs ideal for stoning an adulteress. Tomatoes swimming and dying in garlic. Bread made from cement. Italian ham, prosciutto, tough as the ass of a marble cherub. But Tom Burns did not say for the hundredth time, "Why the procking hell didn't the Vatican take out a franchise from McDonald's?"

"Where's this O'Flynn guy from?" St. Louis wanted to know. "Armagh? A mission territory in Africa?"

Flick suggested he might come from old Ireland.

The learned Runnell joked that this was ominous. "Some old Irish saint, Malachi of Armagh, prophesied that the end of the world was nigh. Having an Irish Pope might make it that bit nigher."

"Got him," cried Burns. "Head of Congregation for Causes of Saints. What're his chances?"

Runnell ran a check on his IBM. "Nil."

But in the first evening session at 4:30, O'Flynn, now rubbing his slightly crossed eyes and scratching his gray cropped head in amazement, took a vote from Ricci and polled two. In the final session of the day he was up to four.

Joke's over, Lord. Popes, like pineapples, don't grow in Ireland.

Some suggested that O'Flynn might come from the back of the field to be a compromise candidate, like Pius X. When the slips were burned, the atmosphere in the Sistine Chapel was brighter than for many a day.

. . .

The U.S. bishops crammed into Runnell's room since Burns's was too close to O'Flynn's. They pooled their knowledge of the Irishman and it came to very little.

Burns's secretary, Father Harry Tickle, a balding giant of a man, was sent to get a bemused Frank Kerrigan. When he arrived, the cardinals circled him like vultures and pressed him down on the only chair.

"Now, Father," purred Burns, putting on a smile as genuine as the Turin Shroud, "where're you from?"

"New York, Eminence."

"Say, what a coincidence. How come we never met?"

"We have," Frank stammered. "Last year you ordained me in St. Patrick's Cathedral."

Burns snapped his nicotined fingers. They gave off a ploppy sound. "Geez, so I did. So you're *the* Father Corrigan I heard so much about."

"Kerrigan, Eminence."

"Listen, son, you level with me and I'll see you're made a monsignor. In fact, consider yourself one here and now"—he touched his breast—"*in petto.*"

The rest nodded approval as the newly promoted youngster ran a trembling hand through his hair. "Thank you," he managed to say.

"Now, *Monsignor* Kerrigan," Burns said, "tell us all you've picked up about Cardinal . . ." He didn't dare name O'Flynn. He wanted to stay clean.

"I've only been with him since the conclave began."

"What sort of a guy is he?" asked Flick, not letting on that he had brought O'Flynn into the reckoning for no other reason than the pain in his backside.

"He's nice," Frank murmured.

"Is that *all?*" they chorused.

"*Very* nice," Frank said. "He says his prayers."

"Don't we all?" sighed Philadelphia, who gave himself a dispensation from the breviary whenever his duties on the golf course demanded it.

More questions were showered on Frank to which he could only reply, "Not sure," or "Maybe so but—"

"His health good?" asked Flick, knowing that some Popes were too damned healthy. It crossed his mind that if he had told the conclave that he, like the sixteenth-century Pope Leo X, had an ulcerous ass, he might have got the job himself in a caretaker capacity.

Frank answered, "He takes no medication as far as I know."

New York removed the Macanudo and flourished it like a holy water sprinkler. Frank flinched as he was spattered with yellow saliva.

"A drink problem, Monsignor? He's Irish." No reaction from Kerrigan. "No vices at all? Come *on*, son, he can't be as clean as the Statue of Liberty."

"I honestly don't know."

"So"—Burns dabbed the air with his cigar, sending sparks flying—"whadya *suspect?*"

Frank said falteringly, "That he's something of . . ."—they hung on his words—"a saint."

"The guy just lost my vote," Flick blurted out. "I mean if ever I'd felt tempted to vote for him."

Sapieha agreed. "Things are tough enough as it is."

Tom Burns bit savagely into his cigar. "So, Corrigan, you're not even an assistant pastor and, presto, you're a procking expert on sainthood, is that it?"

"I may be wrong," Frank said, backtracking and looking for an out. "He's very fond of Charley."

"Charley?" came from eight red throats.

"His dog. Sleeps on his bed."

"On his *bed?*" St. Louis growled. "You've seen this so-called dog, son?"

"No, Eminence. It's a golden Labrador, I think."

"Golden . . . A blonde?" Burns was still mesmerized by Pinturicchio's fresco. "Could be a dame?"

"Right," said Sapieha. "Big boobs, golden locks hitting the floor."

Frank jumped up in a rage. "Eminences, you have filthy minds." He pushed his way through purple to the door. "He's worth the lot of you put together."

29

"I reckon," New York said icily, "you'd better leave us, *Father*."

Frank, who had been a monsignor for all of two minutes, tried to kiss a few rings but the men in scarlet were not in the mood after what he had said of them.

He went to say good night to Cardinal O'Flynn, only to find that from his cell came the sound of gentle snoring.

Chapter Three

Hard bargaining went on behind the scenes. By the following morning, both Ricci and Frangipani had been unceremoniously dropped.

Montefiori, the humblest of men, now headed the conservative challenge while the brilliant Chiarello of Milan, a mere fifty-two-year-old, championed the liberal cause.

In the first ballot, Montefiori gained forty-five votes, Chiarello forty-two and O'Flynn dropped to three.

Now, Lord, you can dismiss your servant in peace.

Flick had withdrawn his support after Frank Kerrigan had accused O'Flynn of holiness.

The Irish cardinal's relief was short-lived. In the next ballot, the others broke even on forty-one and he scored eight.

Hardly anyone went to lunch. O'Flynn found himself at table with Satolli, a deaf old fellow with Parkinson's. He was the one suspected of not voting. In passing the salt to O'Flynn, he spilled it all over him.

"That's lucky," the old boy bawled. "I said, *lucky.*" He grabbed a handful of salt and threw it over his shoulder into the eye of the nun who was serving them. "What's your name?"

O'Flynn mouthed his name.

"I was waiting for a sign," Satolli said, quivering.

I n Runnell's room, the U.S. cardinals were grouped around the computer.

O'Flynn, Brian Aidan

Born: *12 January 1941, Co. Mayo, W of Ireland*
Parents: *Practicing until their deaths*
Siblings: *2nd of 16 (surviving) children*
Studies: *Maynooth, Ireland, 1960–66*
      Irish College, Rome, 1966–71
Ordained: *26 May 1966*
Postgraduate studies: *Gregorian University*
Degrees: *Laureatus in Theology and Canon Law*
Grades: *8 (cum laude) in both*
Preferments: *Bishop 2000*
      Cardinal deacon 2006
Present office: *Head of Congregation for Causes of Saints, currently*
      engaged on process of canonization of Pius XII
Published works: *None*

The Americans were reassured. O'Flynn was no egghead. Top scholars invariably received 10 (summa cum laude) for their doctorates.

Another thing: he was not an Italian. For years, they seemed to have been pacing corridors windier than Chicago, trying to avoid, by day, pockets of foul, garlicky air breathed out by Italians. And dodging, at night, elderly Italian prelates as they made their way to the bathroom with chamberpots running over with something other than the mercy of God.

Flick of Boston was beginning to trust his backside's original intuition. "A good compromise candidate?" he asked.

His colleagues nodded.

"Whose arms do we twist now?" asked Temple, putting on his Frankenstein's monster look.

"Depends," said Flick. "Is he conservative or liberal?"

No one knew. They were at a loss, therefore, whether to consult Montefiori or Rio.

"The trick is," Burns said, his tongue flicking to left and right, "to present him as friendly to both sides."

They divided into two groups. One pounced on Montefiori's crowd in the Courtyard of San Damaso, the other grabbed Rio and company and walked them around the Parrot Courtyard.

At the end of the day, O'Flynn had accumulated twenty-five votes. The other two candidates were down to thirty-three apiece.

As the tabulators counted the slips, they were puzzled. For the first time, all ninety-one slips had been filled in correctly.

At the start of the next session, Montefiori withdrew his name. The electors waited with bated breath to find out which of the two leading candidates would pick up his votes.

Chiarello of Milan polled fifty-two. The surprise was, the remaining fourteen votes did *not* go to O'Flynn—*Lord, you've seen sense at last*—who remained at twenty-five. The fourteen votes were shared among five conservatives, none of whom had a hope. Many electors were plainly confused, not having the faintest idea where O'Flynn stood on ecumenism, clerical celibacy, women's ordination or sexual ethics.

Montefiori proposed that they defer the next ballot to the afternoon to allow time for prayer.

It worked. After intense lobbying by the Americans, the next session saw the back of the weakest contenders. O'Flynn had thirty-two votes and Chiarello fifty-nine, only three short of victory.

It was Christmas Eve. The electors gladly welcomed Montefiori's suggestion that they defer what might be the crucial vote till the Lord's Birthday.

For days now, O'Flynn had been on the receiving end of twisted smiles and fawning little bows from cardinals in the corridors. Chief among his admirers was the influential conservative Cardinal Emilio Ragno, head of the Sacred Congregation of the Sacraments and Divine Worship. He was completely bald, thin and red-faced, and his big beak of a nose supported huge bifocals. He was a bundle of nervous energy, endlessly fidgeting with his pectoral cross, ring, skullcap, tapping his feet, shuffling papers.

At meals, men whom O'Flynn had seen for years in Rome but never spoken to rushed to sit beside him. They insisted he should be served first. And Cardinal Satolli kept sprinkling him with salt like a mackerel.

Chapter Four

In the White House, Roone Delaney, a Republican and the first Catholic President since John F. Kennedy, was in the firelit, sound-muffled Oval Office, concentrating hard. He had drawn the curtains over the eleven-and-a-half-foot-tall French windows while he watched for the umpteenth time a video of his final TV confrontation with Stallone during the previous election campaign. Many theses, a dozen at Princeton alone, had been written about this classic confrontation known as "the Bead of Sweat."

Before the debate, Delaney had been ten points behind in the polls. Six former mistresses had rushed into print, exhibiting their credentials, which gave him an initial advantage. Until the press started asking him, "Where were *you* during the Gulf War?" and coming up with some interesting answers.

He did not respond too well to the questions in the debate, either. He was not too sure where the Solomon Islands were or who owned them. "If only I'd collected stamps when I was a kid," he quipped. He mixed up Iceland with Greenland and didn't know a kiloton from a megaton but conceded they were both on the big side. He got the current budget deficit wrong by $600 billion.

Where he scored was on decisiveness.

According to the next day's *New York Times*, suntanned, silver-haired, paunchy Stallone, with half-moon spectacles to give him an academic look, was no Jefferson. He had a slow, incoherent delivery. He was impressive enough when chewing gum like lumps of toxic waste. But his smile lacked stickum and his teeth were too tough and well capped to let the lies through. He would lead from the middle. He even looked a good loser.

Stallone's hopes of the presidency finally collapsed when he responded to the crunch question in the TV debate.

"If you *knew*, Mr. Stallone, that by pressing the nuclear button you would kill, say, 150 million Islamic Fundamentalists, would you hesitate?"

Stallone, looking older than his mother: "Would I *whut?*"

The interviewer slowly repeated the question.

"Well, uh . . . I guess . . . In answer to your hypot'etical question, I'd uh . . ."

"You'd hesitate."

"I, aw, naw, I, uh, wouldn't hesitate, naw. But . . ."

"But *what?*"

"No buts. I wouldn't hesitate," Stallone said, knowing his lack of hesitation had come too late.

The camera zoomed in and caught that fatal bead of sweat rolling down Stallone's narrow forehead onto his left eyebrow.

His backers swore afterward it was only a dab of greasepaint which melted under the lights. The damage was done. Instant press-button viewer reaction showed he lost 40 million votes and, with them, the election.

"Rocky ain't Rocky no more," was the public's reaction as the networks broadcast the vox pops. "He's a wimp." "The Ham in Hamlet." "This guy's about as much a diplomat as a bilious kid with stars in his eyes is an astronomer." "Betcha he can't spell 'tomatoes.' "

Stallone had done the unforgivable thing: under strain, he *sweated*. Goddammit, one commentator remarked, he has a weak *pore*. If he can't control *that*, how can he control his bladder or his bowels? What's the state of his underpants? If Ayatollah Hourani saw that bead of sweat, he would know that America had no pride. Would a guy who sweats, he'd say, have guts enough to press the button? Would he defend Western Europe or retaliate if the Muslims refused to sell us oil at reasonable prices? No way! Stallone looked as if he believed in a *weak* America. And if, as his backers said, Stallone didn't really sweat, he *seemed* to, which was worse. It meant he *looked* weak even when he wasn't. For Chrissake, that weasel'd be forever sending out the wrong signals. Forget the guy's lips, Muslims would say, *what says his weak pore?* That procking pore of his could bring about a nuclear catastrophe.

Delaney was watching a doctored tape. The worst of his gaffes had been edited out. That was a mistake. They were what endeared him to American viewers. He was no smart-ass. His arguments, like Reagan's long ago, were shallow enough for the voters to follow. The more ignorant he appeared, the more Americans loved him. It's really clever politicians whose stupidity one wonders about.

Delaney always leaned forward in his cream-cushioned armchair at this point. He watched himself leave his place and walk across the stage to Stallone. He shook out his handkerchief, the color of the flag, and offered it to his opponent. It was a masterstroke.

Stallone had a dazed look, as though he were watching one of his old movies. As several doctoral theses pointed out, Stallone was in something of an existential dilemma. If he accepted the offer, he would seem weak and defeated. If he refused, he would appear to be unpatriotic. What did he do? Fumbled in his pockets.

God Almighty, his aides groaned in the wings, he doesn't even know which pocket his handkerchief's in and this *goon* is running for president? Even Dan Quayle could sometimes find his handkerchief.

Eventually, Stallone found it in his top pocket. As he drew it out, a dozen white tablets that looked like tranquilizers flew all over the studio floor. He almost went on his knees looking for them. Glimpsing this on the monitor, he screwed his hankie up in a ball, patted his bead of sweat with it and stuffed it in his inside pocket. It was murder.

A smirking Delaney was asked the same question. "Would *you* hesitate to press the button on 150 million Muslims?"

"Why 150?" he asked trenchantly. "There's over a billion of them, aren't there?"

"I'll rephrase that," the interviewer conceded. "Would you hesitate to barbecue a billion of them?"

"No."

"Not for a second?"

"For no longer than it takes to thank Almighty God for choosing a loyal American like me to do it."

"You really would press that—?"

"As easily as summoning an elevator."

"You'd have no qualms?"

"I'm not a qualmsy sort of guy."

"That is your clear message to the FIR."

"My clear message to them is, they must not now or never be allowed to doubt, query or question but that my impatience is not nearly or remotely now or never inexhaustible."

"Clear enough, Mr. Delaney. But how would you *feel* about the awesome responsibility for, well, deleting so many people?"

"Mighty good."

"No sympathy at all?"

"I wouldn't send 'em flowers, if that's what you mean."

"What I'm trying to get at is—"

"I know what you're trying to get at. Wouldn't I feel just a little bit sorry for, say, innocent Muslim women and children?"

The interviewer nodded.

"Mind if I show you a short video?"

"Not at all, sir."

As the equipment was being set up, Delaney thought it right to forewarn all squeamish viewers to switch off—knowing none would—because they were about to see something even more ghastly than Stallone in search of his handkerchief.

"The late Ayatollah Khomeini, ladies and gentlemen—any kids watching, *please* cover your eyes—Khomeini said, 'We want a ruler who could amputate the hand of his own son if he steals.' This video was smuggled out of Iran. It shows Hourani, President of the FIR, whose three sons were accused of stealing from a bank by forging checks and bonds."

A mesmerized audience saw on-screen the dark face of Ayatollah Hourani as he stood in front of three boys aged about eighteen to twenty. He put a black smudge on their foreheads in the shape of a cross before moving away.

"These are his sons, fine, strapping lads," explained Delaney.

Three doctors stepped forward with scalpels. The three lads stretched out their right hands and the doctors began amputating them without anesthetic. Afterward, the boys screamed even louder as the stumps were plunged in boiling tallow to disinfect them.

The camera turned from the boys' agony to the granite-hard face of their father as he watched, eyes dry as deserts, lips curved in scorn like a scimitar. Viewers had never seen anything quite like Hourani's terrifying stillness.

When the amputations were complete, his sons one by one raised their severed hands aloft to their foreheads to salute their father before tossing them over their right shoulder as though they were branches lopped off a tree.

When the video ended, Delaney, who had almost passed out himself, said, "It mattered little to President Hourani that a month after that deed was done, someone else confessed in a suicide note to having committed the theft from the bank. It was, Hourani said, the will of Allah."

The white-faced interviewer coughed. "So, Mr. Delaney?"

"That's the FIR for you. That old Khomeini guy said in his book *Islamic Government*, 'To kill the unbeliever is a sacred vengeance, a duty of murder.'"

"So?"

"Who's the unbeliever? You, me, the millions of loyal Americans watching. That's why followers of the FIR are not innocents, whatever their age or sex. Skunks who support barbarism such as we've seen, who mock democracy, who approve of terrorism worldwide, who refuse to accept a Christian way of life, they are better off dead."

No wonder *Cosmopolitan* said in its next issue, "The handsome Roone Delaney won the TV debate, why do we need an election?"

He won by a landslide.

He proved himself an even shrewder President than a candidate. He found the formula early on. When the going got tough, he said to his aides, "Cut me some taxes if you can find any. Threaten to send a cruise with a nuclear warhead to blow up Castro's grave or Saddam Hussein's. Write me a speech slamming Hourani and the FIR. Another slamming anyone who culls seals, dolphins or whales. Take my picture with a kitten. Hand me some rhetoric against any non-American who chops down rain forests or opens up chunks of the ozone layer. Get me support in Congress for another fifty of the latest missiles or another twenty B-2 Stealth bombers at a billion apiece. Find me a small inexpensive war I can win in a week or two, the closer to home the better. How's Haiti doing lately, by the way? At most, one or two Americans in body bags so we can have national mourning without too many tears and a ticker-tape parade in New York."

It never failed. He shot up in the ratings. When his popularity sagged while he was running for a second term against Democrats and gays, he took back the Panama Canal.

On his walnut desk, a light showed up on the fifty-line telephone console. Thank God it was not red, meaning maximum alert. If that were to happen, he would be immediately put through, on a scrambler, to the war room at the Pentagon, and, via the Pentagon, to both Strategic Command and NATO headquarters in Europe. The Pentagon might then advise him to proceed to his top-secret bunker or rush aboard the ever-ready-for-takeoff *Air Force One*.

On a nonthreatening line, Bill Huggard, White House Chief of Staff, wanted to update him on the conclave. The CIA headquarters in Langley, Virginia, was forwarding to Huggard twice-daily reports sent by their station in Rome. Advance planning was paying off.

Twenty years before, an Italian art expert who was restoring the Sistine Chapel had been bribed to plant a couple of solar-powered bugs in Michelangelo's vaulted ceiling, a hundred feet up. One was in the gap where the fingers of God and Adam almost meet in the moment of creation. Candlelight would suffice to operate the bugs, which had an unlimited life. They were also virtually undetectable.

The Soviets had four bugs in the Sistine and these were inherited by the FIR when they bought the Russian Embassy on the Via Aurelia for a song.

The British relied on one, a superbug that was state-of-the-art. A pity it ceased functioning after three weeks.

Huggard told the President that Brian O'Flynn's bandwagon was starting to roll. Delaney opened the curtains and the room was flooded with green light. He looked south through the newly installed six-inch laminated, sniper-proof windows, past leafless trees, to the Washington Monument a thousand yards away.

Good for Brian. By a strange twist, he owed him a debt of gratitude. Four years before, Delaney had paid a trip to the land of his forefathers. He had wanted to visit his ancestral home in the village of Ballymuck in County Wexford. The entire Irish hierarchy refused to meet him because they disapproved of U.S. armed intervention in Central America. Jesus Christ, why did God put Central America there except for the U.S. of A. to intervene in it? O'Flynn, probably at John Paul's request, had flown from Rome and stood next to the President for the pictures that meant so much to the wonderful voters back home.

In the unlikely event of that little Irish cardinal making it to the top, Roone Delaney, for one, would not be sorry.

Chapter Five

The same message was spread by several cardinals in conclave, mostly orchestrated by New York. Burns kept saying to everyone he met, "O'Flynn, so obviously a conciliator, an olive tree in our midst, a man of peace."

Burns could see himself standing on the steps of St. Patrick's Cathedral next to the first Irish Pope as the next St. Patrick's Day Parade swept past on Fifth Avenue. Wasn't his archdiocese dedicated to St. Patrick? The cathedral door would bear the papal arms. He'd deck the whole goddamn place out with white and yellow chrysanthemums, turn the huge carved papal throne away from the wall so the Pope could sit in it.

Not just the Mayor of New York, the President himself might attend the parade. He'd get the Waldorf to provide the food on their best gold-service china. All over America rivers would run green that day; they'd eat green hot dogs, drink green beer, even piss green.

Better still, U.S. bishops were having a tough time with gays taking over the parade, priests marrying, divorcing and remarrying without telling them while feminist nuns chased funds for abortion clinics. Mostly of Irish origin, they had shut their ears to an antique Pole. But a Pope from the old country, now, they might just give him a hearing.

This was why Burns was irritated by Kinsella of Armagh, Ireland. Bald-headed Kinsella was so tiny that Burns wanted to pick him up and tap him with a spoon. Kinsella was not at all enthusiastic about O'Flynn becoming

Pope. Maybe it was jealousy but he kept saying in a reedy, sanctimonious voice, "My predecessor in the see of Armagh, God rest him, has a message for the electors."

When he went into that, Burns discovered that the predecessor Kinsella was referring to was a St. Malachi who had lived in the twelfth century. Jesus Chu-rist! he told himself, these Irishmen have such procking long memories. If only they remembered less and worked more. He'd heard that in Ireland, the statues moved more than the people.

At odd moments, Kinsella waylaid Burns to tell him about St. Malachi's many prophecies which had all come true. The saint had provided an enigmatic Latin title for every Pope starting with Celestine II in 1143.

"Until?" Burns demanded, his pointed tongue on the move.

"Until," Armagh whispered, "the end of the world."

"Which is due precisely *when?*" Burns wanted to know so he didn't start dieting if there was no need.

"Very, very . . . soon."

Burns had an almost uncontrollable urge to shove Kinsella up a mouse hole. *"How soon?"*

"Malachi's prophecy is that there will only be two more Popes before Armageddon."

"That gives us a little breathing space," Burns said dismissively.

"No," Armagh said in a sort of whistle. "The last Pope is to be called Peter the Roman. Now, no Pontiff has ever had the temerity to call himself Peter, not even the two Popes who were baptized with that name. Most commentators agree that Peter the Roman is St. Peter himself, who will come with the angels to prepare the world for judgment."

"So the Pope we elect might be the last?"

"He *will* be, Eminence."

Burns thanked Kinsella for the advance warning before rushing away to do more electioneering on O'Flynn's behalf.

Kinsella refused to give up. He squeezed next to Burns at lunch, ousting his Philadelphia buddy, Kammy Sapieha.

"St. Malachi's messages have been very accurate, Eminence. Take Paul VI. Malachi called him *flos florum.*"

" 'Flower of flowers,' " echoed Burns. "So what?"

43

"Paul VI chose three fleurs-de-lis for his shield. Then there was John Paul I. Malachi described him as *de medietate lunae*. Hard to translate, but I think it means 'Pope of the half-moon.' He had but a sliver of a pontificate, so to speak. Only thirty-three days."

Burns nearly choked on his glass of Chianti at Armagh's childishness. "What about John Paul II?"

"*De labore solis*. 'From the labor of the sun.' You would not deny that the last Pontiff of holy memory worked harder than any other. On his many travels, he kept the sun as his companion, so to speak."

"So to speak."

Catching the incredulous tone, Armagh whispered, "One of your own predecessors believed in the prophecies."

This was too much. Burns shot up and was about to leave when Armagh said, "In 1958, Cardinal Spellman of New York—"

Burns collapsed wearily in his chair. "Yeah?"

"Malachi's motto for the next Pope at that time was *pastor et nauta*, 'shepherd and sailor.' You must know what Spellman did?" Burns shook his fat head. "He hired a boat here in Rome, filled it with sheep and sailed down the Tiber."

Burns was about to say he didn't believe a word when it struck him that this was the clincher.

"I might remind you," he roared, causing all heads to turn in his direction. He lowered his voice. "Spellman never made it to the papacy."

"Ah, yes," Kinsella said in his wheedling way, "but the real Shepherd and Sailor was chosen by the Holy Spirit, not by men. Even Protestants acknowledged John XXIII was the Shepherd."

"And Sailor?" Burns said. "How was the little fat guy a sailor?"

"You are forgetting, Eminence, that John XXIII, like Pius X, came from the city on the water."

"Venice," Burns said in a voice that changed register in one short word.

"Malachi's prophecy ends like this: 'In the final persecution of the Holy Roman Church, there will reign Peter the Roman, who will feed his flock among many tribulations. Afterward, the seven-hilled city will be destroyed and the dreadful Judge will judge the people.' "

Burns was now dribbly with irritation and severely short of breath. "The Pope we are about to elect. What is his—"

"St. Malachi of Armagh says he is *gloria olivae*, 'glory of the olive,' a man of peace."

Burns nearly suffered a stroke. He had to be helped back to his cell by his secretary, Harry Tickle. It took him a full hour to convince himself that Armagh's superstition must not be allowed to rub off on him.

He worked off his discomfort by going into a huddle with Rio. He no longer described O'Flynn as an olive tree in our midst, a man of peace, but nonetheless insisted that O'Flynn was the boy.

"But," objected Rio, "will that not seem a political act?"

Burns assured him not. It would be so if they were to elect Kinsella of Armagh, which is in Northern Ireland and under British rule. O'Flynn was from the Irish Republic in the south, which was independent. Furthermore, it was now officially a Third World country.

"It is close to all our hearts," Burns concluded, "in having thirty percent unemployment and foreign debts per person twice the size of Brazil's."

Rio pricked up his ears. "Ah, yes?" This would be like voting for one of his own.

"Remember, too, that the Irish planted the faith all over the world, Africa, India, China, North and South America."

Rio stroked his dark cheek. "Maybe the Irish deserve a Pope after all these centuries." His face clouded over. "A pity he is so conservative."

The suggestion seemed to rock Burns to his considerable foundations.

"Conservative? Just because he refuses to follow the latest fads in theology?"

In point of fact, Burns had no idea where his candidate stood. There was no label on the bottle and inquiries still led nowhere. O'Flynn seemed never to have committed himself on anything, but the signs were he was such a party-liner that his toes hurt. As Temple of St. Louis observed: "He certainly stands *in* in a crowd."

"He is no liberal," Rio insisted.

"Not a rabid one. But flexible. After John Paul II, the Church is not ready for the fast lane. An extremist of right or left would tear the Church apart as it has divided this conclave. Also, Eminence"—Burns switched to a whisper—"Chiarello of Milan is only fifty-two. You want an Italian racing driver for Pope? If we make a mistake . . . thirty to forty years to regret it."

That argument went like an arrow to the target.

"Besides, Chiarello has no firsthand experience of the Curia. O'Flynn knows it from within. They won't be able to pull the wool of the pallium over his eyes."

"Yet, if you will forgive me," Rio said sadly, "he seems such an ordinary man."

"If you will forgive *me*, Eminence, look at the state of the Church after thirty and more years of an *extraordinary* man."

"A man of the middle, you think," Rio murmured.

Behind his back, Burns crossed his yellow fingers. "I am certain of it."

Christmas morning. A solemn concelebrated Mass was arranged in the Sistine for midday. The first vote at 8:00 A.M. was still inconclusive. New York's word in Rio's ear had had some effect. Chiarello had dropped to fifty-three and O'Flynn was up to thirty-eight.

Lord, please be careful. Don't do anything you'll regret.

Montefiori informed the excited assembly that he had invited both candidates to preach at the Mass.

Montefiori, as Chamberlain, was chief celebrant, assisted by Chiarello as deacon and O'Flynn as subdeacon. After the Gospel reading of the Nativity, Chiarello approached the microphone. To the Americans, this was like the final TV debate in a presidential campaign.

Chiarello had a heraldic voice, a superb presence, and his Latin was Ciceronian.

"Jesus is born again today," he began, "in a rapidly changing world. It is vital for the Church to change, too, in order to confront it at every level and convert it. We need a new approach to everything from microbiology, through drugs and sexuality, to the Brotherhood of Islamic Republics, now that the Ice War is upon us."

He told how Islam had moved through Africa, converting to Islam thousands of Catholics who preferred to have several wives rather than suffer what they called the loneliness of monogamy. Males judged the ban on pork was less onerous than the ban on contraception and divorce. And the message of Islam, the *shahada,* "There is no God but Allah and Muhammad is his Messenger," was far easier to comprehend than the Roman catechism.

In addition, Islam had been reborn in the republics of the old Soviet Union and had grown now to 100 million. There were 40 million Muslims in China and in Indonesia 175 million more.

"Not all Muslims are terrorists. Nor, let us be frank, is the West itself free from terrorism.

"For instance, in 1993 the Americans attacked Baghdad to avenge the assumed attempt on the life of George Bush. Mr. Clinton sent twenty-three Tomahawk cruise missiles each with 450 kilograms of high explosive on defenseless Iraqis, including women and children. He even invoked Article 51 of the U.N. Charter, dealing with self-defense! Such hypocrites!"

As to the Church, Chiarello's theme was adaptation. Fundamentals cannot change, but it is vital to apply traditional principles in a new way to a new world. Above all, the Church had to face the menace of Islam as it had faced it in the Middle Ages by means of the Crusades.

He spoke for thirty minutes, and no one noticed the passage of time. At the end, his forehead gleamed with sweat.

His peroration was so majestic, some cardinals had to sit on their hands to stop themselves clapping. It was a hard act to follow.

Lord, O'Flynn prayed, *Chiarello has my vote. I hope he has yours.*

In every way, O'Flynn was a contrast. He moved away from the microphone to speak in a whisper that carried around the chapel.

"My dear friends and fellow sufferers."

Simple, unadorned Italian. This surprised everyone. He spoke it pleasantly with a slight brogue. Chiarello, a kind man, cast a pitying glance at his unsophisticated opponent.

"Our present accommodation, I reckon, enables us to sympathize with Our Blessed Lord."

A ripple of laughter went round the chapel. Chiarello was astute. He realized that a new and magical element had been introduced into the contest: humor. He looked at O'Flynn with a new respect.

"And yet, brothers," the preacher went on, "in God's marvelous providence, might there not be some merit in even Princes of the Church following in the footsteps of the Master?"

The U.S. cardinals, not famed for their sense of humor, did not know what to make of this. Burns whispered to Flick, "For Chrissake, Knife, the nut has procking blown it."

Flick whispered back. "Not sure. He's no saint, Tom. Saints don't crack jokes."

O'Flynn went on to speak of Joseph, the strong and silent defender of the Holy Family; of Mary, Virgin and Mother; of Jesus, God's Son made man for us.

Montefiori's chameleon-like eyes glistened with amusement. With what amounted to a political harangue, Chiarello had missed out. This *was* Christmas Day. Only the seamless Gospel could unite the divided elements of conclave.

"Jesus' poverty," O'Flynn went on, "was real and it was revolutionary, but it was not cruel or strident. It speaks to our consciences. Jesus says, 'I am poor and hungry and thirsty in the poor of the world.' His birth in the stable is a mute appeal to the heart of every rich person. He did not break any windows, so to speak, or spill any blood, but his own. He wants us, as one Irish poet put it—a Marxist, incidentally—'to pray by the straw of the Babe of Bethlehem.' "

Looking around him, the Chamberlain saw that Rio and the other liberals respected this man for his love of the poor. The conservatives liked him because, even in the face of poverty, he spoke of leaving windows unbroken and only praying with faith by the straw of the Babe of Bethlehem.

Above all, the Italians found him *simpatico*. He stuck to the mind-boggling orthodoxies of the faith. His smile was open and warm.

"A nightingale is perched upon his lips," whispered Cardinal Ragno, head of the Sacred Congregation of the Sacraments, quivering all over as he touched his skullcap and shook his head.

O'Flynn's green eyes moved as though he addressed each of them, they shone when he felt things deeply. He made gestures that spoke for him when words were inadequate. A Celt was not *so* different from an Italian.

O'Flynn ended his three-minute sermon with part of the "Breastplate of St. Patrick," sometimes called "The Deer Cry":

Christ be with me, Christ be before me,
Christ be after me, Christ be in me,
Christ be under me, Christ be over me,
Christ be at my right, Christ be at my left,
Christ be in the heart of everyone I speak to,
Christ be in the heart of everyone who speaks to me,
Christ be in each eye that sees me,
Christ be in each ear that hears me.

He sat down completely unaware of the impact of his words. *Now, Lord, choose me in preference to the other fellow and you'll only prove you are, after all, an Irishman.*

Before the final vote was taken, President Delaney was interrupted while practicing his putting on the gray-green carpet which was woven with the Great Seal of the United States.

Huggard assured him that his "old buddy," Brian O'Flynn, would be successor to John Paul II.

"Amen to that," Delaney said, crossing himself with the top of his putter.

He remembered with nostalgia being at home in Mystic, Connecticut, when it was confirmed on TV that he was President-elect. "Christ," he thought, glancing at the small Union flag on his desk, "*that* said something about the democratic process." To think that millions of ordinary dim Americans could be so damn *right*.

On that great day, his wife had come in, nearly crazy, and jumped into his arms, and it took a while for him to realize she was not overcome but terrified. "The FIR!" she screamed. She was convinced a coup was under way: a bunch of hoodlums with guns had surrounded the house and were about to assassinate them both.

It turned out to be two dozen special agents ordered by the chief of the Secret Service in Washington to guard the next Leader of the Free World. By God, he felt important then. Leader of the Free World!

Now Holy Mother Church, the next best organization on earth, was to be led by little Brian O'Flynn. Delaney glanced at the Swedish ivy on the mantelpiece under Washington's picture and thought the green of it highly appropriate.

Chapter Six

C ardinal Chiarello, three votes."

Pandemonium broke out as Chiarello rushed to kneel at O'Flynn's feet. When the electors had quieted down, Montefiori called for a final show of hands to make the vote unanimous.

O'Flynn sat bowed and dejected as the Chamberlain loomed over him. *Lord, you have just made the most terrible mistake of your eternal life.*

It should have been O'Flynn's task as junior cardinal deacon to ring the bell announcing the new Pope. Someone else grabbed it and gave it a loud peal. The chapel doors were whipped open. Secretaries, sisters, helpers raced in. The Secretary of the Conclave, the M.C. and the sacristan joined Montefiori as he inquired:

"Most Reverend Lord Cardinal, do you accept your election as Sovereign Pontiff?"

Frank Kerrigan at the back of the crowd could hardly believe his eyes. Cardinal O'Flynn had given no hint that he was in the running.

Dr. Gadda was running an expert eye over the Pope-elect and liked what he saw. Peasant type, sturdy, surely not prone to nightmares, good complexion, the teeth of an ancient Roman, somewhat cross-eyed. From a distance, he seemed unlikely to disturb Gadda's nights.

Sergio Fantucci, the gardener, took advantage of the chaos to rush to a window overlooking the piazza where his cousin, Mario, was waiting. A prearranged signal meant "number 88," that is, Cardinal O'Flynn.

Mario was astounded. He ran like the wind to phone four bookmakers where he bet in total the equivalent of $25,000—all borrowed—on O'Flynn at odds of around 100 to 1. Each bookmaker smackingly kissed his own hand to thank him for his insane generosity.

In seconds, Fantucci was back in the Sistine, where O'Flynn had still not replied to the Chamberlain. Skullcaps were thrown in the air and everyone was singing *"Ad multos annos, vivat."* Only the Cardinal of Armagh stood apart, voiceless and petrified.

The Chamberlain called for silence and turned to O'Flynn, who was covering his face with his hands.

"Eminenza?" Montefiori whispered hoarsely. "Is it *volo* or *nolo*, yes or no?"

In a cracked voice: *"Accepto* . . . I accept this burden in the name of my Lord who was born to suffer on this day."

Montefiori signaled to the tabulators to burn the final slips without damp straw. Smoke, first gray then white, emerged from the stack.

In the piazza on this Christmas Day, the temperature was near freezing. Only half a dozen Japanese tourists were present to witness the smoke, but TV cameras picked it up. Seconds later, pictures were beamed by satellite across the world.

Brian O'Flynn went to kneel in front of the Blessed Sacrament. He looked up at the awesome figure of the Christ of Judgment painted by Michelangelo.

Lord, I'm really scared. Get me out of this.

Seconds later, having received no answer from above, he nodded, suggesting he had chosen the name by which he would be called as Pope. Cardinals banged on their desks, aides stamped on the felted wooden floor. The whole chapel began to vibrate as though there were a minor quake.

One of the ornamental marble pillars on whose flat top Fantucci had rested a bowl of hyacinths started to sway. Burns saw it first and yelled, "Watch out," but his voice was drowned by the din. Slowly, as if it possessed a malevolence of its own, the three-hundred-pound pillar toppled, striking the new Pope on the right temple. He dropped like a stone, cracking the other side of his head on the floor.

The terrible silence that ensued was split by nuns screaming and shouts of "Call a doctor." One Italian cardinal commented solemnly, "Chiarello of Milan has put the Evil Eye on him." Fantucci was plucking his mustache as though it were a cello. That a Pope might die because of his incompetence was one thing, but what about his $25,000?

The Pope lay prone. There was no blood but he was unconscious. His limbs were limp, his breathing was rapid and shallow. Burns was moaning inwardly, "Is my Pope to have the shortest reign in history?"

Four cardinals struggled to pick the Pontiff up and carry him to his room. One was Flick. The effort was too much for him. His eyes went as red as the buttons on his soutane. A magpie chatter escaped his throat as he suffered a massive heart attack. Sapieha did his best to give him the kiss of life, but he himself was soon out of breath and had to be led away.

Within a minute, Boston lost its cardinal. Had he died a few days earlier, O'Flynn would never have made it to the papacy. And the future of the world would have been very different.

Chapter Seven

Dr. Vittorio Gadda, his face glossy as ceramic, his waxed mustache bristling, rushed forward and took charge. He saw to it that the Pope was not moved but stretched out on the carpet in front of the altar.

In this unprecedented crisis, the Chamberlain showed his mettle. After pledging everyone to secrecy, he cleared the chapel. He allowed only the doctor, the tabulators and Father Kerrigan to stay behind. New York, too, since he seemed to think he had some kind of proprietary interest in the Pope.

To the tabulators, Montefiori said, "Send up plenty of black smoke, *pronto.*"

"But," one protested, "we have already burned the slips."

"Then burn anything, your own soutane, if need be. We need time."

When another objected that he would not tell lies for anyone, Montefiori rounded on him angrily.

"If His Holiness dies, what will the people think of God's guidance of his Church? No, we must not say or do anything until the Pope pulls round, or he dies, and we elect another."

Black smoke, the thickest ever, billowed out of the chimney, and everything in St. Peter's Square went into reverse. Vatican Radio issued a correction. Fresh TV pictures, humble apologies to viewers. Crowds already streaming along the Via della Conciliazione into the piazza turned and went back home to celebrate Christmas.

$$\cdot \quad \cdot \quad \cdot$$

In the mansion of the White House, the President demanded to know what the hell was going on. It was five minutes before he learned the truth.

The FIR also had a keen interest in the election. President Hourani was presiding over a meeting of the Council, which had moved from Tehran to Cairo. The dozen members were seated in an underground bunker annexed to the al-Azhar University, founded in 969 and reputedly the oldest university in the world. Some ignorant Westerners called it Islam's Vatican.

Those present included the Foreign Minister, the chief of Intelligence, the Guardian of Public Morality, the heads of Religious Affairs, Family Protection, the People's Police Force, the Armed Forces, and Revolutionary Affairs. The rest made up the *ulama*, the body of theologians.

No member was allowed to miss a meeting, which meant sometimes they had to be borne to Riyadh or Tehran or Lahore half-dead. One of them did die on the way once: such was the will of Allah. It was written. He was declared a martyr of Islam. The President declared him to be now in a water-filled garden, the Abode of Peace, praising Allah with reason. For he was attended by gazelle-like maidens with dark eyes as, according to the Koran, the martyrs "lie on couches raised on high in the shade of thornless sidrahs and clusters of banana palms, amid gushing waters and abundant fruits, unforbidden, never-ending." There, the houris feed them and minister to their pleasure, though it lasts a thousand years.

President Hourani was giving an address full of scorn for Catholic clerics.

"How account, my brothers, for their wicked preference for celibacy to the innumerable pleasures of the flesh and the sons thereof given by Allah? Why were these Catholic priests born if they think their triple God wants to deprive them of sex here and hereafter? Who would trust a man who is not a man?"

Laughter came from his brethren like the rumble of thunder.

Worse, said Hourani, was their blasphemy that Allah is Messiah, son of Mary, and that he was a god risen from the dead. How could these Christian dogs believe that men could touch and handle the infinite exalted omnipotent Allah? Even Jews were not so heathenish.

As to the Vatican, "It is full of blasphemous pictures and idols, called statues, such as the Prophet destroyed in Mecca. They even pray over dismembered corpses and musty grave clothes."

His chief *alim*, or theologian, confirmed it.

Hourani said he had read descriptions of Christian places of worship like St. Peter's and St. John Lateran.

"How cheap and tawdry they seem, my brothers, compared with the stark and desert-like grace of Mecca or Jerusalem's Dome of the Rock, the Blue Mosque of Omar, which is as beautiful as morning, or the virgin-slender Taj Mahal or the stupendous black onyx tomb of Tamburlaine at Samarkand."

It was strange to him that Catholics chose their leader in an ugly oblong chapel with idolatrous pictures on walls and ceilings, representing creation and judgment.

"As if anyone can picture Allah! As if Jesus, rather than Allah, is, as the Koran says, 'the King on the Day of Judgment.' Ah, if only Muhammad were alive to torch the Vatican and cleanse it of such irreligious filth."

Hourani called on his brilliant Foreign Minister to brief the Council on what was happening in the Sistine.

Sheikh Hamed es-Safy, a Baghdadi, was tiny, with a round face, and clean-shaven but for a walrus mustache. His eyes were dark amber and the end of his nose was missing. He walked with a limp.

The sheikh had been kept up-to-date by a hot line from Cairo to the Villa Abamalek. This was the former vast Soviet walled estate at the beginning of the Via Aurelia, less than a mile south of St. Peter's. From the villa, a tunnel had been dug in the granular tufa, a soft, reddish substance on which much of Rome is built. In the tunnel, near the Vatican, a listening room had picked up the Pope's accident which Sheikh Hamed described in detail.

Afterward, Hourani confessed that he hoped it was Allah's will that

O'Flynn recovered. "The other man's sermon did not please me one little bit," he said.

The meeting ended as always with a line chanted out of the Sura of the Koran in the direction of Mecca: "Make war on those who believe not."

D r. Gadda told Montefiori that the Pope should be hospitalized at once. The Gemelli Clinic was only two miles away, ten minutes by ambulance. John Paul II had been taken there when he was shot in St. Peter's Square and when he suffered various dislocations at audiences and in his bath.

The cardinal shook his head and Gadda said:

"Eminence, cranial injuries are the most difficult to diagnose. There could be irreparable damage."

There was steel in Montefiori's voice. "Do your best, *per favore.*"

Gadda refused to accept responsibility.

Montefiori told his secretary to call a neurosurgeon whom Gadda recommended but not on a Vatican phone in case it was tapped. Nor from the post office outside the tradesmen's entrance at Porta Sant'Anna. There was an espresso bar with a phone a little farther along. The specialist was to enter not by the Arch of the Bells, but at Porta Sant'Anna, so as not to attract attention.

The Pope, still out cold, was transferred by stretcher to Burns's room.

Dr. Tardini arrived within forty minutes, puffing and exuding liquor. A bald, fat man, he and his mistress had been rudely awakened in the middle of their siesta. He immediately consulted Gadda about reflexes, sodium level, signs of metabolic disorder, then carried out his own examination.

Pulse and breathing none too regular, pupils still dilated. He tapped the knees; tendon reflexes feeble. The first outsider to see the new Pontiff was not impressed by his condition.

"Well," Montefiori wanted to know, "will he recover?"

Tardini pointed a pudgy finger at the patient. "Behold the only infallible one, Eminence."

"But the indications?"

"Too soon to say. He could be hemorrhaging internally and might need brain surgery for a blood clot. If he pulls round, he might suffer a complete or partial loss of memory. He might be subject to epilepsy." He joined his fingertips in prayer. "On the other hand, he might wake up in ten minutes with nothing worse than a splitting headache." A baroque gesture to the heavens. "Anything is possible."

Montefiori closed his eyes. *"Miserere nobis."*

Tardini asked if the patient had spoken. Montefiori shook his head but Kerrigan said, "Once or twice he mentioned Charley. That's his dog."

Montefiori came to with a start. "He owns a dog? Go and get him, Father."

As Frank slipped out of the Vatican to look for a taxi, Cardinal Burns was sighing, "Please God, he won't come back with a blonde."

The dog licked his master's face.

For a full minute, the Pope did not stir. Then, in a sort of mumble: "Charley? Go back to sleep."

Prelates and doctors rose as one to their feet.

"You hear me, Charley. Sleep. Go back—"

The Pope opened his eyes and, for the moment, saw only his secretary in a pool of light.

"Hi, Frank."

Frank was too overcome to respond.

"Did I oversleep myself?"

"You had a little accident."

"I did?" The Pope touched the bumps on his head and winced. "Heavens, there's a dentist's drill inside my skull. Another thing." He held up both hands at once. "That's odd."

"What's that?"

"Nothing. It'll pass to be sure."

Frank briefly explained about a pillar falling on him.

"Providence, Frank. I guess that's me out of the running, eh? A crazy notion from the start."

58

"You don't remember, Holiness?" And Frank told him the whole story. *Lord, I just don't believe this.*

"I was elected Pope," the Pope murmured, "and I was damn fool enough to accept?"

Frank went down on his knees to kiss the Pope's hand but Charley beat him to it.

"I am dreaming," the Pope said, still looking strangely at his hands. "I remember nothing since the Mass." He peered around and for the first time saw the other people present.

"Retrogressive amnesia," Dr. Tardini whispered in Montefiori's ear. "Not uncommon after a severe blow on the head."

"Will he remember accepting office?"

"Maybe yes, maybe no. His eyes seem to be looking at each other."

Montefiori said, "They were like *that* before."

Burns stepped out of the shadows and, after kissing the Pope's hand, grabbed Father Kerrigan. "That's my boy, Holiness."

"With your permission," the Pope said, sitting up, "I will continue to borrow him for a while."

"I told him only the other day," Burns said, "that he was going places."

Montefiori gently steered the specialist into the corridor. "There won't be any other aftereffects, Doctor? Derangement, personality defects, things like that?"

"What was he like before, Eminence?"

The cardinal coughed. "No one is quite sure."

Tardini looked at him as if to say, And you elected him *Pope?*

Montefiori returned to the room. "By what name will you be known, Holiness?"

Without a moment's hesitation: "Pope Patrick."

Chapter Eight

Pope Patrick was persuaded to have a good night's sleep. On the morning of St. Stephen's Day, white smoke rose up into the still air and the crowds started massing.

In the sacristy of the Sistine Chapel, Alberto Gammarelli fitted the Pope out from the smallest of his three boxes.

Lord, I still don't believe this.

Alberto helped him on with white cotton socks, white silk soutane, sash, rochet, cape, crimson slippers with embroidered gold crosses, stole and mozzetta. The Pope thought the soutane somewhat heavy, not realizing that an Ollie North bulletproof vest had been sewn into the lining.

The last item to be put on him by the Secretary of the Conclave was the white zucchetto, or skullcap. The custom was for the new Pope to put his own red skullcap on the head of the Secretary of the Conclave, thus nominating him a cardinal. But Patrick, still headachy, did without thinking what he always did at night: he removed his red skullcap and put it on Charley's head for him to deposit it on the dresser.

"*Dio mio,*" everyone sighed, "His Holiness's first appointment is a dog to the College of Cardinals."

When someone tried to remove the skullcap, Charley bared his teeth to show he refused to be demoted.

In the Sistine, Patrick sat on the throne. Before the cardinals came up in order of seniority to offer him obeisance, Charley put his forelegs on the Pope's lap. He it was who received the first and fondest pontifical embrace.

The Pope lifted one of the dog's ear flaps and, with his lips up to his ear, whispered, "Sure to God, Charley, you're the best-looking of the bunch."

Patrick had a smile and a word for each member of the College. Montefiori knelt and symbolically put on the Pope's finger the Fisherman's Ring, which was then removed by the Master of Ceremonies for new seals to be affixed later. Finally, they all sang the Te Deum in thanksgiving.

At eleven, after the Sistine Choir had sung *"Tu Es Petrus,"* over the public address system in the Square came the single word *"Attenzione."* The central loggia overlooking the Square, draped in yellow and gold, began to fill with Church dignitaries; cardinals and prelates crammed into the balconies on either side of it. Then from the senior cardinal deacon:

"I announce to you tidings of great joy." When the cheers subsided: *"Habemus Papam . . .* We have a Pope, Most Eminent and Most Reverend Lord, Cardinal Brian Aidan O'Flynn."

A funny name. Ripples went around the crowd of sixty thousand as they tried to digest this. *"Gesummaria!* Not another foreigner. Haven't we suffered enough?"

Hey, Lord, who is this stranger in a white soutane?

The Dean continued: *"Qui imposuit . . .* who has taken on himself the name of Patrick I."

It was passed from one in the crowd to the next that the Pope's new name confirmed his Irish origin. It could have been worse, an American, say, or a German, or a Pole. The Irish were popular in Rome. First one section of the crowd, then another went wild, singing "It's a Great Day for the Irish."

A group of drunk Italian sailors stripped a beautiful busty blonde of a green dress and waved it like a flag. *"Irlandes, Irlandes."* Two *carabinieri*, with utter disregard for their personal safety, rushed in and arrested the girl.

Lord, why have you done this to me?

The small, stubby figure of Patrick at last appeared and approached the microphone. He was in the very center of the crablike arms of Bernini's colonnade. Crowds, their faces like a giant mosaic, stretched before him half a mile up the Via della Conciliazione. The two fountains in the piazza cast their crystal jets into the sunlight.

61

Seeing the Pope smile, a bull-voiced man below called out, "He doesn't have toothache," and the knowledgeable crowd roared its approval.

But would the new Holy Father address them—John Paul I, who died after only thirty-three days, did not utter a word—and, if so, what would he say?

"*Sorelle e fratelli.*"

Women shrieked with pleasure. Sisters before brothers. They loved him. Cries of "*Evviva il Papa! Evviva il Papa!*" nearly knocked his head back.

The Pope gestured for silence. Then:

"Patrick, the saint after whom I am called, had many names. Patrick was his Roman name. He used to say, 'If you want to be Christians, you first have to be Romans.' Sisters and brothers, I intend to be a good Christian."

Romans, approving his logic, clapped for two minutes.

"Now," the Pope managed to convey above the hubbub, "the first important announcement of my pontificate."

Everyone from cardinal to choirboy breathlessly awaited the first revelation of the mind of the new Pontiff.

"Beware . . ."

"*Dio mio,*" some groaned. Not another Pope threatening them with a wooden gun over contraception.

". . . of pickpockets."

Italians cheered madly, including a thousand pickpockets, who took advantage of the crush to help themselves to a few more purses. That Pope really knows what goes on down here.

Montefiori looked at Rio, who looked at Burns, who looked up to heaven, where the buck stopped.

"From where I am standing," Patrick went on, "I see a river of faces. It reminds me of my dear mother, long gone to God. Near the small cottage in the West of Ireland where I was born and bred ran a river. She used to grab my hand, this mother of mine—I was four years old at the time—and she would say to me, 'Brian, promise me you'll never, *never* get into that river till you've learned to swim.' Seeing you all below me, I realize, in spite of the solemn promise I gave, I must dive in, after all. And whether I sink or swim is known to none but God."

After the mirth subsided, the Pope went on: "Members of the Sacred

College have said that they would like me to be a Pope of peace. Which is why I intend to take as my motif an olive tree in a red lake. The red lake stands for penance. The oil of the olive is balm, it soothes and it heals."

It did neither to Burns, who visibly shuddered, nor to Cardinal Kinsella of Armagh, who had to be helped off the nearby balcony.

The Pope switched to a language which some insisted was an African dialect. *"Beannacht Dé libh."* The few Irish present recognized it as "God's blessings go with you."

"Poor *sagart* [priest] that I am," Patrick said, "I salute all those who dwell in that Green Cathedral of love and mercy called Ireland."

He spoke briefly, too, in English, French, and, with fluency, in Spanish and Portuguese.

All this while, in the Corridor of the Benedictions behind the balcony, Frank Kerrigan was trying to restrain Charley. The dog was sitting upon a red velvet cushion on a large throne. Finally, he broke away and knocked Cardinal Burns over on his way to join his master.

With a bark that resounded around St. Peter's Square, he put his front paws on the ledge of the balcony so he could survey the scene. The sight of a dog with a red skullcap and the face of an English earl was sensational.

Charley, what in heaven's name are you up to?

"My closest disciple," the Pope said above the uproar. "The only one who listens to me without interrupting."

Dozens of magazine editors worldwide saw next week's cover: golden Labrador with doggie coat of gold and white, the papal colors. Miter on dog's head, crozier between his front paws. And the caption? Take your pick. "TOP DOG AT THE VATICAN." "WELL I'LL BE DOGGONE." "ONE MAN AND HIS DOG."

When Frank finally managed to retrieve Charley, the Pope said good-bye to the crowd, asking God to bless them and expressing this hope: "May you all have a grand lunch of *fettuccine al doppio burro* and a glass of Frascati in my honor."

After blessing the Church and the world, he waved a few times and went inside. In spite of the crown of thorns inside his head, he was very happy. The bells of St. Peter's rang out and were joined by those of four hundred other local churches, and a cannonade rent the air over Castel Sant'Angelo.

Children, when asked, said they did not know about the new Pope but they loved his dog. By the side of many a fountain and inside every *ris-torante*, Pope Patrick was spoken of in a string of untranslatable diminutives but which, roughly rendered, meant: "A titchy little, tubby little, a really darling little poppet of a Pope."

Only one man walked away from St. Peter's with a puzzled frown. Monsignor Michael McAleer, Rector of the Irish College, had known Brian O'Flynn for a quarter of a century. Not once had he heard him speak a word of Irish, refer to his mother, relate an anecdote of his childhood, say anything remotely funny in public. Was this the stage Irishman coming out in him at last? Was the Holy Spirit giving him the grace needed to carry out his duties? Or was it something else, more like an illness?

Then something clicked. That was the chief change in Brian O'Flynn: *those hands*.

Part Two

Early
Days

Chapter Nine

President Delaney was casting his eye over the draft of a speech he was due to give at West Point.

"Militant Islamic Fundamentalists have no Christian pity. A Muslim who drinks a beer is liable to a hundred lashes.

"Theft of even a loaf of bread is rewarded with a severed hand. For the second offense, a severed foot. Hourani has left thousands of one-handed, one-legged men in Islamic countries.

"I'm sad to tell you, my fellow Americans, that in Libya and on the Afghan border of Pakistan, there are schools for terrorists. Mostly, suicide bombers. They are the most devout murderers in the world. They fast Mondays and Thursdays from dawn till dusk. On the wall, in elegant Arabic script, is a slogan: 'Pray more to kill more infidels.' That's us. If they die on active service, they're each promised seventy-two virgin brides in Paradise.

"To stop U.S. trade in fifty Islamic countries, these terrorists have poisoned bottles of Coca-Cola and McDonald's hamburgers. A coupla hundred of their own people die in the process but do they care? No, provided they hurt American business interests.

"Hourani and his evil empire have turned many Christian churches and synagogues into garages or bazaars. He refuses exit visas to Jews and there are thousands in Iran alone.

"He has organized pogroms in Tripoli, Baghdad, Aleppo, Damascus, Oudja. His secret police search out dissidents abroad and execute them. In

Sudan, ten Muslim converts to Christianity were crucified. In his pay are hundreds of cane-wielding vigilantes, the *mutawwas,* or religious police.

"I remind militant Islam that I won't hesitate to counter their arms buildup, if need be, by a preemptive strike. Our cause is right and we, the mightiest nation on earth, are ready."

Delaney nodded appreciatively. Underneath the text, he wrote, for the benefit of his chief speechwriter: "Promising, Al. But give me something snappier. Hit these procking Fundamentalists *real* hard."

That was when Huggard confirmed the election in Rome.

"So," Delaney mused, "little Brian made it to the top. Good for him. And good for us."

Cardinal Thompson of Westminster told the Catholic newspaper the *Universe,* "The election of Pope Patrick is entirely the work of the Holy Spirit." He was not to know the contribution of Flick's hemorrhoids. Burns of New York informed the *National Catholic Reporter,* "He has the finest brain I ever came across." Kinsella of Armagh said, "I know St. Patrick is simply bursting with joy on this day."

Vagueness was widespread. Not one Vatican expert had predicted O'Flynn's success. Even with an extra day's warning, *L'Osservatore Romano* had problems. It had to use a picture of Patrick that was five years old.

The international press corps worked hard to fill in the gaps. The only phone at the Irish College in the Via di Santi Quattro was ringing all day. Jack Glynn, *Time* bureau chief, was the first to call.

Monsignor Driscoll, the young vice-rector, revealed that the new Pope came from Mullagh in County Mayo. He played the piano, though he himself admitted it sounded best at a distance. He had picked up Spanish and Portuguese by taking up vacation posts in South America.

"What does His Holiness think of Italians?" Glynn asked.

"That they're a bit overdramatic, I think."

"In what way?"

"I heard him say they'd die twice if they could."

Something to go on, Glynn thought. The new Pope was a distinguished musician with a delicious sense of humor.

"Publications, Monsignor?"

"Well, he has written, so I heard, a sort of a play."

"No shit, a playwright."

"No, no, no. A little thing for children. In Irish."

"About?"

"An elderly pig farmer in the West of Ireland."

"Promising," purred Glynn, as he scribbled away. *"Very."*

"You think so? The pigs have some sort of disease."

"Representing?"

Driscoll, a city boy from Cork, knew nothing about pigs. "Just a disease. And the farmer has to burn them himself on a funeral pyre."

"No kidding. The smell must've been something else."

"But," continued Driscoll haltingly, "in this terrible adversity, the farmer never loses his trust in God."

"Really original. Go on."

"That's it. It's never been performed. Or published."

This was soon to be rectified. All the top Japanese executives in Hollywood bid for the rights to *The Pig Farmer*, unseen. The new owner described it as "a masterpiece reminiscent of the great Anton Chekhov with whom the Pope has often been compared." The studio was arranging for translation into English and thence into fifty other major languages, including Sinhalese. A multimillion-dollar movie, rivaling *Ben-Hur*, was projected, with Bruce Willis as the pig farmer and Danny De Vito as standby. Both were practicing a brogue.

Meanwhile: "You're being most helpful, Monsignor. Now, about his dog."

"Charley?"

"Jesus Chu-rist! Begging your pardon. *Charley*. He really is called—"

"He sleeps on the end of His Eminence's—I mean, His Holiness's bed."

"Pope never sleeps alone," Glynn whistled in a kind of headline. "Animal lovers'll go crazy over this."

He was a prophet. Patrick was the first Pope known to be fond of an animal since Leo X in the sixteenth century took a fancy to a white elephant called Hanno. Pet lovers rejoiced in the idea that the Pope's last duty at night was to give pal Charley a drink. A hundred animal rights groups, including the Friends of Frogs, Toads and Newts, wired him asking him to be their patron. One spokesperson said, "No animal will ever be used in an experiment again. Would the Pope let Charley be chopped up, injected or forced to smoke against his will?"

Tom Jackson, Rome correspondent of London's *Daily Telegraph,* followed up a clue in the Vatican newspaper. Patrick had written two doctoral theses. If he could get his hands on either, he might gain a special insight into the Pope's mind.

He took the archivist of the Gregorian University to a bar for a coffee. He used devious arguments to persuade Giorgio Macchi to provide him with a photocopy of the Pope's unpublished thesis, "Usury in the 12th and 13th Centuries." Next day, at the crack of dawn, he slipped Macchi one hundred Euros in a brown sealed envelope for his trouble. The archivist took the money with a shrug. Jackson was not to know that his was one of 173 requests which had kept Macchi up half the night. Most journalists picked up their copy and promptly dumped it in the waste bin. The thesis was written in Latin.

Jackson was not so easily put off. He faxed the entire text of three hundred pages to his London office. There an Oxford medievalist, Professor Mitchell, went through it page by page. After a couple of hours, the *Telegraph*'s editor burst in.

"Well, Professor, is it well written?"

"The Latin's macaronic."

"Much originality of thought?"

"None whatsoever."

"Is there *nothing* of interest in it?"

"Look," Mitchell said. "This was written before that strange woman Margaret Thatcher became an M.P. It's practically unreadable. The Pope has probably matured since then. I hope to God he has."

The editor picked up the phone and bawled at Jackson in Rome to come up with a better idea.

*P*layboy paid Macchi $50,000 in advance for a copy of the Pope's thesis, "Sexuality in the Middle Ages." It was left to Professor Hans Gerbel of Harvard to deliver an opinion to *Playboy*'s editor, who called him at his home.

"Hi, Ms. Thursby. I'm afraid this t'esis is not in the same league with Henry Miller's *Sexus* or Lawrence's *Lady Chatterley*. It all takes place in bed but nothing happens."

"Anything in it for our readers?" There was no response on the line except a Teutonic gurgle. "*Nothing* titillating?"

"Ms. Thursby, I tell you the truth. This is the unfunniest book I ever have read. Not one laugh. I donunderstand how anyone can write four hundred pages on sex and not one sentence that would raise, well, let's not beat about the bushes, an eyebrow."

That was how two of the brightest publications in the English language failed to appreciate that the two theses they ditched were to form the basis of papal pronouncements that would one day rock the world.

Chapter Ten

The Coronation was fixed for January 1. The Chancellor in Berlin and the President in Paris were among the first to announce they would attend.

In Ireland, the Pope was heralded as Pope Paddy I, the new Brian Boru, and Mayo Man of the Millennium. All the Republic's papers hit on the same rugby image in their headline: "POPE WINS TRIPLE CROWN FOR IRELAND."

Patrick's ancestry was traced back through the Earls of Tyrconnell to Brian Boru and beyond to a couple of important people long before the Flood. Shay Meaney, the only person ever to be awarded the Nobel Prize for literature twice, was asked to write an ode to grace the occasion. Arrangements were under way to borrow the Ardagh chalice from the National Museum and the Book of Kells from Trinity College, Dublin, for the Coronation Mass.

In the Oval Office, Delaney called in his Chief of Staff. "Make all the arrangements, Bill."

"For the Vice President, sir?"

"For *me.*"

"But with these Fundamentalist terror groups around, think of security."

"Have a heart, Bill."

Huggard winced. Aged forty-nine, a native of Yuba City, California, he was reputed to have the warmest heart in Washington. Three years before, he had refused the offer of a heart transplant in space by a robotic surgeon and chose instead a terrestrial implant of aluminum and polyurethane.

"Sir, I've been in contact with the CIA in Rome and—"

"Save me the shit. When all those other Irish bastards boycotted my trip to Ballymuck, which bishop stood by me? Little Brian O'Flynn."

Huggard told him that with Berlin, Paris and London accepting, his presence would mean the four top people were all Catholics. "It'll look like a Catholic takeover of the Western Alliance."

"Bill, I'm going and that's final."

It had to be. Carol, the First Lady, a convert of Cardinal Burns, had already borrowed a couple of dozen dresses from top fashion houses for the trip and told her poodle and three hairdressers to be on standby.

At his home in Kennebunkport, Maine, ex-President George Bush's last days were divided between golf on his carpet, jogging a few yards around the living room, fishing in a goldfish bowl and being wired up, in between exercises, to life support. All the time he kept quacking, "No new taxes. No new taxes," so that even the saintly Barbara couldn't take any more. She warned him if he didn't shut up she would put him on freezehold, that is, cryogenic suspension for the next thousand years.

George was on life support when he got the news of the new papal election. Asked if he intended going to the Coronation, he simply pointed to the encephalograph and said, with characteristic dry humor, "Read my blips."

In Little Rock, Bill and Hillary made it known that home affairs were their specialty. In any case, fifty lawyers and seventy-five FBI agents were finally bringing the Whitewater affair, and one or two others with feminine interest, to a climax.

Dammit, I would like to go, darling, but flying to that ghastly place twice in one month is really *really*."

At Buckingham Palace, in the long salon full of mirrors, Charles III waved his hands like a treeful of rooks after a shotgun has gone off. Camilla stubbed out her cigarette and went fervently on with her knitting.

"No one," she said, "attempted to assassinate you or anything like that?"

"Alas, not with a real gun. It's so good for one's image."

"Provided, darling, they only come at you with feather pillows or teddy bears, I don't mind."

"True. But when I said the place was ghastly, I was really recalling that St. Peter's, including Michelangelo's fantastic dome, was built on the proceeds of Indulgences."

"I did know, dearest."

The King examined his own bald dome in the mirror, the fruit of a thousand years of breeding. "It's not possible to meditate in the middle of all that absurdly scintillating rococo and *nouveau riche* sort of stuff."

"A ghastly carbuncle, would you say, Charles?"

"Precisely. Not at all Gothic."

Camilla nodded as if she knew what Gothic was.

"Besides, I'm writing a sort of encyclical on architecture as well as trying to finish off redesigning the façade of Westminster Abbey. I'm going to thatch the whole thing."

Camilla sighed sympathetically. "The new man's Irish, too. You don't want to seem to support that sort of thing, do you?"

"Good point. It's not his fault, I know. All the same."

"Time for your William to earn his spurs?"

The Prince of Wales, called the Black Prince, now twenty-six, had been to a soft English school called Eton where he had distinguished himself, among other things, by biting off the tip of a referee's nose on the rugger pitch. In spite of this, he was having a bad press.

Columnists were clamoring to have his name removed from the Civil List. He was being compared very unfavorably with his Uncle Andrew, who had lost a spouse like most Windsors but had won the Falklands War for Britain. In the last twelve months, four detectives who had minded William resigned to write their memoirs. He had been Breathalyzed four times, lost his driving license for life and been photographed in the company of a model who had posed in the nude for a certain magazine. Charles, badly briefed, had invited her to tea. It was the girl's hard luck that Prince Philip, nearly ninety, was visiting the palace and recognized her instantly.

"There's no chance yet, Charles," Camilla said, "of you using your influence."

"To get the lad into my old college in Cambridge? Afraid not. You know how dashed egalitarian everything's become."

She could hardly have failed to notice, what with Buckingham Palace open all year to the paying public and the Royal Box at Wimbledon crammed with blacks.

"In the meantime, Camilla, I will send the dear boy to Rome, whatever that awful woman says."

I n 10 Downing Street, there was no vacillation from "that awful woman," Denise Weaver. These days, there never was. Even radio waves had to straighten themselves out before crossing the threshold of that orange-doored establishment.

The first Liberal Democrat to be Prime Minister, Weaver was a forty-year-old handsome honey-blonde with woodpecker lips and good tangible assets. Reputedly an unmarried mother, she was a devout Catholic and feminist. When Roone Delaney called her "the best man in England," she had responded with, "And Delaney's the best woman in America." Aware of the strength of the women's movement in the States, Delaney pretended to take it as a compliment.

"I am going to Rome," Weaver informed the members of her Cabinet, female except for the token male in charge of Environment. The Pope was new to the job. He might need some assistance.

Chapter Eleven

It took Pope Patrick some time to master the intricacies of the Apostolic Palace with its lifts, three-hundred-step stairways, miles of corridors, twenty courtyards and hundreds of galleries, salons and antechambers.

Cardinal Montefiori gave him a tour of the curial offices in the palace. In particular, his own department, the Secretariat of State.

There, he introduced him to Archbishop Umberto Rossi, his *sostituto*, or deputy. Rossi was a small, rigid, emotionless man to whom Charley took an instant dislike. It was mutual. The deputy had thick, gray hair and round spectacles. An expert on U.S. affairs, he had a degree from Catholic University in Washington. He spoke English perfectly with an American twang.

After the tour, Montefiori said confidentially to the Pope, "I realize you know this already, Holiness, but we here inhabit another universe. The earth is its immobile center and the earth's center is the Vatican."

"The *dead* center?"

"Quite dead."

"Very convenient."

"Comforting, certainly. The walls of the Vatican are the only ones visible in the outer space of outer space called heaven. Stars and planets follow here the course we dictate to them. Winds blow and rains fall with our permission, *cum permissu superiorum.*"

"But surely, Giuseppe, the real universe—"

"Holiness, please. *This*"—sweeping gesture, vinegary tone—"is the real universe."

"And the other?"

"A defective copy painted on the air."

"Does God know about this?"

"The Recording Angel is a junior typist in our typing pool."

"I see."

"Hence it is my duty to tell you never to trust anyone in the Curia."

"Not even you, Giuseppe?"

Montefiori's eyes momentarily lit up. "I make no exceptions."

"But if I am the Servant of the Servants of God, surely those in the Curia are servants of the—"

Montefiori cut across him. "Popes come and go. The Curia goes on forever."

"But surely they will occasionally obey the Pope."

"In the Vatican, obedience, like death, is for others. It is unimaginable for oneself."

"Will they at least keep me informed?"

"If they can avoid it, Holiness, they will not tell you the time of day nor the way to your apartment."

Patrick wryly bit his lip. "They will at least keep the Ten Commandments, Giuseppe, for Moses' sake."

Montefiori said, "Commandments they bend like seaweed on the water's edge." He changed to a conspiratorial whisper. "They are said never to give anyone a straight answer."

"Is that really so?"

Still whispering: "Some say yes, some say no."

"What do you say?"

"Yes and no."

"I see what you mean." Getting no response, Patrick added, "I *don't* see what you mean?"

"Holiness, even *I* don't see what I mean."

The Pope sighed. "I'll just have to accept that life is going to be difficult."

"I counsel you, Holiness, against such optimism."

The Pope enjoyed having his leg pulled.

"Giuseppe, has the Curia no saving grace?"

"They take care not to let any ideas in and to let only hand-me-ons out. Beware especially those prelates with a viper's heart and"—smiling sweetly—"a Mona Lisa smile."

The Pope felt quite lost, like someone dreaming in a dream in a dream.

"Of the cardinal virtues, Holiness, they excel in only one."

"Prudence?"

"If that were the only virtue, we in the Curia would all be holier than St. Francis of Assisi."

The Pope spent his afternoons in the Gardens with Frank Kerrigan and Charley, who was a hit with the gardeners.

On his two-mile-long constitutionals the Pope wore a black cassock and a broad, black gondolier-type straw hat. He walked among Lebanon cedars and exotic shrubbery, past orange and lemon trees in ancient pots, past fountains and a Lourdes Grotto, past statues and ancient urns and papal escutcheons, past towers and an unused observatory, through a wood and a vineyard and a vegetable patch and along the high medieval boundary wall.

He inhaled the delicious fragrance of eucalyptus and pine. Sometimes he shushed the bounding, barking Charley while he watched and listened to the song of whitethroats, robins, blackcaps and tiny figpeckers.

On one occasion, he slipped into St. Peter's and sat in a box to hear confessions. A grizzled Franciscan with huge glasses perched on the end of his nose tried to eject him, claiming in strongly consonanted Italian that this was his *posto* and he was not giving it up to anyone.

"I am so sorry," the Pope said.

Only then did the friar recognize him. "Forgive me, Holiness. Hear my confession?"

The Pope obliged. Afterward, the Pope confessed to the friar, beating his breast. He began, "I find it very hard to pray in this place, Father. There are so many other things to do here."

"Ah, Holiness," the friar sighed, "in Rome, it is not easy even to believe."

Father Virgilio—for that was the friar's name—was about eighty. A native of Palermo, he was hard of hearing and very shortsighted. Since he gave Patrick a far tougher penance than he was used to, the Pope appointed him his personal confessor.

Against Montefiori's advice, Patrick agreed to hold a press conference the day before his Coronation. So many journalists applied for tickets, it was held in the Nervi Hall, which straddles the boundary between the Vatican and the state of Italy. Members of the press were searched and let in, only to find the Pope already seated on the stage in an armchair with a lion-like Charley at his feet.

After the pictures—"Would you care to stroke your dog once more, Holiness?"—came the questions.

Charley had starred in so many articles since the conclave, he was top of the agenda.

"Is it true, Holiness," asked the *Sunday Independent*, "that the dog sleeps on your bed?"

"He *is* male and Catholic," the Pope said, taking his pipe out of his pocket by a kind of reflex and tapping it on the palm of his hand.

"You did see his picture on the front of *Time*, Holiness?"

"I did, Mr. Glynn."

"You read our magazine?" Glynn asked excitedly.

"I said I saw the cover. Not a good likeness but Charley accepted it with his customary humility. Incidentally, I didn't care much for your copy editor's line about Charley revising the code of canine law."

"You *do* read us, then?"

"I have to read everything put in front of me. That is one of the disadvantages of being Pope."

"Is your dog infallible, too?" asked the *Sunday Express* of London.

"He's never made a mistake in my hearing. And, see this"—Patrick touched the tip of his dog's wet nose—"best lie detector in the business."

"What do you think of the coverage of your election?"

At this point, Charley sneezed.

"Bless you a hundred thousand times," the Pope said. "I reckon my dog just answered for me."

Montefiori nudged New York, who was sitting beside him in the front row. "The last Pope who wisecracked like this only lived for thirty-three days."

"Your dog," said a Spanish lady, "has no collar on."

"In our place, ma'am, I wear the collar. It's a sign of servitude. I spare him that."

"Has Charley ever sired any puppies?" asked the *San Francisco Chronicle*.

"Certainly not. Have you, Charley?"

The dog shook his head.

"Has he been neutered?" the *London Sun* asked.

"No, sir," as Charley woofed alarmingly, "he is naturally chaste."

"Can you tell us about his pedigree?" the *Sun* persisted.

"I found him several years since wandering in a back street—I had better not mention the name of it."

"Why not, Holiness?"

"Because people might claim they own his relatives."

"Are we Romans such liars?" asked left-wing *L'Unità*.

"I found Charley in Dublin, sir. But in answer to your question, the Romans, I always think, are very like the Irish."

"Liars?" *L'Unità* repeated belligerently.

"They do not know what lying is," the Pope answered evasively. "But they are imaginative. I remember, for instance, a young tennis star coming to Dublin to play—this was in the 1980s."

"McEnroe?" asked *Newsweek*.

"He had an Irish name, to be sure. A nice boy when he wasn't throwing his racket into the crowd or swearing alarmingly at the umpire."

"McEnroe, all right."

"Anyway, when the lad came to Dublin, the promoters received three thousand ticket applications from ladies claiming to be his grandmother. Only half of them were genuine, of course."

The *Miami Herald* put it to the Pope that the weather in his homeland had a bad reputation.

"Among whom?" the Pope asked, astonished. "Eskimos would think that Ireland is blessed with perpetual spring."

The *Cork Examiner* said, "You seem to be working long hours already, Holiness."

"Not at all. It's an old Mussolini trick." The Pope smiled cagily. "The light in my study is on a time switch. It's programmed to go off at three in the morning, even though I'm tucked up in bed at eleven."

"Why three in the morning?"

"My Secretary of State tells me Catholics are somehow reassured by the thought of the Supreme Pontiff working late."

Montefiori blushed.

The *New York Times* felt obliged to lift the tone of the discussion. "What will you miss most now you are Pope?"

"Being able to walk into a store or roam a market like the Campo dei Fiori to buy things for myself."

"Such as?"

"Oh, a few grams of Parmesan cheese or a jar of black olives." Already he sounded nostalgic for days long gone. "That's the first thing, anyhow."

"And the second?" Ms. Daley of *Woman's Own* chipped in.

The Pope grinned. "If my Secretary of State is correct, I will miss never again hearing the truth."

When he was asked about his upbringing, he suddenly saw through the mists of recent years the sharp-chiseled days of childhood, a world of friends, a house smelling of friendship and baked bread. A voice at the half door, his mother's, calling out, "Sean, Brian, Maura, Donal"—naming her children like a litany of the saints—"run and don't be late for school," and Brian ran, looking over his shoulder at her holding both hands in front of her face like in blindman's bluff, though he never worked out why she did it. And there was Cooley, their big black and white sheepdog, tail-wagging around her. How that dear dog would have liked to meet Charley.

The Pope came out of his reverie to speak simply of his life in County Mayo. "You have only to string together some of the place-names and they read like lines from the great Irish poet and songster Tom Moore: Stramore, Gweezalia, Glenagort."

The *Washington Post* asked him if his family had been poor.

"Poor?" he said. "What gave you that idea? There were sixteen of us children, all in good health, living in a three-bedroom cottage. A garden with two beehives, edged by golden furze. Bread, potatoes and turf aplenty. The door ever open to neighbors and travelers. Our girls able to walk the roads by day or night without looking over their shoulder. Everyone went to chapel though some of us had to run fast on Sundays to overtake the Mass, as we say. Yes, now I come to think of it, we were rich, all right." He paused, a faraway look on his face. "No money, of course, but were we poor? We were not."

"And your parents," *Der Spiegel* said, "presumably they practiced their religion?"

"More Catholic than the Pope," Patrick answered, before he realized what he was saying. "My mother accepted everything as God's will. 'Isn't it a miracle of a sunrise, thank God?' Or, in the middle of a storm that blew the legs from under the bull and the thatch off the house into the next county, 'Isn't it a tirrible day, thank God?' "

He explained that he, as the second son, had been singled out from his earliest years to be a priest. He recalled a trip he made when he was a boy to the Burren in the County Clare, a marvelous moonscape of limestone rock.

"When Cromwell's troops first came," he said, "they complained there wasn't enough wood there to hang a man or water to drown him or soil to bury him in. Ah, but the spring flowers. And in summer the countryside ablaze with heather, montbretias, red fuchsia bells; and the air on the heights around the Cliffs of Moher thick with black flies and crane flies mating and dying."

The Irish journalists nudged one another. There was bound to be a massive increase in tourism in Mayo and Clare.

Patrick went on to recall the local schoolmaster and, of course, Father O'Flanagan, the parish priest whose Mass he had served.

"Oh the crowds in the chapel each Sunday and holy day. You couldn't get in unless you were a front-row forward or a pious nun with sharp elbows." And he quoted from the old ballad about "Sagart Aroon, the darlin' priest."

Who in the winter night, Sagart Aroon,
When the cold blast did bite, Sagart Aroon,
Came to my cabin door,
And on the earthen floor,
Knelt by me, sick and poor, Sagart Aroon.

"Your Holiness," said Isaacs of the *Jewish Chronicle*, "may I offer you the best wishes of the worldwide Jewish community?" As the Pope nodded his gratitude: "How do you see my people?"

Montefiori stiffened. Everyone sensed that this question went beyond the agreed limits of the press conference.

Without pausing to think, the Pope said, "Jews and Christians are blood brothers."

"Alas," said Isaacs, "for centuries Christians persecuted my people."

Instantly: "In doing so they sinned against the light. Sometimes even Popes said that all Jews were responsible for Jesus' crucifixion. They were wrong. The Church is made up of sinners and we must confess our sins publicly, as did the Second Vatican Council when it corrected this grave error. It is theologically correct to say that we Christians hold that one loyal Jew, called Joshuah or Jesus, is the Savior of the world." There was a stunned silence which the Pontiff broke by saying, "Anti-Semitism is as much a heresy as was the use of force by the Inquisition to impose Catholic beliefs."

A black-turbaned Arab, representing the *Islamic Daily News*, asked the next question. The latest technology enabled his paper to publish simultaneously in fifty countries with a circulation of 40 million.

"Have you read the Koran?"

"Many times."

"Do you believe, sir, in jihad?"

"I believe in Holy Years, not in holy wars," said the Pope. "Violence, my friend, achieves nothing."

The Arab asked, "Were, then, the eight Crusades against the people of the Book a mistake?"

"No," Pope Patrick said, "a crime. Christians shed blood in trying to recover the sepulchre of Christ which they believed was empty anyway. We should atone."

"Now you think we only are barbarians?"

"Many people, including world politicians, think every Muslim has a Kalashnikov in one hand, the Koran in the other. My own conviction, based on reading the Koran, is that Muslims are peaceable people, full of faith and compassion."

His questioner, as he jotted down notes, muttered in Arabic that Allah would be disgusted that people would not fight and die for his honor.

The Pope added, "I admire the way Muslims pray to Mecca, how even your tents and mosques are all directed there. Would that we Christians prayed to Calvary and all our churches pointed to where Christ died for us. I send brotherly greetings to all followers of the great Prophet Muhammad."

"And to Buddhists?" asked a saffron-robed reporter. And when the Pope nodded, "Are we not atheists?"

Patrick smiled. "My predecessor wrote that once. When he was old."

"It was a mistake?"

"Popes make mistakes. Believe me, I, too, may sometimes be infallible but my daily ignorance is awe-inspiring."

"He was perhaps not subtle enough?" asked the Buddhist.

"Exactly. As people are not subtle enough when they accuse Christians of believing in three gods."

When the quiet laughter died down: "I salute you, my brother Buddhists, for your nonviolence. I salute your Zen poets who see the sun in the midst of rain and scoop clear water from the heart of a fire."

Jackson of the *Telegraph* chipped in with, "Your Holiness will not then follow in the footsteps of your predecessor?"

"My predecessor, sir," the Pope said, detecting a hint of criticism of John Paul II, "was a distinguished man whom I cannot hope to emulate."

"I did not say emulate, Holiness, but follow."

"I don't intend to travel as much, certainly, but I hope to visit Ireland, if God spares me."

The Irish correspondents looked cheerfully at each other.

"Follow him *theologically*, Holiness?"

Patrick said, "John Paul II was, you realize, much misunderstood. For instance, had he said every leaf, every rose, every blade of grass is sacred, he would have been hailed as a mystic. But he only said, every human being

84

from conception to old age is sacred and for that, many people thought him a medieval fool."

"So you, too, are a traditionalist?"

Montefiori watched carefully as the Pope tapped his pipe again.

"Tradition is the anchor of faith."

"You do not intend to change any of your predecessor's teachings?"

"Some things," Patrick said with a heavy emphasis, "the Church can and must change. Others she can never change."

Time took this to mean, "Pope Patrick, a carbon copy of his predecessor," while *Newsweek's* line was, "Patrick, the Reforming Pope."

Both magazines were wildly off target.

Chapter Twelve

On January 1, VIPs drove in one long, glistening bulletproof line under the Arch of the Bells, past the Swiss Guards and round to the rear of St. Peter's. Of the major nations, only China and the FIR had refused to send delegates.

Heads of state were greeted by senior prelates and by a dress-coated prince, assistant to the pontifical throne. A picket of Swiss Guards presented their halberds. National anthems were reduced to a few token bars as heavily armed security men immediately shielded the more important guests and rushed them into the palace.

The Irish party was headed by the President, Miss Jodie O'Reilly, a former Rose of Tralee, accompanied by her live-in boyfriend. The Taoiseach, lean, silver-haired, silver-mustachioed Richard Spring, insisted on a car of his own. He was head of a Labour government in coalition with the PPs, the Pothole Party.

As they both stepped out onto the white pavement of the glass-enclosed Courtyard of San Damaso next to the fountain, neither was pleased to hear the band play "God Save the King" by mistake.

The Archbishop of Canterbury arrived with his wife and three children. He had diplomatically asked his nominated successor, Bishop Marcia Burt of Durham, to stay away in case it gave offense to the Vatican. She had even given offense in the Church of England when her ordination to the priesthood was interrupted for an hour while she gave premature birth to twins in the vestry.

The cortège had long been assembling in the Apostolic Palace. Five hundred clerics from orders founded before 1474 led off. Then came the clergy of the Pope's own diocese, Rome. There followed ushers, courtiers, guards, lay dignitaries with high-ruff collars, chamberlains, privy chamberlains, judges of the Roman Rota.

Nearest the Pope were the Penitentiaries of St. Peter's, and a vast array of multicolored prelates: bishops, archbishops, patriarchs, cardinals, assistants to the papal throne, and finally the two cardinals who would assist Patrick at the Mass.

They were now waiting for the Pope to join them so that the procession could thread its way through halls and salons, down baroque staircases and out into the piazza.

The whole place was buzzing. Half a million in the Square and adjoining streets, as hundreds crammed the roof of Bernini's colonnade.

Lost in the crowd of VIPs was the fragile figure of Lady Margaret Thatcher. She had always immensely admired the last Pontiff—"Old J.P."—for his refusal to make a U-turn. She hoped the new man would be equally *inflexible*. Her own life was ending in frustration: Denise had gone before.

First, zombies in Australia and New Zealand had voted for a republic. Then not only had Britain given up the Falklands and Gibraltar, it had adopted a European currency. She still resolutely opposed the E.U. as a Brussels plot to make foreign countries of Europe part of the United Kingdom. Her very title was nominal after the Labour Party abolished the House of Lords and replaced it with an elected second chamber.

The Via della Conciliazione was jammed so tight, Dr. Ian Paisley, dour Presbyterian minister and former DUP member of Parliament, was unable to move. Round-backed, white-haired, bulbous-eyed, his red face shiny as paint, he was crying out, "Whore of Babylon" and urging his supporters to raise aloft their banners proclaiming, "NO POPERY" and "NO POPE—NO PRIESTS—NO SURRENDER."

Italians, not knowing a word of English, congratulated him on his warm devotion to the Holy Father.

Police with sniffer dogs and antiterrorist search squads were everywhere. Secret servicemen with walkie-talkies mingled with the crowds and manned lookout posts on the colonnade.

In the night, rain had fallen like ripe pears. Now the tin-colored sky was gone. Lesser dignitaries of Church and state sat, chatting amicably in the crisp January sunshine in fifty different tongues.

In the Hall of the Vestments, Pope Patrick was having his first disagreement with his Secretary of State. Montefiori reminded him of the attempts on his predecessor's life.

"No, Giuseppe," the Pope said firmly, "I refuse to wear any protection under my vestments."

"These days, Holiness," Montefiori said, "even the *Pietà* is guarded by bulletproof glass."

"My guardian angel will protect me."

"Experience shows they do not make good bodyguards, Holiness."

Montefiori outlined reports received from the CIA and DIGOS, Italian antiterrorists, about a possible assassination attempt by Islamic militants.

"Always the same bogeymen."

"For the Church's sake, the Pope must be protected."

"Like Goliath the Philistine? Jesus went unprotected to Golgotha. Am I to go in armor to the renewal of Golgotha?"

"There were no automatic weapons in his day, Holiness."

"If I die today," Patrick said a trifle wearily, "I will be in the company of the Master and of St. Peter, who was martyred not far from here."

Montefiori tapped his watch. "Very well. As to the tiara."

"No crown today, Giuseppe, unless you have one made of thorns. Only spiritual symbols." He beckoned. "Frank, make ready the miter and crozier. And for God's sake, keep your eye on Charley till this is over."

In his declining years, John Paul II had been forced to use the *sedia gestatoria*. Vatican aides hoped that Patrick would continue with this ancient practice but he insisted he would walk and carry his staff with a wooden cross on the top.

Three times he stopped while flax was put on burning coals as the Master of Ceremonies intoned in Latin, "Holy Father, thus passes the glory of the world."

In the piazza, the Pope met with wild applause and the waving of thousands of white and yellow flags. After the singing of *"Tu Es Petrus"* and a fanfare of trumpets, he received the pallium, the circular band of lamb's wool, the yoke of his service to the whole Church. Then the members of the Sacred College did him homage.

After he had incensed the altar, the litanies were chanted and the Sistine Choir began to sing Pontifical High Mass. Scripture readings were in Greek and Latin, the highlight being the Gospel read from the Book of Kells.

The Pope's address was a simple hymn of welcome to the world in an age of peace and joy. With shining eyes, he pledged himself to serve all mankind. Hence he had chosen as the theme of his pontificate, "Through penance, peace, *Ex poenitentia, pax.*" This was the motto on his coat of arms under the sign of an olive tree growing out of red water. He threatened no one, scolded no one, attacked no one. He opened his heart wide to all the world.

Among his brief messages was one to his fellow countrymen:

"I send my love to the small windswept land perched on the edge of the Western sea, the little black Rose of Ireland, my Dark Rosaleen. I beg St. Patrick and Mary, Mother of the Golden Heights, to pray for you and for me."

Everything went well until the consecration. The Pope blessed the bread, then, having blessed the wine, he lifted up the Ardagh chalice, muttering, *"Céad míle fáilte, A Thiarna,"* Irish for "A hundred thousand welcomes, Lord."

Meanwhile, a man dressed in a priest's soutane and holding a video camera stepped out of the crowd into the roped-off area. He was in the sights of six high-velocity rifles but no one dared pull the trigger. They might kill a priest at the most sacred part of the Mass, or hit a VIP. Four blue-uniformed civil guards followed the intruder over the barrier, circled and were about to pounce on him when he drew a revolver. The guards now shielded the assassin from their own marksmen.

There was disagreement later as to whether the gunman, only twenty feet from the altar, fired once or twice. Many witnesses swore they saw two flashes.

The attacker was clubbed to the ground, tied up and taken away. The Pope lowered the chalice and continued as if nothing had happened.

To his right, Montefiori hissed, "Are you hit, Holiness?"

Only after the Pope had returned to St. Peter's and given his blessing *urbi et orbi* on the central loggia did events become clear. The would-be killer was a demented Loyalist from Ulster who had been in and out of mental institutions for years. Protestants in the province immediately put out a statement deploring the dastardly deed.

Dr. Paisley, baring big yellow teeth, explained to the press he had no "objuctions" if Almighty God "in his infinite wusdum" struck "Pope Putrick the Fust" dead with lightning. But "NO POPERY" did not mean he wanted the wee blasphemer shot.

The small-caliber bullet missed the Pope and hit the Ardagh chalice, hence the illusion of a double flash. It penetrated one side of the chalice and bounced off the other into the cup. This incident, later known as "the Bullet in the Blood," was unofficially hailed as a miracle in all the remaining convents of the world.

Chapter Thirteen

"Come along." Back in the Apostolic Palace, Patrick beckoned to the U.S. President, who was looking very smart in formal dress. "Will you join me in my apartment?"

Delaney's bodyguards, musclemen with bulging holsters, were aware that the Pope himself had just missed death by a whisker. They promptly pegged the President closer than his wife had in years, apart from inaugurations and birthdays.

The Pope smiled. "It's all right, gentlemen. Your President is quite safe with me. I hardly think my Irish nuns will tear him to bits. Besides, Charley, he's my dog, will protect him."

The President shrugged off his bodyguards and, scowling, they backed away. A young army warrant officer shook his head worriedly. He was in charge of the black thirty-pound metal briefcase with coded bits and pieces for starting a nuclear war should the President be that way inclined.

Roone Delaney pecked at the cheek of the First Lady, immaculate in the Russian lynx coat she had just donned. He was pleasantly aware of dark looks from the likes of Cardinal Burns and British Prime Minister Weaver, who had refused to wear customary black, and chose instead a pantsuit in canary yellow.

"How'd you like a cup of coffee and a bite, Roone?"

"Fine, Holiness."

In the elevator, the Pope said, "I saw your TV debate with Stallone a few years back."

Delaney puffed with pride. "You really *did?*"

"It made a lasting impression."

"Would you *believe?*" the President whistled.

No sooner had they stepped out of the elevator on the third floor than Delaney took the Pope by the hand.

"Holiness, as President of the greatest nation on earth, I shake with you." He dropped to his knees. "As a Catholic, I kiss your ring in filial devotion."

Charley chose this moment to come bounding out of the Pope's study. His swiveling flank knocked the President flat on his face like a Muslim on a prayer mat.

"How very nice of you," the Pope said, helping Delaney to his feet. "I should have warned you about Checkpoint Charley. He frisked you, eh?"

He led his visitor into the small dining room where coffee was set out piping-hot on a carved walnut table.

The President, well used to the trappings of privilege and power, still got a kick out of being admitted to the Pope's humble inner sanctum. After all, the guy was elected for life. This meeting, he decided, would get more than a passing mention in his memoirs which his three ghostwriters were already working on.

"I've stayed in New York a few times," the Pope said, pouring for them both. This was news to Delaney. "In a black district, mostly. Harlem. You know it?"

"Heard of it, Holiness."

"Once in a while I used to stroll along Fifth Avenue. Even Wall Street. Heavens, Roone, that place scared me stiff. The power those fellers wield."

"They scare me, too, Holiness."

They took their coffee into the Pope's private study, a square room full of books.

He suddenly said, "With the FIR talking tough, grave dangers ahead, Roone."

The President settled into an armchair and nodded as he sipped the third-rate coffee. He muttered something he half remembered from a recent speech, about "U.S. bulwark against Islamic terrorists, high spiritual values of a capitalist economy, freedom to grow richer and richer."

Patrick seized on the word "freedom."

"Indeed, Roone, freedom that comes of love and generosity." He took the bent bullet from his pocket.

Delaney eyed it. "I was really sorry to hear about the Ardagh chalice. If the Irish President will permit it, I'll have an expert restore it at my expense."

"No need," the Pope said with a mischievous grin. "I suspect it's perfect as it is. It'll draw an extra million tourists a year to Dublin's National Museum. Wonderful legends will grow up about how that ancient chalice, famous for itself, saved the life of the first Irish Pope."

"I guess you're right."

"Now, Roone, as regards a bite."

Having tasted the coffee, the President was none too keen.

Patrick held up the bullet. "I meant, bite on this. See." He himself bit on it. "Now you?"

The President was dimly aware that the Pope saw some sort of symbolism in this but what it was escaped him. He bit the bullet. Too hard, for he nearly broke a tooth and stifled an expletive just in time.

"Thank you kindly, Roone. Now I'd like you to keep it as a token of friendship between two men dedicated to peace."

Delaney was overwhelmed. That little bit of metal could be worth a million bucks. His handsome face creased in a smile.

"I'll have it framed, Holiness, and keep it in my office."

Uncertain what to give in return, he fumbled in his vest pocket and took out his official ID tag.

The Pope thought it was meant for Charley. Until he read on it: "Delaney, Roone T.—Commander in Chief—O (blood type)—Roman Catholic."

"Roman Catholic," the Pope said aloud. "That's grand."

"Holiness, if there's anything I can do for you . . ."

"How generous."

"I realize that you, like me, have a problem with your budget deficit. Does the Vatican Bank need a helping hand? I could have a word with the Bank of America or—"

Patrick laughed and readjusted his glasses. "I haven't had a chance as yet to look into the bank's affairs but I'll keep your offer in mind."

"Maybe, Holiness, you might like to address the United Nations. Of course, it's not my job to invite you but—"

With the U.S. President, as with the Almighty, all things were possible.

"I might just have something to say to the U.N. sometime. Shall we keep in touch?"

They prayed briefly in the Pope's private chapel, a cool place of white marble and glass mosaics. As they descended in the elevator, the President was delighted. This little Pope was all right. Big on generalities, short on specifics. Uncle Sam could do business with him, yessir. A regular white hat.

"There," the Pope said to the relieved bodyguards, "I brought your man back to you unscathed."

The First Lady, a fancy dresser who never wore the same expression twice, was in a nearby salon, talking excitedly at Denise Weaver. Carol Delaney, for all her faults, was a stickler for protocol. She never went through the bedroom door ahead of her husband. She called him Mr. President even in bed.

She was telling Weaver about a banquet she was hosting at the White House. Liz Taylor had agreed to bring along her ninth and final husband. Barbra Streisand was coming out of retirement again to sing "The Star-Spangled Banner," provided she could read the words on an idiot sheet.

"It's so important to get the best," she said.

"Sweet," Ms. Weaver said sourly.

"And I have to tell you this, Prime Minister, honey. I just went to the ladies' room and would you believe?"

Weaver, who had been left holding the First Lady's white poodle with a blue rinse, heard that Carol Delaney had actually passed water "in full view of a fantastic Raphee-ale."

Apart from the fact that the poodle had meanwhile passed water in full view of a fantastic Prem-ee-er, Weaver was not impressed. She had iron control. After long meetings members of her Cabinet complained that she was prodigal of millions but miserly when it came to spending a penny.

Having seen off the President's party, Pope Patrick invited the British Premier to his library on the second floor.

Chapter Fourteen

My dear," he said, "I'm told that women usually wear black when they visit me here."

"Yes?" said Weaver defensively.

"Your bright outfit gladdens an old man's heart."

Weaver was still sore that Delaney had been given precedence over her. What was America but a once small and ultimately ungrateful outpost of the empire, like Belfast? She also disliked the Pope being "Green" at the Mass. Why the hell did he have to speak Irish at the consecration?

"My dear," he said, offering her a chair, "my role is strictly spiritual. I will never say or do *anything* to inflame any problems you have in Northern Ireland."

This at least was music to the Premier's ears. Lately, his predecessor had provoked all sorts of resistance movements in Poland, old Yugoslavia, Hungary, and Ukraine.

"The IRA style themselves freedom fighters," Patrick went on, "but really they, like their Loyalist counterparts, are terrorists, are they not?"

Weaver nodded.

"The boys in balaclavas have no authority from the people and they're too scared to seek it by democratic means."

Weaver had no idea the new Pope was so well informed.

"The IRA kill men in cold blood in front of their wives and kiddies, even as they emerge from church on Sundays. They rob banks, run protection rackets, intimidate entire communities."

"True, Holy Father," a rapidly thawing Premier murmured.

"Still wanting to bomb the North into reunion. So wrong."

"*Exactly.*"

"Alas, John Paul II went on his knees and pleaded in vain with terrorists to lay down their arms. If I excommunicate them, it'll only add to their glamour."

"Holy Father," Denise Weaver said, completely sure of him at last, "as a Catholic, I pledge you my love and devotion."

"Thank you." The Pope helped her to rise. "Now I have something to show you."

He led her to a wall on which hung a map of the British Isles. A smiling and relaxed P.M. wondered if he planned to grace the United Kingdom with his first trip abroad.

"Would you indulge an old man in a bit of make-believe?"

She positively gushed. "Of course, Holiness."

"Well, just suppose that from the sixteenth century, Ireland was the imperial power and Ireland had colonized England."

Weaver swallowed a grin. "It's hard to imagine."

"Try. Imagine Irish invaders closing all English churches and hunting down clergy and laity like dogs. These brutal Irish refused to tolerate Protestants in Britain, even though they made up ninety-nine percent of the population. From Dublin, they sent over an Irish Cromwell, if anything so appalling can be imagined. This Paddy O'Cromwell put the English to the sword, forbade them to worship according to their consciences. The natives who survived were forced west to the mountains. It was Hell or Wales for them."

"But—"

"Worse, my dear, imagine towns like Durham, ports like Southampton and Liverpool, being handed over to Irish traders. Whereas Protestants—Britons, that is—had once owned all of England, by 1759 they owned but five percent of it, the least productive parts. Ah," Patrick sighed, taking her hand as if in sympathy, "then came the Penal laws. Protestants excluded from government, the professions, the army and navy. No rights of inheritance. The British even had to pay ten percent of their incomes to the Catholic priest who might not have a single parishioner."

It was only her misplaced pledge of loyalty that kept Denise Weaver in the room.

"In the 1840s, a dreadful famine followed in Britain. Well, not exactly a famine. There was enough produce to feed twice the population but the British could only grow potatoes on their little patches of land. Alas, the spuds were ruined by blight. Yet still the Irish invaders exported British grain and livestock to Ireland. Irish priests started promising starving Protestants bread and soup if only they became Catholics. British tenants were evicted by Irish landlords as soon as they failed to pay rent on what was really, you recall, their own land. The Irish wanted to replace the British with cattle, which fitted the landscape better."

The P.M. grimly consulted her watch but the Pope seemed not to notice.

"Millions of Britons starved, millions more fled in coffin ships to America. Even so, the natives grew stronger and demanded independence."

"Holy Father—"

"At Easter 1916, there was a rising in London. The rebels spoke in the name of King Alfred and Magna Carta, Shakespeare and Milton. The rising failed; the ringleaders were shot in the Tower of London, one of them while seated in an invalid chair.

"Finally, Dublin saw sense. After much shedding of blood, it gave the British their independence. Well, not entirely. The Irish government decided—you will forgive me for speaking in riddles or 'bulls,' as we say—they decided that one part of England should remain Irish."

Patrick forced Denise Weaver closer to the map. Taking a felt pen, he shaded a big slice of England in green.

"You recognize these six counties: Cumbria and Durham, Yorkshire and Lancashire, Derby and Humberside. Dublin held on to these and why not? It contains marvelous English cathedrals and cities and landscape."

He gripped her arm even tighter. "Now when the British want to travel from, say, England to Scotland, they have to pass through foreign territory, which, though called Northern England, is defended by Irish soldiers. Not only is everything Irish—tricolors, buses, telephone booths—Dublin sometimes permits things in those six counties that are anathema back in Ireland: like plastic bullets and internment without trial."

Weaver said in her most arctic voice: "I am the British Prime Minister."

"Indeed. You remind me that, in my absurd scenario, the Irish Prime Minister, the Taoiseach, visits Northern England from time to time to comfort Irish Catholics living in the six counties who feel threatened by a growing Protestant minority."

Weaver gritted her teeth so tight they almost sparked.

"Of course, my dear, the small Catholic majority in Northern England have genuine fears. Terrorists stalk the border areas, many go to their funerals disgracefully draped in the Union Jack. In the deprived Protestant ghettos appear ugly graffiti: 'Irish Out' and 'Kill the Green Bastards.' Forgive my language, I've only been Pope for a few days.

"The Irish press accuse you, the British P.M., of granting terrorists sanctuary within your borders. They slam you for saying you cannot give up your aspiration to Northern England without denying your own nationhood. By stubbornly wanting Northern England to be really English and not Irish, you are encouraging violence, they say.

"Naturally, you feel hurt, seeing that it costs Britain a fortune to patrol long and silly borders which the Irish drew, not you. But, in spite of your justifiable anger, you are patient. One day, you hope, Dublin will see the injustice of six great English counties remaining under Irish rule when they are plainly, by history and geography, part of England."

"Over sixty percent of the people of Northern Ireland," the P.M. spluttered, "voted in a referendum to remain British."

"Ninety percent of the people of Hong Kong chose to remain British, but Britain handed it back to China over a decade ago. But, as I was saying, my dear, the Taoiseach seems not to understand your feelings as British P.M.

"You say to him, 'Of course, a majority in the province, because of the way you drew the border, feel they are Irish. I even concede your right to tell them, "Men and women of Northern England, stay Irish for as long as you like." But what you cannot tell them is, "The *territory* will stay Irish for as long as you like." ' And why not?"

Weaver refused to answer.

"I tell you. Northern England cannot *stay* Irish since it never *was* Irish.

The six counties—Yorkshire, Lancashire and so on—are, were and always will be English. Import Irishmen from Dublin, Cork and Galway till they outnumber the native English by a hundred to one, Northern England will remain stubbornly English. Otherwise, we would have to admit, would we not, that every thief who holds on long enough to his ill-gotten gains finally has a *right* to them?"

Denise Weaver made a huge effort to escape his grasp, but he held on to her as though she were a Cromwellian plantation.

"Finally," he said, "—and what a darlin' you are to put up with the whims of an old man—what if all had happened as in my fairy tale? Then surely you, Britain's Premier, would be here with me, Ireland's first Pope, pleading with me to convey a message to Dublin."

"What message?"

"That Northern England is, was and ever shall be England; and it should be subject to English laws and the British Parliament; and its courts should be English courts, dispensing English justice; its flag should be the Union Jack and its anthem the British anthem—and this is so whoever happens to rule by conquest over a part of England at any given time."

Weaver's biggest shock was to come. Pope Patrick suddenly released her and knelt at her feet, saying: "And this is why, Prime Minister, like my predecessor John Paul II, I go down on my knees to those who resort to violence and—"

He got no further, for Denise Weaver stormed out, muttering, "He's mad. The man is stark raving mad."

Chapter Fifteen

That night, Weaver dined privately with Roone Delaney in the Bubble Room at the U.S. Embassy. The walls were lined with lead and the table was inside a ring of electronic gadgetry which scrambled everything they said.

Weaver did not think much of the President. Privately, she told American friends, "Delaney is not prepared to tax anything, least of all your intelligence."

The President brought her up-to-date on U.S. affairs. Over the years, the budget for Star Wars had risen from $200 billion to $1,000 billion.

"But it's worth it, Denise, believe me. We're five years ahead of the FIR. President Hourani must be quaking in his sandals."

"And the latest lasers."

"General Electric has produced high-thermal conductivity diamonds for us . . ."

"Carbon-12s."

"Yeah. A knockout, literally."

He answered questions about the sale of military hardware to China. It was paying off. The Chinese, more militant than ever after the takeover of Hong Kong in 1997, were pinning down twelve Russian tank divisions, five thousand combat aircraft and eight hundred missiles, most of them old SS-24s.

"The Chinese," he said, "are terrified the Russians will drive across their northern plain to Beijing. The Russians are scared out of their wits that Chinese land-hungry hordes will invade them. Either way, we win. Neither of them will bother us for generations."

"And what are the Chinese up to in space?"

"To be honest with you, Denise, we're none too sure."

"And Saudi Arabia?"

The British Premier had been concerned ever since it had become a republic.

"Let's just say," Delaney smirked, "that we came to a rapid arrangement with the fundamentalist regime about the price and accessibility of oil."

Weaver smiled politely. "You can trust Hourani?"

"I got on the hot line to him in Cairo. Told him, 'Just say once the magic words "oil embargo" and make my day.'"

Delaney switched to a topic nearer home. "How'd you find the new Pope?"

"Round the bend."

Delaney had been told the Pope had asked the French President to return the remaining Vatican treasures stolen by Napoleon which were housed in the Louvre. But, he told Weaver, his own experience had been good.

"A wise old bird, in fact. What put you off him?"

Weaver repeated the Pope's distasteful parable in detail.

"What did you say to that?"

"Nothing. What would you have said?"

"Well, frankly . . . it sounds pretty unanswerable to me."

"What?" she shrieked.

"Don't *worry*, Denise." He played footsie with her under the table to calm her down. "Remember our special relationship. When either nation has an impossible case to answer, we stick together, huh?"

The P.M. eyed him stonily. "Listen, Roone, if I were you, I'd fly out of here tonight."

The President turned pale. "Your Secret Service has—"

"No, I mean if you're here tomorrow, Pope Patrick might try and persuade you to give America back to the Indians."

Part Three

Some Surprises in the Vatican

Chapter Sixteen

On January 2, most of the distinguished visitors left Rome. That afternoon, the Pope addressed the College of Cardinals and some senior members of the Curia.

To the ordinary Catholic, all Popes are perfect. The Princes of the Church are more discriminating. They sat in the Sala Bologna like a clan of aging transvestites, hoping for clues to the pontificate that lay ahead. So far, Patrick was as transparent as the marble pillar that almost brained him.

Some recalled how the Dutchman Pope Adrian VI was elected in 1522. The conclave had long been deadlocked when one party, to delay further and hopefully improve their own candidate's chances of success, put forward the name of a complete outsider. Cardinal Adrian of Utrecht was then on an embassy in Spain on behalf of the Emperor, Charles V. To their horror, the opposition immediately seconded Adrian. No one in conclave had ever set eyes on him. As the cardinals filed out and were asked what made them unanimously elect an unknown, they were forced to answer, "It was the work of the Holy Spirit."

Adrian VI turned out to be a disaster. A saintly man, he was stupid enough to try and reform the *popolo grassoni*, the fat cats of the Curia.

Now that another complete unknown was on the papal throne, the bureaucrats were naturally worried about their jobs. Whatever deals are made in conclave, no Pope is bound by them. Christ gives him his power directly, and that power is absolute.

On the other hand, once the bureaucrats were appointed, a Pope might as well shout "Stay there!" to the sun as to try and stop them. They played everything by the book; they exhausted themselves beating other men's breasts. Their ideal world was one in which the Church obeys the Pope and the Pope obeys the Curia.

For several seconds, Patrick calmly surveyed the clouds of vermilion before him. The cardinals all looked to be out of the same warehouse.

Lord, your Son was a young man when he died. How is it that everyone of importance who represents him, including me, is so very old?

Spiritually, Their Eminences were an assorted bunch. Some were saints, some scarcely Christian. Some were so fat they had virtually to be shoehorned in and out of their armchairs. A few openly admitted that Golgotha was not their scene; they were businessmen with insider knowledge, dealing in futures on the other side of the grave. A few said they sold life-everlasting insurance policies to people who were scared to death of dying.

Capalti, a curial cardinal with Ping-Pong eyes and a Buddha-like belly, remarked with unusual honesty, "Jesus had it coming to him." He boasted that, were it in his power, he would refuse an imprimatur to the Gospels for being subversive of all basic decencies. He constantly played an old CD, "They Don't Make Jews Like Jesus Anymore."

Cardinal Chigi, who looked like an aged vaudevillian, claimed, "We only have Jesus' teaching when he was a young man. That is Christianity. Roman Catholicism is the religion Jesus would have taught had he lived long enough to be made a cardinal."

Patrick put aside Montefiori's carefully prepared notes.

"My dear friends and fellow workers, a new Pope is entitled to make sweeping changes in his household staff, in the Secretariat of State, the Congregations and so on."

The face of many a cardinal went pale against the scarlet of his robes.

"I intend to reappoint every one of you."

All of them, saints and sinners alike, clapped like schoolboys after the head has announced a holiday. Some rubbed thumbs and forefingers together as if this were their license to print money. Cardinal Ragno, twitchy head of the Congregation of the Sacraments, beamed in the front row.

"Of course," Patrick added, "if any of you at any time wish to tender your resignation, you have only to tell me."

Those mostly acquisitive old men greeted this with the cracked laughter it deserved. Many shook hands with colleagues around them. They only came to order when the Pope said:

"You may remember that Urban VIII threatened to excommunicate anyone who took snuff in the precincts of the Vatican."

Those cardinals who took the Gospel with a pinch of snuff self-consciously rubbed brown stains on the front of their soutanes.

"And Innocent X banned tobacco."

Many a yellow hand rose to a yellow mouth to check a smoker's cough.

The Pope took out his pipe and put it to his lips. "I would also remind you that Pius IX smoked and he, as you well know, was the first Pope to be declared infallible."

The relief showed.

"However, my dear friends, there is one major decision of Paul VI which I need to reverse without delay."

Consternation. Cardinal Ragno pursed his thin quivery lips. Paul VI, beatified by John Paul II, was remembered for practically nothing but his outright denunciation of contraception.

It was all very well for the new Pope to be liberal toward the College of Cardinals but going easy on the laity was another matter. The silence was tangible.

An Iberian cardinal with a belly on him like an open umbrella looked terrified, as though the Pope was about to ban bullfighting. Popes simply did not reverse the decisions of recent predecessors, not explicitly, anyway.

"My wish is that at the next conclave *every* cardinal will take part, even those over eighty."

The assembly came as close to rowdyism as elderly gentlemen unused to physical exercise can manage.

"After all," Patrick said above the babble, "the under-eighties did not do so well in electing me."

After more appreciative and relaxed laughter he said:

"I also want to reverse an order of John Paul II. For reasons best known

107

to himself, he frowned on the siesta, for others, at any rate. For reasons known to all of us Romans, I hereby reinstate this most hallowed Catholic custom. Notice, I do not impose it."

Curial cardinals wondered at such Solomonic wisdom. The Holy Ghost must be nesting in his ear. He had such a beautiful accent, too, unlike his predecessor, who spoke Italian as if he had lockjaw. Rossi, Deputy Secretary of State, who was sitting next to his friend Cardinal Ragno, applauded more noisily than most.

"Now, my friends"—and they felt by now they *were* his friends—"for those who work in the Curia, I have only one rule which, from now on, will be the first in the code of canon law: Love your neighbor as yourself."

They all gurgled their approval.

"To some people, religion comes before everything, even God. Not so with you. Love God, love your fellowmen, even when they come before you as faceless petitioners on bits of paper."

How extraordinary this new Pope is, the cardinals agreed. A few days ago, he was no more *papabile* than a stray cat in the Forum. Now he sits at God's right hand. How *does* the Holy Spirit produce such a marvel?

"Now, my friends, I have a problem with which you will sympathize because you have it, too." He paused dramatically. "It is not easy being Pope."

The cardinals, none of them acrophobics when it came to the papacy, sighed audibly in sympathy.

"Not easy," Patrick continued, "for the Pope to be like Jesus. Everyone addresses me as 'Your Holiness,' as if I were the essence of the holy. Some, would you believe it, call me 'Holy Father,' even '*Santissimo Padre*, Most Holy Father'? When someone called Jesus holy, he said, 'No one is holy, save God.' Scripture also says, 'Call no one father, except God alone.' In spite of which"—Patrick bit his lip and grinned ruefully—"I am called 'Holy Father.' "

Several cardinals stirred uneasily, unable to help him solve his conundrum. Some snickered, remembering an old Vatican joke that when John Paul II said his prayers, he and God addressed each other as "Holy Father."

"I suppose I will have to live with the irony of it. Then again, I keep thinking that my Master was often hungry, more homeless than a fox or a bird. I ought to live like him. Not easy when you live in"—he gestured roundly—"a great palace. My Secretary of State gave me a map but I still get lost in a jungle of valuables. He has promised me a compass to help me find my way through the thousand rooms of my new home."

The Cardinal of Rio was beginning to enjoy this talk.

"Do you know," Pope Patrick went on confidentially, "no one even lets me open a door. I used to be quite good at opening doors. Until a few days ago I did it regularly. But if things go on like this I will lose the knack.

"The other day, God forgive me, I rebelled against my house arrest. I tried to walk the short distance to the Nervi Hall. I am, after all, not an invalid. Instead, I was bundled into a white limousine as big as the cottage I lived in when I was a boy *and* with more conveniences. When I tried to object, I was shoved in from behind by Tommaso, my chauffeur. Why a Mercedes, when an air-conditioned donkey was fine for Our Blessed Lord?

"On the rare occasion I am permitted to walk, the ground itself is not good enough for the Holy Father. Oh, no, the *sanpietrini* keep rolling out red carpets in front of me. It's as if I'm forever walking on my tongue."

Rio dug Cardinal Burns in the ribs. "This man will do fine, Eminence. He speaks the truth."

Burns's throat vibrated like a singer's but he held his peace. Lies he felt comfortable with. The truth was irksome.

"Next, my titles. More fitting for Augustus Caesar than for the wearer of the Fisherman's Ring. 'Patriarch of the West, Sovereign of Vatican City, Supreme Pontiff, Father of Princes and Kings, Governor of the Round Earth,' and so on. Tomorrow, I intend to mend bicycles."

A few prelates tapped their hearing aids. Others laughed nervously, sensing, correctly, there was worse to come.

"Pardon me for saying so, but, well, your outfits are far more magnificent than mine. I pity you. Ravishing red to my simple white. Even though red symbolizes your readiness to resist evil *usque ad sanguinis effusionem*, unto the shedding of blood, I nonetheless realize how painful you find this. When he saw the Baptist clothed in camel's hair, Jesus said, 'What did you expect of a man of God? Those who dress in purple and live sumptuously are in royal palaces.' I know you are called princes but surely only figuratively?"

Many a grizzled head nodded, without thinking.

109

"The other day, Alberto of the esteemed House of Gammarelli confided to me how much he charged cardinals of the Curia for a hand-stitched silk cassock." The Pope looked around him and, putting the back of his hand to his mouth, whispered stagily, " 'For water-silk outfits, four thousand U.S. dollars,' he said. 'Alberto,' I said, 'you must not pull the Pope's leg. This is not possible.' So he went to check for me, since we all know that of the ten billion people in the world almost seven billion are starving. Alberto came back and apologized for his silly mistake. 'Now, with inflation, Holiness, it is forty-five hundred.' I felt so embarrassed for you, my friends, I wished I had not asked."

So did many of his listeners. Some felt guilty, some did not. Some at least felt guilty for not feeling guilty. One who resembled Enoch's wife hoisted his eyebrows like snowcaps. Another, who began by biting a finger, then two fingers, was now chewing his whole hand.

"Then your titles. *Illustrissimus, Eminentissimus, Reverendissimus*—everything in superlatives, like the top grades of Italian gasoline. My friends, you and I will take turns to weep on one another's shoulders. I marvel at your courage in agreeing to be cardinals when you have so much to put up with. Yet, my dear friends, I do have this slight worry."

They tried to think what this might be.

"If the Carpenter of Nazareth were to walk in here this second"—he pointed so dramatically to the door that many present really did expect Jesus to walk through it—"what a shock, eh?"

Many an elderly prelate shuddered.

"Poor Jesus would feel perhaps a tiny bit uncomfortable in our presence. Like a workman appearing in his working clothes in the front row of the opera at La Scala. Either he or we would have to get changed and, somehow, I doubt if he would."

All shook their heads politely. Most were wretched enough without Jesus being present. But some, like Chile and Guatemala, Sri Lanka and Indonesia, Calcutta and Benin, were smiling broadly, scenting the greenness of a Vatican spring.

"We are quite safe," Patrick went on. "If Jesus tried to enter the Vatican Palace, he would not be allowed in."

The relief was palpable.

"My dear friends," the Pope went on briskly, "we all know it was less heresy that caused the Reformation than the sins of this court. It was a school for scandal. Pontiffs sold Indulgences like postage stamps. Cardinals had many benefices and lived off the proceeds; they exchanged dioceses for more lucrative monasteries, bequeathed bishoprics, like plots of land, to their children and grandchildren. When a new Pope was elected, Romans hoped he was very rich, because they used to loot his palace. Which is why cardinals took their belongings, gold and silver and diamonds, into conclave." He exhaled gratefully. "Things are not like that anymore. I doubt if anything was snatched from the Irish College on the day I was elected. And you, I know, do your best to live like Jesus."

"Our very best," some muttered.

"We must assert our true authority. Superiors must become inferiors. We must not be bothered by tomorrow. We must serve instead of being served and wash our disciples' feet."

Though none of his listeners had washed many such feet lately, they were lulled into a false sense of security by Gospel phrases known by heart. One old curial cardinal even dozed off but immediately woke up with a snort.

"I knew you would back me," the Pope said. "There is a grave priest shortage in Rome. I am sure that cardinals resident in the Holy City will help out at weekends in suburban churches, become chaplains to boys' clubs and mental homes. After all, hearing the confessions of a few holy nuns is hardly an adequate apostolate for men on fire with the love of God, is it?"

When no one answered, he went on: "Now, I'm told we have four thousand employees in the Vatican. Do they work hard?"

"Lazy as Bedouins." The response from Selvaggi, a fat curialist, known as Baksheesh, with reputedly the best wine cellar in Rome, caused a ripple of mirth.

"I want you to meet a friend of mine." The Pope nodded to Frank Kerrigan, who opened the door and ushered in a gardener. He was blushing wildly as he twisted his hat in mud-caked hands.

Rio muttered in Burns's ear, "At least, it's not Jesus."

"Allow me," Patrick said, "to introduce Sergio Fantucci."

Sergio was still on the Vatican's list of employees. Far from being in the money, he had been lucky to cover his bets. Of four bookmakers, the only one who paid up had accepted the smallest bet. One absconded without trace. Another, a former Olympic swimmer, dived into the Tiber, only to be overcome by the pollution. The third threatened to take Sergio's cousin Mario to court for corrupt practices so they decided not to press their claim.

The gardener bowed his curly black head. "*Monsignori*"—and he bowed again.

Some recognized him as the man responsible for nearly killing off the Pope in the Sistine. Many were beginning to have mixed feelings about that.

"Thank you for sparing us a few minutes of your valuable time, Sergio," the Pope said. "Would you mind telling us how many hours a week you work in the Gardens?"

Sergio raised a superb Roman nose to heaven as if to say, only the Recording Angel can add up such vast numbers.

"Fifty, sixty. *Chi lo sa?* Who knows, Holiness?"

"How many *bambini* do you have?"

"*Bambini?*" Again recourse to heaven. At length: "Twelve or so, I guess." He did not include the results of extramarital affairs.

"A grand Catholic," the Pope said appreciatively. He knew that the Italian birthrate was lower than China's.

"Also, my old father and mama live with us," Sergio volunteered, scratching his walrus mustache.

"Ah, what do you feed them on?"

Sergio rolled big black eyes, stiffened his jaw, and opened wide his arms in a gesture of despair. "Pasta."

"Yes, yes, but what is for breakfast?"

"Pasta, Holiness."

"Dinner?"

"Pasta." Sergio lifted his left hand, leaving a minute gap between thumb and forefinger. "A little bit extra pasta, maybe, than for breakfast."

The Pope rose, took Sergio by the arm and led him to the door. "*Grazie tanto*," he said. "*Addio.*"

The cardinals were too shaken to get to their feet.

"Now, my friends," the Pope continued, "with sixteen mouths to feed, Sergio receives only a fraction of the income of a cardinal with no dependents. Also, he cannot say daily Mass for a stipend of one hundred dollars or more a time. We all agreed, did we not, that in the Church, the first must be last and the last first?"

Everyone nodded, most ever so slightly.

"You force me, then, to rethink the Vatican's salary structure. From today, we must adjust the *piatto cardinalizio*, the cardinals' plate. Those of you in the Curia, in keeping with your top rank and closeness to Jesus, will receive a gardener's wage. The rest of you will doubtless insist on having the same salary as your humblest curates."

Their Eminences' dazed looks suggested the Pope had found the perfect remedy for scarlet fever. They had not realized that Christianity had so much to do with them. Under their cloaks, some Italian hands were pointed at him with only the index and little fingers extended.

"Blood of the Madonna," squeezed out Siri, a Sicilian from Mafia country, with phosphorescent eyes and a jawbone that Samson would have coveted. "A bullet for his back, *stoppaglieri*, a cork for his big mouth."

"Archbishops," the Pope said, "will receive correspondingly a little more, bishops a little more and so on, through the whole range of domestic prelates, *Monsignori*, down to priests like my secretary. This will free money to raise the wages of humble married men on the payroll like Sergio. Of course, my friends, when you retire from the Curia, your pension will be based on present salary. That is only fair."

Expressions of relief from every quarter.

"Now, any objections?" Before a forest of hands shot up, he added, "Theological objections."

Only Rio asked, tongue-in-cheek, "And you, Holiness, how much will your own salary be?"

"I am Peter's successor. Obviously, nothing except my keep. This white cassock will be my one and only. I intend to keep it for best. Any more questions?"

There were none.

"Then I thank you for your unanimous support."

Smiling, Pope Patrick blessed them and left with Montefiori, who had sat impassive as a camel throughout.

Outside, the Pope said, "Well, Giuseppe, did I win them over?"

"I reckon, Holiness, the comments of some will not come out of the Sermon on the Mount."

The Sacred College broke up into small, noisy groups. While those from the Third World congratulated themselves on their wisdom in electing a Pontiff with the right ideas, the curialists were positively papicidal. The Pope had hit them below the bellyband.

Madrid checked his watch—it was 5:00 P.M.—and muttered lines from Lorca on the death of a matador: *"Un ataúd con ruedas es la cama / a las cinco de la tarde."* A coffin on wheels is now his bed / at five in the afternoon.

A cardinal from the Rota, a Barbara Cartland look-alike known as the Archangel, used a language that the deaf hear and the dumb speak. His face expressionless to express the utmost contempt, he removed his cloak, held it out at arm's length by his fingertips, dropped it and, without another glance, padded out of the room.

The cull of cardinals had begun.

"The Devil's Chaplain wants a clean sweep, he'll get it," a puffin-nosed cardinal snorted. And another, Miltonesque, said, "Resignations will come thick and fast as the fall of autumn leaves in Vallombrosa." Still another moaned, "How will I be able to pay my subscription to the Acqua Santa?" Sited on the Appian Way, this was the most exclusive golf club in Italy.

Cardinal Ragno, showing the teeth of a Doberman pinscher, said vindictively to Rossi, "I hope Jesus soon wants Comrade Patrick for a sunbeam."

Back at his penthouse suite in the Grand Hotel, Cardinal Burns peered moodily into his martini, casually stirring two olives. He was beginning to regret calling the President and not merely boasting about but exaggerating his role in Patrick's election.

To a near tipsy Philadelphia, Burns said, "I overheard Cardinal Rossi say he hoped Patrick would end up poisoned like Pope Alexander VI."

Sapieha drained his glass again. "Someone told me Patrick's election was *cosa diabolica*, the work of the devil."

Burns mused on that awhile. "Know what, Kammy? Something tells me that we made a mistake."

Chapter Seventeen

Next day, as he had promised, Pope Patrick, dressed in an old black cassock, started fixing bicycles. In the Gardens, Sergio Fantucci had cleaned out a small round-roomed pavilion dating from the time of Leo IV which the Pope found admirable for his afternoon's work. It even had a lion painted on the ceiling with two twinkling stars for eyes.

The first bike he mended belonged to Sergio's uncle. It was an ancient model with which the Pope was familiar. He fixed the chain without difficulty. The steering column was bent but he straightened it out and strengthened it with a clamp. He changed the mudguards. Finally, he oiled the whole machine.

Sergio examined the bike from every angle and took five minutes to say he had never seen such a work of art. In fact, it looked better now than the day it was bought thirty years ago. He persuaded the Pope to let Father Kerrigan take a picture of His Holiness as he handed the bike over to himself as a gift to the poor.

"Strictly for my private album. Tomorrow, Holiness, I will bring you another."

Within a week, a dozen bicycles were stacked in the shed. In the beginning, other Vatican workmen came to the door to watch but they soon got used to it.

"This bike," Sergio said, one afternoon, "belongs to a very poor bloke in Trastevere." He forgot to say it was his own.

"I will give it priority," Patrick promised.

He did not charge for his labor, only for the spare parts, which Sergio brought with him each morning. Frank Kerrigan liked helping out. It made a change from the stuffy atmosphere of the palace.

The attitude of the Secretary of State was different. It took him ten days to discover what the Pope was up to. One warm summer-in-winter afternoon, treading the grapes of wrath, he came out into the Gardens, past the bronze galleon-shaped fountain. He was particularly incensed because of the numerous resignations from the Curia. Three well-qualified prelates had refused to become cardinals, pleading they could not afford promotion.

"Come to help out, Giuseppe?"

Montefiori glared at the bicycles, too furious to reply. This was the place where Pius XII had reputedly seen the same vision as the three children at Fátima in 1917: the sun dancing in the sky.

"This, Holiness," he exploded, *"this* is ridiculous."

The outburst caused Charley, who was taking his siesta in the shade of the Dome, to shiver in his sleep.

Patrick was genuinely taken aback. "Why?"

"Because . . . because you are Pope."

"But, Giuseppe," the Pope countered, trying to avoid a row, "it's only a hobby. Like being infallible."

"It is not fitting for the Supreme Pontiff to behave so. In front of workmen, too."

Patrick rubbed his hands on a greasy cloth. "Is it so bad for people to know that the Pope, too, does manual work?"

Montefiori said, "You have important things to do."

"Important?" The Pope was genuinely mystified. "Is the servant above his Master?"

The cardinal stamped his feet without answering.

"Jesus spent most of his life fixing things. Plows, tables, chairs. Was that wasting time on unimportant things?"

Montefiori chanced to touch one of the bicycles. He rubbed his fingers together to get rid of the grease before examining their smoothness. He remembered his marvelous father, a potter, how rough his big-knuckled hands were and how his fingernails were always packed with clay.

"Once Our Lord's ministry began, Holiness, our Savior gave up those . . . those . . ."

"Foolish pursuits? How do you know he didn't fix Peter's boat after a storm? Didn't St. Paul make carpets when he was founding the churches in Asia Minor? Didn't St. Peter go back to the only trade he knew, fishing, even after the Resurrection?"

Montefiori stood there, heaving. He suspected that mending bicycles was all very well for a disciple of Jesus but poison for the Patriarch of the West.

"Would it help," the Pope said obligingly, "if I took lessons in carpentry?"

Montefiori sniffed noisily and started unbuttoning his magnificent soutane.

"What are you doing, Giuseppe?"

No answer. Cardinal Montefiori, papal Secretary of State, proceeded to blow up a flat tire.

A s Montefiori forecast, news of the Pope's hobby spread across the city and was reported in the world's press. Sergio's uncle had parted with his bike for $2,000. Several poor families were paid similar sums.

Before long, smartly dressed businessmen were jostling one another as they waited outside the Porta Sant'Anna at the end of the working day. They followed Sergio as he went to return the bikes to their owners. The latter were persuaded to give them up "for Yankee dollars, cash." Sergio pocketed 20 percent.

The bikes ended up in some of the most prestigious offices in the world. One was on the wall of Exxon in New York, next to a stone with a hole in it by Henry Moore. Another was at the head office of C&A Clothiers in the Netherlands. Another was at Hoffmann–La Roche in Basel, Switzerland. The brass plates under the glass-cased exhibits bore the inscription "Fixed by His Holiness Pope Patrick." An Irish American executive of IBM kept his papal bike on permanent exhibition next to two hickory chairs made by ex-President Jimmy Carter.

Frank Kerrigan once said to the Pope: "If you gave a pint of blood to the Red Cross, it would end up being auctioned in New York by the milliliter."

Montefiori confirmed it. He reminded Patrick how Pius IX's *valet de chambre* distributed bristles from the Pope's hairbrush among his friends.

One afternoon, Montefiori entered the Pope's private study.

"The bicycle game is up, Holiness." When the Pope said the poor were benefiting, the cardinal shook his head. "Not only the poor."

There were now, to his knowledge, six factories in Naples and four in Turin alone turning out nothing but "old bikes mended by the Pope," complete with the papal seal of approval. These fakes were being sold to tourists at exorbitant prices.

"Shameful as selling Indulgences," Frank chuckled.

Next day, there was a notice in *L'Osservatore Romano:* "Due to pressure of ecclesiastical work, His Holiness Pope Patrick wishes it to be known that he is unable to mend any more bicycles."

When Frank showed it to him, Patrick said, "I see the need for it but it's a pity, all the same."

Harder to bear was the loss of a good friend. Sergio Fantucci was enticed to New York by Sotheby's. His role as the Pope's special adviser was proved by the picture of him and Patrick in the Vatican Gardens. Only he was able to authenticate the 50 to 60 genuine bikes from the 100,000 or so fakes, most of which had ended up in Cologne and California.

An added sorrow to the Pope was that Sergio, kitted out in the height of fashion, his grand walrus mustache thinned to a pencil line, fell in love with a rich divorcée from Fort Lauderdale, Florida.

Patrick wrote to him several times in his own hand, begging him to come home to his loved ones. Sergio did not listen, simply auctioned the letters.

Chapter Eighteen

Patrick did receive one letter that pleased him. From his eldest brother, Seamus.

Dear Brian,

If I may still call you so. Congrats on being made Pope. We are all tickled pink and I bet Mother and Father are buying rounds of Guinness in heaven. Everyone says Ireland feels safe now somehow.

Pope! I knew you didn't want to be, so I prayed you wouldn't be, but God didn't listen. I think he knows best, Brian.

Mrs. Tommy Hennelly in Collins Street, the one who's in church each day till it shuts so she won't have to go through Purgatory, says she always knew you would be. And Father Donal says he hoped you would be, so you could make a saint of Bob Geldof, who did so much for hungry blacks and worked three miracles last year, though the wife of one of them said she didn't really want her man still kept alive.

Of course, we sang the Tedium for you. At Mass, when Father Donal prays for the Pope's intentions, everyone looks at me. They interviewed me sixty times for television and the papers, especially the *Farmers' Journal*, and everywhere I go, this is God's truth, people look at me, so I have to polish my boots and wear a tie. I can guess how *you* feel. Worn-out, I reckon, just by them looking you over.

On the "Late, Late" dear old Gay Byrne suggested if you are only half the man your predecessor was you will bring the Church to the edge of ruin. He didn't mean it, it was only a slip of the tooth, I'm thinking.

It struck me that if you have to pay property tax on that place you live in, Brian, how will you manage?

A funny thought. If I'd died of the croup as was expected when I was three, Da would have wanted you to have the farm and now you'd have the fifty acres instead of being Pope. Doesn't that prove better than anything God exists?

If you ever come back to Ireland you'll be sure to let me know. Pray for your old brother if you ever have time.

Lots of love and prayers.

Yours fondly,
Seamus

Montefiori visited the Pope's apartment every morning and evening to discuss pressing Church matters. He related how John Paul's burning ambition, after his trip to Jerusalem, was to go to China. In fact, he had sent Montefiori to Beijing to explore the possibilities.

"And what happened, Giuseppe?"

"Lee Jing Shang, the Chinese leader, explained that, with his people packed tight like rice in a jar, even two children per couple would be a disaster for everyone. Contraceptives might be against the moral law but they were vital for the survival of the human race. So I asked him if he had ever tried natural methods of birth control."

Patrick was amused at the superb dry wit with which Montefiori told his extraordinary stories. "What did Lee Jing Shang say?"

"That the only natural method that works in China is repeated acupuncture of the genitals with a carving knife."

The Pope had to fight hard not to laugh.

"I said to Lee Jing Shang," the cardinal continued solemnly, "that if he granted John Paul a visa, he would be very discreet. Simply look at the Wall and say, 'I am a Chinaman.'"

"And?"

"Lee Jing Shang said, 'If our people get even a whiff of his doctrine that *every* act of sex must be open to the transmission of life—' A visa was refused."

Patrick laughed till he cried while Charley wagged his tail and fell on his back to share his master's hilarity.

On another occasion, Montefiori told the Pope about something he had read in the *Washington Post*.

Morgan J. Katz, a Democrat from Ohio, had made *The Guinness Book of World Records* for spare-part surgery. Heart, lungs, liver, kidneys, pancreas, gallbladder, hip joints, knees, jawbone, corneas, testicles, brain cells, sense of humor, all had been transplanted. Finally, he had a hair transplant from a suitable donor. "The most painful of all," joked the curly-haired Mr. Katz.

According to the report, this normally amiable man hacked a registered Republican to death with an ice pick on the New York subway. It was a crime committed only for pleasure.

At the trial, his attorney argued that there was precious little left of the original Mr. Katz on which to pin a murder wrap. The killing was attributable to a dead California senator of known criminal propensities whose heart was now beating inside Katz. Should his client be acquitted, as all Democrats were urging, the defense promised that the offending organ would be changed as soon as possible for the heart of a holy old Irish nun.

Katz was sentenced to death.

Montefiori ended by saying, "The Prefect of the Holy Office is wondering if you would care to write an encyclical against this sort of thing?"

"Against what sort of thing?"

"Transplants."

"I'd sooner write an encyclical against capital punishment," the Pope said.

Chapter Nineteen

One evening Montefiori told the Pope that CNN had just reported simultaneous attempts on the lives of four world leaders.

The Belgian Prime Minister was gunned down in Brussels and fatally injured.

The French President escaped a car bomb by chance; he was too unwell to attend a meeting at the Elysée. His deputy was blown to smithereens.

The British Prime Minister's Jaguar was rammed just as it exited from Downing Street on its way to the Palace of Westminster; high explosive, packed in the assassins' van, failed to detonate.

A light plane full of explosives was shot down only one hundred yards from the White House when Delaney was in residence. An alert guard with a hand-propelled rocket launcher saved the President's life.

No one in the West doubted that the FIR was behind all these atrocities.

The Pope asked his Secretary of State to send the necessary telegrams.

Two days later, Montefiori handed Patrick the latest edition of *Time*. It contained a scoop. George Waqif had managed to interview the President of the FIR in an office in downtown Tehran.

Hourani was pictured in profile. He was seated in a gold-inlaid chair, fingering his beads. Behind his head was a large photograph of Ayatollah Khomeini. Hourani, generally held to be the mastermind behind world terrorism, was in an uncompromising mood.

May I begin by asking what you think of the late John Paul II?

123

A sentimental weakling?

That will surprise many of our readers.

He believed lambs and lions can play together.

They cannot?

Lions eat lambs for breakfast.

Some people respected John Paul for being a disciplinarian.

He was a laxist.

Pardon?

He believed in rights for all, even imbeciles and women. The wonder is he did not demand rights for sheep and goats.

What rights do Muslims have?

One only. The right to Paradise.

Some say you are one of the most powerful men in the world.

Power I have none. All power belongs to Allah.

But surely, sir, oil gives your people power on earth?

I do not deny it. I blame the deposed Royal Family of Saudi Arabia for not grasping the meaning of oil. It is not a commodity. Not an occasional blackmail weapon. Not mere wealth. But power. Allah buried the power of Islam in their deserts. Above it nothing but sand and sky. Allah took from his Elect everything that brings them comfort and repose. Instead, he gave them power.

Power for what?

For dominating the great Satan of the Christian colonialist West.

It is true, then, that Islam seeks world domination.

Your Thomas Paine said, "My country is the world." We Muslims say, "The world is my country."

You specially hate Americans?

Yes.

I'm sorry to hear that.

Why? Is it not good to hate what is bad?

If the American President were sitting where I'm sitting, what would you say to him to try and improve relations?

Repent.

And the future of America?

The ash heap of history.

Some say, sir, to achieve your ends you sanction terrorism.

What do you mean by that ugly word?

Killing the innocent.

In that case, all Muslims denounce terrorism.

Are you suggesting it's right to kill those you think are guilty?

Are you suggesting it's right not to?

What justifies killing?

Violating the will of Allah.

What constitutes such a violation?

Read the Koran, it answers all questions.

But is that not a religious book?

It is everything.

Including politics?

Of course.

What is the difference between religion and politics?

None. Only fools think there is. Thus when you two-minded Westerners want to protest, you leave your church and go to political meetings. When we Muslims revolt, we go to the mosque.

So only religious laws are tolerated in an Islamic state?

Tolerated? No, welcomed by all.

Your religion forbids the drinking of alcohol?

Our only wine is poetry and flowers, and neither turns us into brutes.

You are against democracy, I take it?

Ayatollah Khomeini said, "Democracy is a Western word and we do not want it."

Why not?

Only he needs democracy who lacks truth.

How can you be sure you have the truth?

How can you be sure you are alive or awake? By asking that question, you prove you do not know what truth is.

Would you lie to defend the truth?

There is a line in the *Al Tabarani*: "Lies are sins except where they are told for the welfare of a Muslim or for saving him from disaster."

Now that you have nuclear weapons, would you ever resort to a first strike?

Never. Never. Never.

Is that another lie told for the welfare of Muslims?

What fool would lie and admit he lies?

Your critics say you are hard on women.

Less hard than Allah who made them. It is a kindness to make inferior creatures wear veils in public. To hide their shame.

You believe they are a temptation to men?

Erotic women are more dangerous than oil wells aflame. I forbid them to show their navel, for that is the entrance to perdition.

And women in the West?

You allow them to paint their faces like whores and appear naked in public by wearing short skirts and sit knee-to-knee with men at table.

I read you have women flogged for being raped.

Yes. They should not tempt men to do bad things.

You also encourage female circumcision?

For young virgins. It keeps them faithful to their lords (husbands).

What, then, sir, are women for?

Not to enjoy but to be enjoyed and dutifully provide their lords with sons.

Most Westerners think it is cruel to cut off a thief's hand for stealing, say, a loaf of bread.

Is it merciful to let a thief—he spat out the word *harany*—continue stealing?

But—

A hand is a small price to stop theft spreading. Why should guiltless citizens spend billions on prisons?

But a hand?

Sentimentalist! We cut off a hand to make a conscience whole. But chiefly to protect the innocent. Besides, is it not so that in America you execute murderers with lethal injection? Is that not more severe than cutting off a hand?

Sorry, sir, but to us amputation seems barbaric.

Some acts of mercy are the greatest sins.

It's just that Christians take a different view.

You Nasranis (Christians) live still in the Time of Ignorance before Muhammad. But your Jesus agreed with me.

Pardon me. Jesus stood for gentleness and mercy.

True. Which is why he said, If your hand or foot do harm, lop it off. If your eye, pluck it out. Better to go handless and eyeless to heaven than with all limbs to hell.

You would surely give a cup of water even to a heathen?

Boiling water.

You despise Christianity?

For not circumcising Christians like Jesus. For picturing Jesus, a Semite, with a leprous white face and claiming he is the image of a white God.

I read that the Koran forbids the taking of interest on a loan.

So once did Jews and Christians. Usury is theft.

But you take interest on money invested in Western banks.

To take from a brother is a sin but not from hyenas.

That sounds like double standards.

No, we only rob robbers. We take back but a fraction of what colonialists have stolen from us over centuries.

Is there no way to reconcile Islam and the West?

None. Unless the West bows before the one saving faith, the only true *din* (religion).

You are well versed in English and French but only speak Arabic. Why?

Arabic is the language Allah uses when he speaks with angels.

Is it because you don't like the Christian West?

The Koran honors Asya bin Miriam (Jesus son of Mary, the Virgin). Had they lived in Muhammad's time, they would have acclaimed him as the Seal of the Prophets, second only to Allah.

Christians say Jesus died on the cross for mankind.

He did not die on the cross, it was Judas Iscariot.

Christians also say Jesus was divine.

A blasphemy! And the Nasranis condemn Jews for denying it! Christians even claim Allah is one of three! The Koran, Repentance, Sura 9.5, says, "Slay the polytheist wherever you find him."

What proof do you offer for the truth of Islam?

The infallible Koran, our miracle, in heaven. The copy was given by the angel Gabriel to a sinless Muhammad. He read it, though he was illiterate.

Which proves?

That the Koran is Allah's, not his. Only a willful blindness prevents Jews and Christians from seeing these plain truths.

I t is good to know the enemy," Montefiori said, as Patrick put the magazine down with a shudder.

"Giuseppe, Giuseppe," the Pope remonstrated gently, "we have no enemies."

"Then, Holiness, I suggest you watch some of your friends more closely than others."

Chapter Twenty

I t took the Pope some time to get into the swing of things. He had to practice saying Pontifical Mass. At noon every Sunday he said the Angelus and gave his blessing from the balcony. On Wednesdays, he held a general audience in the Square or in the Nervi Hall for upwards of eleven thousand pilgrims. He met the heads of Congregations and Religious Orders and greeted new Ambassadors to the Holy See.

Like John XXIII, he also made a point of visiting the Regina Coeli Prison, where a whole generation of venal Christian Democrat politicians were locked up for life.

Most days, Montefiori brought the Pope bundles of documents to sign.

As the weeks passed, Patrick learned to respect his Secretary of State more and more for his humility, honesty and grasp of world affairs.

For his part, the cardinal developed a grudging admiration for this un-worldly little Irish priest whom God, in his wisdom, had put over his Church.

Not that Montefiori believed, as Patrick seemed to do, that the Gospels always provide a blueprint for how the Church should behave.

He found it annoying that the Pope had given three rooms in his suite to a poor family, the Christinis, from a slum in the Via di San Nicola da Tolentino when his own officials were cramped for space. Patrick frequently removed food from his own fridge to theirs and sometimes ate with them.

The Secretary of State failed to dissuade the Pope from permitting the sale of parochial church plate to feed the poor.

He forecast catastrophe when the Pope allowed priests in Rome to leave churches open all night as a refuge for the down-and-outs. Patrick's argument was simple, conclusive and, in the cardinal's opinion, completely unacceptable.

"Giuseppe," the Pope said, "at night, Jesus lies in a gold tabernacle while beggars sleep on the cold cobbles. How can Our Lord approve of that?"

Beggars streamed into Rome from every corner of Italy.

Soon, two of the most beautiful and ancient churches were burned down, Santa Maria Sopra Minerva and San Clemente. Restoration work on the latter was estimated at $30 million. Though Patrick had to bow to financial pressures of that magnitude, he was not too troubled by the loss of the buildings.

The Irish kept the faith for centuries, he said, when and possibly *because* they had no churches. The faithful knew they, not the buildings, were the Church; the priests and laity, without material concerns, concentrated on spiritual things.

Far sadder than the loss of San Clemente was the fact that Jesus was once more forced to sleep out at night, without food and with no shelter but a cardboard box. That, to Patrick, was an abiding sorrow.

"You sound, Holiness," Montefiori said, "as if you would not care too much if you looked out of your bedroom one morning to find St. Peter's burned to the ground."

"It would certainly not hurt me as much, Giuseppe, as knowing that in the night my Lord died in the piazza for lack of warmth and nourishment."

Another area of disagreement was Patrick's tendency to give precedence to personal letters.

He wrote to a cousin in County Roscommon with advice on how to care for his sick cows when he should have been addressing himself to the problems of the spread of Islam.

Instead of preparing a speech to the Synod of Bishops on the sacraments, he was answering a letter to a Scot whose little girl had died.

Patrick said to Montefiori, "Jesus said, 'Suffer little children to come unto me.' Am I, Christ's Vicar, wasting my time embracing them instead of writing advice to bishops which they wouldn't listen to, anyhow?"

Montefiori's heart softened when he chanced to see that the Pope had quoted lines of Robbie Burns on the death of his daughter.

My child, thou art going to the home of thy rest,
Where sufferings no longer can harm ye,
Where the songs of the good, where the hymns of the blest,
Through an endless existence shall charm thee.

Montefiori, whose passions were Bach and Renaissance art, was far more disturbed when he accompanied the Pope to the Vatican Picture Gallery. As they stood before a Madonna and Child, Montefiori said, "It is so *Catholic*, Holiness." Seeing the Pope's puzzled reaction to something so obvious, he added, "That was being painted when Protestants, like Christian Muslims, started destroying images. They wanted only the written word."

"Indeed, Giuseppe, but *that* is Catholic? To me it is dreadful."

The cardinal jumped as if he had received a bee sting to the soul. Was the Supreme Pontiff a supreme philistine? He remembered what the mischievous English cardinal Gasquet once said to Pius XI: "None of us, Holy Father, is infallible."

"That, Holiness," Montefiori said in his superior offhand way, "is judged by all art experts to be beyond compare."

"Indeed it is. But what has it to do with religion?"

Montefiori, thrown onto the defensive, said, "It lifts the mind and heart to the spiritual beauty of the Madonna."

"You honestly think she looked like that?"

Montefiori did not reply.

"Come, come, Giuseppe. Can you not see Venus in the garb of Mary? Look at her, perched daintily on a cloud. Was Mary so beautiful and stately, with spotless complexion, in gowns of red and blue silk? Wasn't she more likely a poor little Jewish woman from Galilee, dumpy, overworked, wrinkled, just like my mother and, I suspect, yours?"

Montefiori remembered his own dear mother from Turin. He glanced up at Raphael's *Madonna* and stroked his cheek thoughtfully. "Jesus would not have approved?"

The Pope shook his head. "Nor your patron, St. Joseph."

"Maybe we could commission new pictures."

"With Mary holding a scrubbing brush instead of a rosary. And, as a background, instead of a Florentine landscape, why not a few diapers on the line?"

Montefiori gulped. "That might be going a bit too far."

"Then at least have Mary breast-feeding her son as in, say, Joos van Cleve's masterpiece."

"Or *Maria Lactans*. You must know the twelfth-century Coptic mosaic on the façade of Santa Maria in Trastevere?"

"Of course, Giuseppe. That would really encourage mothers in the Third World to breast-feed their babies."

"I'll have a word with some artists I know."

One conflict between the Pope and his Secretary of State was nearer to the bone.

Patrick sent Father Kerrigan to the Vatican's Secret Archive, where over twenty-five miles of shelves held some of the Church's best-kept secrets. Frank returned with the box containing the last, and as yet unpublished, message of Our Lady of Fátima. It was on the Pope's desk when Montefiori came in for his evening briefing. He recognized it at once.

"Holiness, if you would prefer me to leave . . ."

"On the contrary, I want you here as witness."

Did the Pope need comforting? Rumor had it that when his two predecessors read the revelation made to the Portuguese children, they were overwhelmed with terror. But Patrick did not seem in the least perturbed. That was worrying.

"There are far too many superstitions among Catholics, Giuseppe."

"Ye-es."

"Like the last breath of St. Joseph in a bottle."

Montefiori declined to comment on the final exhalation of his patron.

"Did you know that in Catholic reliquaries there is enough wood of the true cross to build six Spanish galleons, and enough of the Lord's blood to float them in? Did you also know that Jesus' circumcised foreskin is in a shrine in Calcate north of here? And his many navels are I forget where."

Montefiori, his suspicions mounting, nodded slightly.

"Then there is the blood of St. Januarius, which is supposed to liquefy on cue. It didn't appear till a thousand years after the saint's death. Scientists say this phenomenon is due to a particular kind of jelly melting when it's mixed, by shaking, with a mineral called molysite, which is common on Vesuvius."

Montefiori, a northerner, was not fond of the Neapolitan miracle but he held his peace.

"Have you ever heard of the Irish saint Malachi?"

Warily: "I have."

"He forecast, Giuseppe, 'At the appointed time, the City on the Seven Hills shall be destroyed and the dread judge shall judge the people.' Nonsense, would you agree?"

Montefiori said, "Strictly speaking, Holiness, the Vatican does not stand on one of Rome's seven hills. It is an extension of the Janiculum and Monte Mario, hence outside the city limits."

"You have not answered my question."

Montefiori said, "Yes, Holiness, nonsense. Now you are going to read the secret of Fátima?"

"No, Giuseppe."

The cardinal relaxed.

"I intend to destroy it."

Montefiori, his great, gray eyes shooting in different directions, rose up like a cobra in his wrath. "You *cannot*. Some things even a Pope cannot do."

"Sit down, Giuseppe. Thank you." The Pope held up a Bible. "God's word to us. Is it or is it not enough?"

"It is," Montefiori said firmly. "And . . . it is not."

"So speaks my Secretary of State. What says a humble disciple of Christ?"

Softly: "The Gospels are enough."

"Good."

"But—"

Patrick waited while Montefiori searched for a reason to stop the destruction of this ancient and revered document entrusted to the Pope's safekeeping. In vain.

"Calm yourself, Giuseppe."

Montefiori tried to.

"The Catholic Church does not need superstitions. God's Son was born for us, died for us, rose for us. Do we need more?"

"Of course not, Holiness."

"It is said that the letter inside this box prophesies that, after the violent death of a reigning Pope, the whole world will be destroyed. As foolish as the prophecies of St. Malachi. Do you believe any of this, *really* believe it, I mean?"

Montefiori gulped painfully. "No."

Patrick took a folded yellow sheet of paper out of the box, lit a match and burned it before Montefiori's widening eyes.

"Nothing is lost, Giuseppe," the Pope said reassuringly. "The world is redeemed."

Montefiori sank to his knees. "That is enough to know, Holiness," he said, as tears scalded his cheeks.

Chapter Twenty-one

Frank could not help noticing that the Pope was very attached to a small old iron crucifix which he kept on his prie-dieu. The face of the Christ was smooth, featureless. One day, Frank suggested he might buy the Holy Father a new one.

Patrick's smile was like a butterfly opening its wings. He would not hear of it. The crucifix had belonged to his father, who, over the years, as he put it, "kissed the face of Christ into anonymity." That enabled Patrick to see in the Crucified the face of everyone who suffers, whatever their sex, age, color or creed.

It might be the face of an Islamic mother whose baby died without warning in its crib. Of a little Christian boy crying for his father lost down a coal mine or at sea. Of a Hindu man who could not afford bread for his family. Of a Jewish wife frantic at seeing her husband in agony from cancer. Of all the victims of wars and accidents. Of prisoners wrongly convicted. Of a priest who, for Christ's sake, gives up the woman he loves, and who loves him.

"You see, Frank, how clever my father's Christ is. He has lost his own features so he can take on the face of suffering people everywhere. And, if it's not heresy to say so, of every suffering creature. Two years ago, Charley was run over."

"Oh, no!"

"Well, the truth is, *I* ran him over when I was backing out of my garage. And it was touch-and-go whether . . . Anyway, when I prayed for him, Christ here actually took on Charley's face. I was surprised, I can tell you. Instead of praying, 'Lord Jesus,' I said, 'Hi, Charley,' and he beamed back at me and d'you know what he said? 'Don't worry, it wasn't your fault.' *Typically Charley.*"

"Sure is."

"Now I think Christ is the Lord because he takes on the faces and the joys and the sorrows not only of people but of sparrows, cats, dogs, even ants." After a moment, he added, "Sometimes, this featureless face is a mirror . . . and the suffering Christ, most humbling of all, is me."

"Your father left this crucifix to you?"

Smiling nostalgically, the Pope said, "Indeed. He died looking at it, y'see. Died as gently as a finger dipped in holy water."

"May I ask," Frank said daringly, "what you ask God for in prayer?"

"Nothing."

Frank was at a loss to know what this meant.

"You see, Frank, when I pray, I can hardly get a word in. God keeps asking me questions. 'Why are you doing this, Brian?' he says in his best Mayo accent for my benefit, or, 'Why are you not doing that?' "

Frank was to remember this conversation when, in the first spring of Patrick's pontificate, a group of Yanomami Indians from the jungles of the Amazon in Brazil came to Rome. Cardinal Gonzales of Rio had arranged the trip so they could meet the Pope.

At ten one morning in early March, a bus stopped in St. Peter's Square and out stepped thirty natives in loincloths and tribal headgear. The women's glossy hair was fringed and they were bare-breasted. Their presence caused quite a stir.

The Pope now dressed regularly in a rough black cassock with a wooden pectoral cross and a white skullcap, much to the annoyance of his *maestro di camera*. Monsignor Giovanni Bertini was a stickler for protocol.

At the entrance to the palace, the Pope warmly greeted the pilgrims. He then led the chief, who wore a huge feathered headdress and a thin stick through his nostrils, up a steep staircase into a quiet, centrally heated room.

After Patrick had embraced each guest personally, the chief, through an interpreter, told His Holiness of his tribe's plight. Meanwhile his people sat in a circle on the floor with Charley in their midst.

In the 1920s, missionaries had come to their land, an island called Marajo in the vast Amazonian delta. His tribe had welcomed Christianity, they lived good lives. Then, from 1984, more and more white men had crossed from Venezuela. These were the gold-hungry *garimpeiros*. By bribing agency officials, they had bought up fertile lands for a song. They had re-moved vast lodes of gold and other precious minerals.

The natives could no longer fish. The rivers were polluted by mercury put into the water by the strangers who panned for gold. Women and chil-dren paddled out in canoes to passing ships to beg and sell their simple wares.

When all the trees had been felled, the men broke their backs planting rice, only to see their branch of the mighty river rise and wash it all away.

Now malaria had struck. In his village of 250, nearly 200 went down with it.

The chief held out his shaky hands. He was one of its victims.

In 1991, they were told they could keep their land but it was a lie. The *garimpeiros* went on destroying thousands of acres with their *queimadas*, or land-clearance fires.

Pope Patrick found it difficult to control his emotions as he listened to this dignified recital. He remembered his own dear land during the famine years of the nineteenth century.

"Twelve sons, my wife bore me," the old chief said in his gravelly voice, "and only one of them still has in him the salt of life. He is a cripple."

The Pope wept openly for the chief, who stood apart, nodding his noble head, and Charley, sensing the sadness, rose and nuzzled up against the chief's bare leg.

"Finally, Holiness, we lay at your feet with respect the cause of our people, poorest in a continent of the poor."

The Pope sat in his chair fully five minutes without speaking. *Lord, tell me what to do. How can I help them?*

Finally, he rose to speak through the interpreter.

"Beloved Chief, my dear sisters and brothers from Marajo in Brazil, I, Servant of the servants of God, welcome you to the city of Saints Peter and Paul. I want the whole world and especially your government to know that the Pope in Rome has listened to you and adds his prayers to yours that you be given the justice due to you as God's much-loved children."

He blessed them solemnly.

Monsignor Bertini, like a wound-up doll, began to usher the Indians out of the audience room when the Pope signaled that he was not finished.

"My friends, we will have our picture taken, you and I. But as Pope I want your families back home to know that the Chief Shepherd sympathizes with you from his heart." He plucked the sleeve of his black soutane. "Stay here a moment, please, while I get changed into something more fitting."

Bertini relaxed. For the first time in weeks, Patrick was going to dress in white as a Pope should.

The official photographer had no sooner arranged his equipment than Patrick reappeared, wearing nothing but a loincloth. Or, rather, a towel tied clumsily around his middle.

Bertini rushed forward to shield the Pope from the gaze of the smiling pilgrims. "Holiness," he spluttered, "this is undignified. It is not fitting."

In a corner, Montefiori did his best to keep a straight face.

"Not fitting?" echoed the Pope, with that now familiar slightly cross-eyed look. "Would you prefer me to be photographed with God's poor clad in gold brocade?"

"At least your white cassock, Holiness," the *maestro di camera* responded heatedly. "This is a *scandal.*"

"You are right," Patrick conceded. "Look." He pointed to a wall on which there was a simple wooden crucifix. "A scandal. Behold your Lord, naked like a slave."

Bertini looked in astonishment from the figure on the cross to the Pope and back again to the Crucified. They were, indeed, very much alike.

"Giovanni," Pope Patrick whispered humbly, "will you not let Christ's Vicar dress just this once like his Lord?"

As Bertini stepped aside, the old chief took off his headdress and placed it on the Pope's head.

That evening, Tommaso, the genial bald chauffeur-cum-manservant, served dinner to the Pope, Frank and Cardinal Montefiori. Patrick said, "This morning Giovanni gave me the impression he had never seen a crucifix before."

"I think," Montefiori said, "he never had. Nor had we."

The Pope thanked him for the kind word.

"And yet, Holiness, what can you, or anyone, do to help those unfortunates?"

"When the time is ripe," the Pope said, brooding, "I hope to become the tongue of a bell as big as the sun, to make a noise for all the noiseless people."

Frank, silent till now, asked, "Why *did* you go native, Holiness?"

"Oh to be sure, I could have written an encyclical on the miseries of the Brazilian Indians. Of the few who would read it, fewer still would have understood it. And of those who understood it, how many would have felt impelled to do anything about it? Within days, my words would have been forgotten. Those pictures shown around the world are my lasting testimony. From now on, no one will ever doubt that the Pope, like Jesus crucified, is the Chief of the Poor."

Chapter Twenty-two

After dinner, Patrick and Montefiori worked on official papers until Frank brought them hot chocolate and a dish of holy water for Charley.

The Pope pointed to a stack of documents still in his in-tray and wiped his brow. "The Curia must send me all this to keep me out of mischief."

Frank and the cardinal laughed.

"For the life of me," the Pope said, "I cannot see Jesus in this or any age letting himself be nailed to a *desk*."

"I think," Frank said, "Jesus would probably have made a rotten Pope."

Lord, your Son would have made a rotten cleric, period. Explain to me how he is chiefly represented by a group of people like me whom he would never have considered joining?

Frank changed the subject. "I got a call from Cardinal Burns today."

"Wanting you to twist my arm in some way?"

"He wonders if you might write something about modern permissiveness."

This jogged Montefiori's prodigious memory. A marvelous raconteur, he recalled how, when John Paul II was approaching eighty-five, he heard that the Miss Universe contest was to be held without bathing suits, as if the young ladies in question were statues in the Vatican Museum. After the midday Angelus, he spoke out against "full frontal and dorsal female nudity."

"I remember what happened next," the Pope said, for Frank's benefit. "The contest was watched on satellite TV by the biggest audience in the history of the planet."

Montefiori confirmed it in his usual detached, almost oriental way. He went on:

"Soon after this, I was with John Paul in the Vatican Gardens—he was hobbling along with the aid of a silver-headed cane that belonged to Leo XIII—when we came across Sergio Fantucci. He was on his knees weeding. John Paul gave him a brief résumé of how wicked the world was becoming. After ninety minutes, the Pope said, 'That so-called Beauty and the Beast Contest the other night. You saw it?' Fantucci nodded. 'But I forbade it under pain of mortal sin. *Why* did you watch?' Poor Fantucci, tired from kneeling, beat his breast. 'Because I am a stinking sinner, Holiness.' The Pope sighed. 'Almost a billion watched it in China alone. How do you account for this?' 'The world is full of sinners?' Fantucci offered. John Paul was about to resume his walk when he said, 'Your wife, she did not watch?' Fantucci nodded. 'And my *bambini*, Holiness. The youngest is two and a half.' John Paul was staggered. '*Why?*' Fantucci shrugged. 'Maybe we all like a good laugh, eh?' 'Laugh,' John Paul exclaimed tearfully. He was out of his depth. '*E quello che era, non sarà mai più,*' " he sighed. "The lovely past was gone forever."

Frank and Pope Patrick practically burst their sides at the sheer brilliance with which this pan-faced cardinal related his story.

Frank said, "Things are not what they used to be," to which Montefiori added, "Young man, things never were what they used to be."

Patrick suddenly developed a headache, though only Charley noticed it. "I think I'll leave permissiveness alone for a while, Giuseppe. I do not want to make it even more popular."

Frank said that Cardinal Burns also wanted him to write an encyclical against divorce. "According to the latest figures, Holiness, every U.S. household has on average two autos, two handguns and three divorces."

"Does New York want me to condemn divorce or approve it?"

Patrick often used Frank as a sounding board for his own views but this question was stranger than most.

"How could you not condemn it?"

Cardinal Montefiori smiled enigmatically as the Pope answered, "No? What, then, is marriage?"

Frank called to mind a definition from moral theology. "An exclusive lifelong commitment of man and woman to each other for the sake of children."

"Do most Americans have that in mind when they wed?"

Frank shook his head. "Lifelong? No. Children? Many exclude them altogether."

"Cardinal Burns should be happy, then. These folk are not really getting divorced because they were never married. They are only dissolving their adulteries."

"So I tell him no?"

"I would probably do more for the Church, Frank, if I said something Cardinal Burns hates to hear. Too many bishops expect me to do their job for them." He suddenly poked himself in the chest. "Who do they think I am?"

One day, without explanation, the Pope asked Montefiori to arrange a press conference. Selected journalists arrived at the palace, only to be led to the roof garden. In John Paul's declining years, this had been transformed into a private swimming pool. It was quite an engineering feat and cost a fortune. Montefiori was apprehensive. He remembered the disgraceful episode some years before when John Paul II had been photographed by *paparazzi* in swimming togs by the pool in Castel Gandolfo.

Bemused journalists, with their photographers, stationed themselves around the pool. When the Pope appeared, Monsignor Bertini's face lit up. He was clothed in his best robes: white cassock, stole and mozzetta.

Not even Frank Kerrigan or Montefiori knew what Patrick had in mind. Only Bertini, who, to make up for the rest of the world, took himself with passionate seriousness, guessed in advance what he intended to do.

"Ladies and gentlemen," Patrick said to the press corps, "for the world's benefit, I, the Pope, am about to walk on water."

The prelates gasped. The reporters, true professionals, did not bat an eyelid. A couple of cameramen climbed an orange tree for a better view. Several scrambled onto the shelves of the diving board.

"Ready?" Patrick asked. Bertini covered his eyes as the Pope signed himself. "Then here goes."

Lord, if it be your will, bid me come to you across the water.

He stepped off the edge at the deep end and he sank like a stone.

Charley barked like mad. A dozen hands stretched out to help as the Pope bobbed to the surface, clearly in difficulties. Frank jumped in seconds after Charley and fished His Holiness out.

"Did they get their pictures?" the Pope gasped.

"Afraid so," Frank said.

After Dr. Gadda had given Patrick a checkup, Frank said, "Don't worry, Holiness. St. Peter himself did no better."

"Thanks for the sympathy," the Pope said, still shivering. "But I did not fail."

"Um. You, er, sank."

"To be sure, but I made my point, did I not?"

Frank drew in a breath. "Which was?"

"That even in matters of faith, the Pope has his limitations."

"You think Catholics don't know that?"

"Frank," the Pope said, gripping his arm, "even my predecessor didn't know that or, if he did once, he forgot it."

Frank, half convinced that this was a cheap stunt which had nearly ruined the Pope's one and only white soutane, said: "John Paul didn't try to walk on water."

"What I mean is, recent Popes spoke and acted as if they were infallible all the time."

Frank was confused. "Weren't they? And aren't *you?*"

The Pope winced. His head ached worse than ever.

"A Pope is not an infallible person. Not in the way he's a short, funny or clever person. He's only infallible when he expresses the Church's faith on the Church's behalf. A question for you. How many times in the first thousand years did a Pope settle a point of faith?"

"I don't know."

"Not once."

That really surprised Frank.

"And when last did a Pope speak infallibly?"

"Sixty years ago. The Assumption of Mary into heaven."

"Correct. Pius XII didn't make that true, simply declared it to be the ancient faith of the Church. But most Catholics and some Popes seem to think a Pope is a sort of divine oracle. As if he can settle points of faith anytime he likes."

"And he can't?"

"Of course not. The Pope above all is a Catholic, not the only Protestant in the Catholic Church. No more than anyone else can he rely on private interpretation. My job is simply to make official what has always been held everywhere by everyone."

Frank, who had had nothing but jolts since he became the Pope's secretary, said, "No surprises, you mean."

Patrick laughed out loud. "Just what I *didn't* mean. Sometimes the Church forgets the most surprising things. The Gospel, for instance."

Frank nodded but he was out of his depth.

"You're still unhappy, Frank, because, like Cardinal Burns, you think I can settle all problems in the Church without bothering to listen. It was to stop rot like that that I gave myself a soaking today."

Chapter Twenty-three

One afternoon the Pope was reciting his breviary in the Gardens when a new friend materialized out of nowhere. As he sat on a seat under an orange tree, with Charley asleep beside him, Patrick became aware of something pressing on his foot.

It was a furry white cat. "Snowflake," for that was the name that sprang to Patrick's lips, insisted on sitting on his lap. He finished his breviary with her peering at each page and purring as if she, too, were praying for the Church and the world.

When Charley awoke, he greeted the cat with the fondness of an old acquaintance. Snowflake, cool and solemn as a star, was not so generous, even when Charley took a lot of trouble to groom her. After submitting hedonistically, she raised a paw and scratched his brown wet nose. Charley, the perfect Christian, did not retaliate.

By the end of the afternoon, the cat was part of the team. She, too, was given the run of the palace.

On St. Patrick's Day, the Pope lunched at his old home, the Irish College, guest of his friend, the rector, Monsignor McAleer. He prayed in the chapel next to the urn containing the embalmed heart of Daniel O'Connell, the Liberator.

In the afternoon, he gave a special audience for diplomats and their families in the Vatican. Sporting a big bunch of shamrock, he spoke of the part it had played in the recent history of Ireland.

Shamrock was the poor people's way of showing respect for the saint when they could not afford green ribbon. A worthy symbol. It was abundant and life-giving like manna, for, in famines, the Irish were forced to mix it with blood taken from cattle and feed it to their children. No wonder the scornful foreigner called Ireland "Shamrock Land."

After his brief talk he went into a huddle with Tony O'Kane, the six-year-old son of the Irish Ambassador. The boy stood on his head to prove he could till his face was apple-red. The Pope, with his arm round his shoulder, told him he would far rather be able to stand on his head than be Pope.

Turning to Montefiori, he said, "Children are so wise. They can teach us all we need to know."

Tony's parents smiled while Montefiori nodded unconvincingly.

"It's true," the Pope said. "We adults have simply forgotten what we knew when we were small. If we hadn't, we would be children forever with a right to enter the Kingdom. Jesus was like a child himself, did you ever notice that? Not just innocent but loving, trusting, hopeful, forgiving and, above all, wise. This child"—he touched Tony's head—"knows what is important. I would like to have a Sacred College of Tonys to advise me on the problems besetting the Church."

"You wish me," Montefiori said evenly, "to make the necessary arrangements?"

"Truly, Giuseppe. We have to suffer a long time to become children again, to live not by works but by grace. I sometimes think old age is God's second offer to us of the wisdom we lost when we ceased to be children. Is that why grandparents and grandchildren get on so well?"

Tony gave His Holiness a picture of himself with his own cat and dog. Word had got round the diplomatic corps that the Pope now had two animal friends and that Monsignor Bertini had a crush on the cat for dressing in white as the Pope should.

The Pope, moved by the gift, promised Tony a picture in return.

He went one further. He not only had his photograph taken with Charley and Snowflake, he wrote the boy a poem for the occasion.

In an accompanying letter, he admitted that he was no W. B. Yeats that's for sure but, with all its faults, he sent the poem to little red-haired Tony with an old man's blessing. He called it "My Dog and My Cat."

I have two friends, a dog and a cat.
Nothing could please me more than that.
He growls, she purrs and this to me
Is better than a symphony.

My dog would never be so rude
As not to show his gratitude.
My cat, I think, is very snooty
Because of her tremendous beauty.

My dog is chummy and when he lies
On his tummy he rolls his eyes.
The glance of my cat is cool and steady
She only comes when she is ready.

Such different pets but once I'd seen them
How could I ever choose between them?
Companions of all moods and seasons,
I love them both for opposite reasons.

Oh, what would *my* life be like now
Without his bark or her meow?
I have two friends, a dog and a cat.
Nothing could please me more than that.

One day, Snowflake, true to her name, vanished as mysteriously as she had come. She probably returned to her original abode, the small bird sanctuary in the Gardens, and refused to come however many times the Pope called her name. The Pope was disappointed but not surprised.

He told Frank, "Charley's a good Catholic, always obedient. Puss is a Protestant. She wants to go her own way."

147

"Ecumenism is never easy," Frank said with sympathy.

"I admire Snowflake for her independence. Sometimes I think cats are what we would all like to be if only we were brave enough."

"She'll come back."

"Maybe," Patrick said. "I shall miss her, that's for sure."

For weeks, Cardinal Montefiori pressed Patrick for decisions on important matters. The clergy wondered where he stood on celibacy; the laity asked if he would reconsider the official harsh teaching on birth control.

The Pope felt he was not yet long enough in the grace of the job to give satisfactory answers on such key issues.

I am still only an apprentice Pope, Lord, in need of prayer and penance.

One evening, he was standing at his window watching the lights come on in the Borgo opposite, when he told Frank there was something that Cardinal Burns would be pleased to hear.

"I am soon to make the first of only two trips abroad, and he can accompany me if he likes."

"Where to, Holiness?"

A distant look came into Patrick's eyes. "Back to his roots and mine. Ireland."

Part Four

A Trip to the Old Country

Chapter Twenty-four

The VIPs waiting at Shannon Airport for the Pope's latest Boeing 777 on a misty end-of-July day included the President of Ireland and the Taoiseach. Prominent in scarlet was the Cardinal of Armagh, trembling lest the Pope's plane crash and bring the world to Armageddon.

Among foreign prelates were Cardinals Thomas Burns of New York and Kamierz Sapieha of Philadelphia. They had flown in on New York's private jet, which Burns, addicted to Macanudos, had bought long ago when U.S. carriers banned even prelates from smoking on their flights. Both had been warned that the Pope came as a pilgrim. The motto of his trip was the same as that of his pontificate, "Peace Through Penance."

Burns told Sapieha he had a story straight from President Delaney's mouth. The Vatican had asked 10 Downing Street to allow the Pope to visit Armagh in Northern Ireland. Denise Weaver replied, "If that old bugger so much as puts a foot on British soil, I'll have him arrested and deported."

"Procking bitch," hissed Sapieha.

Though the airport was sealed off, the surrounding area was black with people armed with flags, some green, some papal yellow and white. After the attempt on the Pope's life at his Coronation the authorities were taking no chances. The first Irish Pope would not be assassinated in Ireland. Security men ringed the apron; tanks and armored personnel carriers, as well as ambulances and fire engines, lined the runway.

As the Aer Lingus plane came into view and prepared for landing,

Sapieha whispered, "You reckon he'll kiss the old sod, Tom, like the last Pope?"

Burns nodded as if to say, No doubt about it.

A buzz went round the VIPs as the plane touched down safely.

Lord, it's so good to be home. The Pope instantly felt six inches taller. As he left the plane, waving two-handed to the crowd, he looked at a green haze of hills. *I am flesh of its flesh, bone of its bone.* He deeply inhaled. *The very air tastes of Ireland.*

By then, the reception committee had received its first shock. As Burns said disgustedly to Sapieha, "He looks like a swan in a procking oil spill."

Instead of dressing in white with a scarlet cape, Pope Patrick was in a frayed black cassock and white skullcap.

TV cameras picked up the prelates' consternation as they wondered how they could face a Pope so much less gorgeously attired than themselves.

As Patrick walked down the gangway, he felt the whole land from sea to sea—lakes, mountains, dwellings, holy wells—rise up to meet him and kiss his lips.

Now the second shock: in place of his Secretary of State, the Pope had brought his Irish dog along. Charley was in a green coat embroidered all over with shamrocks. He it was, not the Pope, who kissed the ground.

After shaking hands with the worthies—Charley, too, stretched out a paw—Patrick asked the President and the Taoiseach to join him in prayer.

They nodded and bowed their heads, naïvely thinking that was all they had to do. The Pope bent down and removed his shoes and socks. The nearest prelate happened to be Burns. As a kind of reflex, he took them from him and immediately passed them on to Frank Kerrigan as if they were a bomb.

"Jesus," Burns whispered to Sapieha, "the guy's even doing striptease."

A microphone was lowered as the Pontiff, Charley sitting beside him with his eyes closed, intoned the rosary. He began with the first joyful mystery, the Annunciation.

A great frown on his deep-lined face, Richard Spring went on his knees. Old prelates also knelt wobbily. Some almost keeled over in a faint. Those with foresight signaled to their secretaries to find them something less conspicuous to wear tomorrow.

152

After five joyful mysteries, the five sorrowful mysteries. His Holiness was not economizing on the prayers.

There was a tense moment as a helicopter approached. In the tower the controller asked the pilot to identify himself.

"You have ten seconds before we blow you out of the sky."

A ground-to-air missile, on loan from America, was in place, an itchy finger on the trigger.

The pilot rapidly radioed that he was carrying a distinguished visitor, old Charles J. Haughey, former Taoiseach. Arriving late from his island retreat of Inishvickillane, he waved regally to the crowd through the chopper's windscreen.

"Permission to land."

"Refused!"

The Pope went to the end of the rosary and beyond. This was Ireland; she demanded the trimmings. There were prayers for the Church, for the world, for bishops, priests, nuns, laity, teachers, the married, the unmarried, the about-to-be married, the never-to-be married, grannies, granddads, children, grandchildren, great-grandchildren, Irish emigrants, descendants of Irish emigrants, those who aided Irish emigrants, those who were unkind to Irish emigrants, the dying, those dying young and those dying old, the faithful departed, dead parents, dead brothers and sisters, grieving owners of departed family pets.

After much more of the same, finally:

"We offer up an Our Father and Hail Mary in honor of God and the Virgin for all poor souls suffering the pains of purgatory. We pray especially for the souls of our own relatives, for every soul who has no one to pray for her or him, and for every soul in great and urgent need. We pray for the last soul to depart this world and for every soul burdened with the guilt of imperfect contrition, or a forgotten Mass, or a penance unperformed. We include every one of them in this prayer. May God release them all this day."

Charley opened his eyes, woofed and clapped his paws. The clergy yelled a great, grateful amen that was echoed by the crowd outside the airport fence. The Pope rose, put on his shoes and socks. He smiled his slightly crooked smile, was cheered, smiled and was cheered again.

He said very little publicly, only that he, as Pope, was more in need of

153

penance than any other Christian. This trip was not just a return to his and Charley's roots, but to prepare for his broader mission to the Church and the world. His one message was: Peace comes from penance. His brother bishops had gallantly agreed to accompany him on his pilgrimage.

In fact, strict secrecy in planning meant the bishops had no idea where they were going or why.

After Patrick, with Charley beside him, had toured the airport perimeter in the Popemobile and they had both blessed the people, the motorcade drove off to his family home in Mayo.

Mayo! The Land of Youth, *Tír na nÓg*. He recalled Blind Rafferty's poem called "The Country of Mayo" with its last great line: "Old age would never find me and I'd be young again."

Ah, wasn't he young again just to feel the sunny Mayo winds and breathe fresh Mayo air and watch clouds lazily float by like goose feathers on a peerless lake and see the grandeur of the countryside with hedges "all drowned in green grass seas" and the occasional Burning Bush of red Mayo roses?

He could not remember when he had been so proud of his race. He belonged to these people. Crowds lined the streets. Thickest around the village where he was born. There his eldest brother lived on a farm which he still owned but rented out to a younger man.

Sturdy, white-haired Seamus O'Flynn, pipe in mouth, waited outside his small cottage. Its neat thatched roof, the only one in the neighborhood, was like a fresh fall of yellow snow. Its walls were white; blue smoke from a turf fire rose from the chimney.

Patrick was suddenly aware of the long pain for which there is but one remedy: home.

Nothing made the past so alive, so present to him, as when he remembered his mother, who smelled of the whole world, of indoors and outdoors, of raspberries and pepper, wet wood and candles, soup and soap.

He was so excited—*I was a boy here*—he practically jumped out of his Popemobile. He ran toward his brother, went on his knees and bowed his head to receive his blessing and, rising, whispered, "And how is every bit of you, Seamus?"

"Grand, Brian," not removing his pipe from his mouth. "Now hurry up so, your supper's ready."

Feeling sad and happy at once, Patrick spoke briefly to the crowd in a voice that betrayed more than for years past his flat West of Ireland tones. He said how happy he was to be back, a sort of returned Pope.

"Charley and myself will be staying here tonight. Tomorrow early, I'll be climbing Croagh Patrick. If any of you care to join us, you'll be very welcome."

He went inside, leaving the press corps scrambling for information.

A local paper provided the press corps with an old issue containing an interview given by Seamus after his brother's election.

Holy Mary, wasn't Mr. O'Flynn proud as a pig in pants!

When Father Donal, the parish priest, politely told him the papal miter would sit elegant on Brian's head, didn't he near need the last rites? He had to make do with a glass of Paddy with which he decently drank the Pope's health.

To think the good God had selected Brian with velocity to top significance. There was a picture of the couch in front of the fire where the Pope slept when visiting. Another of a jam jar full of cock quills for the Pope's pipe.

According to Seamus, God was atrociously biased in Brian's favor, giving him all the brains in the family. Their father used to say he was really too clever altogether for the professors in Maynooth and *drownded* them with his learning. In fact, he took in facts faster than they could deliver, so they wondered how his head could cram in so many bits and pieces.

God gave him holiness, too, so wasn't he always up knitting his rosary earlier than early or kneeling for hours in the chapel pew admiring God?

Indeed, His Holiness did allow himself one Papal Indulgence: he liked the occasional tipple. Never the tough nutriments. Only draft Guinness out of a can since he approved of the big clerical collar at the top, though he was never overtaken by the drink.

He, Seamus, like the Pope, was still a lonely bird, an odd number, since he didn't want a woman coming between his pipe and his pint and, anyway, he didn't like crowing hens and His Holiness understood, saying that when the English were no longer around, what's the point of being under the Penal laws?

In the kitchen, there were prints of the Sacred Heart, the Virgin, Robert Emmet and Patrick Pearse. In the field at the back were a cow and a bad-tempered goat called Beelzebub.

Was His Holiness normal as a boy? Said Seamus, indeed, from the womb, all the mother we had, *Deo gratias*, declared he was not one for the spade but intended for the robes, and even the dog, a real gintleman, knew it. He could hear the dead singing hymns in their graves. When he went fishing, he used to put the line to his ear so he could listen to the trout talking oceanic theology among themselves.

Ever a giggle in his eye and when he smiled didn't the light of it near blind you? And so on.

The clergy chatted in groups before taking off for their accommodation rented in farms and guesthouses in the vicinity.

Frank Kerrigan was billeted in the small stone cottage of Mrs. Hennelly, the lady who attended every Mass said for miles around.

Burns and Sapieha had rented a trailer, the sort used by movie stars when on location. They had also brought along Burns's burly secretary, Harry Tickle, who was a dab hand at cooking. While Harry prepared the meal, the cardinals had a drink, a smoke and a grumble. They both admitted that in the conclave they had gone for the wrong guy.

Sapieha had a guidebook. He looked up Croagh Patrick. Known locally as the Reek, it was, thank the Lord, not far away. St. Patrick had fasted there for forty Lenten days and nights like Moses on the summit.

Burns's tongue flicked in and out in alarm. "We're not expected to procking stay there that long?"

"Says here it's a daily excursion."

Sapieha read on. After his fast, St. Patrick was tormented by demons in the form of blackbirds. He tried to drive them away by reciting the cursing psalms and ringing a bell that could be heard the length and breadth of Ireland. When that failed, he chucked the bell at them and it broke but it did the trick. They vamoosed, leaving Patrick crying his eyes out. An angel came to comfort him but the saint, slyly, would not stop till he was promised blessings for Ireland.

Burns, deep in the financial pages of yesterday's *New York Times*, kept punctuating Sapieha's readings with comments on the Dow Jones and how his stocks were doing.

Sapieha said, "It seems the climbing of Croagh Patrick evolved from the pagan festival of Lughnasa, marking the end of summer." He clicked his fingers. "It says here that in the year 1113, thirty pilgrims were killed on the mountain."

"Jesus Christ," Burns exploded, "I knew there was a catch. How high is this procking mountain?"

"Calm down," Sapieha urged. "It's only two thousand feet or so. Those people died in a thunderstorm."

Burns looked out the window. Black clouds were gathering.

"Don't *worry*, Tom. The disaster occurred on March 17, which is why they now climb in the summer. On Garlick or Garland Sunday, the last Sunday in July. Tomorrow."

Chapter Twenty-five

Everyone was up before dawn. Most prelates had been kitted out with ill-fitting black cassocks. The Pope, who joined them on the brief ride to Croagh Patrick, was in a buoyant mood. He was on home territory.

In spite of the luxury coach, it was a rough ride. Many clerics started to feel travel-sick. The Pope, with Charley in the seat behind the driver, was aware of this.

"We Irish are a penitential people, gentlemen," he said. "We always had three Lents: before Christmas and Easter and after Pentecost, too."

Burns, who sat with Sapieha across the gangway and was still jet-lagged, whispered: "The penance even runs to the procking roads, Kammy. Nothing but shitty potholes stuck together with thin strips of macadam."

Frank Kerrigan, behind the cardinals, was enjoying the snatches of conversation he overheard. He had misjudged them. In spite of their ripe secret language, there was no malice in them. Relieved for a few days of the burdens of high office, relaxed among their peers, they were reverting to the know-all say-all ways of adolescence.

Westport, the town nearest the mountain, was Georgian and still unspoiled, which Burns suggested was Irish for "procking untouched for centuries," while Sapieha said Thomas Aquinas could wander through it and not feel culture shock.

To the guards' consternation, the Pope got out for a few minutes to mingle with the crowd. Charley played with the children and Patrick listened intently to an elderly widow telling him of her husband's recent death.

"I'll say a Mass for the repose of his soul, my dear."

She immediately fished a five-pound note out of her purse.

"No, no, no."

"That's what I always give Canon Dwyer."

"Then give it to the good canon with my compliments. Tell him to buy himself the best bottle of wine in Dunnes or Quinnsworth."

He blessed the people. Then: "Back in the bus, Charley."

The journey had hardly begun again when Patrick exclaimed delightedly, "There she is, Charley. The holiest mountain in all Ireland."

Eagle Mountain, known as Croagh Patrick, rises along the south shore of Clew Bay, ending in a blue quartzite cone. Among the highest in Connaught, it lifts its head above a mighty seascape.

Frank Kerrigan explained over the mike that there would be Mass on the summit at eight.

"It used to be six," Patrick told Burns. "Some people started climbing at midnight with torches, soon as the pubs closed. Not a few poor fellers descended the mountain in twenty seconds."

The motorcade was met by the Archbishop of Tuam on the outskirts of the small village of Murrisk. The archbishop, an old man with side-whiskers, said, grinning wickedly, that he was only sorry his ticker would not allow him to climb with them.

They proceeded to the parking lot just beyond Campbell's, the pub at the center of Murrisk. There was a market atmosphere about the place in spite of the TV crews and dozens of satellite dishes.

The Red Cross and the Order of Malta were present in force in case of accidents. Cars were tightly parked, accents proclaimed that pilgrims had come from as far away as Dublin, Cork and Belfast. Vendors were doing a brisk trade in drinks, crisps, sweets and chocolates. Kids were offering shoulder-high ash plants for a pound apiece.

"You'll need something," the Pope advised Burns, "to help you. I hope you've brought plenty of waterproofing."

It seemed unnecessary. The stars had already faded in a clear sky, leaving the dawn, as the Pope said admiringly, as pink as the inside of a cat's mouth.

"My umbrella will do me as a walking stick," Burns said.

"Please yourself," Patrick said, winking at Frank Kerrigan. He himself

159

wore an ankle-length black plastic mac with a hood and he carried his brother's blackthorn stick.

The Archbishop of Tuam explained that his diocesans were building new toilets up there. He suggested every pilgrim help by carrying a brick to the summit.

The Pope picked one up. Burns, who didn't fancy climbing a mountain anyway, said expansively, "Don't you bother, Holiness. I'll pay for the whole shoot."

"Not at all," the Pope said. "Everyone loves to do their bit. This was how the Oratory was built a century ago," whereupon Burns and Sapieha grabbed a brick. Even Charley had one strapped to his back to show willing.

The guards were getting anxious. The inspector in charge bullishly estimated the crowd at 200,000. The mountain might collapse under the strain, he said. Moreover, how could he protect the Pope in this crush, especially if a group of violent Muslims in disguise were to join them?

"Right, everyone," Frank called out. "Time to go."

No sooner had they started along the path near the pub than Pope Patrick removed his shoes and socks, stuffed the socks into the shoes and tied them by the laces round his neck. He intended climbing barefoot, stick in one hand, his mother's rosary in the other.

"My parents," he explained to Burns, "said shoes hurt their feet. They hardly wore them in the fields and what a waste of good leather on the Reek." He looked up innocently. "But, please, don't do it just because of me."

Frank followed suit, as did most of the prelates. Some, like Burns, had a problem. Their shoes had no laces. With no way to dangle them round their neck, they had to stuff them in the pockets of their soutanes.

The Pope was encouraged by Charley, who raced ahead, then came bounding back, panting, wagging his sleek gold hindquarters, as if to say, Hurry up!

At first, the slope was gentle and the rocks had a covering of mud and smooth gravel. Many a prelate whimpered in pain whenever they happened to step on discarded beer cans.

Charley was not the only dog on the mountain. Several were bounding about whose pedigree was less distinguished than his.

Patrick whispered to Frank, "In case temptation proves too strong, keep an eye on Charley. Don't want him losing his virginity on the holy mountain."

Frank wondered whose reputation was on the line. It would have been a real coup for a photographer to catch the Pope's dog in the act.

Suddenly, from somewhere above, came the strains of a fiddler playing an Irish jig. The Pope, halted in his tracks, thrilled. History floated by on every rapid note.

Lord, I remember nights of music and dancing in my home and at the crossroads in summertime.

In a moment of mountain magic, time's broken tablets were mended. Long-closed doors sprang open; the cuckoo clocks of memory burst forth into song.

He who had never fathered a child was his own son. In the intricate corals of his brain this ghost-son saw peat fires red as cherries, the particular peculiar shapes of potatoes picked from the ridge. He heard again the roar of the old, white, almost human ass, counted the safety pins, her "medals," on his mother's apron, knew even the precise angles of them. Oh, Mother, Mother, you who put out saucers of milk for the hedgehogs and cracked nuts for squirrels and were so neat you peeled and eyed the seed potatoes before you let Father sow them.

The years, Lord, where have they all gone?

In this drowning recollective moment he saw forgotten faces, heard lost conversations, watched little, probably long-dead children, their pet names and surnames linked indivisibly like summer-and-winter, day-and-night, their features, even their hand-me-down clothes, as clear and detailed as when he saw them, sixty years before, laughing, riding bicycles or sneezing as they jumped on hay carts piled higher than a house. Suddenly, everything mortal seemed deathless and deserving.

"Dear God," he said to no one in particular, as the music ceased, "my old da used to fiddle as fast as my mother could knit!" He recalled lines of Yeats's his father used to recite from the "Fiddler of Dooney":

For the good are always the merry,
Save by an evil chance,

And the merry love the fiddle,
And the merry love to dance.

An unmusical and unmerry Burns, a few steps behind, kept treading on what he said was dog shit but was probably mud.

"It's tough on the toes," Sapieha complained. "I've got blisters big as moons."

"Much more of this, Kammy, and I'm gonna kick his lousy dog."

One moment, the sky above was milky white and the view unblemished. The next, a mist brought pitch-darkness. What clerics from abroad resented most was the gossamer-like quality of Irish rain. Soft, relentless, it went through every garment to the skin. To make matters worse, the wind rose of a sudden, clamping them in its cold maw.

Burns tried to put up his umbrella. He might have taken off like a hang glider had not the brolly turned inside out.

"For Chrissake, hold on to me, Harry," he said to his secretary through clenched teeth. "What I procking do for Holy Mother Church."

In the mist, Sapieha kept bumping into him from behind. "Sorry but I can't see your ass, Tom," which was something, seeing it was quite a landmark.

"You want me to wear a taillight?" Burns hissed, as he secretly threw his brick away and took a swig from his hip flask.

Ahead, the Pope stopped. He was at the first of three stations, or places of pilgrimage. These were circles of stones, at which pilgrims walk, stand, kneel and pray. This one was in honor of St. Benignus, Patrick's loyal disciple.

Burns could not remember when he had felt so irreligious.

"Now," Patrick said, "for the difficult part. We're coming to the scree."

A minute later, Burns wailed, "I can't find the path."

"There isn't one," the Pope assured him.

Ahead, on a steep incline, was a desert of small gray stones.

The Pope, not even breathing heavily, said, "This is why I advised you to buy an ash plant. To give yourself a hold."

As Burns dug in his umbrella, the steel tip came off. He was forced to crawl like a baby. All he could see ahead were ghostly figures, all he could feel, apart from the stabbing pains in his feet, were stones rolling down on him.

Sensing the distress behind, the Pope started to sing, "Lead, Kindly Light, amid the encircling gloom."

Before the first verse was over, Burns screamed as he fell over a stone and twisted his ankle. The Pope was attending to him when, out of the gloom ahead, came a terrible screech.

Burns was sure the devil had come for him. But Kammy said no such luck. It was only a donkey descending after carrying provisions to the summit. Harry Tickle, Burns's secretary, had a word with its owner and they came to an accommodation.

Cardinal Burns finished the climb, ass on ass. "God Almighty," he complained to Sapieha, who was hanging on to the tail, "the smell of the beast."

"You don't say," said Sapieha, who was almost passing out at his even closer proximity to unaccustomed odors.

When their despair was deepest, they found themselves suddenly on the summit. It was flat like Tabor. Pilgrims were already gathered there, some smoking, some kneeling for the family rosary. Television cameras were blazing around St. Patrick's Bed, a pile of rocks surrounded by a rectangle of low metal poles that looked like a grave plot.

After making the station, the Pope went to vest for Mass in the Oratory, a kind of glassed-in box. Inside, protected from wind and rain, priests celebrated Mass, their voices relayed to pilgrims by loudspeaker. A door to the left said "Confession," another to the right "Communion." The pilgrims knelt at the wooden rail for communion and then made their exit at the back.

Miraculously, at the homily, the sky cleared to reveal a newly minted sun. The Pope told a hushed gilded congregation that he had last climbed the holy mount in his mid-thirties and he had longed to return. No wonder the Lord spent the night in prayer on the mountainside before choosing his disciples and was on a mountain transfigured. He said he felt nearer to God on Croagh Patrick than anywhere else on earth, including honey-colored and immortal Rome.

"Why, here your head is brushed by angels' feet."

To the northwest, in telescopic light, was Clew Bay, where countless islands dotted the immense sea. Farther north, across the bay, the prospect ended in highlands, from the cliffs of Achill to where Nephin stood to the right in solitary splendor like Nebo, where Moses died. To the south, beyond a valley, was the vast and desolate country of South Mayo and Connemara of the Twelve Pins, its soil spread thinly over limestone rock. To the east, a great plain led to Roscommon. To the southeast, over the waters of Lough Mask and Lough Corrib, were Galway and its famous bay.

This was God's own timeless country, brown bogland and miniature blue lakes.

"If I had faith that could move mountains," the Pope said, "I'd take Croagh Patrick back to Rome with me."

Burns was in no state to appreciate the scenery. The donkey ride had moved his innards and he was taken short. The toilets, he discovered, definitely needed rebuilding. They were not a credit to Ireland. In the company of his secretary, he tottered toward the one marked "Clergy Only."

He tried the door, only to find it was locked from the inside. He was normally impatient but this was something special. He wrenched again. No good.

"Get that guy out of conclave, Harry," he muttered.

Harry rapped on the door. "Would you come out, please?"

Silence.

"Come on out," the secretary hissed. "There's a cardinal wants to take his seat."

"Not possible," came back a steely voice.

"If you don't come out," Harry said, "you'll be in deep trouble."

"Don't you threaten me," said the occupant, "I'm an immovable parish priest."

Incensed to hear the old joke at this delicate moment, Burns brushed his secretary aside. "Come out, Father, and I'll see to it you're made a monsignor."

"I'm already a monsignor."

"Jesus Christ!" Burns moaned. "I'd excommunicate the guy if we weren't on procking holy ground."

He switched from leg to leg, but he had to contain himself for one more minute before he heard the blessed sound of the water closet being flushed.

164

He didn't even wait to curse the previous occupant before rushing in and exploding in relief.

Minutes later, his secretary, still nearby, heard:

"Har-ry?"

"Eminence?"

"That shitty guy used up the last of the toilet paper."

"I'll do my best, Eminence."

The secretary went through his pockets but found nothing serviceable. He searched the ground outside and came up with an empty packet marked "Jacob's Crackers." That seemed very appropriate, except it was sopping wet.

"Sorry, I can't find a thing."

"Har-ry, don't you have your pocketbook?"

Tickle reluctantly went through it. He only had hundred-dollar bills.

"Jesus," he thought, "it'd be cheaper to tear strips off my new shirt."

He kissed the bill good-bye and slipped it under the door, sighing, "That's one in the eye for Ben Franklin."

"Thanks." A minute later: "Har-ry. D'you happen to have another hundred bucks?"

I t was even tougher going down. They slid down the scree, cutting only their hands, because now the Pope alone went barefoot.

"Ah," he exclaimed, "this holy mountain is making a new man of my feet."

In the parking lot, vendors were selling pictures of St. Patrick clad in green vestments, crozier and miter. Against a background of green hills and round towers, he stood astride a rock with serpents at his feet.

The clergy were more interested in the food carts that sold burgers and French fries. Burns's secretary presented him with a triple burger.

He was about to bite into it when he became aware of an urchin with black face and black curly hair nudging him and looking up longingly. He pretended to take a huge bite but, at the last moment, handed the burger to the boy.

"For you, kid."

Frank Kerrigan came across and whispered to Burns, "That rascal had his hand in your pocket, Eminence."

"Nothing in it but air, Father." He called his secretary over. "Harry, see this snotty-nosed kid? Give him a few bucks."

Harry had just got change from the burger. He handed a five-pound note to the lad with the bulging mouth.

Burns stooped down and murmured in the lad's ear. "You a Catholic? Fine. Know who I am? No. Fine. Your name? Bobby. Fine. Listen, Bobby, I want you to go to confession and say you tried to pick the pocket of a holy Yankee priest who told you that if you ever do a thing like that again, Bobby boy, he's gonna"—Burns suddenly screamed—"knock your procking head off."

The boy yelped and flew off like the wind.

Harry Tickle meanwhile handed Burns the burger he had bought for himself. Burns was about to sink his teeth in for the second time when the Pope said:

"Do none of you want to join me for the rest of my pilgrimage?"

Burns stopped in midbite like an electrified snake.

"Next stop," the Pope explained, "is Lough Derg."

"That's fine by me," said Burns in his ignorance.

"The thing is, you have to be fasting from midnight."

Burns looked longingly at his bun before dumping it in the nearest trash can. The rest followed suit.

"Ah," said the Pope, as he put his shoes and socks back on, "this is far too much fun to be called a pilgrimage."

The prelates climbed miserably into the bus, which took them to the outskirts of Westport, where a fleet of helicopters was waiting to take them to their next destination.

Chapter Twenty-six

From the air, the clergy had their first view of Lough Derg. The Red Lake, in south County Donegal, is three miles by two, with a peninsula and several small islands.

The helicopters dropped them off outside the village of Pettigo. Coaches were waiting to transport them the last few miles.

On the coach, the Pope kept telling Charley of the good things ahead. He stretched across the gangway and explained to Burns and Sapieha that people once thought Eden was where the sun rose and Lough Derg, in its western remoteness, was where it set. "So there was nowhere to go but *down*, so to speak."

"Then," said Sapieha apprehensively, "Lough Derg is where this world and the next meet?"

The Pope nodded. "St. Patrick himself came here in 445. And, d'you know, some ancient maps of Ireland have only Patrick's Purgatory marked on it?"

Burns had his nose in Sapieha's guidebook and did not like what he read. A great Irish warrior, Finn McCool, had here defeated a giant serpent and cut out of its belly a fully armed knight whom it had swallowed. The dragon's ribs are the rocks off the shore of Station Island. The dragon's blood had stained the lake's waters their present red.

"Jesus!" Burns hissed. "*A palm tree in a red lake.* Forget purgatory, pal. We're gonna go through hell."

"According to legend," the Pope was saying, "it was here that St. Pat, the new Finn McCool, cast the snakes out of Ireland. You'll see the saint's footprints on the stones."

He went on to say that Dante borrowed his ideas on purgatory from this place.

"Ghosts, too, arise here from the underworld. Remember Hamlet: 'Yes, by Saint Patrick . . . Touching this vision here / It is an honest ghost, that let me tell you."

Burns, looking out onto a cold, damp summer's day, could well believe that this place bordered on the nasty.

The Pope took over the public address system. "Gentlemen, you'll soon realize why, for the Irish, purgatory and hell are not hot places, but cold, wet and windy."

The laughter greeting this was not hysterical.

Round a corner, the lake came into view. Rain was pitting the surface, a mist off the bogs and surrounding hills swept over it. A few clerics, led by the Cardinal of Armagh, clapped limply. An Irish bishop said, " 'Tis a real Lough Derg day and all."

The Pope told them that in 1879 a Canon O'Connor wrote a book on the Lough and sent a copy to Leo XIII.

"He couldn't read English, so, to give him the flavor of the place, the canon sent him a specimen of the oat bread which is all we shall feed on while we're here."

Burns's chin nearly hit the floor. "I'm procking starved already," he muttered.

The bus halted. Station Island, the place of Patrick's Purgatory, bulked gloomily half a mile from the southeast shore. They could just make out the basilica, with its pointed dome.

The clergy alighted and were greeted by the prior, Monsignor Ryan, a small bent man with a white beard. After the introductions, he pointed to a notice beside the pier. Pilgrims were expected to take part in all the exercises. He issued the clergy with gray metal tokens, marked "Lough Derg Boat Ticket." A launch, the *Saint Patrick,* licensed to carry fifty passengers, was purring beside the pier.

"Now, pilgrims," the prior said through a bullhorn, "this lake separates us from the busy world. Please respect the peace and quiet of the island."

"Remind you of anything?" Sapieha hissed, as the boat pulled out. Burns shook his head. "Charon's ferry across the Styx?"

Burns recalled only too well Michelangelo's picture of the Last Judgment, in whose shadow he had made the biggest mistake of his life.

Monsignor Ryan was saying that Station Island is a mere 126 yards by 45 at its broadest, with thin and rocky soil.

"Penitents have been coming here since the twelfth century, inspired by St. Malachi. Since then, it has been shut down only once, in 1497 by Pope Alexander VI."

Burns muttered, "Good for procking Borgia."

"It reopened six years later under Pius III at the request of the Archbishop of Armagh."

For a few seconds, pride overcame Armagh's apprehension that the boat might sink and bring about Armageddon in his own backyard, so to speak.

"In 1642," the monsignor said, "the English closed St. Patrick's Purgatory as being a 'poor beggarly hole.' It was only a few feet deep, they said, and big enough for a mere half dozen people. They filled it in. Not that pilgrimages ceased even during Penal times. This whole area was in the center of the Scottish plantation and pilgrims were fined or publicly flogged. But that didn't stop them flooding in. In the rest of Ireland, worship was in secret—in woods, under hedges, on hills—but not at Lough Derg. Priests and bishops came here disguised as merchants and said Mass *openly*."

Frank Kerrigan, even Burns and Sapieha, sensed that they were approaching the real Ireland, Ireland the indomitable, Ireland poor, rugged, yet enduring.

As to Pope Patrick, he was lost in pride at the unimaginable pain borne there by so many unremembered saints.

Christ of the Three Nails, watch over this, my country.

"This demesne," the prior went on, "was once owned by the Magrath family. One son, Miler, was a simonist with a difference. When the reigning Pope refused him the see of Clogher, he became, would you believe, the first

169

Protestant Bishop of Clogher? He also took a wife. Later, he was for nine years Catholic Bishop of Down *and* Protestant Archbishop of Cashel. His tomb is at Cashel of the Kings, where he died aged one hundred."

Everyone chuckled, including the Pope.

As they neared the island they could see a green postbox and pilgrims walking and praying. There was little grass, and not one bush or flower.

"The church of St. Patrick, pilgrims, is the only basilica in these isles, a privilege it shares with Lourdes and Montmartre."

As the boat bumped against the pier, the monsignor warned, "You have all fasted from midnight. You will fast for three days altogether, except for one meal per day of black tea or coffee and dry toast."

A scared Dr. Gadda, who had mysteriously missed the climb of Croagh Patrick and reappeared, whispered to the Pope, "Far too tough for you, Holiness. At the most, half a day of fasting, eh? I write you a certificate of exemption."

The monsignor shook the hand of each one of them as they disembarked, saying, "Good luck and God bless."

A t reception, they were given a ticket for the men's dormitory. The Pope's read: "Cubicle 10 Bed A." Burns's was 10 Bed B. His was the top bunk. There was a hook for their clothes, a shelf for their belongings and a washbasin filled with lake water which Charley was already lapping up.

Burns, reminded of the miseries of conclave, wasted no time in clambering up on his bunk to test it out. The mattress was hard as an atheist's heart but he was tired after Croagh Patrick.

No sooner was he on the horizontal than the Pope dug him in the ribs. "*Verboten*, Eminence. No sleep the first night."

Burns shot up. "What?"

"Tonight that bunk will be occupied by a feller who didn't sleep last night."

The Pope took off his shoes and socks. A shocked Burns and Sapieha did the same before joining him outside on the cold wet stones. Most of the day's pilgrims had started at eleven o'clock. The clergy were over an hour late and had a lot to make up before 9:20 that evening.

After a visit to the Blessed Sacrament in the basilica, they went out to St. Patrick's Cross, where they knelt to say one Our Father, one Hail Mary and the Creed. Afterward, they kissed the rusted iron cross atop the remains of a fluted column.

They walked to Brigid's Cross on the outside wall of the basilica and said three Paters, three Aves and one Creed. Standing with their backs to the cross, arms outstretched, as if crucified to the wall, they three times renounced the devil, the world and the flesh.

Burns did it but with a few mental reservations.

The next exercise was to walk around the basilica, silently saying seven decades of the rosary followed by the Creed. The flagstones, though cold, were easier on the feet than the scree on Croagh Patrick. Oilskins and plastic macs kept out the worst of the wet, and there was something soothing in the cries of gulls.

Now it was time for the first Bed, that is, the remains of a cell or oratory of an ancient monk. St. Brigid's Bed was near the bell tower.

Burns and Sapieha, who had not lined up for anything in years, queued with a few slow old ladies. Here the rocks were sharper. Soon Burns was complaining to Sapieha out of the corner of his mouth about his procking bunions. His knees, too, for there was a lot of genuflecting.

The routine was to walk three times round the outside of the Bed by their right, saying Paters and Aves and the Creed; kneel at the entrance and repeat the prayers, then walk three times round the inside, saying the prayers again. Finally, they knelt at the cross in the middle for the final bout of prayers.

That first station took an hour and, by the end of it, Burns was exhausted.

This was repeated at the beds of Saints Brendan, Catherine and Columba. Only the Pope seemed to appreciate the rain, claiming that it was the friendliest thing and without it would Ireland be Ireland? It would not.

"Are you enjoying this, Eminence?" the Pope asked Burns, as he took a huge breath of fresh air. "God's own country." And he recited aloud, " 'Round Lough Derg's holy island, I went upon the stones / I prayed at all the stations upon my marrow-bones.' "

St. Patrick's Bed, near the men's hostel, was bigger than the rest and the prayers correspondingly longer. Afterward, they headed for the Bed near the water's edge.

Some pilgrims, including the Pope, stepped into the lake to refresh their feet. After reciting the rosary to the Glorious Maiden Mother, they returned to St. Patrick's Cross. More prayers. The station ended in the basilica with five Paters, five Aves and the Creed for the Pope's intentions.

Heavens, would you believe, that's me?

"Christ," Burns said in an undertone, "this parquet floor feels good."

By Sapieha's count, they had already recited 99 Paters, 162 Aves, 7 Glorias, 26 Creeds. If they ever finished Lough Derg, they would have said at least 891 Paters, 1,458 Aves, 63 Glory Be's and 234 Creeds. And they had to recite their breviary in between.

Time for refreshments.

In the bright low-ceilinged refectory, they were served black coffee out of a metal pot, a piece of soggy toast and as much as they wanted of Lough Derg soup: hot water sprinkled with pepper and salt. It went down, according to a famished Cardinal Burns, like "The Battle Hymn of the Republic" sung by the Mormon Tabernacle Choir.

Night came. The sun went off in search of America. Lanterns on the lakeward ramparts came on and, at dusk, bats appeared. The Pope sat with Charley, Dr. Gadda and a few clergy on the pier bench, looking out across the lake to the softwood plantation on the shore.

To cheer Burns up, the Pope said, "They say the devil personally sharpens all the stones at night."

After too brief an interval, they limped into the basilica for night prayers and benediction. The Vigil Candle, lit for the previous day's pilgrims, was now a stump. Over the altar was a Penal cross on whose base was a cock. The Pope explained that this was the cock that crowed three times when Peter denied his Lord.

"On the day after Christ was crucified, it was killed for the pot, but when

Christ rose, so did the cock then roasting on a skillet. It flapped its wings and sang the praises of God. Isn't that a grand legend, now?"

For Sapieha's benefit, Burns quietly went, "Cluck, cluck, cluck," before seeming to expire.

Hymns were sung, including "Nearer My God to Thee," "Hail Glorious St. Patrick" and "Abide with Me." Incense mingled with the smell of damp clothing.

When night prayers finished, the prior told the second day's pilgrims they were free to go to bed. They left, too tired even to cheer.

He introduced the rest to the Vigil. It began with a Holy Hour, during which the doors of the basilica were symbolically locked. After that, the stations would be held inside the basilica.

"I need hardly tell you, pilgrims, that on no account must you relax. If you see anyone dozing, be a good Christian and poke him in the ribs. Now I'm going to light your Vigil Candle. May you burn as loyally."

This was to be the longest night of Cardinal Burns's life. He'd not thought of Flick of Boston for weeks but now he saw Knife's heart attack as a blessing from God.

The night was a chloroformed blur of unending prayers, kneeling, moving along the benches, standing. He felt alternatively drugged and delirious.

The fourth station began at 12:30. At 1:30, some went outside to the shelter for a smoke. Burns and Sapieha crept away to the lakeside for a cigar and a swig from Burns's hip flask. As Burns slapped a swarm of midges that were eating him alive, the flask slipped out of his hand. As he tried to catch it he lost his balance and went into the water. Only the lower part of him got wet but that was bad enough because, when he returned to the hostel to dry off, he found it locked for the night.

"For Chrissake," he roared, as he banged the door to no avail, "don't they trust even a cardinal around here?"

The bell rang for the fifth station. It was 2:00 A.M. Burns shivered until the break at 3:00. The sixth station followed at 3:30 with a break an hour later.

Pope, Frank and Charley went out to see the birth of the morning. In lettuce-crisp air, the last bats were skimming the water. In the west, the moon was ready for milking while eastward, over the rim of the hills, the sun was signaling its presence, a pearly light hovered over Kinnagoe.

As they watched, a wind arose. Waves tossed and beat against the shore. Yet the sky was clear and God re-created the world in front of their eyes. Out of chaos and dark night distant mountain ranges appeared, treeless except for a few stunted pines on the lower slopes.

The Pope absorbed everything, drank in the remoteness of the place and its desolation. How he loved the brown bogs, the moorlands, the wet gray mountains, the remote yet strangely familiar farmhouses.

Frank groaned, "No sleep for another seventeen and a half hours."

At five, they went inside to find the light beginning to reveal the colors in the windows. It was time for the seventh station. This hour, spanning the dawn, was the most difficult. The Pope had to dig Dr. Gadda in the ribs constantly and stop Charley from disturbing everyone with his snoring.

Many a bishop claimed he was killed dead. One confessed he would sell his soul for half a plate of porridge. "Mephistopheles, where are you?"

For morning prayers at 6:30, they were joined by the other pilgrims, who, after a good night's sleep, looked like members of a different race. Sapieha declared he would like personally to strike a match and burn every procking one of them.

Priests sat on chairs behind the altar rails, and pilgrims went up and knelt beside them for confession while the organ softly played.

The Pope took his turn at confessing, with Charley, as ever, beside him, listening attentively but without surprise.

Cardinal Burns, too, confessed; all he remembered was calling himself a lump of purple shit who deserved to be in purgatory till the place shut. He didn't mean it. It was only his lost, true self speaking, like a horn in an impenetrable forest.

The prior invited the Pope to give the homily. Only he could possibly have aroused a spark of interest in the first day's exhausted pilgrims.

"My sisters and brothers in Christ," he said, with all eyes fixed on him, "every moment we spend here is the fruit of a millennium. Enough faith has been exercised here, enough pain has risen in sacrifice from the soles of feet that have walked here, to heal the world a hundred times.

"My dear mother made this pilgrimage twenty times, my father a dozen at least before, as he said, he ran out of Lough Dergs. Not entirely, for as his coffin was lowered into his warm grave he bore two Lough Derg pebbles on his breast. With millions of others, in times troubled and untroubled, they hallowed this place and, if you will pardon an Irish bull, they handed on their sturdy feet to me.

"You are tired, so was Christ. You are hungry and thirsty, so was Christ. For a thousand years and more, Christ has walked the paths of Lough Derg hungry and thirsty on the bare and bloodied feet of believers.

"My sisters and brothers, we are privileged to be here. Let us be glad and rejoice."

As he stepped down not all shared his happiness. The acclamation after the consecration was, "Christ has died, Christ has risen, Christ will come again," causing Burns to whisper, "*Christ* may come again, Kammy, *I* certainly won't."

In the precious free moments between the stations, Burns and Sapieha wandered around together like babes in the wood. Looking at the Soviet-bare stalls, Burns complained there was nothing to buy except the Infant of Prague, Our Lady of Lourdes, silver medals of Padre Pio and procking garden gnomes.

Sapieha pointed. "*And* crucifixes for a happy death, Tom. Six pounds each."

"I'll take three," said a miserable-looking Burns, "so at least I die laughing."

They finally had access to the drying room. Burns was able to wring his socks out and make Christians of his feet again. Too soon it was back to the basilica for more prayers.

There, they found the Pope kneeling on his hands as an added penance.

Burns's idea of self-denial was to examine his conscience from a discreet distance, not to beat the daylights out of himself as the Irish liked to do.

"I hate the procking Celtic gloom of the place," he told his pal.

Sapieha replied with, "Amen, Sweet Big-Assed Angel of New York, amen, am-*en*."

With the next station outside the basilica, they knew the second day had begun.

At noon there was renewal of baptismal promises. A malarial-looking Burns remembered little of that interminable day except when, without expressly intending it, he lunged at Charley with his foot. Charley responded with a snap at the plump left pillow of his bum and he said that lousy dog should be put down with a cleaver here and now pilgrimage or not and the Pope said he must have done something to annoy Charley whose love and understanding of humans went beyond words and Burns said his procking ass was bleeding like a stuck pig and the Pope denied it saying Charley could bring in pheasants without creasing a feather and never bit anyone in his life only gave gentle warning touches with his teeth but Burns solemnly excommunicated Charley just because it felt good before lying flat on the ground moaning I wanna be put down myself while Charley repentantly licked his several rank cigar-smelling chins.

That night, Burns, whose request for euthanasia had been turned down, only had time to notice that the Pope was not in his bunk before he himself hit the hay like a hammer.

Patrick knelt by the water's edge with Charley, his excommunication lifted at the highest level, next to him, fast asleep. The sound of lapping water rested the Pope's soul. The sun, red as blood on snow, had long set behind Croagh-Breac, leaving an undressed moon to cast a broad silver sheen on the upper reaches of the lake.

I will be sad to leave this place, Lord. I feel safe here. If only I did not have to bear the burden of the Church.

To the surrounding dark he whispered, "Not my will, Father, but thine be done." He whispered it again and again until the dove-eyed dawn turned the sky overhead from black to blue-gray porcelain.

Burns must have left his bunk when the morning bell rang but he did not remember it. He had the look of a man who'd spent the whole day gazing at the sun from its rising to its setting. He came to at the last station. Soon the misery would be over. This was worse than six years' hard labor in a seminary.

Before the pilgrims caught the boat back to the mainland, the prior said, "You're obliged to keep the fast till midnight. The good news is, you can drink to your heart's content as soon as you're off the island."

Ah, but it was good to get back into shoes and socks. What an underrated luxury! The pilgrims' laughter rang out as they said good-bye to the prior.

"Thank you, Monsignor," the Pope said, clasping both his hands.

"And thank *you*, Holiness." The prior also shook Charley's extended paw. Out of respect, he called on everyone to sing "Hail Glorious Saint Patrick" on the way across.

The Pope, in effervescent mood, said to Cardinal Burns, "Did you notice how much merriment there was on Lough Derg?"

Burns admitted it had not struck him forcibly.

"It reminds me," Patrick said, "of what a great Irish poet said once: 'Tragedy is only undeveloped comedy.' "

Burns, who felt inches away from pneumonia, thought that his tragedy had an awful lot of developing to do.

"A word of warning," the Pope said. "Legend has it that whoever looks back on Station Island will one day return."

Cardinals Burns and Sapieha looked stolidly ahead of them toward the shore. And, with very different emotions, so did Pope Patrick.

Chapter Twenty-seven

They flew by helicopter to Kilkenny. This city, the Pope assured them, was one of the glories of Ireland.

The first call was to the Norman Castle. Not exactly to the castle but to the grounds south of it. A brief walk brought them to a picturesque graveyard, surrounded by holly and beech trees. Consecrated in 1894, it had belonged to the Butlers, the most famous family in that part of the world.

Buried outside the cemetery railings was a dog called Sandy. Charley's bark indicated he knew he was in the presence of a kindred spirit.

Burns was staggered. They could have been visiting the Cliffs of Moher or the Rock of Cashel. He asked Sapieha why they had come all this way, three hundred yards, to check on the bones of a procking dog. But Frank Kerrigan sensed that the Pope was thinking ahead to the day when he and Charley would be parted.

Sandy's headstone faced inward to the grave where later his master had been buried. He was James Edward William Theobald Butler, 21st Earl and 3rd Marquis of Ormond, who had died on October 26, 1919. On the dog's gravestone, his master had inscribed:

In Loving Memory of
SANDY
The Most Devoted and Beloved
Little Friend and Companion
For 17 Years

Born at Loch More April 1895
Died June 4th 1912

There are men both good and wise
Who hold that in a future state
Dumb creatures we have cherished here below
Shall give us joyous greeting
When we pass the golden gate.
Oh! How earnestly I pray it may be so.

The marquis, who had entertained two monarchs, Edward VII and George V, at his castle in Kilkenny, who had shot with them on his enormous estates, sailed with them at Cowes, attended on them at state functions, must have dearly loved his little dog.

After kneeling in prayer, the Pope said, "It's odd that Sandy was not buried nearer his master."

The local Church of Ireland bishop who had welcomed the Pope said, "You mean *inside* the graveyard?"

"Why not?" The Pope pointed at Charley, who did not seem to be trespassing. "Consecrated ground means a baptized person has the right to be buried there. Not that a nonbaptized creature cannot be granted the privilege."

"But," the bishop said unhappily, "I thought dogs had no souls, Holiness."

"Maybe not like ours." Under his breath: Maybe better.

As Patrick stooped to pat his dog's noble head, Frank remembered that the Pope had once seen Charley's face on the figure of the Crucified.

"But surely," Patrick went on, aloud, "the God who makes animals can remake them if he likes? He is Almighty, is he not?"

After a few moments, the bishop said, "I'll see to it."

The Church of Ireland permitted the Pope to celebrate Mass in its beautiful cathedral of St. Canice. Kilkenny was named after the Kill (or church) of Canice. This was the first Catholic Mass in the cathedral since the Reformation. For many years there had been warm ecumenical relations between Anglicans and Catholics in the city. This cemented them.

After Mass the Pope was entertained to dinner in the Long Gallery of Kilkenny Castle. In one of the finest rooms in Ireland the Irish Youth Orchestra played Mozart and Brahms. Burns appreciated the food, the wine and—he was sitting opposite the President of Ireland—the sparkling company. He was now almost over his regret at coming on pilgrimage.

The President, an Irish beauty in a green gown, rose to say, with many expressive gestures, that the election of His Holiness, who was a resource for the whole world, was an honor to him, but also to Irish men and women who had planted the faith throughout the world. She felt his election was a symbol of the kind of new Ireland she wanted to present to the world. She spoke fluently for twenty minutes without notes, which, with notes, might have taken two.

The Pope refused to make a speech. He had prepared only one for this trip and he would deliver it in Dublin.

There were sighs of disappointment until he said, "But, if you will indulge the sentiments of a nostalgic old Irishman returning to his homeland, I'll recite a few verses for you from a favorite poem of mine."

Everyone settled down as Pope Patrick recited softly with deep patriotic feeling "Dark Rosaleen" until its final verse:

> O, the Erne shall run red,
> With redundance of blood,
> The earth shall rock beneath our tread,
> And flames wrap hill and wood,
> And gun-peal and slogan-cry
> Wake many a glen serene,
> Ere you shall fade, ere you shall die,
> My Dark Rosaleen!
> My own Rosaleen!
> The Judgement Hour must first be nigh,
> Ere you can fade, ere you can die,
> My Dark Rosaleen!

There was no applause when the Pope finished. It was some time before the conversation picked up again.

Next morning, the Pope traveled in his Popemobile from Kilkenny eastward along country lanes to Glendalough. This, too, was a security nightmare. The terrain was splendid bandit country. The lanes were narrow, lined with lush trees and thick hedgerows.

Outside the village of Rathdrum in the Garden of Ireland, the Pope insisted on a brief unscheduled visit to Avondale. This was the family home and birthplace of the "Proud Eagle," Charles Stewart Parnell.

As they entered the grounds, only Frank Kerrigan was close enough to hear the Pope whisper, "Oh, have you been to Avondale / and lingered in her lovely vale, / Where tall trees whisper low the tale / of Avondale's Proud Eagle?"

The gray house was in an idyllic setting of 550 acres of grand old Irish and exotic foreign trees. Parnell, a Protestant, was, some said, the greatest of all Irishmen. The clergy contributed to his downfall when he married a divorced woman, Kathleen O'Shea.

Patrick stepped out of his Popemobile in front of the dignified Georgian building. He fell to his knees, stretched his arms out wide and prayed for five minutes.

The Irish prelates wondered. Was he praying to atone for what Parnell had done? Or for what the clergy had done to him?

The only hint Patrick gave was when, on leaving, he signed the distinguished visitors' book in the hallway. Under "Comments," he simply quoted Parnell:

"No man has a right to fix a boundary to the march of a nation. No man has a right to say 'thus far shalt thou go and no further.'"

It was only a few miles from leafy Avondale to Laragh. Soon Glendalough appeared, the Glen of the Two Lakes, at the very heart of Wicklow.

Because of the crowds, it took half an hour for the Popemobile to cover the last few hundred yards to the Royal Hotel and across the narrow bridge over the swift brown River Glendasan. The Pope stepped out of his carriage and walked through ecstatic crowds under the ancient gateway arches and into the former Episcopal city of the Seven Churches.

Dominating everything was the thousand-year-old Round Tower. Steps led up to the opening, which was ten feet high. The Pope ascended a specially constructed staircase. From one hundred feet up, through four windows which looked onto the four winds, he had an uninterrupted view of one of the most beautiful sights in creation. Instinctively, he gave his blessing *urbi et orbi*.

To the west were the rippling waters of the upper lake. On one slope, thirty feet up, gentle barefoot St. Kevin had made his "bed." Around him legends had grown.

One was of a blackbird that nested in his outstretched hand. Another was that men working on the cathedral had to rise with the larks, which, unfortunately for them, happened to soar and sing earlier than any others of their species in the land. Out of pity, Kevin bade them be quiet. Alas, thereafter, over the waters of the lake no larks ever sing.

The west lake was separated from the smaller east lake by a strip of land caused by silt deposited by the great jade waterfall of Poulannas. That strip of grassland was now invisible beneath a vast concourse of people on each side of the Dosan River. Hills, green from top to bottom, circled the landscape in a massive colonnade more stunning than any Bernini dreamed of. A great variety of trees was to be seen: silver birch, rowan, hazel, pine, alder, white hawthorn.

Most wonderful was the world below him, a haunted city of monks and saints.

Kevin died at the age of 120. He asked for a church dedicated to God's Mother to be built to house his remains. "My sons," he said, "cut away the thorns and thistles around a shepherd's grave and make a beautiful spot on this place." In the Church of St. Mary, he awaits resurrection.

Laurence O'Toole, Ireland's first canonized saint, was abbot there, before becoming Archbishop of Dublin.

But the ancient monastic city tugged at Pope Patrick's heart for another reason. It became desolate after the Norman English invaded Ireland in force in the early thirteenth century. The churches were left roofless. The tombstones of great Irish chieftains, the O'Tooles and the O'Byrnes, had been made sport of and broken. The thick stone walls were fragmented and holed. Yet, even in its desolateness, the place spoke more eloquently of God than any modern city.

Pope Patrick celebrated the Eucharist on a temporary altar under a roof of blue sky in a cathedral dedicated to Saints Peter and Paul. The Mass, the first said there for centuries, was relayed by television to tens of thousands around the city enclosure and on the greensward between the lakes.

Frank Kerrigan, who acted as M.C., guessed that the Pope was happier there than anywhere. When Patrick spoke the prayers of the Mass, Frank felt as if he were running alongside him with a strong wind on his back.

Cardinal Burns read the Gospel with unaccustomed emotion. The reading told of how Jesus sailed across the lake to avoid the great crush of people and finally fed them with a few loaves and fishes.

Then to everyone's delight, the Pope preached. It was the briefest sermon many of them had ever heard.

"Sisters and brothers of Ireland, when, long ago, I visited this thrice-holy place, I was struck by an inscription on the ancient gravestone of Luke Toole of Annamoe. It read: 'He was Friend to the Uncomforted, Father to the Orphan. His door was open to the Poor.' That is a summary of the Gospel of Jesus Christ. I, your Pope, your proud yet humble fellow countryman, have nothing to add except may God bless and keep you all."

The applause threatened to make another rift in the mountains.

After Mass the Pope planted a yew tree in the shadow of the cathedral before heading for the capital.

Chapter Twenty-eight

It was not to Dublin Castle that the Pontiff went. Nor to the Dáil, that is, the Irish Parliament. Nor to Trinity College, the ancient university of Ireland. Nor to the President's Mansion in the Phoenix Park. There was only one place left on his itinerary.

Kilmainham Jail to the west of the city still had a grim aspect, with an image of chained serpents above the entrance. He was given a tour that included the rarely seen torture chamber in the basement, but he seemed to know the place as well as the curator did.

He was specially interested in the places associated with the Easter Rising of 1916. He prayed in the chapel where young Joe Plunkett, one of the leaders of the Rising, wed his wife, Grace Gifford, a few hours before he was executed. He visited and blessed in turn the cells of Patrick Pearse, Thomas MacDonagh, Tom Clarke and all their comrades, who, in May 1916, met their doom at British hands.

He made his way down iron steps, along gray corridors with rusted gas pipes and time-damaged doors, to the Stonebreakers' Yard. In this high-walled ellipse-shaped enclosure, so like a ruined cathedral, the men of 1916 had been executed.

As dignitaries of Church and state lined the yard the Pope once again took off his shoes and socks. He planted a red rose tree in the earth bared by the removal of a flagstone. He knelt and prayed the rosary next to a cross which marked the spot where all but one of the leaders had been shot by firing squad. He said the final decade, the Resurrection, sitting in a straight-backed wooden chair by the cross at the far gate-end. There it was that James Connolly, a Marxist who had made his peace with God, was shot bound and sitting because his wounded leg made it impossible for him to stand.

The Pope's tiny figure, his bare, bruised and bloodied feet, created an unforgettable impression. Frank Kerrigan felt that simple chair suited him better than the papal throne in St. Peter's.

Patrick handed the rosary he had been using back to the jail's curator. Thomas MacDonagh had worn it round his neck when he faced the firing squad. It had been his mother's.

Patrick stood and turned to the cameras. He spoke this, his only public address, without notes.

"Ladies and gentlemen, even Popes make bad mistakes."

Frank Kerrigan glanced at Cardinal Burns, who looked as if *he* were facing a firing squad.

"I refer to a letter from a predecessor of mine. Known as *Laudabiliter*, it was written in 1156 by the only English Pope, Adrian IV. The only Irish Pope thus far wishes, nearly a thousand years late, to apologize for it.

"John, Bishop of Salisbury, whispered in the ear of his close friend Adrian IV. He persuaded the Pope to make Ireland an heirloom in perpetuity to the Norman English King, Henry II.

"Henry pretended he wanted to invade Ireland to purge it of paganism and make it loyal to the Holy Catholic Church.

"He spoke thus of a land that fifteen hundred years ago produced the likes of young St. Ciarán of Clonmacnoise and St. Kevin of Glendalough. That sent missionaries abroad like Columba and Aidan. That was a seat of civilization when Rome itself was overrun by barbarian hordes. That had a Celtic Christian culture when the English wore nothing but animal skins. Dr. Johnson was right to say, 'Ireland was the school of the West, the quiet habitation of sanctity and literature.'

"John of Salisbury went to the Pope at Benevento and asked him if Ireland could be English. The Pope said yes, and gave him a gold ring adorned with a gorgeous emerald. With this ring the King was invested with the alleged right to govern Ireland.

"In *Laudabiliter*, Pope Adrian said to Henry: 'It is beyond doubt that Ireland and all the islands upon which Christ, the Sun of Justice, has shone and which have received knowledge of the Christian faith, are subject to St. Peter and to the most Holy Roman Church . . . For this you are ready to pay one penny (a denarius) from every household as an ancient tribute to St. Peter, and to preserve the rights of the churches of the land whole and inviolable.'

"So it was that an Englishman, Pope Adrian IV, wrote a Bull in favor of another Englishman, King Henry II, at the prompting of another Englishman, John, Bishop of Salisbury."

The British Ambassador, Sir Geoffrey Smith-Burlington, all stiff upper lip and quivering lids, could take no more. TV cameras followed him as he made for the exit, muttering, "Damned impertinence of the man." He paused momentarily to hear:

"I tell you solemnly as Pope, this was massive English wrongdoing. The Donation of Constantine, on which Pope Adrian based his right to give islands away, was a forgery. In any case Kings of England broke the terms of the Bull: they did not preserve the churches' rights. On the contrary, by stealing land from the Irish and distributing it among their cronies, they set in motion the great wheel of violence that still crushes this poor country. Not all *Angli* were *Angeli*.

"No wonder the great cathedrals and churches of Ireland fell into decay, their treasures pilfered, their manuscripts tossed to the winds. No wonder the holy place where I said Mass this morning, Glendalough, once known as 'the Rome of the Western World,' is now prey to wind and rain.

"In time, the Strangers, having squandered their own spiritual wealth, tried to steal from the Irish their most precious heritage: the Catholic faith. They strove, with cruelty, to break their allegiance to the Pope and the Church universal over which the Supreme Pontiff presides in love.

"Happily, they failed.

"I, the first Irish Pope to visit this my country, have no hesitation in declaring that the document on which John Bull based his right to Ireland is null and void. The English have not the right, never did nor will have the right to *a single inch* of Irish soil. They came as usurpers; where they remain on Irish soil, it is as usurpers.

186

"This Stonebreakers' Yard is the most poignant spot in a poignant land. It is the altar of Ireland where the bravest of the brave died honorably and in uniform, as soldiers should, to make Ireland Irish once again. Here, I solemnly revoke *Laudabiliter*. And here I bless and bless and bless again the hallowed spot where they gave their lives.

"*Requiescant in pace*. Green be their graves."

The Pope put on his shoes and socks, bowed to both crosses in the yard and spoke not one more official word on his trip to the old country.

Back at the Vatican, he realized that, while away, he had not had a single headache. And that night, in the Apostolic Palace, he slept more peacefully in his iron-framed bed than he had slept in a long time.

Part Five

Coming to
Terms
with Sex

Chapter Twenty-nine

The Pope's headaches returned. He still remembered nothing about his election. Sometimes, he told Dr. Gadda, who was in constant attendance, he felt as if he was living in a dream.

He made regular visits to the parishes of Rome to confirm children. Afterward he distributed sweets and chocolates to them out of the pockets of his soutane. These outings lifted his spirit.

Charley, who had a special place in the Popemobile, was a hit with the kids. They kept feeding him the wrong food, so, in spite of his Lough Derg fast, he was getting rather fat.

The Pope's honeymoon with his diocese continued, especially as he was bringing tourists back to the city. And, when he preached, they sensed he was defense not prosecution.

One day, Cardinal Montefiori told His Holiness that the prefects of the Congregations were again breathing down his neck.

"The question of priestly celibacy," he said, "requires your immediate attention."

He detailed John Paul's approach in his later years. He did not believe in letting priests marry. He also took years to dispense from celibacy any who resigned. This made many of them so bitter that they left their posts to marry civilly.

"Lately," Montefiori said, "we have received a flood of requests for laicization."

"Hundreds?"

"Two thousand since you took office."

"You make it sound as if I am responsible, Giuseppe."

The cardinal lowered his gaze. "It could be they think you will be more . . . merciful."

"What do *you* think?"

Montefiori chose his words carefully. "If you dispense too easily, many priests, young ones especially, might give up the ministry at the first temptation."

Patrick looked dreamily out of the window across the busy piazza, over the many spires and domes of the city where swifts darted here and there in shafts of sunlight. "I remember how it was when I was a young priest. Many times I fell in love."

Montefiori coughed in embarrassment.

"Don't worry, Giuseppe. I hadn't the courage to do anything really bad."

"Courage?"

"I never had lurid dreams like St. Jerome in the desert. Nor did I take a couple of mistresses like St. Augustine." He laid his hand reassuringly on his Secretary of State's arm. "I suppose I wasn't destined for the heights of holiness."

"No, Holiness."

"Even now I have to blindfold my eyes and fig-leaf my imagination, so to speak, when I walk through the galleries and see Venuses and Nereids, all naked and—"

"Quite, Holiness."

Patrick turned serious. "If the matter's so urgent, I will give guidance. But I must listen to the Church first."

Montefiori faxed letters to metropolitan bishops throughout the world asking them to consult their hierarchies. They, in turn, were to consult priests and laity. All findings were to be sent to him well before the Synod of Bishops met in Rome.

Chapter Thirty

Patrick was indirectly responsible for a live TV debate between President Delaney and Ayatollah Hourani of the Federation of Islamic Republics.

Tension was high. A U.S. double-decker superjumbo with eight hundred passengers aboard was downed by a missile over the Persian Gulf. There were no survivors. No one accepted responsibility, but NATO blamed the FIR.

When the Pentagon made bellicose noises, the Pope urged both sides to step back from the brink and talk with one another.

Ever since Delaney won the catechism prize in fourth grade, he thought himself an expert on religion. So, when the U.N. Secretary General invited him and the Ayatollah to discuss their differences, he accepted. His ratings at home were low; this, he reckoned, was one way of lifting them.

He called Cardinal Burns to ask for prayers. Burns advised him to stress in the debate that Christians, being civilized, are against all forms of torture. "Though," he quipped, speaking from the heart, "it might be no bad thing, Roone, to give crooks in jail a daily enema."

"Did I hear you right?"

"Yeah. Five gallons of treacle and lemon juice. Would wipe out crime overnight."

"Hell, Tom," Delaney said, "they'd all plead the Eighth Amendment and opt for the electric chair."

The President asked the Pope to bless his upcoming contribution, which, against Montefiori's better judgment, he did.

. . .

Half the world switched on the debate. In the USA, where Hourani was the man Americans most loved to hate, the audience was over 80 percent. They remembered him for hacking the hands off three of his sons.

Patrick, who had never seen the man the media called "the Pope of Islam," stayed up till three in the morning to watch with Frank and Montefiori.

Delaney was shown seated in the Oval Office, the Stars and Stripes on his desk, the bullet that nearly killed off the Pope framed behind his head.

The Ayatollah spoke from the Holy Iranian city of Qum. In a tent, bare but for the red, black and yellow tricolor of the FIR, he allowed himself to be viewed only in profile.

An unseen bilingual M.C. was in a studio in Geneva. After the two national anthems were played, he called on the Ayatollah to make his initial contribution.

Instead of the expected harangue, Hourani simply said, "Unto Allah be all glory, the Lord of all worlds."

When Delaney, sooner than he had anticipated, was asked to give his address, he began by waving a piece of parchment at the viewers. He thanked His Holiness Pope Patrick, acknowledged spiritual leader of the West, for sending him his blessing.

For the next twenty minutes, in a speech marvelously crafted by his aides, he bitterly attacked the FIR. It was behind most terrorism in the world, like the recent destruction of an American Super-Jumbo. It espoused rebellion against lawful governments. At its bidding, militants had overthrown the state in Iran, Algiers, Turkey, Iraq, Libya, Egypt, the Royal House of Saudi Arabia—to name but a few.

The black-clad Hourani listened impassively to the translation through an earpiece. Then in his rich low voice:

"Did not your own nation, Mr. President, become a republic by an armed rebellion against a tyrant King? You do not answer me. Was not George Washington a rebel and your own famed Declaration of Independence in 1776 an act of treason?"

Pope Patrick whispered to Montefiori, "A clever feller, this Hourani."

Hourani went on, "I recall what a wise man said: 'A little rebellion, now and then, is a good thing.'"

"You call that *wise*," humphed Delaney.

"Words of Thomas Jefferson. And Abraham Lincoln, no militant Muslim, said in his first inaugural, 'Wherever the people grow weary of the existing government, they can exercise their constitutional right of amending it—'"

Delaney cut in, "Through the ballot box."

"'Or,'" Hourani went on evenly, still quoting Lincoln, "'the people can exercise their revolutionary right to dismember or overthrow it.'"

Delaney knew he was in some scrap. He responded by detailing how the U.S. Constitution fostered equality for all.

"Pardon me," Hourani intervened softly. "Does not your Declaration say, 'All men are created equal'?"

"Damn right."

"*All?* Including Indians?"

"Yes."

"Whom you massacred and ejected from their lands?"

"They *are* American citizens."

"Since 1924, true. Also, in your Declaration, I find no mention of women."

"'Men,' as Pope John Paul used to say, 'includes women.'"

"Though they only got the vote in 1920."

Delaney, after a swift glance at his off-camera advisers, agreed.

"And slaves, are they too included in 'men'? You do know, of course, that an early draft of the Declaration condemned slavery but it was struck out by Jefferson as being unacceptable."

Another glance by Delaney at his advisers, followed by a second grudging nod.

"Unlike the FIR," he blustered, "there's no slavery in the United States now."

"I doubt that. Even so, have you not made slaves of most of the Third World?"

Pope Patrick whispered, "Yes, yes, yes."

"Let's stick," Delaney said, "to the United States."

"Very well. How can all Americans be equal when millions of you are poor and hundreds of you multimillionaires?"

"At least, we have a free press, which our founders said is like a second government to us."

"Who," asked Hourani, "runs this second government? Barons who own every newspaper, movie company and TV station. Can a press be free when it is owned by a few moneyed tyrants?"

"I'd have you know, sir, that our press, unlike yours, is free to print what it likes."

"Am I, a devout Muslim, expected to applaud their freedom to tell lies, spread error, blaspheme against God?"

"At least no one here is imprisoned because of his religion."

"Even if his religion offends God?"

Delaney went into a long spiel about the benefits of separation of Church and state, democracy, due process of law, trial by jury and the absence in America of cruel or unusual punishments common in Islam.

To which the Ayatollah dryly responded, "I realize that had past U.S. Presidents been liable to execution for adultery, as in Islam, few would have died in their beds."

"I resent that," Delaney said hotly.

"If only your Supreme Court had not decided in 1878 that polygamy is irreligious and violates Christian ethics, if only it had adopted our sane custom of having four wives, then . . ."

"Then?"

"Some of your Presidents might not have needed to sleep with whores."

Delaney vehemently protested against such a justifiable slur on, well, his predecessors. Then it was Hourani's turn to expand on the theme of democracy.

It was the invention of the devil. Islam had nothing but contempt for majorities, for those who honor incompetents and bow before the infallibility of ignorance.

"Where in Islamic countries," objected Delaney, "is there an opposition party?"

"Whom would it oppose? Allah? Are we expected to put up opposition to the Koran for the fun of it?"

Christians, Hourani went on, despise Muslims for cutting off the hands and feet of thieves, for stoning adulterous women who have offended the *'ird*, the honor of their husbands.

"And yet, Mr. President, in our lands, theft, adultery and drug taking are virtually nonexistent. Why? Because we punish the godless. By contrast, in your country citizens cannot walk their own streets without fear. When you ran out of buffaloes you started shooting each other. You have riots, arson, rapes, muggings, abattoirs for babies—"

"I *beg* your pardon," Delaney said heatedly.

"I refer to your abortion clinics. In recent years, America has slaughtered more babies than Adolf Hitler."

Once more the Pope sadly said, "Yes."

"Your pregnant mothers," Hourani went on, "poison their unborn with drink and drugs. Children are having children. Children are murdering children. If a severed hand or two can stop this mayhem, is it not worthwhile?"

Frank said, "That'll go down with the law-and-order lobby in America."

Delaney, on the run, said, "A daily enema . . ." then had second thoughts about it.

Pope Patrick laughed. "What say you we record the rest and put the day to bed?"

Montefiori glanced at his watch and agreed. The Synod of Bishops was beginning within a few hours.

As Frank switched off the television, the cardinal said wryly, "You should have taken my advice, Holiness."

"I only sent him my blessing for a happy death."

Frank said, "He'll be needing it right now."

"It only goes to prove," Patrick said, "how unreliable a papal blessing can be." He chuckled. "I should've known. John Paul gave me one and look where it landed me."

Chapter Thirty-one

Patrick listened intently as two hundred bishops set out the problems of their dioceses. The phrase "vocations crisis" kept cropping up.

Third World bishops were worried by a shortage of priests. Many had left to marry. There were no replacements.

Most Western bishops were in the same boat but they stressed that to laicize priests too easily would lead to an even bigger exodus.

After a week, the Pope called a three-day halt to the discussions. He wanted time to pray about the issue.

One evening, after Tommaso had served supper, he broke his silence to ask Frank Kerrigan what he thought about priestly celibacy.

"I think it should be optional."

"Would *you* marry?"

"No."

The Pope was surprised and pleased by the speed of his reaction.

It was some time before Frank was able to explain.

"A couple of years ago, my parents, both under fifty, were killed in an air crash. I was an only child so it made me kind of lonely."

"I'm sure," the Pope murmured. "There was a whole houseful of us."

"I found among my mother's papers a letter written to her by my father on their silver wedding anniversary. He said—and it's etched into my memory—'If I had a hundred lives I would ask you to marry me in every one of them.' Underneath, she had written, 'I accept a hundred times.' "

Patrick lifted his hands in approval.

"That, Holiness," Frank said, as though he had given it much thought, "is what love is all about, isn't it? Not unto death but beyond death, beyond all death, forever. My parents had that kind of love. I envied them and wondered how I could live without it, how face the long loneliness ahead."

"It is not good for man to—"

"A year later, not long before my ordination, I fell in love with a girl from Ohio. Very beautiful she was. I thought so, anyway."

Patrick returned his pained grin before asking, "Who gave up who?"

"Mutual. Jody said she couldn't take the responsibility of stealing me from God."

"And now you know you would never—"

Frank surprised the Pope by suddenly leaving the room. He returned a minute later with a small white cardboard box tied with pink ribbon.

"Wedding cake, Frank? I see. When—?"

"It came a couple of months ago. Since then I've been trying to summon up the courage to throw it in the Tiber."

There was a long friendly silence between them before the Pope laid his hand on his secretary's. "Wish I'd known. I could at least have—" He joined his hands in prayer.

Frank blinked to clear his eyes. "It's over. Really. I now know that if I had a hundred lives, I'd choose celibacy for the love of Christ in every one of them."

The Pope jerked his head back, as if to say even he might like to experiment in one or two of a hundred. Then:

"Thanks, Frank, you've helped me see this celibacy thing much clearer. Now, I wouldn't mind some cake. Just a tiny bit to save it from the Tiber."

The Pope summoned the bishops again. Montefiori announced, "Since this Synod was called, another fifteen hundred priests have written to the Holy See asking to be laicized."

The Pope looked around him solemnly. "An unhappy, wavering priest will not spread the joy of the Holy Spirit."

Everyone murmured agreement.

"It would be easy for me to bend the rules made by my predecessor. But the Church's plight is far too critical for that."

Cardinal Burns and the rest of the conservatives breathed more easily.

The Pope went on: "Obligatory celibacy is not a dogma but a discipline. Never wholly successful. In the Middle Ages, and later, priests and even Popes, cardinals and bishops took mistresses."

Many prelates, well aware of this, were still upset that the Pope should call attention to it in public.

"And what about today, brothers? I have received hundreds of letters from priests who, in their own strange words, are forced to live in sin.

"Some say their housekeeper is their wife and they have children whom they love.

"Some admit that when their lovers conceived they paid for them, sad to say, to have an abortion. Many women, to hide the priest's shame, acquiesced.

"Some wrote to me about fellow priests who, unable to cope with their vocation and their love of a woman, committed suicide.

"Some told me of confrères who, because of enforced celibacy, never grew up in their sexual lives. It led them to seduce young boys and girls, sometimes a hundred victims.

"You have read of dioceses in the New World becoming bankrupt after paying legal compensation to poor little kiddies whose lives were ruined. Many priests are scared to wear their clerical collar in the streets because of the stigma attached."

There was an appalled silence in the room as the Pope spoke freely about misdemeanors which many bishops had taken pains to cover up for years.

"The strange thing is," Patrick went on, "though these priests and, yes, quite a number of bishops acted thus, they saw no need to resign. Yet not so strange. Canon law demands a priest be celibate but he has no equal duty to resign if he is unchaste. In fact, many priests use their privileged position to live like Casanova. They have innumerable affairs, sire many children whom they neglect, and still they do not resign." He looked around him miserably. "What is wrong with our education that such men behave like alley cats?"

No bishop was prepared to give him an answer.

"What shall we do?"

A ripple of red but no one spoke.

"Shall we change canon law so that any priest who is unchaste, even once, has to resign?"

A brave Filipino bishop rose to say, "If so, we will have no priests to run our dioceses."

"Precisely," said the Pope. "Many bishops have confessed to me that every one of their priests has a liaison with a woman. Is not this hypocrisy? And absolutely contrary to the Gospel?"

Many bishops were forced to concede the point.

"I ask you, brothers, how many times shall we allow a colleague to break his pledge to Christ? How many children is he allowed to sire or murderously abort before we say, enough is enough?"

No one answered him.

"Shall we," he challenged, "allow a priest one child, two, ten, sixteen?"

Silence.

"I heard of one priest, a loud defender of celibacy, who has nine children by nine different women and now sleeps with a tenth. Another has had affairs with thirty-seven women. Neither has offered his resignation. I ask again, what changes shall we make to canon law to stamp out this behavior?"

Once more, the bishops treated this as a rhetorical question and maintained a brittle silence.

"I have said I will change whatever is possible and necessary. However, in spite of all these misdemeanors, I do not propose to tamper with clerical discipline."

"Good," muttered Cardinal Ragno of the Congregation for the Sacraments, who was all for the status quo.

"I intend to change it back to what it was in the beginning. From now on, priests will be allowed to marry if they so wish and remain in the ministry."

Suddenly, there was uproar in the hall. The Pope was throwing out a rule that was a thousand years old.

Someone yelled, "A celibate serves God with an undivided heart."

"St. Paul says that," the Pope responded, "and so do I. The apostle was speaking of *all* Christians, not priests. But what if the heart of a priest with no gift for celibacy is divided more cruelly by a desire to marry?"

Cardinal Burns yelped, "Even in the Orthodox Church men aren't allowed to marry *after* they're ordained." Konstant, a tall, bald English bishop, said, "Holiness, surely those already ordained must stay celibate. Any changes can only apply to future candidates?"

"That seems logical," the Pope conceded, "but it leads to strange results. We would not let priests marry and continue in the ministry. On the other hand, we would ordain men already married. We are doing that already in regard to convert clerics. But if a married man can become a priest, why can't a priest get married? If it's fine to drink whiskey with water in, why not water with whiskey in?"

When the hubbub died down, Patrick added:

"I assure you, brothers, every bishop will be free to accept only lifelong celibates. If some of his priests choose to marry, they can join another diocese."

Bishops were already saying infallibly whether they would or would not accept married priests.

"When I came to this decision," Patrick said, "I was struck by this fact. In the last forty-five years, Catholics have more than doubled while the number of priests has declined. Now, celibacy, as we all know, can do wonders for the individual soul. But what if it harms the community?"

"Harm," Cardinal Ragno shouted. "How can celibacy *harm* the Church?"

The Pope said he did not regret the word.

"I would remind Your Eminence that the rule of celibacy is man-made whereas the right to marry is part of natural law. Celibacy is an option for the Church, the Eucharist is not. Without the Mass, our people starve. When did our poor decide on a Eucharistic Hunger Strike unto death? Suppose there were a famine in Italy and vast quantities of food had to be imported. What would Italians think if I insisted that only celibates could distribute it? And if millions died as a result, would I not be to blame? The same sin lies on me if there is a spiritual famine in the Church, a shortage of the Bread of Life, and I do nothing."

The Pope turned to Montefiori, asking for statistics on ordinations.

The cardinal said that in Holland, last year, one man ordained; in Germany, five; in Ireland, seven, in the United States forty and so on.

Finally, Patrick said, "As Chief Shepherd, I cannot stand idly by and do nothing. Surely, the center of our faith is the Mass, not priestly celibacy."

Chapter Thirty-two

There was a break to allow the bishops to digest the Pope's words. Some were delighted. Others, like Cardinal Ragno and Archbishop Rossi, Deputy Secretary of State, who as usual sat side by side, were in a rage.

Frank managed to whisper to Patrick, "If only you had been Pope a few years ago."

When the bishops reassembled, Cardinal Gonzales of Rio congratulated the Pontiff on a brave and momentous decision.

"I take it, Holiness, we may now ordain qualified married deacons as priests?"

"As soon as I sign the necessary documents."

Cardinal Rottweiler, the old Prefect of the Holy Office, got to his feet to growl, "This is a slippery slope."

"Eminence, the good Lord himself set man on the slipperiest of slippery slopes when he gave him free will."

Cardinal Burns rose to ask sourly, "How will mission territories be able to provide the right sort of training for these married men?"

"The apostles," the Pope answered, "did not go to a seminary. Take Peter. A married man, incidentally, who, like the other apostles, took his wife with him on his missionary journeys. Read I Corinthians 9:5. Though a fisherman, he was smart enough to preach Christ crucified. My guess is, St. Paul himself would not have grasped the intricacies of scholastic theology. But I'm not sure priests need that in favelas and shantytowns."

Cardinal Gonzales of Rio stamped his feet, the only way he could register his approval above the din.

A Dominican bishop jumped up, very agitated, to ask whether religious priests—Dominicans, Franciscans, Benedictines—would also be dispensed from celibacy.

"Why not?"

"Because we religious take vows of poverty, celibacy and obedience. Rescinding a *vow* is quite different from changing a law."

"I take your point," the Pope said. "But I suspect that many men become monks and friars to live in a community where they can protect the celibacy imposed on all priests. If they want to marry, I would not hesitate to dispense them from their religious vows."

"But," the bishop wailed, "it will decimate our religious houses."

"If so, brother," the Pope said firmly, "it will prove, will it not, that there is something wrong with your houses? If religious are dedicated to God with an undivided heart, how will even a Pope's decision disturb them? I am allowing them to marry, not forcing them."

"But, Holiness—"

"Brother," the Pope gently said, "can you not see that priests who cannot be celibate need a helpmate, someone to whom they can confide their deepest anxieties and sorrows, someone to hold and caress them in the night? It is not sex but solace that these priests chiefly need." Glancing at Frank Kerrigan: "A priest who even contemplates marriage has never said in his heart, 'I want to be celibate forever.'"

"The Church will die," wailed O'Halloran, the new Archbishop of Boston.

"I hope so," the Pope said.

"I thought it was meant to live forever," said a shaken O'Halloran.

"No, Eminence. It was meant to die and rise again, over and over."

Passions intensified when the Bishop of Vancouver asked whether His Holiness had considered the ordination of women.

Patrick said, with a smile, "I have never found any theological reason against it."

Several red-faced bishops jumped to their feet. They were content that Burns said on their behalf:

"There were no women among the Twelve."

"Nor Gentiles," Patrick replied evenly. "The time was only ripe for men, Jewish men. All circumcised."

Several bishops squirmed involuntarily at hearing one of the original qualifications for the priesthood.

Cardinal Ragno said, "John Paul decreed in 1996 that ordaining women is against our entire tradition."

"Not at all," Patrick said evenly. "Just because we never did something doesn't make it untraditional. Only those things which we always said we never could do are untraditional. After all, brother, why cannot the Church ordain women?"

"Because," Ragno said shrilly, "a priest has to represent our Lord, and Christ was a man not a woman."

Rio stepped in to support the Pope. "Are you saying, Eminence, that a priest's genitals somehow endow him with the capacity to say Mass?"

Ragno was too incensed to reply.

"Surely," Rio went on, "Jesus saved us because he was human like all of us, not because he was male like only half of us."

The Pope said, "I agree. Besides, Cardinal Ragno's argument would prove too much. If Jesus only saved us because he was male and is our great High Priest because he is a male, Christianity as we know it is impossible. How could a girl or a woman put on Christ in baptism, become a member of Christ's body?"

"Exactly what I think, Holiness," Rio said. "When our Lord said, 'I am hungry and thirsty, naked and lonely,' did he mean only in all destitute males?"

"Every person," a black bishop said, backing Rio, "can become another Christ and represent him every second of every day. Why, then, cannot a woman represent him at the altar?"

"Holiness," the Bishop of Vancouver said, clearly pleased, "can you see women being admitted soon to the ministry?"

"We are well into the third millennium, brother. It is sad that the Church, bestower of Christ's freedom, is the last great society to treat women as a caste of Untouchables."

"Except for Islam," said Rottweiler.

"Indeed," the Pope said, smiling. "I do not know if you say that with approval?"

Rottweiler did not enlighten him.

The Pope went on, "There have been women Prime Ministers and Presidents in Britain, Ireland, Iceland, Canada, Scandinavian countries, also in Sri Lanka, India, Pakistan, Turkey, before Ayatollah Hourani intervened. There have been women Supreme Justices in almost every country of the world. I put it to you, when the Church is starving for lack of the Eucharist, how can we go on excluding half, some would say the holier half, of the human race from serving the Church as priests?"

"*Married* women?" a conservative asked caustically.

"I am no prophet," the Pope said, "but I foresee the day when there will be a black woman, married and a mother, on the Chair of Peter. After all, which of you ever thought to see an Irish Pope?"

The Archbishop of Dublin had to be carried out.

After a five-minute interlude for running repairs to a few prelates, the Pope went on:

"As far as I am concerned, every Catholic is basically entitled to all seven sacraments. But I leave the decision about women priests to you. In some places, women have not yet attained social equality. Elsewhere, they will surely make the sacrifice and offer themselves for ordination. Especially the sisters, many of whom are far better qualified academically than I am."

A frail, elderly cardinal with a pendulous purple lower lip wondered aloud in a piping voice whether women were quite suited to the rigors of the job.

The Pope was not the only one to smile.

"Women endure the pains of motherhood. I suspect they will be able to cope with the strains of the priesthood. In my view, the Church needs women, married and unmarried. For centuries, most of human experience has been blocked off from the ministry. Married people have not been allowed to share with the Church their knowledge of family life. Celibates have made all the rules, which is strange, seeing that they must, in the nature of things, be sexually illiterate. Any married person has more experience of married life than all of us clergy put together."

"One thing bothers me," said Buenos Aires. "Can our poorer churches support a priest with a spouse and children?"

"If a community is desperate for priests, Eminence, it will find the means. New priests may have to supplement their earnings, of course, by manual work. Like Jesus and St. Paul."

"But," the cardinal went on, "won't married priests be looked on as second-class?"

"I have thought of that," Patrick replied. "That is why I intend to hold a big ceremony in Rome. I will personally conduct the weddings of all priests who come here for that purpose. In this way, the whole world will know that married clergy are integral to the Church's life."

Chapter Thirty-three

No papal decision in centuries aroused so much excitement. The Church, which in the last pontificate had seemed moribund, felt the stirrings of a second spring.

But knives were out for the Pope, especially in some curial offices. Misogynists declared the idea of women hearing confessions obscene; the weaker sex would be forever breaking the seal by tittle-tattle or by the lifting of a painted eyelid. It would mark the end of aural confession.

Rome, the greatest rumor machine in the world, reported that a small group of cardinals met in secret conclave in an expensive restaurant on the Piazza del Popolo.

They first toyed with the idea of calling a Council to depose the Pope. This was judged impossible, since by canon law only a Pope can call a Council and sanction its decrees.

Next, Ragno suggested that the Pope's bump on the head had caused irreparable brain damage. The archphysician should examine him and, hopefully, diagnose insanity.

The rest of the world saw things differently. Television companies budgeted for the ceremony in St. Peter's. What kind of ladies would priests' spouses turn out to be? And how many sexy clerics would have the nerve to come out of the sacristy?

Letters for and against the Pope's decision poured into the Vatican.

Protestant Churches praised him for admitting, after five centuries, that their revolt against priestly celibacy was justified.

Orthodox Churches, on the other hand, strongly disapproved. Rome had made it harder for them to refuse marriage to ordained ministers.

Lay Catholics accepted the change without a murmur, convinced it heralded a more enlightened papal attitude to contraception. In mission lands, there was jubilation that Mass and the sacraments would soon be available to all.

The majority of Western prelates flew home from the Synod in a foul mood. Married priests, they knew, would not be as easy to deal with as clerical eunuchs.

Some bishops did not care a fig about their clergy's sleeping arrangements, provided they accepted orders from Bishop's House as coming from God.

The Archbishop of Dublin made it clear on the tarmac that, whatever others did, he would never tolerate married priests.

A pity, commented the *Sunday Independent*. The relaxation of the rule of celibacy could reduce Irish unemployment by at least fifty thousand.

The clergy's response to negative noises from bishops was immediate. Priests' conferences warned their lordships that if they didn't play ball, there would be even more priestless parishes in their neck of the woods.

In New York, where Burns declared his unwillingness to employ married clergy, two hundred priests immediately gave notice of wanting to be transferred elsewhere.

Chapter Thirty-four

At the first briefing after the Synod, Montefiori put it to His Holiness that he was acquiring the reputation of a liberal.

Patrick was upset. Labels encouraged a party spirit. He wanted to unite the Church after John Paul's divisive policies.

"Me, a liberal?" he said. "But I have simply returned to the more ancient tradition. Besides, it's obvious that we need priests more than we need celibates."

"True, but you are alienating conservatives. For instance, Cardinal Ragno of the Congregation for the Sacraments is very worried, as is my deputy, Archbishop Rossi."

Montefiori suggested that Patrick take counsel from two men on opposite wings. The first was the hard-line former Prefect of the Holy Office, Josef Rottweiler. The second was Francesco Frangipani of Venice, noted for his progressive views and one of the original favorites to succeed John Paul II.

Patrick liked the idea and acted on it at once.

Toward the end of one meeting in the Pope's private study, Cardinal Frangipani said:

"You do realize, Holiness, that the entire Catholic world is awaiting a word from you on birth control."

"That was decided once and for all forty years ago," Rottweiler said testily.

Rottweiler, in his eighties, with thinning white hair and hollow eyes, tapped his fingers on the arm of his chair in vexation. He did not trust this Pope, not since his decision on celibacy.

"Decided once and for all?" asked the Pope. "You *are* referring, Josef, to Paul VI's *Humanae Vitae?"*

Rottweiler nodded.

"Surely, Paul VI made it plain he did not issue that encyclical infallibly."

"True, Holy Father," Frangipani affirmed briskly.

"Then," the Pope asked, "how can it have been settled once and for all?"

"Because the tradition of the Church is constant on the matter," Rottweiler said. "Not even a Pope can contradict it."

"Circumstances change," Frangipani said. "So can the Church's response."

"Nonsense," Rottweiler spat out. "Not when something has been taught universally. Give me one instance where the Church has permitted contraception."

"How is it, then," Frangipani countered, "that discussion is still going on in the Sacred College itself?" He turned to Patrick. "And doesn't the practice of the faithful count for anything? Surveys show that most Catholics use artificial methods of birth control."

"Most people tell lies," Patrick said gently. "Does that make lying right?"

Frangipani shook his head. "The point is, the laity see nothing wrong in controlling births in this way."

"Few liars seem ashamed of lying. But please go on."

"Forty years ago, Holiness, Vatican II said couples have the right and duty to limit their families."

"Indeed they have," the Pope said, "with overpopulation threatening the world."

"But how *can* they limit their families with only the so-called rhythm method, which has been dubbed 'Vatican Roulette.' "

"The latest natural methods are quite reliable," Rottweiler said.

"How," Frangipani asked heatedly, "can women living in a hovel with a dozen children use thermometers, calendars and temperature charts? Some of them can't read and haven't any electric light."

The Pope nodded. "A very strong point."

Rottweiler was horrified. Having thrown away the jewel of celibacy, was he about to discard the immutable teaching on contraception?

"Do you know," Patrick said, "John Paul, presumably under your guidance, Josef, said something that horrified me."

Rottweiler himself looked horrified at this. "Yes, Holiness?"

"He said a husband with AIDS has the right to sex with his wife, provided he does not use a condom."

Rottweiler was astounded. "How could John Paul permit the use of a condom?"

"How could he permit murder?"

"Holiness," snapped Rottweiler, "I really think—"

"My dear friends," the Pope said, feeling a horse-gallop in his head, "may we leave it there for the time being?"

Cardinal Rottweiler went away and immediately typed out a letter of resignation from the Sacred College in case he needed it.

Chapter Thirty-five

The media were first to get wind of the invasion. When they called to make reservations in Rome's normally quiet October, hotels had no vacancies. They tried boardinghouses, seminaries, convents. These, too, were full. Many distinguished journalists had to book bed and breakfast in private houses. The number of priests who wanted the Pope to marry them had to be enormous.

It was true. Applications from priests who wanted to be dispensed from celibacy rained in after the Synod. Many clergy announced their own marriage banns from the pulpit, often to tumultuous applause.

What upset old curial officials like Rottweiler was the number of high-ranking prelates who sought dispensation.

"John Paul," Rottweiler thought, "must be spinning in his grave."

The final tally of those on the path to Rome was 22,000, including 4 cardinals, 20 archbishops and 225 bishops. Many wanted, in the language of the courts, to regularize unions of long standing.

The Pope was disappointed but not dismayed. "I was right," he said to Montefiori. "Many priests were wild to get married. Celibacy was *not* working."

Montefiori made no comment on that. But:

"An additional complication, Holiness. Among the brides chosen by the clergy are large numbers of . . ."

"Yes?"

"Brides of Christ."

"To be expected," Patrick said calmly. "After all, the clergy do have close contact with the good sisters."

"Perhaps in future, joint ministries for husbands and wives," Montefiori commented. "His-and-her vestments, that sort of thing."

"It may well be so, Giuseppe. In my experience, nuns make excellent Catholics."

The clergy not only brought their future spouses with them but, in many cases, a huge retinue of family and well-wishers.

Hundreds of Filipino and Latin American parishes had held collections to send their priests and dependents to Rome. Honor demanded it.

One holy old friar from Sicily, renowned for the marks of crucifixion on his body, proudly appeared with his beloved, his nine children and twenty-seven grandchildren. His puzzled superior was reported as saying that Fra Antonio had richly earned his stigmata.

In thumbing through the list—thick as a telephone directory—Patrick said, with a twinkle, to his Secretary of State:

"Remember Martin Luther. When he first wed, he awoke with surprise to find a pair of plaits beside him on the pillow."

"I suspect," Montefiori said, "that most priests on that list are long over their surprise."

"Well, Giuseppe, you know the old limerick:

"There was an old monk from Siberia,
  Whose life became drearier and drearier,
  Till he rushed from his cell
  With a hell of a yell
  And eloped with the Mother Superior."

Whether because he disapproved of the sentiments, or because his English was not up to it, Montefiori was not amused.

215

• • •

Because of the sheer volume of applicants, the Secretary of State recommended three ceremonies. The first for cardinals, archbishops, bishops, abbots and heads of religious orders. The second for domestic prelates, canons and deans of chapters. The third for the lower clergy.

For several days prior to the Great Weddings, confessions were heard in three Roman churches: St. Peter's, St. John Lateran and St. Mary Major. Confessors were specially empowered by the Pope to release priests and religious from their obligations and censures.

Many an aged and venerable confessor was seen emerging from his box after a three-hour stint, perspiring madly and clutching his head in disbelief. The laying-on of hands had acquired a new meaning.

Some clergy, having been shrived once, belted back into the box in search of fresh cleansing for once again warming the marital bed too soon.

At the first nuptial Mass in St. Peter's, in front of a noisy, smiling congregation of fifty thousand, the Gospel was read by an eighty-one-year-old cardinal who was marrying an eighty-year-old abbess.

In a short kindly address, Pope Patrick took as the text for his address St. Paul's words to Timothy:

"A bishop must be above reproach, married but once, sober and sensible. He must manage his own household well, keeping his children obedient and respectful in every way. If a man cannot manage his own household, how can he care for the Church of God?"

He congratulated all the couples present on having a vocation from God denied to him and other celibates. Marriage is the cradle and nursery of love and humanity. It is a gracious vocation shared in by the first Pope—Patrick gestured to his left where stood the famous bronze statue to St. Peter—and probably by the rest of the apostles.

He praised all the couples for opting for a calling that required such self-sacrifice. Yet, he assured them, there is much comfort in the abiding com-

216

panionship of man and woman which was God's original plan for the race. In one another they would have their best friend.

"Listen to each other," he counseled them, "as you would sit beside and listen to the running of a river. How good it is for man and wife to sleep together, wake together, work together from daybreak to sunset in the service of the Lord. I trust"—he cast his eye over those to be wed—"that you priests and your devoted wives-to-be will give daily expression to the love that Christ and his beloved Bride the Church bear eternally toward one another."

In words that caused a stir throughout the huge congregation, he stressed that in this time of massive overpopulation it was up to partners of childbearing age to decide for themselves the number of children they should strive for under God.

Cardinal Ragno, at this point, found a pretext for storming out of the Basilica.

Some, the Pope said, would decide to have no children, some one or two: some, trusting in the bountiful blessings of God, might choose a dozen.

"What is important is that each couple should decide for themselves in spiritual freedom their future life together and trust in God's providence."

He ended with the words:

"Be not afraid. Go hand in firm hand from this altar as perfect equals, embracing joy and pain, with no guilt or gloom but only love in your hearts, hoping in all your shared tomorrows."

The few protesters who railed at the Pope for betraying the Church were outcheered by the rest of the congregation. Never had St. Peter's witnessed scenes of such old-fashioned romance.

Each couple was photographed at the altar as they took their marriage vows. The grooms, in their usual clerical attire, looked even more splendid than their mostly somewhat ancient brides. Many an elderly son, including twelve members of the Italian Parliament, gave his mother away to his bishop father. Many a bishop came away from the altar wearing two rings.

On that night and the two following nights, Rome of *la dolce vita* saw celebrations and fireworks displays never to be forgotten. There was a feeling abroad that after two thousand years of giving Eros poison to drink, Rome had at last come to terms with love and sexuality.

One drunken old reveler was arrested for dancing goatily in the Trevi Fountain before adding his own prodigious liquid contribution. The authorities were only dissuaded from pressing charges when he was identified as the recently married Cardinal Angelo Pavese, who had a medical condition.

Poggi, the socialist Mayor of Rome, put in a formal complaint to the Vatican about these disturbances of the peace. Sour grapes, was the general verdict. He was annoyed at the favorable press the Church was getting.

And it was true. Because of Pope Patrick, the Catholic Church was at the height of its popularity.

Chapter Thirty-six

Rottweiler, who had listened tremblingly to the Pope's addresses in St. Peter's, had his letter of resignation in his pocket when he rejoined Frangipani in the Pope's study.

"Last time," the Pope began, "we discussed contraception and, in particular, the safe period."

Rottweiler nodded grumpily. Back at the German College near the Piazza Navona, his cases were already packed for the flight home to Munich.

"It *is* odd, is it not, Josef," the Pope said, "that women use thermometers and calendars to avoid conception when a pill or a piece of rubber would have the same effect? Why let them use mathematics and not chemistry and physics?"

Rottweiler was too hurt to reply. The Pope was hinting that there was no difference between natural and unnatural methods of controlling birth. Was he a theological simpleton?

By contrast, Frangipani was bubbling with excitement. The ban on contraception had led to mass defections from the Church in the West. It had contributed to the population explosion, widespread sterilization, abortion and grinding poverty in undeveloped countries.

Rottweiler finally found his voice. "You are not suggesting, Holiness, that our teaching needs to be amended."

"I am, indeed. Principles cannot change but we must apply them in the light of modern science and medicine."

"Precisely," Frangipani said.

"But," Rottweiler cried, close to tears as he saw all the achievements of his long life crashing around him, "the Church cannot go against itself, against a teaching two millennia old."

"I agree with you both," the Pope said.

The cardinals looked at each other, wide-eyed and openmouthed.

"Josef," Patrick said, "as former Prefect of the Holy Office you often defended the right of couples to use the safe period."

Rottweiler nodded. "Pius XII taught that. So did Paul VI in *Humanae Vitae* in 1968. John Paul repeatedly said the same."

"Now, Josef, please be very frank. Did you never find something odd about allowing sex in the safe period?"

"Well . . ." Rottweiler paused. "To be honest, yes."

"Ah." Frangipani was enjoying his rival's discomfort.

"Explain yourself, Josef."

"Well, Holiness, for centuries the Church taught it was a sin to separate sex and procreation."

"That would happen *when?*"

"In *coitus interruptus*, when the man withdraws and spills his seed outside the woman's body. This was Onan's sin for which God punished him by death."

"When else did the Church say intercourse is wrong?"

"When the wife is already pregnant."

"Why was that a sin?"

"Because," the old theology professor intoned, "when she is pregnant, her husband's seed is wasted, as it was in Onan's case. It is like throwing good seed on a field already sown."

"Who taught that?"

"Every Father of the Church, every Pope and respected theologian."

"What about women who are sterile or beyond the childbearing age?"

Rottweiler said, "All said that sex in such cases is some sort of sin because it is taking pleasure for its own sake and not to have a child."

"Why is that a sin?"

"Because the only purpose of sex is the child."

The Pope smiled. "You did say the *only* purpose?"

Rottweiler nodded. "The Church did not say the child is the primary purpose of sex but the only one."

The Pope said, "By the Church, you mean . . . ?"

"Every Father of the Church, including Clement of Alexandria, Justin, Jerome, Ambrose and Augustine. Every Pope including Leo the Great, Gregory the Great, Innocent III. Every theologian, including Aquinas and Bonaventure."

Frangipani was irritated. Why bother to regurgitate all this old-fashioned stuff?

Patrick said: "I agree with you, Josef. My thesis, 'Sexuality in the Middle Ages,' showed that no Churchman *ever* said it is right to separate sex and procreation because sex has only *one* God-given aim, the child."

Once more the two cardinals turned to each other. Whose side was the Pope on?

"A problem for you, Josef. The Church always said: Never, and I mean *never for any reason whatsoever,* separate sex and procreation. Isn't that precisely what happens when couples use the safe period?"

Rottweiler squeezed out a yes.

"It is done deliberately?"

"That is the whole point of the exercise."

"What," Patrick said, "do you think of such an *exercise?*"

"Well, um, I am not too unhappy with it. Not too happy, either. Even St. Augustine had a primitive knowledge of the safe period."

"What did he say about it?"

Rottweiler shrugged disconsolately. "He condemned it. Unreservedly. As a mortal sin of lust. He said it could never be right to separate sexual pleasure from having children. It made the husband an adulterer, the wife a whore and the marriage bed no better than a brothel."

"And St. Gregory the Great?"

"He said, 'Sex in marriage is only without sin when the child is intended.' "

"And St. Thomas Aquinas?"

" 'The only aim of marriage is procreation,' " and, " 'to have intercourse for pleasure only is a grave sin.' "

The Pope underlined the point. "You mean our greatest teachers said that using the safe period is *always* a grave sin?"

Rottweiler muttered something about these men having lived a long time ago.

"All the more important for the Church's witness, Josef. You are unhappy, I suggest, because Catholic teaching, repeated by John Paul over and over, is this: *Every* act of sex must be open to the transmission of life."

Rottweiler nodded miserably.

"And having sex during the sterile period aims at stopping the transmission of life."

"But," Rottweiler insisted, "nothing unnatural is done."

"No? Surely our whole tradition stressed that all methods of frustrating the one lawful aim of sex are the same? That the safe period method is unnatural in *fact* and in *intent* even though there is no mechanical interference?"

"Yes," said Rottweiler. "When my parents married they were told it was a big sin to use the safe period. The Church does seem to have—"

"Changed," Frangipani put in triumphantly.

After reflection, Rottweiler nodded firmly. "An act can hardly be open to the transmission of life if couples deliberately restrict it to times when, by definition, the transmission of life is impossible."

"Bravo," the Pope said warmly. "It is as preposterous as saying a man is free to eat off an empty plate or that he can fill a can with water when it is full of holes."

Once again, Rottweiler signaled agreement.

Seeing his distress, Patrick said kindly: "I put it to you, using the safe period has led many Catholics to argue, 'If we take all this trouble to avoid a child and it doesn't work, why not use simpler methods, say, the Pill or the condom, which do work'?"

Rottweiler said, "Many, I think, have reasoned like that."

"And why not, Josef? They are deliberately wasting seed anyway by copulating during the sterile period."

Rottweiler nodded.

"And they take pleasure in sex while making sure that procreation cannot take place."

"Yes, Holiness."

"And turn the most sacred of acts into a cheap guessing game?"

"Yes, yes, yes. Such *heftige Liebe*, passionate love, is wrong."

"And the fertile period, the only time when sex can achieve its purpose of creating life, is curiously labeled by moralists as 'dangerous' or 'unsafe'?"

Rottweiler said, "It is odd, I grant."

"So odd it is contrary to all Catholic tradition."

Rottweiler, who saw a conflict of authorities, was rattled. "Three recent Popes permitted the use of the safe period."

"I do not deny it. But were they right so to do?"

"I took it for granted they were."

"Understandably because everything any Pope has said since Vatican I in 1870 has a sort of infallible mystique."

"There was another reason," Rottweiler said. "The safe period, however inadequate, helped some couples who had to limit their families."

Patrick took out his pipe but did not light up. Dr. Gadda had warned him that smoking and coffee would make his headaches worse.

"Tell me, Josef, what do you think now?"

Rottweiler fingered the letter of resignation in his pocket, not sure what to do with it. "Maybe using the safe period is also a form of permissiveness."

Frangipani, who was enjoying Rottweiler's grilling, laughed aloud. Rather than admit that the current teaching on birth control was nonsense and needed root-and-branch reform, the old archconservative preferred to say that recent Popes, even fierce old John Paul II, had encouraged *permissiveness!*

"Holiness," Frangipani said, "aren't you saying there is no moral difference between the so-called artificial methods of birth control and the so-called natural method of the safe period?"

"Correct."

"So," Frangipani said, full of hope, "they are both all right?"

"Precisely what I did *not* say."

"You don't mean—"

"Both methods deliberately separate sex and having a child, but of the two methods the safe period is more degrading. Imagine, women go to all that trouble, have all that anxiety, and for what?"

"To avoid conception," Rottweiler said dazedly.

"Indeed, Josef. To do what the Church has always forbidden. How anti-Christian this is. No wonder the Orthodox Church never accepted this method."

"Oh my God," whispered Frangipani.

The Pope said:

"Suppose my father, God rest him, a small farmer, had waited for the year's first frost or for six inches of snow to fall before he sowed his wheat, barley, potatoes. We, his children, would have asked him, 'Why, Father?' 'Oh, so I do not have a harvest.' We would have thought him crazy. Why waste his precious seed? And yet human seed is much holier, since it is intended for the harvest of God's children. Can you really imagine that God wants a Catholic couple to choose deliberately the times and seasons when the divine seed cannot bear fruit, when it will rot in the ground, so to speak? Can you see him wanting married people to use the procreative act specifically in order *not* to procreate? Isn't this the worst sort of trivialization of sex?"

Frangipani said, "Then, you are only thinking of banning the safe-period method, which few use today, anyway?"

"Only!" Rottweiler said morosely. "Even that would be considered a huge change in some quarters."

"You are both wrong," Patrick said, adding to their bewilderment. "You are forgetting something."

They looked at him inquiringly.

"We need to apply our unchanging principles in the light of modern scientific understanding."

"Understanding of *what?*" Rottweiler wanted to know.

"Of the safe period."

"But," Rottweiler said, his exasperation showing in his high color, "you said it is degrading to make use of the safe period."

"To *avoid* conception. Not to *achieve* it."

Both cardinals shrugged, still not cottoning on.

"Why, Josef, did science investigate the infertile period in the first place?"

Rottweiler said, "To help women who failed to conceive. If they knew their infertile period, they could avoid that and only have sex during the fertile period."

Patrick banged the desk. "Precisely. The holy aim of the research was to increase the accuracy and fruitfulness of the acts of intercourse."

Frangipani went goose-bumpy all over. "You are intending to declare that sexual intercourse is *forbidden* during the safe period."

It was Rottweiler who grasped the full extent of the horror. "You mean, Holiness, sex is *only* permitted when the woman is *not* safe?"

The Pope finally relaxed. "How slow two of my best men are to see the implications of Catholic teaching in the light of modern findings."

Chapter Thirty-seven

Pope Patrick's first encyclical, *Splendor Vitae*, was a mere six pages long but it rocked the Church and the world. And that included Cardinal Montefiori.

After a sneak preview, he said bluntly, "It will not make you popular. As we Italians say, 'Bed is the poor man's opera.' "

The Pope had replied, "I am not in a popularity contest. You cannot expect me to go down in history as the Pope of the Nine Commandments."

When Montefiori suggested he was asking too much of human nature, Patrick said, "Every person has a wealth of glory and greatness locked up inside him," at which Montefiori confessed dryly he had not noticed.

"Any suggestions, then, Giuseppe?"

"Yes, Holiness. Tonight after dark, I could let you down the Vatican wall in a basket."

Rumors of a change on birth control circulated for some time. After the Pope's address at the Great Weddings, liberals hoped that the Pope would at last permit contraceptives, as the Anglican Church had done eighty years before. Conservatives steeled themselves for some "adjustment" to traditional teaching from a seemingly reformist Pope.

But this was as surprising as seeing angels climbing up and down ladders, smoking cigars.

Splendor Vitae began with an acknowledgment that the world desperately needed to curb its numbers. The only moral way to achieve birth control was self-control.

There were thousands of ways of loving, but having sex while deliberately negating life was not one of them. Sex must always and only be in the service of life, otherwise it ceased to be a loving act and became its black shadow, namely, lust.

This meant a ban on *all* forms of contraception as well as a ban on sexual intercourse whenever couples knew or suspected that it could not issue in new life.

"Intercourse," the encyclical went on, "must be restricted to the fertile period. Only then will sex always be open to the transmission of life, which is the one divine purpose of sex.

"For sex is not about pleasure but about love. It is about selfless love, a selfless love of God, of the partner and of the next generation.

"Sex, as all Catholic tradition tells us, is only holy and loving when its aim is solely procreative, that is, when a devoted couple intend under God to produce a child of God who will enjoy the vision of God forever."

He called a halt to the immature and often frenzied search for unnatural ways of avoiding conception, whether by pills, condoms, intrauterine devices, or by using computers to spot gaps in female fertility in order to copulate with no effect save sexual pleasure.

"The only mature and moral way to avoid conception is the same for the married as for the unmarried: perfect chastity and respect for the partner. Mary, who is rightly held up as the Perfect Mother, is also, as Jerome and Augustine taught, the model of the Perfect Wife. Not wanting another child, she and Joseph, her spouse, remained holy and abstinent."

He prayed that further scientific research would pinpoint ovulation.

"Then it will be morally obligatory to restrict intercourse to a precise day, perhaps even a precise hour of day. Only then will sex be completely humanized in accordance with the glorious design of the Creator."

It was with very real regret that he was obliged to censure Pius XII, who was the first Pope to endorse the safe period in his Address to Midwives in

227

1951. He had seriously contradicted the Church's constant teaching on a critical issue of morality.

Many Popes and General Councils had condemned certain Supreme Pontiffs as "heretics." Patrick felt bound to follow them and declare Pius XII a heretic.

Paul VI and John Paul II, who had repeated his error unreflectingly, could not escape censure, though Patrick stopped short of excommunicating them. At least Paul VI in *Humanae Vitae* and John Paul II in *Veritatis Splendor* had made it plain that they were not speaking *ex cathedra*, that is, infallibly.

Patrick kept the biggest sting for the tail.

"This teaching is so plainly in line with two thousand constant years of tradition that I have no hesitation in defining it as the true irreformable Catholic doctrine."

Chapter Thirty-eight

The world's media, originally stunned by *Splendor Vitae*, had to admit on reflection that the Pontiff's argument was consistent. If couples were trying to avoid having children, the methods made no moral difference. Catholics in their millions had already accepted that argument by choosing, without guilt, techniques more reliable than the so-called safe period method.

The *Times* of London said: "Since Pope Patrick has reaffirmed the Roman doctrine that sex is only for breeding, all Catholics would now be well advised to use the Pill. Better be really safe than sorry."

The *Chicago Tribune's* editorial comment was: "Pliny said elephants are chaste because they only copulate when they require offspring and wash themselves afterward. This Pontiff wants Catholics to imitate elephants."

Der Spiegel predicted a mass exodus from the Roman Church. "Does the Pope, in his ivory tower, really think Catholic couples will live like Adam and Eve before the Fall? Does he expect them to restrict intercourse to a few weeks or days of their married lives?"

The English daily the *Sun* printed a picture of a big-bosomed page-three nude inside a huge condom. An editorial said the Pope made Ayatollah Hourani look like a feminist. It cheekily recalled what happened after John Paul's lying in state in St. Peter's. Cleaners found as many colored Benetton condoms in the sunken area in front of the high altar as are tossed on a summer's day in the Trevi Fountain, though the Vatican tried to say this was a token of repentance.

Left-wing papers in Italy accused Patrick of not grasping the Italian way of doing things, which takes bribery and corruption in its stride. "Why does this inflexible old Irishman not go bite his elbow?" You have to bend a bit, they reasoned, even with Brother Satan.

All over Rome, posters, with digitally forged photographs, depicted Pope Patrick in the arms of a beautiful naked blonde.

Feminists came down hard on the Pope. They had lately campaigned with way-out slogans. They disapproved of marriage, they said, as a cure for virginity. Marriage was all right if people were that way inclined but definitely no marriage before glorious pleasurable sex.

One such Catholic publication in California said of the Pope: "What does this genderless, nonbegetter know about *love?* He's never cradled anything softer than a telephone. And this celibate cartoon tells us women how to lead our lives. A bear might as well teach bees how to make honey."

The *Universe,* an English Catholic weekly, remained steadfast.

> *Roma locuta est, causa finita est.* The vacillation that has marred the Church since Vatican II fifty years ago is ended. Loyal Catholics have long awaited a definitive statement of the Church's position on contraception. Pope Patrick has given it. This outstanding encyclical will separate sheep from goats. We humbly pledge His Holiness our total loyalty.

This from a goaty editor whose wife and mistresses had been on the Pill for years.

The Netherlands weekly *De Tijd* announced it was closing down.

> This Pope has made his narrow, male-oriented perversion of sex into a dogma and anyone who denies it a heretic. Theologians will do their best to soften the impact of *Splendor Vitae.* If the past is anything to go by, they will not resign their posts. If the Pope had defined that there is no God and Jesus was a legend, they would still have

managed to square these "infallible truths" with their personal religious beliefs. For myself, I am relieved to go.

Theologians proved to be quite as flexible as forecast. They went at the encyclical like ten top toreadors who tormented and finally gave the coup de grâce to a tired old cow.

Ireland's bishops who for years had lauded the safe period method of contraception acclaimed the profound wisdom of the encyclical.

In *Intercom*, the Bishop of Kerry said there was now at last firm medical evidence that restricting sex to the safe period caused nausea and severe mental illness. It was demeaning to women and far from being really safe.

> What is undeniable is that every child resulting from the use of the safe period is an *unwanted* child. Could anything be more reprehensible than that? Thank you, Holy Father.

Many theologians saw signs of hope in *Splendor Vitae*. Patrick did not say it was mortally sinful to separate sex and procreation. The use of pills and condoms, hitherto regarded as mortal sins, might now be looked on as only "probably mortal." Some daring scholars even said they were now "possibly only venial," like telling little lies or stealing pennies. Contraception remained sinful, otherwise the Church would deny itself, which it could never do. But contraception no longer—probably—barred Catholics from communion.

Chapter Thirty-nine

Harry Tickle from the New York archdiocese appeared on the "Today" show. He had recently been promoted by Burns to monsignor in gratitude for services rendered in the men's room on Croagh Patrick. A balding giant, he contrasted rather badly with the interviewer, fair-haired Adonis George Dole.

Tickle was no great shakes at theology. He had, though, written a highly regarded doctoral thesis for Fordham, the Jesuit university in the Bronx, which proved that a rapist who wore a condom sinned more gravely than one who did not. Tickle was now the front man for the Catholic hierarchy when the bishops hadn't the stomach for the job.

As a performer, he was deft. Tap-tap-tap. He could outdance Astaire.

Dole began by asking him how it was possible for one Pope, Patrick, to condemn another, Pius XII, as a heretic.

This had also been news to Tickle before he read the encyclical. Several Popes, it seemed, had been guilty of heresy and condemned for it after their deaths, but it was not something the Catholic Church boasted about.

"What I don't understand," Dole said, "is how one *infallible* Pope can condemn another *infallible* Pope."

"Easy," said Tickle, brushing the sleeve of his jacket. "The heretic Pope was not speaking infallibly."

"The Pope who condemned him *was*."

"You read me."

"I am just getting over the wire," Dole said, "a report that the body of Pius XII is being removed from St. Peter's for reburial somewhere else. Do you know where that somewhere else is, Monsignor?"

"In unconsecrated ground, certainly. You can't leave no heretic, no dead heretic, in the vault of St. Peter's."

"I thought I read somewhere, Monsignor, that you were campaigning last year to have Pius XII canonized."

"Not at all. I put forward his name to the Holy See for a decision. Obviously, it would have been negative."

"Obviously?"

"It was obvious to me. The guy smelled."

"Before or after death?"

"When he died, before they buried him. His face turned green. His body ballooned and grew flatulent and inside his coffin he made noises like a firecracker. How could the Holy Catholic Church have canonized *that?*"

"But didn't you say once, Monsignor, that he deserved to be canonized for defending the Jews from the Nazis?"

"Pius XII never did defend the Jews from the Nazis."

"That surely was your point. You said that he defended the Jews by not defending them."

"If he had defended them, the Nazis would have persecuted them all the more."

"But six million Jews died. How could the Nazis have persecuted them more?"

"Please don't try and sidetrack me, Mr. Dole, by talking about my Jewish friends."

"Really, I wasn't—"

"The point of this encyclical is the one the Pope didn't make."

"Really," said the handsome but flustered Mr. Dole. "So its chief purpose was to leave something out?"

"You catch on quick, son," the monsignor said affably. "It takes an expert to see what isn't there, as it took a Sherlock Holmes to grasp the significance of the dog that *didn't* bark in *The Hound of the Baskervilles.*"

"What was left out of *Splendor Vitae?*"

"That contraception needn't be—I don't say isn't—a mortal sin."

233

Dole paused to impress on the audience that he was thinking: Isn't that a rather important thing to omit?

"Bingo."

Dole really *was* having to think now. "D'you suppose that Pope Patrick will one day write an encyclical on sex and put *in* what he most wants his Church to understand?"

"Unlikely."

"I don't see why."

"You're not a theologian, son. You see, it's by not saying important things that Popes draw special attention to them."

"Is this a peculiarity of your Church, Monsignor?"

"*Pec-ul-iar-ity.*" Tickle's great jowly face went even blacker. "I resent the anti-Catholic prejudice behind that remark."

Dole trembled. With his dry tongue, twisted features and a necktie that had shifted to one side, he looked as if he were hanging from the boom mike.

"I'm sorry if I offended you."

"It don't matter about me, sir. It's the 65 million Catholics out there watching you I'm sorry for."

"I really didn't mean to be anti-Catholic."

"That, sir, is the most insidious of anti-Catholic prejudices: the unspoken sort. By *not* saying it, you have drawn everyone's attention to it, and, incidentally, proved my point."

"All right, Monsignor," said an ever more shaky interviewer. "Your Church is not peculiar. It's others that are."

"I accept your apology," Tickle said. "I can't speak for non-Catholics watching us. By the way, are you Jewish?"

"Certainly not," said the blue-eyed, golden-fleeced Dole.

Tickle's face registered horror. "You're *anti*-Jewish!"

"Am I anti-Jewish just because I deny I'm Jewish?"

"You didn't just deny it, sonny. You took offense."

"How would *you* react if someone accused—I mean, asked you, yes, *asked* you—if you were Jewish?"

"I'd first say, 'Are *you?*' "

"If he said yes?"

"I'd say, 'Nice of you to inquire, but, unfortunately, no.'"

"And if he said he *wasn't* Jewish?"

"I'd shake his hand."

"That is hypocritical," said Dole, aware he was fast losing his cool and, possibly, his job.

"With your anti-Jewishness, you are assuming that by shaking his hand I am *congratulating* him. In fact, I am *sympathizing*."

Dole turned desperately to the camera. "I want to assure Jewish viewers that I'm in no way anti-Jewish."

"Proves my point," Tickle rumbled. "You won't allow Jewish people to forget for one minute, even on a breakfast show like this, that they're Jewish. I mean to say, there are Bolivians out there, Ukrainians, Turks. Do you ever say to them, 'I want to assure you folks that I'm not anti-Bolivian, anti-Ukrainian, anti-Turk'? *No*, only Jews. You have to prove you're anti-Jewish by denying you are anti-Jewish."

"But—"

"Let me get a word in, boy. I bet all day long you're mumbling to yourself, 'Thank the great Jehovah *I'm* not Jewish.'"

"This is ridiculous," bawled Dole. "I never give a procking thought about being Jewish."

"Mind your language in front of the children, *boy*. Now let's be serious. You expect anyone to believe you are not anti-Jewish when you jump down my throat for respectfully asking you if you are Jewish?"

"Please—"

"Your sort creates this image of Jews, ordinary, kind, lovable Jews in New York and San Francisco and elsewhere, as somehow peculiar people whom you don't want no truck with. Well, let me tell you, Mr. Clever-Pants Dole, it's dirty tricks like this that led to Nazi concentration camps and the Holocaust, which that great, great Jew, Steven Spielberg, revealed to the world a few years back."

"Please, will you—?"

Monsignor Tickle shot out of his chair, tugging off his neck mike. "I refuse to sit here," he said with massive dignity, "and listen to you maligning Jews, non-Jews and everyone else on God's earth. You started on Catholics,

235

then it was Jews. Next you'll be slanging Poles, Germans and all the Irish just for being Irish like our beloved Pope Patrick. These people all happen to be friends of mine."

The camera followed his broad back as he stomped off the set.

In his dressing room, Tickle took a stream of calls from grateful Jews, Catholics, Poles, Germans, Ukrainians, Bolivians, Turks and Irish. He was specially touched by the sixteen bishops who called to congratulate him.

"Thanks, Harry," said Cardinal Burns, "for taking the heat off that procking encyclical."

"What procking encyclical?" Tickle wanted to know.

Chapter Forty

Cardinal Burns called up his crony Kamierz Sapieha in Philadelphia.
"Glad you didn't go in for holy bedlock, Kammy."

"Thought about it, Tom," Philadelphia replied. "But I guess I'm too old for liftoff. Besides, my favorite Reverend Mother ran off with a procking bishop from Tennessee."

They briefly discussed *Splendor Vitae*, decided it was garbage but it would make no difference, anyhow. The Pope might as well try selling pork chops to Orthodox Jews or burying a hole.

"They paid no attention to the Polish sausage," Burns said, "why should they listen to the leprechaun?"

Sapieha had read that only one sex act in two hundred results in conception and yet the world was grossly overpopulated.

"And the Pope wants one hundred percent of them to be fertile. He is out of his tiny mind."

They agreed something had to be done about this, so they authorized a joint-pastoral supporting the Pope up to the hilt.

A surprising number of favorable letters arrived at the Vatican. The general tenor of them was: About time the Church finally made its mind up about sex. It is disgusting, *period*. The Pope's teaching has about it the beautiful consistency of truth. He is without question the moral leader of mankind in a crusade against contemporary all-pervading smut.

The average age of the letter-writers was seventy-five.

The Pope, reading some of the mail, said to Frank, "I had to do it. Three recent Pontiffs were slipping in a fundamental change in tradition and not admitting it. Not to have corrected them would have been hypocrisy."

Not all letters were positive. Many clerics, recently dispensed from celibacy, wondered why they had bothered. According to the Archbishop of Glasgow, *Splendor Vitae* was already undermining his marriage. It was not just for homemade haggis and polite pillow talk he had married a nun way past the menopause.

When Denise Weaver took a call from the President of the United States on arms control, she brought up the matter of the encyclical.

"I'm glad I'm no longer a hot-blooded youth," Delaney quipped, presuming the P.M. would notice the irony in his voice. "Mind you, the First Lady reckons this *Splendor Vitae* thing is a charter for women."

"Didn't I tell you, Roone," Weaver hissed, "that old man is crazier than a retired general."

"Don't worry about him."

"Not *worry?* Christ, that monster's a lamb with lion's teeth. Think of the hassle he caused in Belfast over his 'Ireland for the Irish' speech in Kilmainham Jail."

"Yeah, that was too bad, Denise. I just pray God he stays away from the U.S. of A."

He was not to know that a letter from Patrick, written in his own right as Vatican head of state, was already on its way in a diplomatic bag, asking him to arrange that little address to the United Nations.

Part Six

Filthy Lucre

Chapter Forty-one

Rumors were whipping around Rome that the Pope intended selling off the *Pietà*, the only one of Michelangelo's statues on which he carved his name. Though not the best—Jesus' body was far too small in comparison with Mary's—it was the best-loved sculpture in the city. This sale, added to Patrick's teaching on sex, meant that his honeymoon with the Romans was over.

His pictures in church porches were pulled down and sometimes burned. A world soccer match between Ireland and Italy due to be played in Rome was canceled because the police could not guarantee the safety of the Irish team.

Even Charley, known for his Irishness, suffered. He was puzzled that no one stroked him anymore. Whenever he showed his nose, people booed.

One Sunday afternoon, Cardinal Montefiori was with the Pope when the red carpet was replaced by red paint.

"Romans like blood even in their oranges," the cardinal said, ignoring the paint in his own hair to wipe the spots off Patrick's soutane. "Remember, Holiness, God chose this place as the diocese of the Popes to keep them humble."

"I only told them the truth, Giuseppe."

"Truth?" the cardinal exclaimed in mock horror. "In this city, they are not interested in truth. They would only accept an encyclical if it had stamped on it, 'Free Pass for the Trains.'"

In New York, Cardinal Burns took calls from the directors of a dozen galleries, including three from Japan. If ever the *Pietà* came on the market, they told him, they'd be very interested.

Burns telephoned Frank Kerrigan to ask what the hell was going on. Frank was tight-lipped, even when he was promised the rank of auxiliary bishop for his cooperation.

Rumors had begun as soon as Pope Patrick paid a surprise visit to the Istituto per le Opere di Religione (IOR), otherwise known as the Vatican Bank.

Pius XII had set up the IOR in 1942 with a handwritten letter. Bishop Paul Marcinkus had joined it in 1969. He was in charge in 1982 when, to the Vatican's embarrassment, the Banco Ambrosiano, which had strong links with the IOR, went bust with debts of $1.2 billion. Soon after that, Roberto Calvi, chairman of the Ambrosiano, was found hanging under Blackfriar's Bridge in London.

Even in the 1990s, the IOR had sold $60 million worth of government bonds given as bribes to leading politicians and refused to return its 10 percent commission.

The Pope, accompanied by Charley and Montefiori, went to the new IOR, a spectacular skyscraper of steel and glass, which had replaced the sixteenth-century building in the Sixtus V courtyard near the Porta Sant'Anna. The current president was Bishop Pawel Radowski, a silver-haired, Stanford-educated Pole.

On the way, Montefiori tried to entertain the Pope by more of his droll stories. He told how John Paul, after he had his appendix out, acquired a passion for canonizations, including three thousand Poles.

He had made a saint of Lucia dos Santos, a Carmelite nun and last of the three shepherd children who had seen Our Lady of Fátima in 1917. Nothing wrong with that, except, as his memory faltered, he had wanted to canonize her three times.

Montefiori also had to work hard to stop him decanonizing two women saints, Bridget of Sweden and Catherine of Siena, for daring to give Popes advice during their exile in Avignon.

John Paul's most controversial decision centered on Paul Casimir Marcinkus. For years, the Italian Court of Cassation tried to have Marcinkus extradited from the States to face charges of fiscal corruption.

"John Paul," said Montefiori, "showed his disdain by making Marcinkus a cardinal. Then, Holiness, while Marcinkus was playing golf outside Chicago, for the first time in his life he holed out in one. It led to a massive heart attack. When I told John Paul, he instantly canonized him to encourage Marcinkus's fellow Lithuanians. However, the new saint lingered on for three more days. Since no one can be declared a saint before death, it is doubtful whether the canonization was valid. This may explain why no statue has been erected in his honor, not even in Lithuania."

Normally, Patrick would have laughed heartily at Montefiori's superb gift as a storyteller, not today. His mood was grim as they were ushered by a uniformed attendant into a superb hall of white Carrara marble.

In seconds, an elevator whisked them to the twelfth floor where Marcinkus's successor had *the* office of the future. The latest electronics linked it to every financial institution in the world.

When they were comfortably settled, Radowski purred, "What would you like to know, Holiness?"

"Everything, Pawel."

Radowski touched a button and a wall screen showed facts and figures: Deposits, Loans, Net Income, Stockholders' Equity.

"We are worth, you see, several billion dollars."

"And our investments, Pawel?"

"Safe," Radowski said proudly.

"I don't doubt it. But what are we invested in?"

Radowski pressed another button.

"We seem," the Pope said, "to have interests in casinos."

Radowski cleared his throat. "Las Vegas and Atlantic City."

"Oh, yes? And we are into electronics."

"The corporation in which we have a controlling interest, Holiness, is subcontracted to Boeing, USA."

"What does it make, this electronics firm of ours?"

"I believe, er, missile guidance systems."

"Really? And I see we are into pharmaceuticals. Medicines?"

"Pills, certainly," Radowski said evasively. "We are the main shareholder in the Istituto Farmacologico Serafico."

"What sort of pills?"

Radowski reddened. "Headache pills." Pope Patrick brightened. "And, er, birth control pills."

"What for, Pawel?"

"Um, for controlling births, I guess, Holiness. I have not inquired too closely. The fact is, we own five percent of all shares quoted on the Italian stock exchange and we choose the best."

"Best?"

"Those that give the highest returns. We hold money in trust for our creditors and shareholders, you understand."

"No abortion pills?"

"Certainly *not*, Holiness."

The Pope pondered a moment. "I am told, Pawel, that many clients bank here to avoid paying Italian income tax."

Radowski shrugged. "I do not fill in their returns."

"But they *might* invest with us for that purpose?"

"It is conceivable."

The Pope waved airily at the screen. "What do stockholders think of these . . . investments?"

"They never say, Holiness."

"They come to meetings and never open their mouths?"

"I mean we do not, er, hold stockholders' meetings."

"But surely they sometimes query the balance sheet?"

Radowski coughed to rid himself of a tickle in his throat. "We do not publish a balance sheet, Holiness. We have never been asked for one."

He rushed on to statistics about gold reserves held in Fort Knox and the

Bank of England. The IOR had very friendly connections with big foreign banks like Barclays of Britain, Sumitomo of Japan, Union Bank of Switzerland. "I also represent you, Holiness, on the board of twenty Italian banks."

"Me?" Patrick was astonished and even Charley seemed to blink. "Why?"

"Because you have substantial holdings in them."

The Pope threw his hands up in surprise, disturbing Charley's contemplation. "Forgive my asking, but where do I get all this cash you invest for me?"

"Apart from holdings in equity markets around the world, we also provide certain, well, services."

"Tell me more."

The Pope has the mind of a seminarian, thought Radowski, who was finding his questions embarrassing. As St. Paul Marcinkus so wisely said, "You can't run the Church on Hail Marys."

"Well, Holiness, we channel money to hard currency havens."

"Such as?"

"Switzerland, chiefly."

"And it comes from . . . ?"

Radowski gulped. "It is often wired to us from abroad."

"From where in particular?"

"It could be from anywhere, from anything."

"Gambling casinos, Pawel, racing tracks?"

"Perhaps. Well . . . yes."

"I see. This money from abroad, is it—?" Patrick made a gesture with his hand.

"Hot?"

"Whatever hot is, yes."

"It is money, Holiness, which is, shall we say, acquired in an unspecified manner and which its owners do not want to be traced?"

"By unspecified, you mean crooked?"

"No, no, no, Holiness. I mean I honestly do not know its origins and I have no legal right to ask."

The Pope looked mystified. "But . . . but, Pawel, it might come from mobsters, pimps, illegal gamblers, burglars, kidnapers, drug smugglers, arms dealers—and you might be helping them place the proceeds into legitimate businesses. Don't you *want* to know about this money you are transferring?"

Radowski had an urge to say that bankers are not father-confessors.

"I assure you," he spluttered, "we do nothing illegal." He hurriedly pressed another button. "As you see from this graphic, the IOR is approximately the size of the Bank of Montreal and—"

Patrick looked up at the crucifix above Radowski's head.

Lord, forgive us for we know not what we do.

Abruptly: "Close it down, Pawel."

"The computer?"

"The bank."

"How long for, Holiness?"

"For good," the Pope said.

Chapter Forty-two

B ack in his quarters, Patrick could not hide from Montefiori his disgust at what had been going on under the auspices of the Holy See.

"It might not be so easy to close the bank, Holiness. Profits help the Vatican's deficit, which amounts to several million dollars. You may have noticed that Vatican City is beginning to look rather like Jericho after the trumpet blast."

"What about Peter's Pence?"

"Dried up during the last years of John Paul, even from Cologne and Boston. Collections here in Italy would not buy you a tutti-frutti ice cream." The cardinal sniffed. "To be honest, many prelates are pining for the good old Mafia-like days when the Church sold 'protection.'"

"I beg your pardon."

"Indulgences," Montefiori sighed. "What a system that was. High prices, infinite demand, endless supply, and no outlay to speak of."

"Your suggestions."

"You could sell raffle tickets at general audiences. Or do advertisements for soft drinks. 'The Pope Drinks Coke' sort of thing."

"Be serious, Giuseppe."

"Very well, Holiness. In the short term, the Vatican Bank is likely to have a liquidity problem."

"Then," Patrick said bluntly, "we will sell our assets."

247

"Not enough to pay off the creditors. Radowski tells me most of the money is out on long-term loans."

"Then we will raise the money some other way."

"How?" Montefiori asked, scowling. "By selling off St. Peter's to Americans so they can take it home brick by brick?"

That was when the *Pietà* came into the reckoning.

"We will have to sell off works of art, Giuseppe."

"Not so easy," Montefiori said, as steadily as he could manage. "Sell off too many at once and prices will plummet on the world market."

The Pope remembered a recent article in *Time*. Turner's long-lost *Juliet and Her Nurse*, left in the will of an old lady from Buenos Aires, had fetched a record $250 million at an auction in New York. The irony was, it was destroyed two days later in a fire before insurance terms had been settled.

"Is the *Pietà* in that class, Giuseppe?"

Montefiori puffed out his chest. "Better."

"Find out how much it is worth, please."

On such a topic, no inquiry coming from the Secretary of State could be called discreet. He came back to report:

"At least $400 million."

The Pope was astonished. That was five times as much as the Vatican received in 1929 to compensate it for property confiscated when Italy was unified in the nineteenth century.

Montefiori said haughtily, "The *Pietà* is surely worth a couple of jetliners. After all, it has already lasted five centuries, which is about 480 years more than the old jumbo jets."

"But who could afford it, Giuseppe?"

"A consortium, I dare say. But you cannot be serious. You would never be forgiven."

"Will God forgive me for keeping open the Vatican Bank? He has given me the task of preaching the Gospel, not being the curator of a museum."

"If you are still short of cash," Montefiori said, "you could always rifle the Picture Gallery."

It was meant as sarcasm but, minutes later, he was by the Pope's side when he asked, "This Pinturrichio, what do you reckon, Giuseppe?"

Montefiori went ahead without answering and stood in front of

Raphael's *Madonna of Foligno*. After gazing at it for a few moments without comment he moved to *The Transfiguration*.

"Raphael's last work, Holiness. He was aged thirty-seven and dying. It was reckoned by Sir Joshua Reynolds to be the greatest panel painting of all time."

Montefiori was bearing up bravely. After all, not long ago he had witnessed the burning of the last secret of Our Lady of Fátima.

"The *Pietà*, together with these two masterpieces, Holiness, should be enough for your present purposes."

Chapter Forty-three

The Pope received a visit from three South American cardinals: the metropolitans of Brazil, Mexico and Argentina. Word was that they had come as a group to complain about *Splendor Vitae*.

When Ayatollah Hourani heard of this trip from his Foreign Minister, he went black with anger.

When Washington heard of it from the Rome station of the CIA, there was interest bordering on alarm. What if the cardinals had not come to discuss sex and birth control but something else?

President Delaney failed to pick up the hint. He had troubles enough elsewhere. In Senate hearings, his latest nominee to the Supreme Court, Theobald Boyce, who, he said, was as straight and reliable as they come, confessed to having had a sex change from her to him when she/he was twenty-three, after bearing two children. He was also a kleptomaniac, the proof being he had stolen two golden eagle bookends from the Oval Office under Delaney's nose.

The CIA alarm over the Pope was more than justified.

The three cardinals flew to Rome at Patrick's request and the encyclical was not even mentioned. For the four days of their stay, the Pope closeted himself away with them. Not even Montefiori was allowed in.

Gonzales of Rio, Brazil, represented 200 million Catholics; Ernesto of Mexico, 100 million; Fonseca of Argentina, 48 million.

Through videos, they showed the Pope how their people were massed in slums and shantytowns without basic necessities. No bread, no drinking water. The air, no longer healthy and invisible, was a lethal yellow. Tens of thousands of children had measles, gastroenteritis, cholera.

In one film, the Pope saw a mile-long line of abandoned babies. On the streets of São Paulo, 2 million urchins tried to scrape a living. Girls as young as eleven were already washed-out by prostitution.

"Why, my friends?" the Pope asked, stroking Charley's hard-boned head for comfort.

The cardinals traced their misery way back to the 1970s. International banks were flush with OPEC deposits. They preferred to lend to countries, known as "ever-greens"; unlike private companies, they could not renege on their debts or disappear overnight. Billions of dollars poured into Central and Latin America.

"My country," said Mexico, "borrowed $13 billion in 1982. We had good collateral. Oil, silver and copper."

Brazil and Argentina said their countries, too, had received jumbo-sized loans. It was a disaster. There were three world recessions, oil prices dipped. Borrowing led to massive inflation. Soon, developing countries could not pay back their loans. Worse, they could not even afford the interest on them.

So they kept devaluing and borrowed ever more to service their loans. As a result, debts grew from hills into mountains.

They asked for a second loan just to pay back the interest on the first. They borrowed money on paper only to give it straight back on paper to the lender. They cut back on social services, on schools and hospitals. They raised taxes sky-high. It did no good.

"However much our people sweated and starved," said Rio, "the debt grew. Our civilian government was only twenty years old when it was ousted by the military. Our starving millions did not object. What is freedom without bread? Besides, only a fascist dictatorship could stop them rebelling against impossible living conditions."

In spite of destitution, the International Monetary Fund kept saying,

"Cut! Cut imports, federal budgets, housing subsidies, social services. Raise! Raise taxes, the price of gasoline and electricity."

"Why, my friends?" the Pope said with added anguish.

"To pay back the gringos, Holiness."

"The bankers?"

They nodded. "From Germany, Japan, Britain, but mostly from the USA."

"By the 1980s, we owed $49 billion," said Argentina.

Mexico owed $95 billion, while Brazil topped them all with debts of $102 billion.

Ten years into an economic miracle, after squeezing their own poor for nearly three decades, Latin America owed on average 80 percent *more* than at the beginning.

"Our people," complained Argentina, "are the best educated on the continent. We are self-sufficient in oil and the third biggest grain-exporter in the world. Year after year, we export far more than we import, and we get steadily poorer."

"How about you?" the Pope asked Mexico. "Is not your country part of the North American Free Trade Agreement?"

"Disaster," the cardinal said. "Yet we, too, are awash with oil, 64.5 billion barrels of reserves. PEMEX, our state-owned petroleum company, makes a fortune each year. For foreign bankers. Now the government is talking about selling it off, with our state electric company, to foreigners in violation of Article 27 of our Constitution."

Rio, white-faced, said: "Holiness, you know my country well. We export steel, coffee, grain, soybeans. We have a trade surplus each year of billions of U.S. dollars. Yet still our little ones starve."

"Terrible," the Pope kept saying, and Charley, sensitive to Patrick's every switch of mood, shook his head in disbelief.

Inflation in the three countries ranged from 600 to 2,000 percent.

"My country," said Brazil, "was the last in the world to abolish slavery and now we are enslaved worse than ever."

"No one saves a cent in my country," said Argentina. "After President Menem brought inflation down, it went back up to two thousand percent.

252

Top executives club together so that, from their combined salaries, this month one of them will have a TV set, next month another and so on."

"Again and again," said Mexico, "we have rescheduled our debts. Very harsh terms, Holiness. During the peso crisis of 1994–95 we borrowed another $26 billion. We couldn't repay, so we borrowed again."

"Why do you try to repay?" the Pope wanted to know.

Argentina answered him. "Our Minister of Finance once said on TV, 'We will pay no more.' Within the hour, he got a call from U.S. Treasury Secretary Donald Wilks. He said, 'Sure, Miguel, you are okay for oil and grain. But what about when your cancer patients scream out for morphine, your diabetics go into comas for lack of insulin? When you have no kidney machines, no heart-lung machines, no anesthetics for pulling teeth or taking out children's appendices? When your currency is no longer quoted on the world markets, when no one will buy a grain of wheat from you, and your ships are not welcomed in any port and no one will sell you tanks or airplanes, tractors or cars? Miguel, how will you explain *that* to your people?' That is why, Holiness, we try to pay."

Pope Patrick listened for four days, and thought about what he had heard through each long night. He prayed with the cardinals and said Mass with them. Afterward, he explained to them what he intended to do.

Newsweek said, "The three Latin American cardinals left the Vatican white and speechless with rage. They had been unable to budge Patrick on the contents of *Splendor Vitae*."

The truth was, they knelt and kissed his hand, saying, "Only you can help us, Holiness." They pledged him their undivided loyalty.

Chapter Forty-four

Rottweiler and Frangipani were more wary than ever when the Pope summoned them for another consultation.

"Business ethics, gentlemen," he said.

Frangipani, the naïve liberal, was relieved. A boring subject but far less explosive than sex.

In answer to the Pope's "What is usury?" they replied jointly, "Lending money at interest."

"And what does the Bible say about it?"

Rottweiler, the expert on sin, said, "That it is wrong."

"You remember what Aristotle called usury, Josef?"

"The birth of money from money."

"Yes, economic incest," Patrick said. "Even pagans knew that taking interest on a loan is a crime."

"True," said Frangipani, who didn't care one way or the other.

"Jesus said, 'Lend, hoping to gain *nothing* thereby.' Who gave permission for what the Lord forbade? Not the Church. She followed his teaching from age to age. What happened to a Christian who charged interest on a loan?"

"He was made an outlaw," Frangipani said, still uninterested. "He was refused absolution and Christian burial until he made restitution."

Patrick took a thick yellow document out of a drawer and slammed it on his desk. Both cardinals eyed it with suspicion.

"My doctoral thesis on usury," the Pope explained. "Every Father and great theologian, every Council of the Church, every single papal document dealing with the taking of interest said it is *wrong*. And Dante—"

"He put moneylenders in the hottest place in hell."

"Exactly, Francesco. Those were the only sort of people the Lord got violent with when he threw them out of the Temple." Patrick looked solemnly from one cardinal to the other. "Without exception, without qualification, every age of the Church said usury is wrong."

From boredom, the cardinals switched to apprehension. Rottweiler knocked over his coffee cup.

"Who was it, Josef, first taught it was all right to take interest on a loan?"

"Calvin."

"Precisely. One of the first Protestants in what is still the most Protestant city in the world, Geneva. Now, why did *we* betray our great tradition?"

"Hardly *betray*," objected Frangipani. "We *developed* it."

The Pope responded heatedly. "Was it not a betrayal to turn our backs on two thousand years of Catholic teaching?"

"It really *is* more complicated than that," Frangipani began. "It was only after the Middle Ages that people saw that money actually made money. Why shouldn't the lender gain something from his money when the merchant to whom he lends it makes a profit?"

"There," the Pope exploded, "speaks common sense, even when it is against the whole Bible, including the Gospels."

Frangipani was taken aback by the fierceness of the Pope's reaction.

"Tell me, Francesco, your authority for denying the Lord?"

"You mean a statement of Pope or Council?"

Patrick nodded.

Frangipani shrugged. "I haven't one."

"How could you have one? Benedict XIV in an encyclical *Vix Pervenit* in 1745 attacked usury in exactly the same terms that Paul VI attacked contraception in *Humanae Vitae* in 1968. Benedict said whoever takes interest on a loan, no matter how big the interest, no matter what reasons he gives for taking interest, sins against justice and must repay the borrower. Any exception is unthinkable."

Frangipani was puzzled. "When, then, did the change take place? Because obviously the Church has changed."

Rottweiler explained. "In 1830, the Holy Office, with Pius VIII's approval, said that whoever charges a fixed rate of interest on a loan is not to be disturbed."

"*Really!*" the Pope said. "A *fixed* rate of interest. The implication being, if the rate is fixed and not too high, it is all right."

The cardinals nodded.

"Pius VIII might as well have said," Patrick continued, "that anyone who tells an occasional lie or sleeps with a prostitute only now and again is not to be disturbed."

Once more, the cardinals looked at each other, worriedly.

"The Church, my friends, always dealt more harshly with the usurer than with liars or fornicators. No Christian burial for *him*. He was worse even than an adulterous Pope."

Rottweiler had to admit that the Church had never said that charging interest was right. On the contrary, it had always said officially that usury, like contraception, was *in principle* wrong.

Patrick tried to keep calm. Dr. Gadda kept warning him that too much excitement would make his headaches unendurable. He lowered his voice as he said:

"The Church could hardly say otherwise, could it, Josef, in view of its tradition? No, in 1830 was sown the seed of the Church's present tragedy. From then on, downhill all the way. Pius IX entrusted the Patrimony of St. Peter to the Rothschilds and ordered nuncios to invest Vatican funds with foreign banks at the highest interest."

"I must object," Frangipani said.

"On what grounds, Francesco? Can you not see the sorry consequences of leaving bankers with a quiet conscience? Why, we even had a Vatican Bank, which is rather like a Vatican Whorehouse or a Vatican Abortion Clinic."

Frangipani tried to interrupt. "Holiness—"

"Wait! Popes and bishops themselves have acted as bankers and charged interest on loans. A hundred years before Marcinkus got involved with crooks like Sindona and Calvi, Leo XIII was not just gambling on the stock exchange, he tried to found the Union Général, an international Catholic Bank. Incredible! Thank God it went bust with debts of a million lire."

"I'm sorry to disagree," Frangipani said, "but where would we be without banks?"

"I'll show you where we *are* because of them."

The Pope played them the videos left him by the Latin American cardinals.

"These," the Pope said finally, "are the results of usury in the modern world. I have been speaking with Radowski. Bankers do not ask, 'How can I help the poor?' but 'How can I squeeze them further—regardless?' By their fruits you shall know them. These"—he indicated the videotapes—"are the fruits of the banking system."

There was a long, pained silence. The cardinals shared in the Pope's great grief while Charley looked up at him soulfully. At length:

"The terrible truth is, my friends, we, especially recent Popes, have, by our silence, condoned the greatest of all sins. Yet Christianity is the religion of a Poor Man who sided with the weak and the hungry. If only we, his disciples, had seen Christ in the poor as clearly as we see him in the Eucharist! If only our faith had seen him in the lack of bread as clearly as in the Bread!"

Rottweiler was thinking he had never had such a theological lesson when the Pope added:

"Make no mistake about it, it is more urgent for us to be on the side of the poor than to say Mass or celebrate the sacraments." He put his hands to his burning forehead. "I and my predecessors have condemned contraception and remained silent in face of the Great Sin, the oppression of the poor."

"It is true," Rottweiler mused. "We have endlessly attacked what people do in bed and said almost nothing about what wicked businessmen do in the marketplace."

"Be careful, Holiness," Frangipani warned. "If you attack the banks, you will seem to be the enemy of capitalism itself."

"And rightly," Patrick replied with white heat. "Whether Jesus was a socialist is debatable. One thing's sure: he was no capitalist. What *is* capitalism? Maynard Keynes called it an infinite hunger for riches. Yes, it is absolutely irreligious."

"But, Holiness," Frangipani almost whimpered. He could not continue. The implications of the Pope's views were too terrible to contemplate.

"Capitalism, Francesco, puts not God and his poor in the first place but mammon. It spreads the idolatry of wealth. Happy are the greedy for they shall possess the earth. Happy the violent, the proud, those with souls like broomsticks. God bless Dives and God help hungry, lice-infested Lazarus at his gate."

He paused momentarily.

"The strange thing is, capitalists see no connection at all between religion and economics. Maybe not *so* strange. We, the Church, handed over economics to Satan. As if there is natural law for sex but not for commerce, except to make the most money in any way you like. Even though millions starve in consequence."

Frangipani was tempted to argue that the Pope's views went out of fashion with Gothic cathedrals, but he could still see in his mind's eye the video of black and brown children with empty potbellies and spindly legs.

"Capitalism," Patrick mused, "is the perfect form of colonialism. It is *the* way to take over a country. No need for an invasion, that is far too costly in money and men. Just lend a country enough cash, charge a high enough rate of interest, and the great-great-grandchildren of those foolish or needy enough to borrow will go on paying back forever and ever."

"And no amen." Montefiori had slipped into the room and heard the tail end of the discussion. "What do you intend to do about it, Holiness?"

Lord, did I not put on a loincloth and proclaim myself Chieftain of the poor? Help me to help my friends from Marajo and all like them in the continents of the poor.

"Holiness?" Montefiori repeated.

"I am writing an encyclical to be called, *Defender of the Poor*. Also, in spite of President Delaney's attempts to thwart me, I intend to address the United Nations."

Chapter Forty-five

"You look upset, Holiness."

Frank and the Pope were having a rare hour of relaxation at the billiard table.

"I guess I am, Frank."

He expressed dismay that bankers, desk murderers, tyrants in pin-striped suits, should have the power to ruin the lives of people far away. They would steal the pennies from dead men's eyes. They reminded him of the absentee English landlords who had bled his people dry and confiscated all their produce during the great famines of the 1840s.

"Worst of all, Frank, allowing interest just sort of sneaked into the Church, like the safe-period method of avoiding conception. Not a whimper of protest from anyone. Not even when the rich took control of arithmetic, giving subtraction and division to the poor and keeping addition and multiplication for themselves."

Frank, having missed an easy red, said, "Paul VI wrote about the imperialism of money in *Populorum Progressio*. Didn't he say capitalism keeps the poor poor and the rich rich? And didn't John Paul II speak of brutal forms of capitalism?"

"True. But neither got to the root of the problem: the evil of interest, which is far worse than contraception; the truth that *all* forms of capitalism are brutal. I worked in South America, I saw the results firsthand. Once-beautiful lands no longer fit for people. Kiddies playing in gutters and feeding

259

off garbage like rats. Communities living in cardboard cities. Whole nations virtually kidnaped and held to ransom."

The Pope shook Frank by interrupting his shot to ask:

"How *can* people be rich without mortal sin?"

"You mean that, Holiness?"

"You've read the Gospel. It's harder for a rich man to get into heaven than for a camel to squeeze through the eye of a needle."

"My father was a multimillionaire."

Patrick's face creased into a grin. "With God, impossible things are possible. Besides, with a son like you, how could your parents *not* get to heaven?"

Frank smiled, thinking fondly of his parents.

After making a lucky cannon the Pope added, "I knew your family was rich."

Frank blinked.

"I heard, too, that you had given all your money away. It didn't surprise me."

Frank gestured as if to say, How could even a Pope know that?

"What gets me, Frank, is that a dealer in New York can press a button and make more in a few seconds by playing the money markets than most men could make by the sweat of their brows in a hundred lifetimes. Some speak as if insider dealing is what is wrong. No. Whatever ends in such massive injustice must be wrong."

"American enterprise," Frank chuckled.

"Don't misunderstand me. I love the States. It was my people's refuge in the dark old days of the scatter for America. But the Bible is right when it says, '*Love of money* is the root of all evil.'"

"My father was a broker," Frank admitted. "He loved the idea of growing rich in his sleep. When the Nikkei or the Dow Jones fell a point or two, it was like a death in the family."

When the Pope laughed, it made him wince. "There is half a million people in the States with over $2 million and 40 million on food stamps. When did your bishops write a pastoral on that?"

"Cardinal Burns never did." Frank hesitated before adding, "You make it sound as if capitalism is worse than old-style communism."

The Pope missed his next shot. "Both godless. Yet, to be honest, I feel capitalism is more so. It has wrecked more lives than Stalin ever did. It's handed over millions in the Third World to a slavery worse than anything Abe Lincoln condemned in the old cotton plantations. If capitalists could market the elastic their consciences are made of, they'd make another fortune."

"Are you saying you regret the passing of communism, Holiness?"

The Pope peered into the middle distance. "You know, sometimes I wonder whether the Church missed its big chance when Lenin picked up Marx before we did."

Frank said, "From each according to his capacity, to each according to his needs."

"Who said that first?"

"Lenin?"

"No, Frank. St. Luke in Chapter 2 of the Acts. The first Christians sold everything and distributed the proceeds to the poor as any had need of it. And Chapter 4 says, 'There was not one needy person among them, for whoever owned land or houses sold them and brought the proceeds to the feet of the apostles and distribution was made according to the needs of each.'"

"Christian communism," Frank said.

"Surely. The only communism left in the world. You know, Church Fathers had the same idea as your native Americans. The earth, the air, the rivers, the land are God's gifts to all his children. It's an obscenity to think that a few can grab whatever they want for themselves."

The Pope went on to speak of a poem, written years before by an Irish communist, Liam MacGabhann. He was from Valentia Island off the coast of County Kerry. The islanders burned his books for their un-Christian sentiments.

"Ah, well, Frank, other times, other values. His poem shows how good the heart of man naturally is."

Leaning on his cue, Patrick began to recite in his gentle Mayo accent:

"I have seen rich men go feasting and making din,
 I have seen the rich men's homes and the wealth therein.

261

And I would that their wealth and wares to the winds were hurled
For the poor of the world, O Christ, the poor of the world.

Eyes at the rich men's windows watch and want,
Hearts to the rich men's music leap and pant,
Oh, I would that this wine and gold on the streets were hurled
For the poor of the world, O Christ, the poor of the world.

They call You kind, O Baby, weren't you born
For the sceptre of barren reed and the crown of thorn?
Have you no hosting spears, no flag unfurled
For the poor of the world, O Christ, the poor of the world?

I would smash the panes of the rich men's windows in,
I would mingle the cry of the poor with their callous din.
But I only pray by the straw where a Babe lies curled,
For the poor of the world, O Christ, the poor of the world."

"I like it," Frank said, genuinely impressed. "A bloodless revolution in the style of Christ."

"Indeed. I quoted a bit of that poem in conclave. I don't think they really grasped what I was getting at."

That misunderstanding was soon to be rectified.

Chapter Forty-six

It finally got through to Roone Delaney that the Pope was up to no good. Intelligence sources told him that the Vatican Bank had closed *sine die* and was disposing of its assets. The heads of all the top U.S. banks asked the White House for an explanation. Abe Cornberg of Citicorp called the President personally.

"Roone, don't you see that the failure of any bank anywhere is a procking worry in these troubled times?"

After the call, Delaney needed something to take his mind off things. He was no great brain. In fact, he was not qualified for anything except to be President of the United States. He switched on his tape of the "Bead of Sweat" debate. He was his own greatest fan.

"Jesus," he whistled, "Stallone looks as if he's using one hand to juggle with his balls, the other to squeeze toothpaste back into the tube."

Stallone had just proved he hadn't the beef to fill a bun let alone the presidency by hesitating to zap 150 million Muslims, whereas he, Nuke Delaney, had drooled at the prospect of wiping them all off the face of the earth.

"After all," the TV Delaney said, "they're all in favor of chopping off hands and legs, aren't they?"

His viewing was interrupted by Bill Huggard, who bore the third request from the Pope to address the United Nations.

Delaney had been advised by his own aides, as well as by Prime Minister

Weaver, to refuse the little guy from the Vatican entry to the land of the free. He immediately drafted a reply to the Pope.

Unfortunately, he told him, he had promised more than he could deliver. The U.N. was resisting pressure these days from the only superpower. The President regretted, etc.

It made no difference. The U.N. Secretary General was a Brazilian. A quiet word from Cardinal Gonzales and a date was fixed for the Pope to make his second trip abroad, this time to address the General Assembly in New York.

He made no plans, as Cardinal Burns had hoped, to visit St. Patrick's, the pseudo-Gothic cathedral on a block between Fifth and Madison. There was to be no papal Mass in Yankee Stadium. He turned down a meeting with President Delaney, who offered to fly in from Washington for a chat and photo session in the Waldorf-Astoria.

The Pontiff gave no advance script. Without fuss, accompanied only by Cardinal Montefiori, Frank Kerrigan and his doctor, he left Rome's Fiumicino at midday, wearing his white cassock and scarlet cloak. From Kennedy Airport in New York he was immediately transported in a limousine along streets no more crowded than usual.

Cardinal Burns, who was watching on television, said to his secretary, "Did you see that, Harry? He takes his shoes off every goddamn place like he was Japanese, but not in New York. He doesn't even have the decency to invite me to sit next to him in the U.N. What have we procking done to deserve *this?*"

The motorcade stopped outside the U.N. building in Manhattan. Patrick was greeted by the Secretary General. He prayed briefly in the nondenominational meditation hall before being whisked up to the thirty-eighth floor for a mineral water.

There were to be no frills, no distractions from the discourse he was to give.

At the appointed hour, the Secretary General escorted him down the center aisle to the platform. The hall was filled to capacity with three thousand delegates and distinguished VIPs. The Pope sat in a large beige leather chair while he was greeted formally by the Secretary General.

Now it was his turn. *Lord, be in my heart and on my lips.*

He did not give the expected polished hour-long address. Instead, he preached a brief and simple sermon in thickly accented French, which was instantaneously translated into forty-two languages and beamed by satellite across the world.

Standing at the green marble rostrum, the Pope, who never once raised his voice, began with this text: "Give to him who asks and from him who would borrow from you do not turn away.

"My sisters and my brothers, I speak for the poor as Jesus did. I also speak against the rich as Jesus did. For the rich have become rich at the poor's expense.

"In the Third World—once called developing but developing no longer—country after country is being systematically exploited by a few rich Western nations.

"In particular, I censure those nations' bankers. The Church has been silent for too long. It has allowed the greedy to charge huge interest on loans to the poor of the world.

"These bankers force men, women and children to live in slums and on sidewalks, to eat off garbage dumps, so that they themselves can live in luxury in New York and London, Paris and Berlin, Tokyo and Zurich.

"In the words of the great Abraham Lincoln, they are 'wringing their bread from the sweat of other men's faces.'

"Many of these crushers of dreams call themselves Christians. They are not. Rather, barbarians, slave traders, thieves of liberty, destroyers of civilizations. They are pirates at the Lord's Supper and their creed is greed.

"Even a Christian cannot be charitable toward avarice or forgiving of brutality. The Sermon on the Mount does not commend loan sharks and bloodsuckers. There is no Christlike way of starving babies for profit.

"Without rancor, indeed with deep compassion for men on the brink of Hell, and in order to bring them to their senses, I call them before the entire world the *enemies and crucifiers of Christ.* For two generations, they have descended on Africa and South America like plagues of locusts. They have plundered lands and, with iron jaws, skeletonized nations. They would charge the poor rent for their bodies, if they could, charge a levy on their breathing and tax their tears.

"I admit, to my shame, that for years the Vatican owned a bank. I have ordered it to be shut. Any proceeds will be given to the poor in reparation.

"To Catholics who have done wrong in this respect, I say, Take your greedy hands out of the pockets of the poor and your feet off their necks. Take your big spoons out of the orphans' soup bowls.

"As Martin Luther King said, 'Stop spending millions storing food surpluses and store them free of charge in the wrinkled bellies of the poor.'

"In Jesus' words, 'Repent and do good.'

"You have stolen billions; you must repay billions. Build roads, schools, hospitals, sewage works, factories, in atonement.

"If you refuse, I order the Catholic clergy, as of old, to refuse you absolution, communion and Christian burial. It would be a denial of the Gospel to grant you such blessings when you continue to victimize Jesus in the person of his poor.

"To debtor nations, I say, *Act together and you are invincible.* Do not connive at the injustices done to you. You have paid more than enough. I, the Pope, forbid you to sin by paying one more penny.

"Instead, demand compensation of those robbers who have colonized you and brought your once-proud lands to penury. End this slavery of your people. Drive out these financial *conquistadores.*

"Jamais plus l'injustice aux pauvres! L'injustice aux pauvres, jamais plus!

"To governments of the downtrodden, I say, Choose: either pay the international robber bankers *or* feed your starving people. Where does your duty lie? Do not be afraid. Remember scripture: God made the Dragon that He might laugh at him."

The Pope raised his right hand aloft, as if he held over the suffering world a lamp of hope beside a golden door.

"Remember, finally, you poor, you downtrodden, you huddled masses, that the Poor Man of Nazareth who died and rose again, stands beside you on bloodied feet, with his pierced workman's hands around your shoulders.

"God bless and keep you and grant you the liberty of the children of God."

The address, riveting in its quietness, had been too short, too imperious, for anyone to interrupt. Suddenly there was a burst of applause from the Brazilian delegation, followed by clapping and stampeding from Mexico, Argentina, Chile, Venezuela, Nigeria, Haiti. The Cuban representative put his fingers in his mouth and whistled. The delegation from Nicaragua burst through a security cordon to shake the Pope's hand.

The U.S. Ambassador, who had sat through the speech with a ruptured look on his face, went into a huddle with his British counterpart.

For the first time in months, the Soviet and Chinese representatives were seen deep in conversation.

The Ambassadors of Islamic nations left the hall, stony-eyed, giving nothing away.

Delaney had been watching on television. He felt out of luck, as though he had been hit by a meteorite. Several times during the speech, he screeched the name of his Lord. Afterward, he bit a leaf off the Swedish ivy, swallowing in the process a few red spider mites.

No sooner was the address over than his telephone started ringing. And ringing.

SHUT THE BANKS" was the headline in the Wall Street Journal. "POPE SAYS: STOP BURYING BANKERS," said the New York Times.

Patrick was accused by the media of meddling in matters outside his brief. He was called an economic pygmy or a crypto-Marxist. The *Los Angeles Times* wrote off the U.N. address in one word: "Bunk."

London's *Economist* said:

> The Pope's ineptitude in economics is inspired. Does he not realize that, if Western financial institutions stop lending to the Third World, the first victims will be the poor? And if the financial institutions go bust, as the Pope seems to want, what will become of the billions invested world-wide by pension and insurance funds which hold money in trust for ordinary working men and women? Does His Holiness have no fear of the dire consequences of his naïveté?

Some publications were less sure. In editorials, deep questions were asked: Is Western society as Christian as it imagines? Do not banks share the responsibility for keeping the poor in their poverty? Isn't it time that the Church turned its attention to social and economic problems instead of concentrating on personal morality and nostalgic festivals? Maybe the Pope is the conscience of the age.

Bishops and theologians thanked the Pope for restating the tradition of the Church—while doing their damnedest to soften its impact. Church finances could be badly hit by his U.N. address and *Defensor Pauperum* that soon followed it.

The encyclical impartially pleaded for justice for victimized peoples: the aborigines of Australia, the Maoris of New Zealand, the nationalists of Northern Ireland, the native Indians of North America. Their plight was a sin calling out for heavenly vengeance.

He pleaded with every rich parish to adopt a parish in the Third World. "Life is so short for doing good in, for being kind to one another."

The big surprise was his condemnation of both Pius IX and Leo XIII for speculating on the stock exchange and lending money at interest. Pius XII was criticized again for founding a Vatican Bank.

Even John Paul II was heavily censured as an à la carte Catholic. Against all Catholic tradition, he had not only welcomed the safe period, he was the first Pope in history to give even a grudging welcome to capitalism in his 1991 encyclical, *Centesimus Annus*.

Pope Patrick promised to use his influence to help close down all financial institutions, including banks and building societies, that did not lend money free of charge. He forbade Catholics to pay interest on loans: this encouraged loan sharks to persevere in their sins.

Excommunication for Catholic bankers meant they were to be refused the blessings of the Church, including the right to a Requiem Mass and Christian burial.

M urderous discussions went on in the boardrooms and offices all over the globe: in finance companies, stock exchanges, above all in banks.

The Pope had said they were barbarians? Jesus, they had Picassos and Renoirs on their office walls, and sometimes they even looked at them.

Lending without interest? That was as self-contradictory as boiled snow.

Already, some U.S. bankers were making wild predictions about the effects of the Pope's mischievous interference.

The predictions were not nearly wild enough.

Chapter Forty-seven

"Jesus Christ!" said Abe Cornberg of Citicorp.

Assigned a seat in an anteroom at the White House, he could not keep still. He walked up and down, chewing viciously on his Corona Corona while he waited to see the President.

Crammed into the smoky room were a dozen hard-faced, white-knuckled, eight-ulcered executives who represented the major banks in America. Wired up like puppets, they wore an earpiece and a mike in their lapels to keep them in touch with home base. Fluent in expletives, they tried to outshout each other in their abuse.

"That warped Irish chicken-plucking Pope-fart."

"Lousy soft-nosed son of a bitch, calling *us* loan sharks."

"Tit-nosed harp."

"*Mamzer*, prick, punk, court jester, nutball, John Brown, tea bag, *schmuck* of a commie bastard."

"Judas Iscariot, wanting to knock us out of the ballpark."

They spoke with utter sincerity. The world would not turn without them. They *were* civilization.

"I warned you long ago, okay?" The speaker was Tom Willows, the bearlike but amiable Chairman of the Federal Reserve Board. To Cornberg: "Told you not to make huge long-term loans to Brazil. What is it, still forty-five percent of shareholders' equity?"

Goldie Grubb, head of Chase Bank, was in shock and held his big belly like a medicine ball. "We have forty-nine percent exposure, forty-nine *per-procking-cent*, donchaknow, in Mexico? This shithead of a Pope should be strung upside down outside his cathedral like Mussolini."

He got on his phone to order a sandwich from a takeout till he remembered where he was.

Tom Willows had said over and over that the sixteen or so leading U.S. banks had broken all the rules by lending long and borrowing short. They had compounded their stupidity by borrowing from a few big lenders who could practically yank their money out at a minute's notice.

"The Pope's not so persuasive," said one squint-eyed banker with a beard and hairs coming out of his nostrils like severed electric cables. "When did he get Catholics to stop using contraceptives?"

"I reckon," Cornberg chipped in, "he could persuade atheists to stop paying their bills. I can even see millions of Jews converting overnight and claiming financial asylum."

Bill Huggard opened the door. A dismal man with a nose redder than a traffic cone, he wore a wet wispy mustache that looked as if it objected to being there.

"The President will see you now."

Angry bankers rushed down the hall into the Oval Office as the sun peeped in through the French windows. The White House horticulturist was meanwhile carrying out the Swedish ivy.

Delaney stood next to Treasury Secretary Donald Wilks, who looked as if he had just died and become the ghost of his former self.

"Well, gentlemen," the President began breezily, after giving each a Jell-O handshake, "you have something to say."

"Yeah," said Cornberg. "Congratulations, Roone, on being the last Catholic President of the United States."

"Address the President as Mr. President," chief aide Bill Huggard demanded fussily. In his starched shirt, he looked like a turtle with diarrhea.

"Gentlemen, is this some kind of a joke?" said Delaney, confronted by just about the unfunniest sea of faces he had seen since his one and only summit with the leaders of Russia.

Cornberg acted as spokesperson.

"Mr. President, since the Pope's case of shit-and-run at the U.N., the U.S. of A. has been in deep trouble. This could be worse than 1929."

"Keep calm, Abe," the President said, looking like a fan dancer without a fan. "I'm no Herbert Hoover."

"Listen," Cornberg said, struggling to control himself, "that Irish guy of yours—"

"He's not *mine*," Delaney cut in, as if the Pope were an illegitimate baby. Gazing at the gold-framed bullet which, alas, had narrowly missed the Pope, he gulped, "It's still Washington on the dollar bill. Well, isn't it?"

Only that morning, the *Post* had reminded its readers of Pius IX's infamous words that America was the only country in the world where he could be King.

Cornberg pressed home his attack.

"The word 'bankrupt' takes on a whole new meaning when it's applied to *banks*. We trade in confidence. Every time that guy in Rome opens his mouth we feel the breeze."

His hot breath hit Delaney between the eyes.

"I tell you," Cornberg said, "that procking Pope will have us all belly-up if debtor nations renege on us at once."

"Delete 'procking,' " said Huggard.

"So, Abe, we blackball them."

"We can't blackball the entire Third World," Cornberg almost screamed.

Jenkins, president of the Bank of America, who had forgotten to put on his hairpiece so he looked like his grandfather, intervened. "The Pope has 600 million supporters in Latin America alone and he's told 'em it's a *sin* to pay what they owe."

"He's recommending a debtors' cartel," Cornberg explained. "It only takes three of the big ones, say, Brazil, Mexico and Argentina, to refuse payment at the same time and—"

"The whole U.S. banking system," Jenkins concluded, "will go down the tubes. Ditto every state and city in the Union that owes money. We won't even be able to afford oil."

"Gentlemen," the President pleaded, as his back twisted into knots, "alarmist talk. We've heard this bilge for thirty-five years and more."

"It's happening *now*," said Cornberg. "Almost every nation is threatening to withdraw funds from the U.S. and switch them to Frankfurt, London, Paris and Geneva."

"Why to there?" asked Delaney, turning as white as the Washington Monument.

"Because they're good Protestant places like West Virginia," said Cornberg, "and the Pope's a procking Catholic. Like *you*, Roone."

"Mr. *President*," Huggard insisted.

Cornberg ignored him. "Let's face it, you talk more about Jesus and God than any bishop. You don't hear the Chancellor in Berlin or the P.M. in London talking endless shit about God."

"Delete 'shit,' " said Huggard.

"All I said, Abe, was God bless America."

"Well, he ain't been listening," said Grubb of Chase Bank, known as Goldie because his mouth was full of bullion.

"Roone," said Cornberg, "the Arabs are not subtle like us. When you talk drivel about your faith in Jesus Christ they think you mean it. How're they to know you're even more irreligious than Jack Kennedy or Richard Millstone Nixon?"

"One word from President Hourani and the whole Islamic world will kiss us good-bye," said Grubb.

Cornberg was tapping his earpiece. He could not sleep at night without something in his ear; it did not feel right. He'd picked up an item of news.

"I wondered why Hailey of J. P. Morgan isn't here. He's just resigned."

"No!" came from a dozen throats, as though eighty-year-old Hailey had just raped the First Lady on the White House lawn.

"The nut told a press conference that, as a sincere Catholic and Knight of Columbanus, he can't continue in banking after what the Pope said to the U.N."

"I'm a Catholic, too," the President protested, "but does that stop me doing what is right?"

"Procking Patrick," said the squint-eyed banker, "worse than Gaddafi ever was."

"D'you *mind*," cut in the President, in a mosquito whine, "you are talking about the Holy Father."

"Holy Father?" shouted Cornberg. "Holy Shit!"

"Delete 'Holy Shit,' " said Huggard.

"Look, Roone," Cornberg said, "the Arabs know there are 65 million Catholics in the U.S. and you are the chief layman. They really think you might try and shut down the banks with all their petrodollars in it. Or go soft on debtor nations, mostly Catholics, who renege on their debts."

"Money's really tight, Mr. President," put in Jenkins of the Bank of America. "If the Arabs pull the plug on us—"

"The price of gold is up seventy-five dollars an ounce." Cornberg passed on information from the head office. "And, yeah, wait a second, the run on the dollar has begun. Telegraphic transfers to the Cayman Islands, Singapore, Bahamas, Luxembourg, even procking Liberia. In the last half hour foreigners have cashed in two billion sweet ones they had on call."

"So?" asked Delaney, whose business experience was limited to his father's ball-bearing company.

"If they next cash in their weekly, monthly and three-monthly deposits, we'll be out of funds. Far too much is on long-term loans to the Third World and now they might not even cough up the procking interest."

"Delete 'interest,' " said a confused Bill Huggard.

"Will someone delete this procking asshole of an aide?" snarled Cornberg.

The rhubarbing stopped as further news was awaited.

These top financiers, who thought they controlled the U.S. and, via the U.S., the entire world, were finding that someone was in control of *them*. They were not quite sure who it was, the plush Arabs or the poverty-stricken South Americans.

What difference did it make? The seemingly impregnable fortress of U.S. finance, after one short sermon from a sick old Irish priest, had proved to be a house of cards.

Cornberg announced that the World Bank and IMF buildings in downtown Washington had been set on fire and it wasn't militant Islamic Fundamentalists doing it. "The Pope satanized those places," he grumbled, "so no wonder."

"And the foreign exchanges?" whispered Delaney.

"The dollar's dropped five percent since opening," Cornberg replied. After twisting his earpiece: "Correction. It's now six and a half."

Donald Wilks of the Treasury, tight-lipped till now and swallowing tablets like it was his religion, suddenly shrieked, "They're dumping Treasury bills. By the million. Foreigners all liquidating. We're gonna be left with a paper mountain."

Before the implications of this had sunk in, news broke of small investors in every state of the Union pulling their savings out.

There were panic lines around every bank from New York to faraway Los Angeles where banks were not open yet and where people were camping on the sidewalk in the dark. NBC found that 70 percent of those lining up said they were loyal Catholics obeying the Pope.

"Remember the troubles of the eighties," groaned Goldie Grubb. "Continental Illinois, Ohio, savings and loans. Jesus, we're going to have zero liquidity."

"What's the problem here?"

Cornberg was shocked at such ignorance even in a President of the United States.

"Let me put it in a way you can follow, Roone. Take a different kind of run. Suppose every man, woman and child in America had an uncontrollable urge to shit at the same time—"

"No man would give up his seat to a lady, that's for sure," interjected Grubb.

"On the contrary," Cornberg said, "men would take over the women's rooms by force."

"You exaggerate," said Delaney, a ladies' man.

"No, Roone. Say this emergency happened in the rush hour. The driver and all the passengers in the New York subway wanted to shit *now*, as an imperative."

Huggard wanted to delete "shit" but realized there was now far too much of it around.

"The driver'd stop the train, Roone, and off they'd all go in a mad Gadarene rush for the johns. More crap in the streets of New York than Calcutta. Owners of limos telling their driver to step on the gas, a hundred bucks, no, he can name his price, if only he finds them a throne in time—and the driver equally urgent on his own account. In the courts, judge and jury and everyone else suddenly rush for the rest rooms. On the Hill, Congress suspends one sitting to take up another. At the North American Aerospace Command, personnel leave America defenseless while they all scramble for the thunderbox. In private homes, offices, restaurants, even nuclear plants, everyone knocking down doors for the privilege of a seat in a blessed water closet."

"What *is* all this about shit?" a dazed President wanted to know. "That couldn't happen, could it?"

"By the law of averages, no. Blastoff times are staggered. That's why we don't have one toilet per person at home, school and work. That'd mean nearly an extra billion in America. But suppose even one city or state were poisoned, there'd be hell to pay, people'd all instantly demand a toilet of their own and practically murder to get it."

"Come to the point, Abe."

"The point is, the entire American banking system has been poisoned by that little prock of a Pope. Everyone is shitting their pants to get their money out. It shouldn't happen. Banks run on the principle that it *can't* happen, that if even five percent of money is taken out at once it's a *disaster*. If all depositors want all their money out at once, as when there are rumors of a bank's collapse, or as now, when *all* the banks seem on the verge of collapse, the system can't take it. There ain't enough tellers or cash to pay 'em. In a word, there's just too much shit. You follow?"

Delaney nodded miserably. He wanted to go to the bathroom himself but feared it might cause a stampede.

The next item to appear on the bankers' wrist TVs was not unexpected. The Dow Jones had lost 518 points in a free fall. That was a guestimate. The Street's computers had gone haywire with thousands of transactions as yet unrecorded.

There was a massive dumping of blue-chip stock, including Boeing, General Motors and IBM. The exchanges sensed the big corporations were going to be short of funds. A hundred big companies were buying up their own stock to try and steady the market. A famous bit of old New York had become a second Wailing Wall.

276

All this while, Willows of the Fed sat silent and expressionless. He came to, to find all eyes fixed on him.

He smiled, shrugged his broad shoulders and readjusted his glasses, big and thick as flying goggles.

This hadn't crept up on them like a Stealth bomber. One day, he had said before several House committees, the world was going to tear up the USA's credit card. In spite of Newt Gingrich, the federal budget deficit was $2.5 trillion. The day of reckoning had arrived.

"C'mon, Tom," said Delaney, squirming in his swivel chair, "tell us what to do."

This was an ironic twist. By law, the President was forbidden to tell the Fed what to do. Besides, the Fed only guaranteed part of the loans of private investors, it didn't insure the banks themselves.

"Okay. This is not a crisis, Mr. President."

"Great, Tom!" cried an astonished Delaney. Lighting all those candles last night in the Virgin's honor had paid off.

"No, sir. You can manage a crisis. This is a meltdown."

"What's the solution?"

"Some problems don't have one."

"We've got to do *something*."

"Well, if I were you, Mr. President," Willows purred, "I'd get straight on the box and tell your fellow Americans everything's gonna be okay—"

"Really?" said Delaney.

"Because you've left your Church to become a devout capitalist."

"For Chrissake, Tom, be serious."

Tom Willows lifted his glasses and replaced them. "I don't know, Mr. President, what suggestion from me will be any more agreeable. The dollar's under strain. Our emergency funds can't cope with hemorrhaging on this scale."

"Give us the options," Delaney ordered.

"Okay. Double interest rates that are four percent too high already— that won't attract buyers anyway, only crush business confidence at home."

"Forget it."

"Okay. Go for a quickie tax cut which Congress won't pass in time, if at all."

277

"You said it."

"Okay. Print money to pay the small investors—"

Delaney tried snapping sweaty fingers in approval.

"But if we do that," Willows warned, "a guy'll need a cabful of dollars just to buy a can of Coke. Other countries'll avoid the greenback like an old whore with the clap. No one'd do business with us anymore."

"They can't do without America." The President's first article of faith came out wobbly.

A news flash. Heads of state from Brazil, Mexico, Chile, Panama and Argentina had arranged to meet in Brasília.

Willows commented, "*They* seem to think they can get by without us."

"If those procking Mexicans try defaulting on their loans," said Jenkins, knowing the size of his bank's portfolio south of the border, "we'll just take 'em over. We did it to Texas and California for less, didn't we?"

"Okay, we could freeze all foreign assets," Willows mused aloud. "We did it to Iran and Iraq a few years back."

Cornberg jumped in. "Who'd do business with us again?"

"Granted," Willows said, and the Treasury Secretary added that it was also against federal law.

Another news flash. Michelangelo's *Pietà* had been sold for $750 million.

"Should have asked for gold," grunted Grubb. "By this time tomorrow, it won't buy an entrance ticket to Disneyland."

"Sold to an Arab," Cornberg informed them.

"He'll probably give it pride of place in his harem," Jenkins muttered in disgust.

"Or," said Cornberg, "he'll hammer it to bits in accordance with his religion."

"So you reckon, Tom," the President picked up, "if we print more money—"

"We'll have Third World inflation here, at two thousand percent," Willows said. "And our kids'll be eating out of trash cans."

"That'd please the Pope," Cornberg said, through yellow teeth. "That procking commie bastard wants us to eat dirt, don't he?"

278

Chapter Forty-eight

After consulting his Defense Secretary, Secretary of State and the head of the CIA, Delaney got on the phone to New York.

"You alone, Tom?"

"Completely." Thomas Cardinal Burns glowered around him. "Even my guardian angel's deserted me."

He had lost $225,000 (personal) on the stock exchange in one day's dealing.

"One word, Tom. 'Tyrannicide.' "

Burns nearly choked on his Macanudo. "What?"

"You're the theologian, Tom. You even converted my wife."

"Don't blame *me*, Roone."

"As your Commander in Chief, I demand to know *when* a tyrant can be bumped off and *by whom*."

"Did you have someone special in mind, Roone?"

Minutes later, Frank Kerrigan received a call from Cardinal Burns.

"Listen carefully, son. I have received information that an attempt is to be made—sure no one else's on the line?—on the Pope's life."

"But, Eminence," Frank gasped, "how . . . why . . . ?"

"The CIA doesn't make mistakes, son. The attempt may take place in a private or a general audience, at Pontifical High Mass. It may even come from someone within the Vatican itself."

"But that's not—"

"John Paul I was assassinated, was he not?"

"I really don't know."

"Believe me, son, he was. As were many Pontiffs before him. Knifed, strangled, suffocated, poisoned."

Frank gulped. "I'll tell Cardinal Montefiori."

"Do that. And remind him of Jesus' own words: a man's enemies may be of his own household."

"You don't mean—"

"I do mean. It could be an archbishop, even a cardinal."

"Were any names mentioned?"

"Do you know a Cardinal Ragno? And an Archbishop Rossi?"

"Eminence, please—"

"It's up to you to keep your eyes skinned, son. Whether our Holy Father lives or dies may depend on you. But just keep my name out of it, you hear?"

After replacing the receiver, Frank switched on his computer. He had on it the entire *Annuario Pontificio*. Almost three-quarters of its two thousand pages were made up of the members of congregations and committees.

When he did a cross-check he found to his horror that Ragno and Rossi sat on exactly the same twenty committees. He remembered that Charley, whose nose was endowed with perfect intuition, had never been fond of either and he had to restrain him in their presence.

He rushed downstairs to discuss this latest information with Montefiori.

B y now, Delaney had telephoned Paris, Tokyo, Geneva and Berlin, saving the final call for Denise Weaver in London.

"Yes," she confirmed, "it's all happening here."

She had spent the day meeting with the Chancellor of the Exchequer, the governor of the Bank of England and the chairman of the stock exchange.

"The bank," she told the President, "is staying open at the weekend for only the third time in history."

"Don't tell me."

"Everything's gone wild in the money markets. As you know, the price of gold's gone through the roof. The yen has risen to the skies, causing the Chinese to hate the Japanese almost as much as the Russians. The European currency is up alarmingly, as if we'd all found huge new oil deposits. We'll never be able to sell a damn thing outside the E.U. We've dropped interest rates by three percent and still cash is pouring in."

"I know where from," Delaney sighed.

"I thought you looked green, Roone." She longed for the old days when you didn't have to see people you talked to on the line. "Wait a moment."

The P.M. was being briefed by an aide.

"Got it. Roone, Hourani has called for OPEC to meet in Riyadh tomorrow."

"What in blazes for?"

"Either to quadruple its oil price to compensate for the dollar's decline or, more likely, to move to a new currency for oil, maybe the E.U.'s."

"Gee-*sus!*"

"And you've heard about the meeting of debtor nations."

"Yeah. In Brasília."

"No, a further development. The South Americans are joining others in Lagos. Poland'll be there, and Romania, as well as Russia, Peru and the rest of the wogs."

"The Arabs couldn't be more pleased," Delaney said, "if Muhammad rose from the dead."

"Maybe he has, Roone."

"Right. How else can you explain the mess we're in?"

"Oh, well, Roone, this bugger of a Pope's made war on sex and money, what's next?"

"Oh my God."

The President slapped his forehead, nearly knocking himself out. He had just guessed.

Part Seven

Soon, Soon, Armageddon

Chapter Forty-nine

Dr. Gadda was so concerned about the Pope's failing health that he gave up using his luxury apartment near the Spanish Steps and lived more or less permanently in a room set aside for him in the Vatican Palace. As a result of Burns's phone call to Frank, Montefiori had alerted the entire staff to the possibilities of danger.

Gadda, more attentive than ever, took to giving the Pope a quick checkup as soon as he arose at six in the morning. He also got Frank's permission to serve the Pope's Mass. This was providential. Only Gadda's professional eye prevented a calamity.

One morning, he had poured the wine into the chalice at the offertory when, to the Pope's, Charley's and the nuns' surprise, he grabbed it from his hand. Having closely inspected the contents, he declared:

"Holiness, you risk drinking from a poisoned chalice."

Cardinal Montefiori was summoned. Gadda told him he suspected the wine was contaminated with white cyanide. The gritty contents of the cruet and the wine bottle were sent for analysis, which proved positive.

Dr. Gadda must have gone on pure intuition since white arsenic has no taste or smell. It was, he said angrily, a throwback to the time of the Borgias. Worse, it was a liturgical sacrilege. The Pope was about to change poisoned wine into Christ's Blood, which, instead of being his salvation, would bring him instant death.

Cardinal Montefiori immediately offered the Pope his resignation. "I said from the beginning, Holiness, you must not trust anyone in the Curia, not even me."

When Patrick told him bluntly not to be so foolish, the cardinal, on the advice of Security, insisted that the Christini family who had rooms in the Pope's suite had to be moved out. Also, several of the Pope's assistants had to be transferred to other jobs in the Vatican. They included his chauffeur-cum-waiter, Tommaso, and the Irish serving sisters.

No one thought these had knowingly done wrong. One of them might have planted a bottle of wine poisoned by a killer posing as a devout Catholic.

Montefiori also forbade any member of the Curia to enter the Pope's private suite in future, including Cardinal Ragno and Archbishop Rossi, his deputy.

Even the Pope's confessor was told his services were temporarily suspended. "After all, Holiness," the cardinal said, "Don Virgilio comes from Palermo, Mafia territory. And he did hear your confession in your private chapel the night before the outrage."

The Secretary of State wanted Security to sweep the Pope's rooms for bugs but Patrick said no. Who would make sure they didn't *plant* bugs instead? Before long, experts would be checking his soap, his aftershave, the air fresheners, the drinking water. They would all end up in a maze of mirrors with no way out save through madness.

Days of investigation led nowhere. The wine bottle in question was the third in a crate delivered three weeks prior to the near-fatal Mass. It was the only one contaminated. There were no fingerprints on the bottle except those of the sacristan, seventy-eight-year-old Sister Moribunda, who had had no contact with the public for years. It was a mystery why white arsenic was used, since there were equally lethal poisons which left no trace.

Frank was grateful that the "killer," whoever he was, had botched his first attempt. He phoned Cardinal Burns, who asked him to congratulate Gadda on his behalf.

"And get Montefiori, son, to double security. The CIA assures me the assassin is not going to call a halt now."

Charley, ever sensitive to mood, whined pathetically against Sister Moribunda's skirt, as she came to the Pope's study to say good-bye. Tommaso got the same sympathetic treatment. When they had left, Charley snuggled up against Patrick and looked up at him misty-eyed to assure him of his support.

Frank said, "If you wish, Holiness, I'll stand down, too. I had the opportunity and—"

"So did Charley," the Pope said. He would not hear of his devoted secretary sacrificing himself futilely in this way.

The second attempt on the Pope's life hurt far more.

After he had preached in a crowded St. Peter's on the evils of usury, a man in dark glasses, dressed as a Capuchin, with an almost waist-length white beard, stepped forward to receive the Pope's blessing. Suddenly, he raised a white cane and out of the end of it shot a nine-inch blade.

Charley, a few feet ahead of his master, must have seen a glint of steel or smelled something on the man's skin different from that of hundreds of other pious people in the vicinity.

As the fake friar lunged at the Pope, Charley leaped in the way. The blade, the point of which was poisoned, went clean through his heart, killing him instantly. A moment later, the halberd of a Swiss Guard split the attacker's head down the middle.

A pilgrim took a picture of the Pope, his white cassock stained in blood, as he knelt in anguish. His left arm was round his dog's limp neck—*O God, O Charley*—and his right hand was raised in absolution over his would-be assassin.

The "Capuchin's" beard was false. He was closely shaven and had a crew cut. Under the brown habit he wore the uniform of an Italian sailor. In his pocket were forged identity papers and $5,000 in small bills.

The Italian authorities said they could not understand how the Capuchin had smuggled his weapon through the new metal detectors at the entry to St. Peter's. They gave the affair priority and promised the Vatican that the magistrate's report would be completed within four years.

The Arabic features of the dead assassin prompted the Americans to accuse the FIR of being behind this attempt. Independent commentators thought this was a smoke screen and that it had been masterminded by the CIA.

In fact, it *was* an FIR plot. Contrary to what Denise Weaver had said to Roone Delaney, Islamic Fundamentalists were far from pleased at the Pope's antics. It was not in their interests to have the balance between the superpowers upset at a critical moment in history.

The U.S. was spending 15 percent of GNP on armaments, 1 percent more than during the Korean War. Its satellites could not only track FIR subs underwater, they could direct smart bombs, shells and missiles right on target.

It had developed nuclear-powered booster rockets which could intercept an eagle in flight. It had replaced all its B-1 bombers with ninety-five B-2 Stealth bombers. The final batch of MX missiles was in place. One call from Delaney releasing nuclear codes, a couple of keys turned simultaneously in underground silos, and, from Arkansas to Arizona, America would spit out death on an unprecedented scale.

The same story on the seas. Seven *Nimitz*-class carriers of ninety thousand tons had been launched. Poseidon subs had on board twenty Tridents with the latest D-5s, accurate over six thousand miles.

Europe, including Germany, was bristling once more with ground-launched cruise missiles and the latest Pershing-3s were equipped with multiple warheads. There were enough explosives in six West European countries alone to blow up several worlds.

Far more worrying to the FIR was the fact that the USA was years ahead in space. It had cost America dear, making it the poorest superpower the world was ever likely to see. But its profligacy had paid off.

FIR Intelligence reported grimly on America's X-ray laser-based Star Wars system. Contrary to all arms-control agreements, the technology was already being tested; it would be operational within weeks.

. . .

For their part, Islamic nations needed a *sound* America to feel secure themselves.

Sound economically: Islamic nations needed the U.S. for their technological equipment. Also, as a safe haven for their petrodollars. Europe and Japan could not provide the financial services they needed.

Further, if the U.S. stopped producing, who would buy oil? Again, if the dollar continued its headlong fall, it would cost Islam billions in lost interest and the real value of oil revenues. Some Muslim countries might be reduced to penury, like Russia and its former satellites.

Sound politically: if the USA were destabilized by the pious rantings of the Pope, it might be tempted to make a preemptive nuclear strike. Delaney, a madcap Catholic, was capable of anything.

Hourani had never felt more threatened.

The Council of the FIR met in the famous Mosque of 'Amr in Old Cairo. Within is a pair of close columns. Legend has it that only true believers can squeeze between them. They were relieved that even the fattest of them was able to thread his way between the columns because they had a sacred duty to perform.

For this, they retired to their electronically operated underground bunker near the university. Though it was mid-November, the weather was still very warm.

Hourani took his seat under a massive portrait of Khomeini. The twelve adopted their usual formal pose, solemn and upright, while he presided, a hawk among buzzards.

The Foreign Minister, Sheikh Hamed es-Safy, expressed concern at the damage being done to U.S. capitalists and neocolonialists by the Pope's pronouncements.

"Brothers," Hourani said, "this is, indeed, bad for us. This Pope who rules a billion is ruled by his own tongue."

Hamed es-Safy added, "A tongue longer and more lethal than a lizard's."

It was he who had proposed evil for evil, namely, the Pope's elimination "before he whitens all our beards."

Hourani closed his eyes and said: "Item 1: the Pope. I propose that this reactionary irreligious pest be purged at once. *Fatwa*," and they all echoed, "*Fatwa*."

Without a pause. "Item 2: Method of Purging."

The Defense Minister, Sheikh Rasheyd Halim Mahmud, suggested Plan 3-B. This involved activating a Palestinian agent who had been trained in Libya in the halcyon days of Gaddafi and who had fought with distinction in Afghanistan.

"His origins are untraceable. He speaks several languages. He is a master of disguise and a ruthless assassin."

"Passed unanimously."

This superspecial agent had lunged vainly at Pope Patrick when a super-annuated halberd cut his head in half.

Charley it was who died.

Charley was a dog but not just a dog. Patrick, tired-looking and old, victim of ever more severe headaches, walking heavily in shoes weighted with years, buried his friend and guardian angel in the Vatican Gardens—*I really loved you, Charley*. He was assisted by Frank Kerrigan and Cardinal Montefiori.

Frank knew that, for the Pope, not only did Christ crucified take on Charley's face, Charley sometimes took on Christ's.

The pine coffin was draped in the Vatican flag with the crossed keys. At the head of the grave, a simple wooden cross in green willow bore the words "No Greater Love Than This."

Thank you, Lord, for my loyal, sensitive, sentimental friend. Quite shameless he was in showing affection. He gave me the good of his life. But I'm so tired, Lord. Nothing left.

Frank remembered with a stab of pain the dog's grave in Kilkenny which the Pope had been so interested in.

At the end of a ceremony of gratitude, when the Pope was tossing the earth in, feeling his own heart was down there with Charley, a miracle occurred. Something stirred against his left leg.

Snowflake, somehow sensing that her rival was dead, had come back. With her, the Pope's energies returned. He smiled. He was ready for the extra mile.

Your grace comes in strange guises, Lord. From the bottom of my poor weak wavering heart, I thank you.

Owners of Cemeteries of Animal Companions throughout the world sent messages of condolence; several thousand elderly animal lovers applied to join the Catholic Church.

Chapter Fifty

The Pope's weekly allocutions, now televised live, centered on the iniquities of nuclear weapons.

"If only one-twentieth of the cash spent on arms were spent on agriculture, starvation on this beautiful planet could be eliminated."

The FIR, he noted, had pledged itself, like the old USSR before it, never, never, never to be the first to use nuclear weapons. NATO, on the other hand, stated repeatedly that it would not hesitate to use "tactical" nuclear weapons should the FIR attempt even an oil blockade of the Mideast. But such tactical weapons would trigger off a full-scale nuclear response from the FIR.

"What would we say," the Pope asked, "if a nation or group of nations, who were threatened by an aggressor, promised to bayonet a million babies to death? Nuclear war will destroy far more babies far more horribly than that."

After each session in the Nervi Hall, the Pope returned to his study exhausted, and walking as though on ice. Razor-thin, he coughed incessantly. When he swallowed, his Adam's apple rose and fell like a gull on a wave.

Dr. Gadda, the faithful archphysician, now hardly left his side. Dressed in soutane and surplice for each papal ceremony, he inspected the coals and incense in the censers in case they gave off poisonous perfumes. He encouraged the Pope to wear thick underwear, ostensibly to keep him warm, but into which was sewn a flak jacket to protect him against a sniper's bullet. He persuaded the canons of St. Peter's to deny visitors access to the dome in case someone, from the outer balcony four hundred feet up, took a potshot at Patrick when he strolled in the Gardens.

Ever since he returned from Ireland, the Pope had eaten nothing but boiled potatoes mixed with butter and milk. *Vive la pomme de terre,* he always said.

Gadda coaxed him into drinking glucose and personally bathed his feet in warm water and iron salts each night. He was ever consulting top physicians by phone and they recommended new medication. It had little or no effect. He told Frank Kerrigan to plead with the Pope to go for a checkup at the Gemelli.

Lord, how can I go into hospital for a checkup when you have given me so much to do?

"Thank you," he said to Gadda every night, as the doctor plied him with medicines and pink pills to help him sleep. "Thank you for keeping me alive one more day."

Tears clouded Gadda's eyes. "It is not me, but God himself, Holiness."

The allocutions were having an effect. Desertions from the U.S. forces outnumbered defections during the Vietnam War. There were massive peace marches on Washington.

NATO plants in Germany and Holland were under siege, violence was commonplace. Greenham Common in Berkshire, England, was once again an American air base. U.S. military police broke all the guidelines when they shot dead twenty-seven protesters who scaled the perimeter fence to strew flowers on a cruise missile site. The incident sparked off riots in a dozen British cities.

. . .

Frank Kerrigan, a loyal American, once asked the Pope, "Why do you never criticize the FIR over *their* arms buildup?"

"Would Muslims listen to the Pope, Frank, when I'm an infidel to them? Besides, it's NATO that's pledged to the principle of first strike."

"But, Holiness, that is only a threat. We Americans would never go for a first strike."

"Pardon me, Frank," the Pope said, "you already did."

In the Oval Office, there were frequent, frantic meetings between the President and his National Security Council, which kept him informed of the dire consequences of the Pope's speeches. Its members told him they were planning for every eventuality against a background of a steadily deteriorating economy.

The dollar and real estate values hit an all-time low. U.S. banks had received not one cent of interest from debtor nations since the Pope's address to the U.N., and eight thousand out of the country's fifteen thousand banks were in trouble.

Brokers who escaped being shot by bankrupt clients were jumping out of windows and pooling their brains on the sidewalk.

There were lines five miles long around gasoline stations. Schools and hospitals closed for lack of fuel. Medicare was bankrupt. Crime rates were up like it was Prohibition. Murders in Central Park quadrupled. Unemployment was at 17 percent and rising. NASA was closed for lack of funds. Exxon fired twenty thousand employees and there were no handshakes, golden or otherwise. General Motors was strapped for cash. Coke sales were down by 60 percent. Farm prices were at their lowest since the Civil War.

U.S. jets in foreign airports were refused refueling until the airlines paid in cash. Las Vegas was a ghost town. The Top Ten was filled with songs of the Depression. Cinemas, even Broadway theaters, played to almost empty houses. TV stations showed nothing but black-and-white repeats.

The lights in the White House were on for only six hours a day to set an example to the nation. There was talk of impeaching the President.

Hate mail swamped the White House. Secret Service men logged a thousand threats to the President's life every hour on the Internet; the bad spelling proved they were not made by Muslims. Delaney picked up a telephone for company and the line was dead as a dodo.

The grass on the front lawn was a foot long; he thought of keeping a cow on it like Mrs. Abe Lincoln during the Civil War, but who would milk it?

He invited top congressional leaders to breakfast at 7:15, only to be told their appointment books were full. Even Republican senators ran a mile just not to shake his hand. He was the best man in Washington not to know.

He tried to address a special joint session of Congress on measures to tackle the crisis but was refused entry.

He offered to give a televised fireside chat but no channel would give him airtime and, anyway, no one in the White House was willing to light the fire.

Off duty, his bodyguards hired bodyguards to defend them. Cartoons in the papers and on billboards showed him with his pockets turned inside out, fingering his rosary beads while drinking from a faucet marked "Lourdes Water: Miracles Guaranteed."

The First Lady, dressed permanently in black down to her silk frillies, painted even her toes black. Her feet looked like specked potatoes. She bought herself a single burial plot and kept hinting at divorce by rushing through doors ahead of the President shouting, "Geronimo!"

The country was falling apart. First Hawaii, then California and Texas were bellyaching like Baltic States. They wanted out of the Union so they could raise an army and print their own sound money. That would mean not just another Civil War but several such.

Delaney was a patriotic man. There was nothing he would not do for his country short of resigning. Even that was not necessary. No one else wanted the job.

When Denise Weaver called to say every means must be taken to shut the Pope up, short of nothing, Delaney repeated his assurances that the procking Irishman was being taken care of.

The CIA called its Rome station once again to ask why the Pope was still operational.

Day after day, the Pope spoke out, passionate as Tolstoy, gritty as Gandhi. Slogans he despised. Fighting for peace, he said, was like raping for virginity. Jesus, a complete pacifist, had insisted that it was better to die than to kill, that those who live by the sword would die by the sword. But mankind had not learned. Living by the bomb, it would die by the bomb.

Devices detonated in the stratosphere had left 200 million tons of radioactive debris filtering down on a fragile earth. The bombs dropped on Japan at the end of World War II proved that nuclear weapons could not discriminate between military targets and innocent civilians.

"I once visited Hiroshima," he said. "In that place, a man-made earthquake left a man-made desert. Human beings were turned into shadows and burned on the surfaces of flat rocks. Even the stones wept in Hiroshima after what the Japanese call the *pika-don*, lightning-thunder, a scream louder than any the world had heard before.

"In my nights, I see visions of my fellow human beings, little ones too, vomiting blood, their hair falling out, their eyes turned to water, purple patches all over their feather-light bodies, their bones thin as the ribs of autumn leaves.

"Oh, my sisters and my brothers, I heard of red mountain flowers, shaped like trumpets, blossoming out of walls in the blasted streets of Hiroshima. Seeds, long buried in the mountain clay from which the walls were made, had been released and given new life by the heat and rays of the bomb. Let that be a symbol of resurrection. But let there be no more deaths. For next time, there will be not one Auschwitz but a hundred thousand across the earth."

In a nuclear war, victory, he said, was impossible; the guaranteed effect was mutual destruction. Hadn't Einstein said that in such a war, "human society will disappear in a new and terrible dark age of mankind, perhaps forever"?

296

He also quoted the lament of Dick Diamond, U.S. Secretary of Defense: "If only God had made a bigger world. This one is far too small for our bombs."

Newsweek asked the Pope if it was wrong to threaten with nuclear weapons.

"If it's wrong to use them," he replied, "it must be wrong to threaten their use. It must also be wrong to test, manufacture and keep them."

"And stockpiles?"

"They must be destroyed."

"Unilaterally?"

"Of course. Just as Christians have to decide unilaterally to give up adultery or murder."

"But what if the result is to bring about the nuclear conflagration the superpowers are trying to avoid?"

"My friend, we must never do evil though good may come of it; we must always do good, even if evil results."

"You mean," the interviewer said, "you will insist on unilateral disarmament, even if it ends in catastrophe?"

"Our task is to do what is right," the Pope said. "The rest is up to God."

The Council of the FIR was even more disturbed by this than Washington. The white crow in the Vatican was disturbing the balance of power painstakingly built up over the years.

The Pope did not relax in spite of rapidly failing health.

Lord, keep me safe till my work is done. I have tried to protect your poor from exploitation. Help me save the world from Armageddon.

"Nuclear catastrophe," he once told Montefiori, "could be started by an error in judgment, by the malfunction of a piece of electronics, by sabotage. Some drunk or sleepy person might misread a bleep on a radar screen, thinking a test is an attack, with results that cannot be imagined."

Scientific innovation in the nuclear sphere had outpaced information technology. In one address, he said:

"One false step and, behold, a nuclear winter. The sun blotted out, crops rotting in the fields, people melted down, radiation sickness, hurricane winds blowing across a barren earth, congenital defects among the few unfortunate survivors."

In another address, he asked:

"If a powerful nation, by some vile experiment, risked the extinction of all the roses in the world, or all the cats and dogs, what would we think of it? And what should we think of nations that risk the extinction of *all* life on this planet, *now and forever?*"

He revealed that he was working on an encyclical dealing with nuclear weapons. "If God spares me, it will be finished in a few days."

Roone," screeched Denise Weaver, "you've only got a few *days.*"

"Jesus Christ," the President said, "the guy must have made a pact with the devil. Long ago he should've been like Humpty-Dumpty after the fall."

Chapter Fifty-one

"Muoio e non posso morire," Patrick said in a soft voice. "I am dying, yet I cannot die."

Frank Kerrigan knew it was not a lament, more a cry of defiance.

The Pope, feeling he was already, as he put it, riding on the rims, worked on day after day long after the sun had made its final genuflection. He went on into the early hours until the lightening sky turned jade over the Janiculum. This was the culmination of his pontificate, his last service to mankind.

I have to finish it, Lord, if for nothing else, then for Charley's sake. Ah, but I am tired.

His eyesight had nearly gone and several teeth were loose. Life was a few trembling butterflies in his thin frame. His past he saw as a featureless plain. Ahead, the mountain, ten times higher than Croagh Patrick, absorbed his thoughts. And the years passed like nights, swifter than a weaver's shuttle, full of unremembered things. He *must* climb and climb.

Once, when he dozed for a moment in the early hours, he had a dream. Rome was like old Pompeii. Everyone was dead. In the palace, all dead. In the great gold cavern of St. Peter's, a vast congregation, dead.

O God, what if I am responsible for all this?

Crossing the piazza in an electric yet shadowless glare he was stupefied to see the Obelisk falling like a weightless log. Then the 182 statues, each eleven feet high, dived off Bernini's colonnade like swimmers in a pool and landed with a noiseless splash.

In a louder-than-thunder silence, he moonwalked the dense city streets. Into the thronged Piazza Navona with its bubbling fountains where big dogs raised their heads and howled silently to the sky. Along the crowded brown-skinned Tiber. Along the Corso, where nothing, not even discarded cigarette packets, stirred and everyone, including the police on traffic duty, was dead.

Shaky as Goya's horse on a tightrope, he made his way to the Piazza Venezia and coaxed his tired frame up the white marble steps of the "Wedding Cake monument" erected in honor of Victor Emmanuel II, only to see the building turn brown and shrivel before his eyes.

He looked west toward the Vatican and saw a bolt of green lightning, *pika-don*, strike the cupola, which burst like a bubble without a bang.

On to the eyeless Colosseum, where he remembered the words of the eighth-century Venerable Bede, *"Quamdiu stat Colisaeus . . .* While the Colosseum stands, Rome stands; when it falls, Rome falls; when Rome falls, the world falls."

From heaven an archangel descended and, with protruding eyes and bulging cheeks, blew on a sixty-foot-long brass trumpet the Last Trump, making no more sound than a glassblower.

Auschwitz! Hiroshima! *Otonawa-baku*, all of us bloody fools, all burned like shadows into rocks.

O God, was he to be the last Pope, destined to give *urbi et orbi*, to the city and the world, not his blessing but the last rites?

Patrick watched in horror as the Colosseum's huge blocks of travertine started weeping before they collapsed silent as leaves and crumbled into dust.

He went to touch his cheek and his fingers went straight to the bone. That was when he realized, amid all the desolation, that he was the one who was dead. They were all dead to him.

But, Lord, I cannot die.

He needed a few million more heartbeats added to the 3 billion in an average lifetime. He still had to go on climbing that mountain, to go on, on, on, on, on. *"Veni Sancte Spiritus."*

F inally, *Mundi Holocaustum* was complete.

To Frank's surprise, Patrick told him he wanted a tiara. He had not even used one at his Coronation.

"The one given to your predecessor by Napoleon?"

The Pope smiled. "Make one out of cardboard, if you can, and cover it with gold paper."

Frank did his best. As he handed it to Patrick, his attitude suggested, Why?

"Innocent III," the Pope said, winking painfully, "called the tiara the symbol of world domination."

He held the encyclical aloft and, in a kind of reverie, spoke words that Frank recognized as part of the ancient rite of Papal Coronation:

"Remember you are the Father of Princes and Kings, Pontiff of the round Earth, and Vicar of our Saviour Jesus Christ over the whole Church."

After Patrick had retired to bed with a pounding head and a bad nosebleed, Frank took a peep at the encyclical. The early part contained no surprises.

"Those who make, keep or threaten others with nuclear weapons are no less criminal than genocidal figures of the past: Genghis Khan, Joseph Stalin, Adolf Hitler.

"Nuclear war cannot be won. Weapons of mass destruction contradict, at every point, the nonviolence of the Gospel which says: 'Do unto others as you would have them do unto you.' No possible good could outweigh the immeasurable evil of such weapons."

The Pope dealt firmly with the argument that they had kept peace between the superpowers for over seventy years.

"You can deter little boys from stealing apples by cutting off their fingers. Is this a moral thing to do?"

As to keeping the peace: for what? To give the superpowers license to carve up the rest of the world and colonize it militarily or economically or religiously. Even that was no longer possible with several smaller nations in possession of nuclear weapons.

Frank read: "Possessing nuclear weapons is not a safeguard but the craziest gamble ever made. Suppose those weapons keep the peace for another two hundred years, after which there is nuclear war. Would the deterrent be judged a success then?"

It was the last few paragraphs of *Mundi Holocaustum* that lifted the hair on Frank's head. It was a history lesson that explained the miter.

Pope Patrick reminded Catholics that in the eleventh century, Gregory VII had proclaimed his right to depose Emperors and Kings.

In the thirteenth century, Boniface VIII went further: "We declare, announce and define that salvation demands that every creature be subject to the Roman Pontiff."

In 1558, Paul IV said in a Bull: "The Pope has full authority and power over nations and kingdoms."

Twelve years after that, Pius V used this power to excommunicate Elizabeth I of England. He also deposed her as Queen, absolving her subjects from allegiance.

The encyclical concluded:

"Since it is the wickedest crime imaginable to manufacture, retain, use or threaten to use nuclear weapons, I am sadly obliged to exercise my supreme authority as Roman Pontiff. Unless Catholic leaders—and this includes the heads of government in Berlin, Paris, London and Washington—immediately and unilaterally destroy their nuclear arsenals, I excommunicate them and absolve all Catholics from obeying them. They will effectively be deposed."

In Rome, it was three in the morning. Frank called Cardinal Burns in New York, as promised, and told him the news. At 10:15 P.M. local time, Burns called the White House.

Mundi Holocaustum divided the free world. Some hailed the Pope as peacemaker and saint. The rest thought him quite insane.

A fter the biggest peace march on the Pentagon since 1963 during the Vietnam War, President Delaney went on television to reemphasize his pledge to zap a billion Muslims without hesitation if need be.

The Catholic heads of state hastily met in Washington. Unanimously and unreservedly, they condemned the Pope for meddling in politics. Whatever their religious convictions, they said, they would not swerve by one iota from their stated military objectives. To defend their people, they would, if need be, wipe out all the nations belonging to the FIR.

I t was in the Federation of Islamic Republics that the major shift in strategy took place.

Chapter Fifty-two

The Council flew in from the countries of the Muslim world to Riyadh. "How is your health and how your journey?" Hourani asked each formally, as he embraced them. And they replied, "It is good, Allah be praised."

After ritual washing, they went barefoot into the vast space of the mosque that was as cool as a desert at dawn. They stretched themselves on their mats and prayed, soaking up life and strength from Allah, as lizards, coming up from their sand dens after a freezing night, return slowly to life by drinking up the sun.

When, their prayers completed, Hourani heard the latest grim tidings from Rome and Washington, he took the unusual step of transferring the meeting to Mecca.

His heart thrilled as he saw, from his chauffeur-driven limousine, the steep decline into the city. From the heights he saw right through the open gates into the Great Mosque. He wondered again at the aloof *Kaaba* with its minarets topped by onion domes. He saluted the gold dome over Zemzen, well of bubbling waters. This desert miracle had been shown by the angel to Hagar to save her baby Ishmael from dying of thirst. All Muslims were descended from his loins.

The Council met in a building decorated within to look like a pale-gold air-conditioned *mudhif*, or tent. It had a ribbed roof and traceried windows. There was a fountain and a waterfall. There were roses red as flaming lamps;

exotic trees presaging those in Paradise whose leaves are singing birds. Above them, in the galleries, flew white Iraqi house doves.

Reclining on cushions of embroidered satin, they ate a swift silent meal of rice and mutton, Bedouin fashion, from a single dish into which they dipped their right hands. Hourani, as host—"Be the guest of Allah"—ate last.

After dates and lime tea, Hourani took a melon, honey-skinned like a harvest moon. He sliced it with his dagger so that each of them received a dripping segment, which, when eaten, left in their hands the crescent moon like that which ends the fast of Ramadan.

After this, they sparrow-splashed their fingers in water poured into a silver ewer.

Finally, they took strong bitter coffee in a coffee bower, its floor covered with Baghdad rugs strewn with rose petals.

Afterward, the members bowed to Hourani: "The Lord be gracious unto thee," and he responded with, "Go in the peace of the Lord."

S eated around the conference table in the *mudhif*, there was a brief analysis of the papal encyclical by their head *ulim*, or theologian.

"By my mother's milk," he concluded, "this heathen, who does not know north from south, has put terrible pressures on the man in the Black House."

Foreign Minister Sheikh Hamed es-Safy summed up: "Brothers, this is as welcome as news of an Ayatollah asking for baptism."

Hourani concurred. "The Satan of all Satans is now utterly destabilized. I know this infidel President of the United States like my own stallion. They deny they are a theocracy yet Rome and Washington want to colonize the world together. Delaney's religious madness makes it impossible for him to govern his country."

Members around the table nodded.

"For us, the situation is critical."

Once more, Hourani explained how the FIR's finances were imperiled if international banks collapsed and no one could afford to buy oil.

Worse, Islam had waited more than a thousand years to fulfill the Prophet's dream. Now, when it was within their grasp, the Pope had undermined it by throwing the U.S. and its allies into confusion. If he continued, there would be irresistible pressures on his stooge, Delaney, to go for a first strike before he became politically impotent.

"Tyrants only hold on to power at home by making war abroad."

"And," said the Foreign Minister, "after he has nuked us, as the *Americanis* say, the debtor nations will pay their bills to the U.S., all right. Two birds with one bomb, so to say."

Hourani pressed a buzzer and in came their chief strategist, Amir Stebelkov, former Soviet general from Kazakhstan, a convert to Islam.

"Tell us of their Star Wars project."

Using models, Stebelkov explained the working of the American project known as Brilliant Pebbles. The system consisted of a thousand precision rockets 36,000 kilometers above the earth in permanent orbit. They had on their outer surface giant mirrors.

"Laser beams of electron particles," the general said, "bounce off these mirrors, *so*. These beams have very high energy levels. They are able to catch and neutralize all our missiles still rocketed, alas, by conventional fuel and which travel only three hundred kilometers above the earth. As soon as our missiles are in the boost phase, they—" He threw his arms out wide.

"Like throwing pomegranates against a wall," said Hourani.

"Yes, Mr. President. We are weak as water in comparison. Our own bombs would annihilate our own lands." Stebelkov looked solemnly around the table. "Intelligence tells us we have a few weeks at the most."

The President nodded. *"Weysh aad,* what are our chances of knocking out this defensive screen of the infidels?"

"Quite good," Stebelkov said. "Except our maneuvers would be detected by U.S. satellites. They would go for a first strike. We would retaliate."

"And?"

"There will not be a World War IV, Mr. President."

Hourani said, "It would be like the two wolves in the legend fighting and eating each other till nothing remained of either."

When the general had bowed and left, the President sighed, *"Eigh! Eigh!* This papal son of mischief who would bite a mad dog has thrown sand in our eyes."

Someone said, "Allah curse the father and mother of this *mesquin,"* this pitiful person.

Hourani nodded solemnly. "Doubtless the Americans have first targeted Mecca and Medina."

Everyone around the table stirred and frowned. One said, "That is *harram,"* forbidden, and another chanted, "All our roses now are thistles and our nightingales no more sweetly sing than falcons."

"We must put into operation," Hourani said, "the last plan on our list code-named Hegira." He put a hand to his face and peered through the bars of his fingers. "Can one of my brethren see an alternative?"

One by one they reluctantly shook their heads.

Hourani quoted grimly from the poet Zuhair, "Our destiny, like a blind camel, tramples us in the dust." Then: "Write this, my brothers, with an eagle's quill, we are defeated."

The brethren nodded.

Hourani, taking a deep, deep breath:

"I remind you that, according to Plan Hegira, we will fly to the chief capitals of the West and explain why the FIR, for humanity's sake, has decided unilaterally to destroy its nuclear arsenals. The days of bluffing are over."

For a moment, no sound in the chamber but the cooing of doves.

The Council members lost their formal pose and eyed those next to them. They saw their faces turn a gypsum white. They knew their people would complain that once again the pride of Islam had been brought low by Western colonialism.

They broke into some cursing and some Koran around the table, and one said, "Would I could make a Muslim of this Pope with a gelding knife," another adding, "Then would he squeak, 'There is no God but Allah.' "

The President told the Council that all intelligence operatives abroad must obey orders instantly, without question.

The head of Intelligence promised. He got from the President in return a solemn pledge that whatever happened, the Pope would remain target number one.

Hourani nodded. His cold gaze swept around the table.

"It hurts, ah, it hurts, I know it," he said, and a sob came from his great hollow throat.

Sheikh Hamed es-Safy, pecking at his stunted nose, asked in a lament, "Must we smoke our sweet leaf in a foreign land? Take the hand of the heathen? Oh far easier to fall upon my sword than partake of bread and salt in the tents of Satan."

"We must drink to the dregs our misery," Hourani said, "for if we act not *now*, the colonialist dogs will preempt us. Either at once, or, more likely, in a few weeks' time when their Star Wars system gives them immunity. We would be annihilated and all Islam's great achievements since the days of the Prophet would be lost."

All agreed. This was the will of Allah. It was written.

A dove flew down and perched on Hourani's shoulder. He detached it gently, stroked it—"Salam, my friend"—and tossed it lightly back in the direction of the gallery. He went round the table personally pouring out for each a glass of strong, green peppermint-flavored liquid.

He said, "You will make arrangements within three days, as demanded by Plan Hegira. Take your eldest sons with you, though, for reasons you know of, I must leave my Ali here."

"And our *hareem?*" asked the Foreign Minister.

"As you wish." Hourani's dark face darkened further. "When this wretched time is over, the *Islamic Daily News* will tell our peoples that we only acted thus to bring the Prophet's dreams to fulfillment."

"Books and books will be written about us as the Saviors of Islam," said Sheikh Hamed es-Safy.

"Yes," Hourani said. "They will remember us unto good. They will tell to all ages how we made the infidel kneel like a camel before us and how we planted an earthly paradise for our children and our children's children."

The twelve Council members bowed and roared in unison, "*Allahu Akbar,* Allah is great."

. . .

Having changed into white calico robes, bare-headed and half-naked, they retired to the Great Mosque, purified themselves and entered the sacred shrine. Slender were its pillars, its walls and floors covered with finest mosaics. Overhead hung hundreds of glass chandeliers.

Onward they went to the open-aired sanctuary. There, though unfasting, they joined thousands of *hajjis*, pilgrims from the far corners of the world. They swirled around the Black Stone, the meteorite set in the shrine of the Kaaba by the Prophet himself. The shrine was covered with black Persian cloth, embroidered over and over with the Great Confession.

Those pilgrims became a huge white whirlpool as they walked round the enclosure seven times counterclockwise, as though to symbolize that they were putting back the clock of time, trying to reach back to the golden age when Muhammad walked the earth.

Seven times they kissed the sacred stone set in the wall with gold at its heart. All was done under the stern gaze of a red-bearded attendant. His shiny skin was black as the Stone and on his right arm was strapped a pointed dagger. Other ebony attendants from time to time cleansed the golden ring with oil of roses.

Afterward, when all members of the Council were refreshed, Hourani said to them:

"This is to be our Hegira, the year of the second Migration, O my friends, matching the first in 622 of the Christian era when the Prophet fled from Mecca to Medina."

They understood only too well what he meant when he added, "The Crescent will soon once more defeat the Cross 'in sha'Allah—if God wills."

An hour later, a fleet of black-curtained stretch limousines took them one in each car to the edge of the Blissful City. There, wrapped in heavy cloaks, they set off in pairs, not riding high in pride but walking humbly and barefoot like the prophets of Islam, leading each a prize white pilgrim-camel.

Sunward they walked toward a horizoning mountain range, ever near but never nearer. Red Sea-ward they walked in silence, save for the shuffling tread and heavy breathing and burbling of the camels.

They walked past the last ocher orchard wall with a gazelle therein and the last garden with its slender dusty female palms. Past vast sacrificial herds of sheep and goats, lambs and kids, all bleating. Past black goatskin tents from which came the sounds of tambourines and drums, the grinding of green coffee berries and the piping voices of children. Past a woman milking a ewe near a fire of thorns and dried camel dung whose sparks landed like red seeds in the sand. Past the last ass tethered and loaded down with tents and bedding and the last stray dog, its bark like slivers of glass in the pale air. Past a rusted sixty-years-abandoned steam engine, upended and almost drowned in sand. Past a brook inhabited by seemingly Arabic-speaking frogs. Past a group of snails that raised their long necks vertically out of their shells in the scrub grass so they looked like perfect tiny mosques.

Silence now and theirs the only shadows and they fast lengthening. A lone buzzard above, only scuttling and slithering below. Otherwise, emptiness and a giant sun.

Finally, when they seemed to melt into that swimming sun, they came to a desert place where there was nothing but Allah. Slashing the backs of their hands with a dagger, they smeared their faces with their blood.

After they had sworn a solemn oath, they saw a portent in the early sunset sky of winter. In dewless golden-aired Arabia, behold, far off, like a ghostly white lizard, the flicker of thunderless lightning.

Hourani kissed his hand toward it, saying, "God's Angel," to which the Council members answered, "*Lubbeyk! Lubbeyk!* To do thy will, O Lord."

Hourani bent down and gathered two handfuls of purifying sand. He stood up and threw them with a scattering underarm motion high in the air.

"Why worry we, O my brothers, when Allah knows where each grain of sand will fall?"

Day's end. Sun's end. World's end.

The Council members, with bloodied lips, knelt and prayed the fourth, that is, the sunset prayer, with their heels to the blinking light.

Intrusive and unreal those voices in the desert wastes.

Afterward, in the gloaming, with the rising of the wind, each turned his camel toward Mecca and imitated Hourani as he ordered, *"Ikh-kh-kh,"* and touched his beast with his pointed camel stick, the scepter of the desert.

The camels, now silhouetted in the sudden cold blue night, went on their knees groaning, their languid eyes as empty as the wilderness, their smoky jaws moving sideways as they chewed huge cuds.

Another signal from Hourani to his fellows and each put his left arm round the neck of his couched camel in a harsh embrace and slit its throat in sacrifice.

M r. President," Bill Huggard said breathlessly, "you are wanted on the Number One videophone by the President of the FIR."

Delaney would have thought this a joke, coming from anyone but Huggard. The FIR had not been on the hot line for months.

"What the hell does he want?"

"Atwa, sir."

Delaney jumped. *"Fatwa?"*

"No, sir. *Atwa* apparently means a truce."

Delaney, trembling, picked up the phone.

Hourani said: "As President of our great Federation, I send you salutations. We, devoted Muslims, fear that the world has lately become disagreeably unstable. I propose to address the United Nations on my plan for peace. Afterward, with your permission, I will take the shuttle to Washington to take bread and salt with you and negotiate with you face-to-face."

Delaney was almost too shaken to reply.

"About?" he got to say.

"A complete rundown of nuclear weapons."

"How complete is complete?"

"The Council of the FIR has decided that His Holiness Pope Patrick has both increased the possibility of war between our two great peoples and made it imperative for us to come to a final solution. In three days' time, at the United Nations, I will demand that all nuclear weapons throughout the world be scrapped. And we, Mr. President, will lead the way."

Delaney had the White House Cabinet Room swept for bugs and called a meeting. Everyone important in State, Defense and the CIA was present, as well as the Vice President and the Attorney General. Tom Dickey, the President's National Security Adviser, had brought with him members of Jason, a team of top scientific experts.

Delaney was inclined to think this was the best thing that had happened to him since he failed to graduate from Harvard. His advisers to a man took a different line. No white flag here, rather the assassin's knife.

They told him that the FIR initiative stank to heaven. Militant Muslims had been financing international terrorism for years, blowing up trains, ships, planes.

"Christ, Chief," Dickey said, "this is the guy, remember, who tried to knock out the White House with you in it."

Their Islamic expert, Professor Gilder, said, "According to our psychological profile, sir, Hourani is nuts."

Dickey took over. Now that Islam had nuclear capability, New York and San Francisco would change places if they weren't careful. He spread out a big map of the world on the table. "Take a look at this."

He dabbed at key strategic points held by Islamic nations.

Four of the most important zones of Africa: the Straits of Gibraltar, the coasts of Libya and Morocco, the horn of Africa.

In the Mediterranean, the coasts of Egypt and Syria.

In the Mideast, Istanbul on the Black Sea. Both sides of the Persian Gulf, along the shores of Saudi Arabia and Iran, with Iran also on the Caspian together with Azerbaijan.

Farther east, Pakistan, Afghanistan, the Indonesian archipelago with strategic islands like Java and Sumatra.

"With their ability to move missiles around unseen," Dickey said, "and send 'em East or West, we sure better keep our guard up."

Delaney was advised to take the black box with him when he went for a shower.

"Isn't it fishy," Dickey asked, his eyes blazing like headlights, "that this move comes just a few weeks before our Star Wars system is operational? Don't bank on that Ayatollah guy stepping on American soil."

Jason advised the President to save the hallelujahs and put all the armed forces at home and abroad on triple alert. They might just all be sitting with their asses on a live volcano.

Delaney called Downing Street. Denise Weaver said her head of the Joint Intelligence Committee agreed with Jason. Every single nuclear bomber crew at every Strategic Air Command base of the Western Alliance should have their fingers on the red button that arms the bombs.

By this time, the President's helicopter was serviced and *Air Force One* was fueled and ready to go at Andrews Air Base in case of a crisis.

Chapter Fifty-three

Something sensational was happening. Delaney was informed by the CIA and the FBI that the Federation of Islamic Republics had pulled all its spies out of the countries of the Western Alliance. An entire espionage network, built up piecemeal over fifteen years, was being dismantled.

Risking certain disclosure, FIR spies who had been in place and sleeping in some cases for years had broken cover. They had left the countries in which they worked and were seen openly in Tehran, Karachi and Cairo.

Even double agents, who had been watched without their knowledge by allied security forces for over a decade, were called home to Islamic countries. The Ice War seemed to be over.

The press was at first indignant that there had been Muslim spies in top jobs in the U.S. Six in the CIA and five in the FBI alone. Even the President of the IMF and chairmen of two congressional committees had been secret converts to militant Islam.

So had the one male member of the British government. After selling his story to the *Sunday Mirror*, admitting he was a transvestite, he at least had the decency to blow his brains out, though Denise Weaver regretted he had done so at a Cabinet meeting in Number 10. So terribly messy.

Press bitterness evaporated when security experts pointed out that the FIR had made it impossible for its agents to operate in the free world in the near future.

A further friendly development. The FIR head of Intelligence tipped off U.S. security that two small nuclear devices had been planted "by a hostile government" in the World Trade Center and in the underground garage of the Chrysler Building in New York. The parts had been smuggled in and assembled, needing only to be primed. The FIR had saved America from a catastrophe.

It was, however, only when Delaney saw the TV pictures that his doubts finally left him. The Council of the FIR had split up and, accompanied by their families, were flying to Berlin, London, Paris, Dublin, Tokyo. Hours after seeing the FIR Foreign Minister being mobbed in London, he watched Hourani alight from a Saudi Arabian plane in New York.

The Ayatollah was accompanied by his pride and joy, his eldest grandson, six years of age.

Chubby, brown-eyed Ruhollah was dressed in white robes like a sheikh with a dagger in his belt. He was substituting for his father, the President's eldest son, who was reputed to be ill. A year before, Ruhollah, instant darling of the media, had reached his maturity by slitting the throat of his first infidel.

For Delaney, this was a dream above all dreams. He was not, after all, presiding over the eclipse of America but over its rebirth. The American Dream was *now*.

Kennedy's courage in facing down Khrushchev at the time of the Cuban missile crisis was child's play compared with his own feat in annihilating Hourani. In time to come, he would take his place alongside Lincoln. No, *above* him. After all, hadn't he just eliminated religious slavery worldwide? They would rename the Washington Monument "The Delaney." Wow, wow, *wow!*

Bill Huggard sucked his wispy mustache and pumped Delaney's hand. "Procking hell, sir," he drooled. "Congratulations."

"We did it, pal." There was a throb in Delaney's voice. "Peace through superior strength has paid off."

The address of the President of the FIR to the United Nations was televised worldwide, except for China and the Islamic republics. Pope Patrick watched it in his dining room, as he sipped glucose, next to Dr.

Gadda and Frank Kerrigan, who, for all his joy, was consumed with secret guilt.

"Salaam, peace be unto you," Hourani said. There were no strings to the FIR's offer, no dagger inside his robe. He wanted to sign an agreement with all nuclear nations, but especially with America, for a total ban on such obscene weapons. Someone had to make a move. History would show the peace-loving peoples of Islam were the first to sacrifice their military might to stop the annihilation of the planet.

"I have already issued orders," he said, "for the dismantling of *all* FIR missile sites. U.S. satellites will confirm this. It will take perhaps three years to complete but peace has already broken out.

"I have ordered our air alert to be grounded for the very first time in over ten years. The FIR will also permit free and unfettered inspection of all our missile sites."

Admittedly, important ideological differences between the two super-powers remained. He went on:

"To reduce mutual suspicions, we intend also drastically to reduce our conventional forces. We pledge ourselves never to permit an oil embargo to the West, and will give written guarantees of such to the United Nations. Peace, we have always said, can only exist between equals."

U.S. satellites would verify that the FIR was already withdrawing its conventional forces from all the trouble spots—for instance, on the borders with Israel.

Finally, why peace? Because, since the breakdown of the nonprolifera-tion treaty, many nations had acquired enriched plutonium for making nu-clear weapons. The risk of accidents had increased in proportion.

"And let me be honest with you, my friends," Hourani said. "Within our own borders, we have already experienced the lunacy of meddling with such power.

"Two years ago, a hundred miles south of Cairo in the El Minya, there was a leak in a nuclear reactor. It did far more harm than even the infamous Chernobyl. Western media got wind of it through satellite pictures and distant fallout, but the full horror of it I will now proceed to show."

In his study, the Pope leaned forward with horror as the FIR leader showed a video.

316

Twenty thousand people in a town on the desert's edge nearest the reactor died instantly. Thousands more suffered from radiation sickness and were dying daily. This was a thousand Three Mile Islands in one. Tributaries of the Nile and aquifers would be contaminated for tens of thousands of years.

"I have to tell you, sirs, that my own first son, Ali, father of my dear little Ruhollah, visited the area to comfort the sick and bereaved. Ali, child of my youth, my best poem, tall and straight as a reed, was himself contaminated and is now dying a slow, painful martyr's death in a Tehran clinic."

The assembly uttered a deep sigh of sympathy and the Pope prayed in his heart for him.

"Allah demands," the FIR leader said, "that this madness should cease. My own little chick"—he pointed to Ruhollah—"must not die young like his father. And now I have a gift for the Secretary General."

The Pope's mouth opened wide as he saw Hourani hold up a black box.

"This is no ordinary briefcase. It contains the top-secret nuclear release codes which control the entire FIR arsenal. It has been in my company for the six years I have been President. I knew, and you knew, no one could ever give the order for a nuclear attack. Not just the United States but the FIR, too, would have been annihilated by either a first or a retaliatory strike. That is why I pledged that never, never, never would we Muslims sin by a first strike."

There were tears in Patrick's eyes as the Secretary General approached the podium.

"Sir," Hourani said, "I give our codes to your safekeeping."

To the Pope, this was the most dramatic gift since the Magi offered gold, frankincense and myrrh to the Infant Jesus.

In a silence deeper than any who were viewing had ever known, Hourani said:

"The Federation of Islamic Republics is now completely vulnerable. To use an English phrase, we have chanced our arm by offering it in friendship to America and the whole world."

He was almost finished.

"We Muslims, too, have had to make a choice, so to say, between butter and bombs, between life and death. Ultimately, between survival and annihilation. I speak for all the compassionate people of our great republics when I say, *We* choose peace!"

He was given a ten-minute standing ovation.

T he only blot on the landscape was Jews picketing outside the U.N. building with placards, "Let my people go."

After his address, Hourani eluded security guards to mingle with protesters outside the U.N. His message was translated by an aide and spoken over a bullhorn.

"*Shalom* to all my Jewish friends.

"I issued orders before leaving Mecca that members of your revered race who wish to leave the lands within the FIR may do so. Any Jew living in Islamic territory who wants an exit visa will be given one *immediately* to go wherever he wishes.

"Telephone your relatives—the lines have been restored—and find out for yourselves. I have drawn back the final curtain. I accept the two Helsinki agreements in full. It is not 'next year' but '*this* year in Jerusalem.' "

He was applauded by all the Jewish protesters, who asked which direction Mecca was in so they could utter a prayer of thanksgiving.

H ourani took the shuttle to Washington, where he was honored on the White House lawn in spite of Dickey warning Delaney, "That bastard'll probably have ten pounds of Semtex wrapped round his waist."

The President, having practiced for hours, was able to greet Hourani with, "*Salaam alaikum,*" Peace be with you, to which Hourani replied, "*Alaikum as salaam,*" With you be peace, said with a face as impassive as a rock.

A band gave a lively rendition of "Happy Days Are Here Again." There was a twenty-one-gun salute. Flags of the FIR flew everywhere alongside the Stars and Stripes.

An ecstatic President Delaney hugged his distinguished visitor. There was an accidental bumping of noses. Delaney came off worst. He shook Hourani's hand as if he wanted to wear it out. Afterward, Hourani pinned on his chest a gold medal struck for the occasion.

The First Lady, her face painted like a medieval manuscript, grabbed the hand of Ayesha, the first of Hourani's wives, a small woman, swathed and almost invisible in black.

It was calculated to bring a tear to the eye of a New York cabdriver.

Hourani said: "Between our two peoples, it used to be like this"—and his grandson held up two clenched fists like a prizefighter. "Now it is like this"—and Ruhollah opened his hands, spreading his palms toward the cameras.

"I promise you, Mr. President," Delaney said, smiling like a stewardess, "there will be an appropriate response from the U.S. on this historic day."

He was jubilant. He and every American watching realized that militant Islam, for all Hourani's rhetoric, knew it was licked. The Ayatollah was behaving like old Khrushchev when he was forced to withdraw his missiles from Cuba long ago. This, too, was surrender.

Only much later that evening as he fingered the bullet that nearly killed the Pope and which he had taken to wearing as a lucky charm around his neck did Delaney remember to tell the CIA to cancel Operation Shamrock.

"Our information is, Mr. President," the Director replied, "the killer is on-site, the process irreversible."

"Jesus Christ!" the President groaned. "Maybe I ordered dead the man who saved the world."

For the first time since 1995, when his ball-bearing firm nearly went bust, Roone Delaney sank to his knees and prayed.

Part Eight

A Time
to Confess

Chapter Fifty-four

Messages of congratulations poured into the Vatican, including one from the Cardinal of Armagh: "Thank you, Holy Father, for saving the world." The New York Times, in an uncharacteristic purple patch, claimed the Pope had rolled back the Stone of Universal Death and Eastered the world. Time chose him as Man of the Century. The Nobel Committee in Oslo wrote offering His Holiness the Peace Prize unopposed. The Dalai Lama sent a message: "You are, alas, sick, Holiness. The morning glory which blooms for an hour / Differs not in heart from the giant pine / Which endures for a thousand years."

Patrick received two important telegrams. The first from Marcia Burt, Archbishop of Canterbury, addressed him as "Vicar of Christ." The second, from the Orthodox Patriarch of Constantinople, spoke of him as "Supreme Bishop."

It looked as if the two great historic divisions of Christianity in East and West were about to be healed. Patrick was beyond question God's choice as Bishop of Bishops.

Thousands gathered in St. Peter's Square each day, including Poggi, the socialist Mayor, to cheer the Pope, who had scarcely the energy to drag himself to the window to wave.

When I wake up, Lord, I reckon I won't even be a cardinal nearly killed by a pillar, only a pious little boy from Mayo in a big bed with three of his brothers.

The only sour note came from the Chinese People's Daily. The Beijing leadership felt isolated and imperiled by the rapprochement between America and the FIR. In a violent outburst, Lee Jing Shang attacked the peace proposals emerging from Washington as a conspiracy against China.

Newspapers showed satellite pictures of FIR tank and infantry divisions pulling back from the borders with Israel. Reports kept coming in of FIR Council members being feted in the capitals of Europe.

Street parties were held in every town and village in England. There had been no celebrations like them since 1945.

Denise Weaver had the pleasure of hosting the FIR Foreign Minister, Sheikh Hamed es-Safy. She invited him to stay a couple of weekends in her country home, Chequers.

Weaver confided to her Cabinet that he was about "the queerest-looking whiskered little sod" she had ever come across. But she appreciated his bluntness.

When she asked if she might call him Hamed, he said no. When she asked if he was the one who nearly had her blown to bits outside Downing Street, he said yes. No regrets about that now? Only that the bomb never went off.

Even as he sipped a drink of sugared tamarind and tucked into the best roast lamb served on solid silver dishes, he kept babbling, "I remain till my dying daylight a proud Muslim. You know, I really hate you colonialist swine with all my—how you say?—procking gut."

"How charming," said Weaver. "I'm sure you say that to all the girls."

In Washington, Delaney had found the end of the rainbow. The decade's best-selling CD featured an Irish tenor singing "Delaney Boy" to the tune of "Londonderry Air."

He was reminded of a dream he had when he was a kid of ten. His whole house was made of ice cream, and he went from room to room licking, finally finishing off his father, who was composed of his favorite strawberry, right down to the soles of his shoes.

The press pictured Delaney as he walked arm in arm with Hourani in the Rose Garden, as he sat with him one night on the Truman balcony, watching the stars.

Professor Gilder, his Islamic expert, told Delaney that once an Arab had exchanged peace with another and shared bread and salt with him, he was his friend for life. Even Dickey said, "Chief, you read the entrails right."

Editorials described Delaney as "more popular than Andrew Jackson," as "the greatest President in this or any age." "He could run again unopposed," the *Post* said. "In fact, if he says the word he can have the job for life." "To coin a phrase," said the *New York Times*, "now he belongs to the ages."

He had only to be gunned down in a theater or assassinated in Dallas and he would go down as the greatest man in history after Jesus Christ.

His only problem was the First Lady. She insisted on three birthdays in one week.

D r. Gadda confined the Pope to bed. Father Virgilio was once more allowed to hear his confession. It was a general confession, ranging over his whole life. Montefiori brought him a fresh batch of telegrams.

"Congratulations, Holiness," he said, "for working the greatest miracle ever witnessed in Rome." Before Patrick could object: "Even the cardinals are praying for your recovery."

Frank served Patrick his lunch but he was too weak to eat. A spoonful of mashed potatoes went down like cactus leaves. He did not so much breathe as suck the air, causing his pared body to spike his pajamas, now here, now there. His neck was wooden, his eyes sunken and white as the eyes of a grilled fish. His joints were decayed, his fingers autumn-painted chestnut leaves, knotted, twisted out of shape. Like a leper, Montefiori thought. Or like Christ crucified.

Lord, I seem to be heading farther west than sunset toward the land with lots of time.

He read a few of the greetings and was cheered especially by the one from the President of Ireland. The new spirit of cooperation between the superpowers delighted her.

The mountain has disappeared.

The cardinal said, "You saved the world," and the Pope replied, "No, the world is always being saved because more people tire of hating than tire of loving."

He brushed away the tears behind his glasses, telling Montefiori, "Only the mountain mist, Giuseppe."

Softly: "Holiness, I have to admit there were times when I doubted the wisdom of your decisions."

"I know. Thank you for your loyalty, my sweet man. *Go raibh míle maith agat.*" He took the cardinal's hand in his. "You have the rarest form of wisdom and love."

The unemotional Montefiori was really surprised.

"You teach, you heal, you love . . . by listening."

The Secretary of State shook his head. "No, Holiness, you had a secret no one else had. You took the Gospel seriously regardless of the consequences."

Patrick had one request. "Please see to it that I am cremated."

The thought of the Pope's death and such an aftermath upset the normally stolid Montefiori. "But why cremation?"

"I do not want to take up too much room when I am dead. A pinch of me for St. Peter's, the rest to surround the red rose tree I planted in Kilmainham Jail."

The cardinal smiled. The Pope, as Jesus commanded, had grown up to be a little child long before the approach of death, which makes sucklings of us all. Still, he regretted this decision. This humble little man was the Michelangelo of the papacy. He would be remembered alongside Leo I and Gregory the Great, Popes who had preserved civilization itself. It would have been nice to see whether the body remained uncorrupted, the certain proof he was a saint.

"Understood, Holiness." He saw on the Pope's face the serenity of a man whose important death is already behind him, and bent down. "Peace, Holy Father." He kissed the palms of his hands. *"Bacio le mani.* You have my word you will be cremated."

Chapter Fifty-five

*L*ord, *my soul is a September swallow straining to fly away.*

Frank helped Patrick into a clean pair of pajamas. He pitied him his boniness, the sheer transparency of his mangelike flesh, eyes floating in dark little ponds, his forehead one moment blazing like a fire, the next cool as a blade. Yet this Irishman had a keyhole view into everything, into wood and stone, into people's hearts and heaven itself.

Thumbing his rosary, the Pope said, "Time I made my will."

Too tired to write, he dictated it. It came out so smoothly, Frank guessed he had stored it in his head a long time.

"I, Patrick," the Pope began pipingly, "a sinner, the most unlearned of men and least of all the faithful, offer my thanks to the Trinity.

"I was like a stone lying in thick mud when the Lord who is mighty came and in his mercy lifted me up and placed me, the most contemptible of men, on top of the wall.

"I dreamed a dream in which I heard, 'He who gave his life for thee speaks within thee,' and so I awoke full of joy to do God's work.

"I am worn-out now and beyond repair, but, small in the world's eyes, God inspired me beyond all others to serve the Church, which Christ's love conferred on me. By his grace, I have lived as a poor man in the midst of wealth, knowing that poverty suited me better than riches. But was not Christ poor for our sakes, he who is my heart's Sun which never sets?

"I ask forgiveness of all whom I have offended. Now, as I make ready to

327

depart this life, I hand over to my Lord, the King of Friday, all my cares for his Church. May he be blessed forever and ever. Amen."

Frank put down his pen. He knew it is much easier being a martyr than a saint but Patrick was both. He said:

"That is beautiful, Holy Father."

The Pope smiled. "Most of it comes from my great patron, St. Patrick."

When the testament was signed and sealed—it was an effort—a final burden was lifted from him. He now had the face of an onlooker.

"Take care of Charley's grave for me, eh? You know that dog treated me like a Pope before I even became Pope." He winked. "He was grand, was Charley. Never felt sorry for himself. Never faked a thing or gave in to hypochondria."

Wincing, Frank said, "Trust me, Holiness."

"Sprinkle some of my ashes next to his, eh? And don't forget to feed Snowflake—cream on feast days. This is a Vincent de Paul ending, Frank, so my only memento for you is my crucifix, there, the magic one with the faceless Christ. There's nothing else, though I'd be obliged if you'd see to it my brother Seamus gets my rosary. It was our mother's."

Frank, who knew the Pope's reign was coming to an end, dropped to his knees beside the bed and began to cry.

"Forgive me, Holiness." Before Patrick could interrupt, he added, "I have a confession to make. I . . . I betrayed you."

The Pope smiled incredulously. "You are the best thing to come out of America since the potato."

"I'm a blighted potato. I called Cardinal Burns and told him about your last encyclical in advance."

Patrick stroked Frank's thick brown hair, assuring him that this was no betrayal. Burns was his bishop and the news was bound to leak out, anyway.

"I think, Holiness, he would have stopped you publishing *Mundi Holocaustum* if he could."

"Well, it has all turned out well in the end."

Frank did not argue the point.

"Shall I tell you something, Frank?" He looked him straight in the eyes. "I never liked anyone as much as you."

Brushing his tears aside, Frank said, "Apart from Charley."

"Seriously. There are pots and pots of honey in my heart for you. Before you came I was a complete loner and proud of it. Now I'm so glad not to have ended my life without a close friend." After a silence, Patrick said, "You *will* remember me?"

"How could I forget *you!*"

"I don't mean remember Pope Patrick. But your friend, this funny little Irishman who, for all his titles, is only shallow writing in the sand."

Frank promised, then prayed the Te Deum with him and read him a passage from John's Gospel: "I am the Light of the world, he who follows me walks not in darkness but has the Light of Life."

After: "Ah, Frank, God is always the glory just over the brow of every hill," to which Frank replied, "I think, Holiness, God has let you see over the hill already."

Chapter Fifty-six

An hour later, there was a surprise visitor. Dressed in an ordinary black soutane, Cardinal Burns had flown in, posthaste.

"Holiness," he said, dropping to his knees. "I have come to congratulate you and beg your forgiveness."

The Pope insisted he get up. "Forgiveness for what?"

"Everything. You made me see my whole life has been a sham. I never listened. I've traveled through life without paying my fare. Who'd have been first to scramble aboard Noah's Ark? Tubby Tom Burns." He beat his breast like a carpet. "I was even jealous of your dog."

"You excommunicated him."

"That was nothing. Twice a day I excommunicate God."

Patrick grinned. "God," he said hoarsely, "finds it as easy to forgive as to create the world."

"My good friend, Sapieha of Philadelphia, feels like I do. He's resigned his diocese so he can give his last years to the poor of Ecuador. I wish I had the courage to do the same. But"—he gestured miserably—"I am weak."

"It's a strength to know one's weakness."

"I've given up smoking and drinking, though." Realizing that he still reeked of both, he explained, "I had my last cigar and glass of Irish just before I came."

"And you are staying where?"

"At the Grand. My secretary made the booking in a hurry. Just for tonight."

"Excellent." The Pope tapped Burns on the arm. "Tom."

Burns was touched to hear the Pope speak his Christian name. "Yes?"

"I have a terrible confession to make to *you*." Burns looked at him, puzzled. "I know I shouldn't have but on the trip to Ireland I overheard quite a few of your conversations with . . . Kammy."

Burns's tongue forked in and out as if in search of his exiled cigar. "I'm sorry if I shocked you."

"I enjoyed it, O Sweet Big-Assed Angel of New York."

Burns coughed in embarrassment. "Oh, by the way, Holiness, a little present for you. From the President of the United States." He took out a miniature bottle of whiskey. "As old as America. May I pour?"

"One for the long road, I guess. You won't join me?"

"I've given it up." Burns kept the biggest surprise till last. "I've booked myself into Lough Derg for next year."

And they say, Lord, the age of miracles is past.

L ate that night, Dr. Gadda, trailing his usual aroma of peppermint-cum-Gauloises, came in to give the Pope his checkup.

Afterward, he whimpered, "The rich music of your life is being played on a single string."

"Don't upset yourself, Vittorio, I have never been so happy."

Gadda went down on his knees. "I am a vile wretch, Holiness, because I failed you."

"Nonsense." Patrick was upset at being the cause of so much guilt. "Get up, please. No one could have done more for me."

"Not true, not true."

"It is. You kept me alive until my great work was done. I intend making you a Knight of the Order of St. Gregory."

Gadda's eyes swam with tears. "I . . . I poisoned you."

The Pope looked blankly at him. "What are you saying? You *stopped* me being poisoned."

"That was only a game. *I* put the arsenic in the chalice."

"But why do that and then tell me?"

"So, Holiness, no one would ever dream that I was, well, poisoning you . . . in a more discreet way."

The Pope, who saw that he was to die like Alexander Borgia, was speechless. *That* was how Gadda knew the chalice was poisoned. *That* was the reason for the firecrackers in his entrails.

"After I went with you to New York, Cardinal Burns called me. Said you were the Antichrist and loco like Caligula. Said you were too good for the world's good and you would bring Church and world to ruin. Said it was my duty as a good Catholic . . ." He gestured inconsolably.

Be a good Catholic by killing the Pope?

"Listen, Vittorio, Cardinal Burns was the one who informed my secretary that he had been alerted by the CIA about—"

"A smoke screen, Holiness, to distract attention from the real . . . agent on-site, namely, me. After I saved you no one could possibly have suspected me."

"How, Vittorio?"

"The pink pills, Holiness. Cardinal Burns said the CIA Chief of Station in Rome would deliver them to me. He did. Better even than atropine, he said. No more traceable than the love of God. He's a cynic, too, you see."

"Cardinal Burns was just here."

Gadda pursed his lips and gave a dry spit. "That Judas came to confess?"

"Yes. But he never mentioned you or pink pills."

Gadda became very agitated. "He is a stinking liar. I knew I could not trust a word he said."

The Pope's head was in a whirl. *Lord, which of the two is lying?*

"Those pills were not to help me sleep?"

"Yes, permanently. They weakened your heart so it is now . . ." Another eloquent gesture suggesting the membrane of a mosquito's wing.

"No hope?"

"None, Holiness. It was a miracle you survived till now. The doses I gave you would have killed a team of mules. I really hate that guy from New York for what he did to me."

"Maybe I should go to Lourdes?"

Gadda laughed briefly.

Patrick sank back on his pillow. There was no rancor in him, even though dear old Father Virgilio had been under suspicion and Tommaso, too. His dear Irish nuns had been sent packing for nothing. "God's will, Vittorio."

Gadda fell to his knees again and the Pope made the sign of the cross over him.

"You did what you thought right, and I forgive you from"—he took a deep breath—"my heart."

"You will tell no one?"

"I will treat it as a confessional secret and take it to God with me."

Gadda kissed the Pope's cool hand again and again. "Saint, Holiness. You are a saint."

Lord, if only you were as keen to canonize me as some mortals are.

Patrick closed his eyes in amusement. He jerked them open to ask Gadda if he would mind examining the whiskey bottle by his bedside. "Smell it, Vittorio."

Gadda uncorked the bottle and sniffed appreciatively. "Excellent stuff."

"It doesn't smell of, say, arsenic?"

"Arsenic has no . . . You are pulling my leg, Holiness."

The Pope was not sure whose leg was being pulled anymore or by whom. He said, "I must be getting suspicious in my old age."

Gadda agreed to analyze the whiskey professionally. After an appreciative swig and a look that said, See how I risk my life for my Pontiff, he coughed in apology. "I hardly dare ask this but . . . may I still be a Knight of St. Gregory?"

The Pope nodded.

Lord, you judge him, I haven't the wit or the energy.

"You *will* put it in writing, Holiness. Just in case you . . . forget."

The Pope took a pad from his bedside table. So shaky was his hand, he had, as it were, to paint a note of appointment.

As the doctor prepared to leave, Patrick said, "I hate to ask this."

"Anything," the newly knighted Gadda said magnanimously.

"Did the CIA offer you any, well, remuneration?"

Gadda gave him an off-balance, one-leg-in-the-pants look. "Nothing. Well, a little but I haven't seen it yet."

"A little?"

"Ten million."

"Lire?"

"U.S. dollars. In a Swiss bank. Only the tiniest rate of interest. The Vatican Bank is closed, but you know that."

"Vittorio." The Pope almost giggled. "Vittorio."

"I would have done it for less, Holiness. To prove it, I have decided to give the bulk of it to charity."

"That is nice. But," the Pope added, concerned, "will the Americans pay you, seeing you failed to—how shall I say?—kill me soon enough?"

Gadda looked hurt. "I am Italian. I made them cough up in advance."

"Good-bye, my friend. Let us pray for each other, eh?"

When the doctor left, Pope Patrick opened the drawer by his bedside. In it were three or four dozen pink pills.

Lord, thank you for rewarding my disobedience.

He had taken one each night to help him sleep. But not the prescribed four a day.

In one thing, Dr. Gadda was not fibbing. He had already promised his wife to settle $1 million each on his six lazy sons.

Frank Kerrigan showed in one more visitor that day, an old colleague of the Pope's, Monsignor Michael McAleer, rector of the Irish College.

"Mike," the Pope whispered, "so good of you to come."

The rector went on his knees to kiss the Pope's ring. "Holiness."

"Holiness?" the Pope echoed. "I'm little Brian O'Flynn, remember?"

"I'll try to . . . Brian."

"Thanks, Mike. My own name again. The best gift you could give me, my own identity, so to speak. D'you know, in this place, I've always felt something of an impostor."

"I'm sure every Pope feels like that."

The Pope, remembering how Nero died thinking he was a great actor who had been playing the part of a Roman Emperor, wrinkled his nose as if to say his friend was probably right.

"In any case, Mike, I shall soon be going where there aren't any titles. Oh, to be an ordinary Christian in the Land of Youth, without all eyes on me like I was a leopard in a zoo."

McAleer was overwhelmed with emotion, seeing his old friend half-in, half-out of the water with the Angler's hook in his mouth. Brian had really amazed him. Before his election he had been remote, living in a quiet bureaucratic zone of his own. He should have been only an off-the-peg sort of Pope and yet there now beat inside him the heart of the world.

He remembered the story of a little Irish girl who looked each day through the window of a sculptor's studio. She became ever more amazed as he carved the statue of a little boy. Finally, she said to her mother, "Mammy, how did he *know* there was a boy in there?" McAleer's turn to be amazed at what only God knew was hidden in the rough stone of his friend's being.

He said: "You'll never be ordinary, Brian, not even when you get through Peter's Gate. I've never been so proud to be Irish and a Catholic."

They talked for a while about the old days. Toward the end, McAleer said, "One thing has puzzled me since you first appeared on the loggia after your election."

"What's that?"

"Well . . . I hardly know how to put this. You were always right-handed and you seemed to react to the crowd, waving and so on, as if you were left-handed."

The Pope gave a soft, low chuckle. "It's true. I had a fierce bang on the head soon after I was elected, and when I came round, not only could I not remember accepting, I found myself doing everything with my left hand. I even wrote letters that way. Bits of my brain must have swapped places."

"Astounding!"

"And do you know, Mike, only now, at this very minute, am I right-handed again. And, good heavens, only now do I remember what happened just before that pillar fell on me. I was going to call myself John Paul III."

"I'm glad you didn't, Brian."

"Me, too, Mike. Me, too."

Chapter Fifty-seven

In Washington, the Islamic President received sad news. Little Ruhollah, his eyes like stars on a frosty night, whispered one word in his grandfather's ear: "*Mat*," and Hourani sighed, "Fadeth away the world, *ed-dinnia fany*."

Ali, his eldest son, was dead.

Though Hourani was the father of a flock, he said in grief, his tongue touching his palate, "When your first son dies, who cares if the world dies?"

Instead of rushing back to Cairo for the obsequies, he insisted on staying to conclude the negotiations which were so important to the whole world.

The two Presidents were seen watching the TV pictures of the funeral together. Both grieved in an unprecedented show of solidarity as the corpse, shrouded in skins, was sprinkled with soil from Mecca and Zemzen water.

Hourani knelt on the floor, swaying to and fro, and recited the first verse of the Koran, hands joined. Sometimes he keened, "My son, O my son," and sometimes, "Earth, O earth, thou host that slayest all thy guests."

"Abdallah," Delaney was overheard saying, as they watched the interment in a rock tomb in a hillside, "I pray that God may soon grant your dear son life everlasting."

Hourani stopped weeping and frowned. Did this heathen not know that his son was among the *shahud*, the martyrs of Islam? Ali did not need prayers to a false and triple God in order to escape some Nasrani purgatory. His heart had stopped here on earth to beat forever in eternity. His beloved Ali had been clothed by bosomy houris in green silks, and was enjoying with Muhammad the luscious fruits and tinkling waters of paradise.

In his office in Citicorp, Abe Cornberg groaned aloud. "Jesus Chu-*rist*, the guy is at the God-crap again."

The top-level talks moved to Camp David in the Maryland hills. The two leaders had adjoining cabins. They walked the leafy woods and ate together in a heated cabin by the pool or in Laurel Lodge. The U.S. party was overwhelmed by the FIR's flexibility. They were ready to compromise on every issue.

A subcommittee negotiated a five-year meat and grain contract with excellent terms from the U.S. standpoint, provided the cattle were slaughtered in accordance with Islamic law. Wilks, the Treasury Secretary, told Delaney it was the best deal for America since the Louisiana Purchase.

If it raised his stock with Democratic farmers, Delaney would not shed any tears.

True to his word, Hourani ordered the speedup of exit visas for Jews. He even provided free transportation. Hundreds arrived in New York each day and thousands in Israel. Delaney became an overnight Jewish and Zionist hero.

The FIR delegation suggested a treaty between themselves and the USA. Each people pledged itself to defend the other in the event of an attack.

The Grand Alliance was taking shape. Delaney felt that, if he suggested a Christian prayer meeting, Hourani would have led it.

The Treasury Secretary summoned Cornberg and Tom Willows of the Fed. Hourani proposed that the new joint Arabic currency, the real, should be quoted for the first time on the foreign exchanges. Why should not Islamic money become, in time, a reserve currency like the ecu and the dollar?

The Americans were specially pleased that Hourani backed them in standing no nonsense from debtor nations. He would, he said, "fondly beat them like a woman." Nonpayment would ruin commercial confidence internationally.

When this was leaked to the *Wall Street Journal*, it was rightly dubbed "the scoop of the century." The dollar shot up in the foreign exchanges. Cash started pouring back into New York from every quarter. The Dow Jones jumped 400 points in an hour.

"Jee-*sus*," Cornberg whistled. "The FIR is making America strong again. Delaney has brought good out of evil like vaccines out of microbes. God bless him!"

The President went on TV, grinning like a man to whom God had just given sole franchise to sell iced drinks in hell.

"My fellow Americans, the world felt threatened when our country and the Federation of Islamic Republics were hostile. What blessings for the world now we are friends and allies!"

Chapter Fifty-eight

In the Vatican, as Christmas decorations were being put up and the first anniversary of his reign approached, the Pope suddenly took a turn for the worse. Was that whiskey, of which he only drank a thimbleful, poisoned, after all?

From his bed, he watched snow fall in thin flakes and strained to hear a group of Irish pilgrims in the piazza lustily singing carols—"Unto us a child is born." He began to see things, not in dreams, for he was no longer able to sleep, but as a kind of vision out of hell. Three times he heard the banshee scream like a cock; everything darkened as though blackbirds were blotting out land, sea and sky.

Two malignant prophecies seemed to be merging, those of Fátima and St. Malachi.

"See, amid the winter's snow."

The Pope gripped his shawl about his shoulders as he was blasted by a *tramontana* from beyond the grave. The blackbirds shrieked and disappeared, taking the snow with them. Then, out of a clear blue sky, it rained blood.

Not rain; it came down in huge cataracts. Blood redder than Chianti, redder even than the blood on a bull's back.

He glanced at his wall in horror. The eyes of his parents in their oval-framed picture streamed with it. The palm tree of his escutcheon turned red; the red lake ran over. "O, the Erne shall run red, / With redundance of blood."

Oh, save me in my Judgment Hour. Oh, save me, my Dark Rosaleen.

The overflow hit the floor and started to rise in the room. Soon, it would be as high as the bed. He, Pope Patrick, was destined to be washed away in a river of blood.

Outside, it was no better. Seas, lakes, streams were filling with blood, so that, not in forty days and forty nights, but in a few seconds, the world drowned in it.

God, where are you, God?

Sudden subtraction of all air. The sun at its zenith, not just eclipsed, but plucked from a cloudless sky. One moment, God—air, sunlight—was everywhere; the next, nowhere. And himself, Patrick, savior of the world? Rather, its destroyer. Humble? No, prouder than Beelzebub.

Words of the poet W. B. Yeats came into his mind. "Things fall apart; the centre cannot hold; / Mere anarchy is loosed upon the world, / The blood-dimmed tide is loosed, and everywhere / The ceremony of innocence is drowned . . . Surely some revelation is at hand; / Surely the Second Coming is at hand."

He rang his bell. Frank Kerrigan came running. Saw the Pope's condition. He said he was going for Dr. Gadda. Patrick shook his head. He wanted Montefiori.

The cardinal's soul, as he came, cried out, though he knew not why, *Hic est enim calix sanguinis mei.* No sooner had he entered the bedroom, splashing knee-deep through blood, than Patrick whispered in a fearful voice, "Something terrible, Giuseppe."

Seeing the Pope's orphaned look: *"Dio.* What is it, Holiness?"

In a ewe-bleat of a voice: "I have lost . . ."

"O come, all ye faithful."

". . . my faith."

To Montefiori, this was the biggest shock in a pontificate of surprises. "Not possible, Holiness. I—"

The Pope blanketed his objections. "I no longer believe."

The cardinal gulped. "No longer believe in what?"

"The Creed, the Trinity, the Holy Catholic Church."

Montefiori drew up a chair. He removed a small purple stole from his inside pocket and draped it round his neck. "I will hear your confession, Holiness."

"Pray, Father, give me your blessing for I have sinned."

Montefiori blessed this dove among crows while thinking, "Absolve him? As well whitewash snow." He had never known anyone as sinless as this gladiator for good who had hungered with the hungry, whose labors had reduced him, body and soul, to thistledown. He had grown imperishable gold harvests on icebergs of the heart. He had been the Church's Moses, bearing all the burdens of the world and the Church on his back. He was now destined to die just before entering the Promised Land.

"I have lost my . . . entirely . . . a castaway . . . I cannot pray . . ."

"When did this begin, Holiness, my son?"

"From the moment I remembered my election, things started . . . And now I can't see . . . Blood, blackness everywhere."

Perspiration beaded Montefiori's forehead. It had been hard at the beginning having a Pope who might die before his Coronation but far worse to have a Pope who might die an infidel, without Christian faith at all.

"This is part of your illness, Holiness," Montefiori said, anguished that the chief Shepherd had become a lost sheep. "You are far from well and the devil plays nasty tricks at times like this. He is making you see only the wrong, crazy side of the tapestry."

Patrick said, very slowly, as the bloody lake pressed up on him like lead from below the bed:

"I have heard the cock crow thrice. I do not believe in God. I do not believe I am Pope or priest. I am just a human being, Giuseppe, who has been suffering from a terrible delusion. I always said riches are what you take with you when you die. My spirit is empty now. I am leaving the world poor and naked."

Montefiori whipped off his stole and knelt beside the bed. *Eloi, Eloi.*

He suddenly realized the meaning of Jesus' last desolate and despairing cry to an absent God. This was how the Lord himself had died, stripped to the nothingness beneath blood and bone, without faith or hope, believing without faith, trusting without hope, alive only through a tremendous and invulnerable love.

The cardinal's frame trembled. Tears rushed down his ribbed cheeks in a torrent. No longer cardinal-confessor to a Pope, he was just a Christian praying for a poor fellow Christian in his final and most awful agony. Without knowing why, he began to hum Bach's "Sheep May Safely Graze."

Montefiori stopped and opened his damp eyes as he became aware of another presence in the room. Something moved. Something white. Something as silent as a butterfly. He wondered if one of Bernini's stone angels from the nearby bridge across the Tiber had etherealized and taken wing to comfort the Pontiff. Yes, a seraph must have come to strengthen God's great Servant, Patrick, as he neared the Throne of Grace.

It was Snowflake.

In one graceful bound, she was up on the bed, licking her master's hand, and, with searching, intelligent eyes, mewed in his face.

Patrick stroked her soft flank, then fondled each furry ear in turn. The sea of blood turned, ebbed, vanished. Not one blob left for a robin's breast. Only two seedlings turned to red bugle flowers which bloomed out of the white walls of his face.

He looked at his shy dry-eyed parents. Then at his shield on the wall: a green palm tree in a tame red lake. Ahead of him stretched a golden road into a land that looked suspiciously like Mayo.

Montefiori watched in wonder as doubt and despair left the Pope's heart—*Hello, God*—saw him smile the old confident smile in the future. In the lush green of his mind woolly lambs were playing with lions. Yes, the Lord had won his soul finally, and forever.

"So you have come."

The cardinal realized he was talking not to him nor to Snowflake. He was communing with an unseen visitor.

Patrick saw this bearded, bronzed giant of a man in a fisherman's smock. The Key Bearer. The stranger who was no stranger said, "It is all right, Patrick. I am here. You have done enough. The Church is safe in my hands."

"Thank you," Patrick whispered.

The Pope said, "It is all right, Giuseppe." And Montefiori smelled a wonderful aroma in the room, the scent of oranges and roses. *Upon this Rock.* He knew now all was well and all would be well.

Patrick stroked Snowflake as the two great churchmen recited the Creed together with a fervor neither of them had ever known before.

Afterward, the Pope quietly gave his apostolic blessing to the city and the world. He then took the still shaky hand of his brave colleague—"Silent night, holy night"—saying, thankfully, that now he felt safely parceled up for heaven. *Nunc dimittis.*

The cardinal fondly pressed his forehead to the Pope's but they did not say farewell. In the catacombs, the word *vale* never appeared. For those living and dying in Christ there is no good-bye. He was content to see that the Pope's death was like the family dog at the back door. Quiet, patient. Just waiting to be let in.

When Montefiori left, the Pope, his face a shining monstrance, was smoking a pipe for the first time in months, a white clay pipe from which smoke rose in white halos. And, a last gesture, typical of the man: he removed the Fisherman's Ring and laid it on the table beside his bed for easy access.

Chapter Fifty-nine

In the United States, the parties returned to Washington from Camp David. What better time, Delaney thought, to sign a bilateral agreement than at a Christmas dinner in the White House?

The entire Council of the FIR, together with their eldest sons and senior wives, had flown in from Europe and the Far East. The Islamic leaders were dressed in white and, against the wishes of Security, had daggers in their belts, the same with which they had slain their camels in the desert of Arabia. They sat down with key male members of the U.S. administration.

Also present were VIPs from abroad. Included were the President of France, the Chancellor of Germany and, in a unique coup, the Emperor of Japan, though this meant that Lee Jing Shang of China boycotted the assembly. The Russian President sent his regrets, he had an uprising or two to deal with. But, as a gesture of reconciliation, the Prime Minister of Israel had been specially invited by Hourani.

The only woman present was Denise Weaver, though she had been persuaded to dress in a long black dress and was seated at the farthest point from Hourani. It was either that or nothing.

It was a black-tie affair but not the occasion the First Lady had anticipated. Islamic rules obliged the women to eat in a room apart.

Carol Delaney, dripping with jewels, and in a scarlet Dior gown guaranteed to make a cardinal swoon, ushered the Muslim ladies, invisible save for eye slits in their veils, into the dining room.

Christ, she thought, if only I had these girls for a few days, I'd teach 'em a thing or two!

To Hourani's first wife: "Tell me truly, darling, under all that drabbery, are you Julia Roberts or Claudia Schiffer?"

She gestured to little Ruhollah to come with her but he fiercely shook his head, refusing to let her put a finger on him. He was a man, his place was at the table next to his grandfather.

She smiled sweetly at him. "Suit yourself, you little bastard."

In the main dining room, Delaney and Hourani sat side by side, top center of the horseshoe table. They pulled a cracker together. "Thank God, or should I say, thank Allah," Delaney joked, "that's the only explosion likely to take place between us."

The cracker had a whistle in it, which Hourani appropriated, and a party hat, which Delaney rammed down on his own head.

The meal of roast lamb served with disgusting nonalcoholic beverages out of deference to the guests was over now. They were at the toast stage.

Ayatollah Hourani was first on his feet. To everyone's delight, he handed his grandson his whistle.

"There, heart of my heart, first of my first, my baby dove, do my bidding." Ruhollah blew the whistle for silence.

Great stuff, they all agreed, though Delaney knew in his heart that he was the one who had blown the whistle.

Hourani's first sentence caused the entire Islamic delegation to bang on the table. Some Americans thought this was war until the translation came:

"Allah knows this to be the proudest day of my life."

To please Delaney, Hourani emphasized again that debtor nations had to repay their debts if business confidence was to revive. "Otherwise, I take a camel stick to them."

He praised his own great Brotherhood of Islamic nations. He spoke movingly of Ali, his eldest son, whom he had loved beyond all love and would surely join soon.

"I put on record a special tribute to Pope Patrick. In a thousand years, when historians look back on the events of this day, a day when the blood feud between your people and mine was finally ended, they will know whom to thank.

"Your President tells me His Holiness is very sick, so I have just sent him this telegram: 'Allah bring thee to thy journey's end and reward thee according to thy deserts.'"

Delaney, not a little guilty, led the applause.

Hourani finished his touching speech by holding his glass aloft.

Leaving aside for the first time in his life the language with which God addresses the angels, he said in broken English, "On this silent night, this holy night, I give you a toast: God help America," so that many Americans, even as they downed their sherbet, found it hard to stop the titters.

It was Delaney's turn. His party hat was in the shape of a red dragon. He was short of sleep but he meant every word when he praised Islam's President and people.

He turned to Hourani and was about to give him a résumé of the story of Bethlehem when Bill Huggard poked him painfully in the back.

"Mr. President, your presence is urgently required."

Delaney looked daggers at him. Who knew, he might be on the point of converting Hourani, like a latter-day Emperor Constantine, from paganism to Christianity. The Pope would baptize him in St. Peter's with good old Roone as godfather.

"Later, Huggard," he hissed. "Scram, vamoose, get outa here."

Huggard switched off the mike and practically dragged him out of his chair. "Emergency."

Delaney made a mental note to fire the idiot and send him home in a procking ambulance to Yuba City.

"NCA matter, Mr. President," Huggard whispered.

"Oh my God," Delaney whispered back, his Adam's apple turning into a marble lump. He apologized to his chief guest. "My aunt, I mean, my uncle. Not too well, I'm told."

"I am so devastating," Hourani murmured sympathetically in English.

The M.C. motioned to the band, who struck up "Three Cheers for the Red, White and Blue," to cover embarrassment. Huggard pushed the President past the VIPs out of the dining room into a soundproof closet nearby.

"Huggard, what the shit?" In that dead atmosphere, he seemed to be speaking inside a burial vault.

"Shut up and listen," Huggard ordered, fighting for breath like someone plunging down a roller coaster. "It looks like a decapitation attack."

The President went into vertical traction. "A *what?*"

"NORAD has just informed the National Command Authority that a double or triple nuclear explosion has gone off high in the atmosphere."

"Thank God," gasped Delaney. "I thought you were going to say San Francisco just went up—"

"For Christ's sake, *listen*. This explosion high in the atmosphere has set off fantastically powerful electromagnetic impulses over thousands of aerial miles."

"Get to the procking point."

"The procking point is, the control center at NORAD—"

"You *are* talking about the North American Aerospace Defense Command in Colorado?"

"Yeah. Well, it ain't working."

"Impossible. It's Christmas procking Day. Someone's sunk his head in a whiskey barrel."

"Subsidiary nerve centers with infrared sensors giving advance warning of missile attacks have ceased functioning. Our listening posts, all dead. Radar systems—Cobra Dane Station in Alaska, our Bear Paws from Cape Cod to Sunnyvale, California—all dead. The Canadians in the Arctic Circle, British GCHQ in Cheltenham and their reconnaissance over the North Sea, all—"

In barged the Assistant Secretary of Defense, Chuck Bealand, who was responsible for computer security.

"The Pentagon's computers are all sick as parrots, Chief."

"*Si-ick?*" echoed Delaney, as if only VIPs like him were entitled to get sick.

"A virus," Bealand explained, "must've survived our inoculation procedures and got through the gate into our Military Command and Control System. It's acting like an electronic shredder. Our computers can't talk to each other."

Bealand's boss, Dick Diamond, rushed in next without knocking.

"Chief, this could be the prelude to a hostile attack on the U.S. and our European allies."

"Prock the allies," roared Delaney. "Who's behind all this? Think, for Christ's sake! All the top people of the U.S. and the FIR are in one place. So are the other leaders of the Western Alliance and the Emperor of Japan. It's gotta be either the Russians or the procking Chinese."

"We're none too sure who's behind it," Diamond admitted.

"Not procking *sure!* The Chinese have gone on testing nuclear weapons."

"True, sir. But we have no evidence that that's their patch of sky."

"It can't be the FIR," the President said. "Hourani gave the U.N. his black box."

Diamond said, "I didn't think to tell you, sir, but—"

"But *what?*"

"This morning, we put an agent in the office of the U.N. Secretary General. He opened up the safe, then the FIR box and—"

Urgency bordering on panic: "What did he find?"

"An explosive took his head off, sir. So we still don't know if the case contained their nuclear codes or the insides of a transistor radio."

"It *can't* be the FIR," Delaney said in a wail. "Their first target would be Washington, *us*. And their leader's in the White House with his little grandson next to him, about to sign the end of the Ice War. For Chrissake, can you see that prick's finger on the button?"

"You could ask him," Huggard said inanely, before retiring to a corner where, eyes closed, he softly hummed, "Om."

"An accident in space," Delaney said. "Could it be that?"

Diamond shrugged.

"That *must* be it." Delaney crossed his fingers. Perspiration drenched his Cardin shirt, his bowels liquefied, he badly needed a drink. "The FIR would hardly start a nuclear war with their entire Council having dinner next door, would they? What sort of a procking trick is that?"

Diamond did not answer. Seeing Delaney frantically searching for his handkerchief, he took it out of his top pocket and handed it to him.

"Our pants are down, Chief. No alert flights. Planes, ships, nuclear subs, all celebrating in home or friendly bases. Whatever you do, don't hesitate."

"Don't *whut?*"

Delaney rubbed the sweat off his brow. Over Diamond's shoulder, he saw a warrant officer clutching the briefcase with the codes for launching a nuclear attack. His head felt hard-boiled. He could not even remember the act of contrition, let alone the combination of the lock and, in any case, who the hell was the enemy?

Diamond said, "If those bombs in space were designed to put NORAD out of action and nullify our entire satellite band in preparation for a pre-emptive attack, you originally had eight minutes to react." He checked his Rolex watch. "Now, Chief, you have three minutes ten seconds left, and counting."

Delaney was suddenly boneless and dribbling. What a decision to have to make on Christmas procking Day! Where was Carol? Where in prock's name was that Papal Indulgence for a happy death?

His party hat still on his head, his handkerchief between his teeth, the Commander in Chief of the U.S. armed forces, madly signing himself, down-up and right-left, for the second time in a few days, sank to his knees in prayer.

Requiem, requiem, O requiem aeternam. Cardinal Montefiori, sadder than ever that this smiling Pontiff had asked to be cremated, tapped Pope Patrick's head with a silver hammer and said, "Brian Aidan O'Flynn, are you dead?" at the precise moment when, practically unopposed, FIR missiles, leashed from submarines in the Atlantic, from silos in a broad band from Morocco to Pakistan, started annihilating the free world.

To the Reader

If you enjoyed *Pope Patrick*, why not recommend it to your friends?
But, please, do not spoil their enjoyment by revealing the ending.
Thank you.

About the Author

Peter de Rosa, a former Catholic priest, is the author of the bestselling *Vicars of Christ: The Dark Side of the Papacy* and *Rebels: The Irish Uprising of 1916*. His first novel, *Bless Me Father*, was a bestseller, which he adapted into the enormously successful British television series of the same name. He lives in County Wicklow, Ireland.